TROUBLE BOYS

WHITE LIGHTNING SERIES, BOOK 5

DEBRA DUNBAR

J.P SLOAN

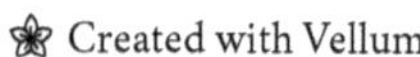 Created with Vellum

Hattie stared over the water of the Chesapeake Bay, not really seeing the sunrise as she leaned over the rail of Raymond's boat. Waves lapped against the hull, washing her thoughts into a pool of distraction. Reaching one hand into her pocket, she felt the sharp edge of an envelope.

"Alright, now," Raymond grumbled from behind the helm. "You been brewin' up a storm cloud since we left the slip. What's got you in a twist?"

"Nothing." She pulled her hand from her pocket and gripped the rail.

"Is it the job?"

Hattie shook her head. Two-bit gangsters she could handle, but this…?

"You ain't said more'n two words since we let out," Raymond prodded, rounding the controls to join her along the railing. "If you're feelin' blue, that's alright. I just wanna make sure I hadn't put you in a mood."

She turned to smile at the man who over the years had

become more of a best friend than a coworker. "What would *you* have done to put me in a mood?"

Raymond shrugged. "Don't think I did nothin', but four years of marriage taught me that don't mean much."

Hattie smiled and waved him off. "You're fine, Raymond."

"*You* ain't."

"Just in my head today, is all. Truly, I'm fine."

"You say 'fine' like that means somethin' I don't think it means."

Hattie shook her head. "You're set to pester me until I cheer up, aren't you?"

"It's why you brung me, right?"

Hattie turned to face Raymond, the envelope oddly heavy in her pocket. "You think we're making a difference here? Doing this?"

Raymond squinted. "What, knocking over the Crew boats?"

"Aye. It feels… I don't know. Small. Ineffectual."

"If things go good today, this'll be four, maybe five barrels off their hands. And a couple of their boatleggers."

Hattie nodded. "Is this sort of thing enough to hurt Vito Corbi, is what I'm wondering?"

Raymond shrugged. "That's a you decision. I just drive the boat."

She sighed. "True. I'm just talking my way through it."

A vulture circled the boat overhead, tilting its wings against the rising sunlight. Hattie peered at the bird and straightened her spine a little.

"Give him room," she said, easing Raymond back as the vulture took a dive toward the boat.

It snapped its wings wide as it swooped low, and with a flurry of feathers and the popping of joints, the bird transformed into the grizzled, red-bearded image of Charley. He landed on the deck with a thump of his boots, rubbing his shoulder with a groan.

"Gotta stop with them hot dives," Charley drawled. "Not getting any younger."

Hattie nodded in sympathy. "Any sign of them?"

"A-yep. Fishing boat with a green hull. Looks to be about six barrels. Heading south out of the Patapsco."

Hattie nodded again and reached a hand to Raymond.

He passed her a revolver, which she held into the air. She squeezed a shot into the sky, its report bouncing off nearby trees.

The air thumped with a soft, deep rush as Blake popped onto the deck.

Raymond jerked, shaking his head.

"Man, I never get used to that."

Hattie chuckled. "Aye, we're a right freak show." She turned to Blake. "Boat's inbound. Six barrels."

Charley added, "Only two goons manning the tiller."

Blake clapped his hands and rubbed them together. "Sounds like our best-case scenario, right?"

Hattie asked, "Everyone set on the haul-away?"

Blake nodded to the shore. "Ready when you are."

"Okay. Keep your eyes peeled, then."

Blake gave her a two-finger salute to his brow then blinked back to his position on the shoreline.

Charley asked, "You want me in the water?"

"No. Stay with us. We'll need to move fast if they get a case of the nerves."

He nodded and took position behind Raymond.

"You sure you don't wanna get the rifles out?" Raymond asked, leaning in toward Hattie. "We got lucky last week, I think."

"No guns," she said, pocketing the revolver. "I promised Vincent."

Raymond sighed. "What've these thugs ever done for him, anyway?"

"It's not about paying *them* back," she said. "Vincent knows these men. We're about to deprive them of a job. The least we can do is leave them intact."

She strode to the bow, eying the horizon. Before long a green-hulled fishing boat appeared around the bend of the Chesapeake, its rigging cutting a ragged silhouette against the brightening sky.

"We're on," Hattie announced. "Try not to move too much."

She closed her eyes and extended her powers in a wide cone behind her, bending the light around the boat. Then she opened her eyes, satisfied that the boat was invisible to the Crew boatleggers approaching. She didn't bother with anything more than visuals. The gangsters were moving too fast to hear the waves lapping the side of the boat. By the time they were close enough to notice, it'd be too late.

The fishing boat angled to the center of the bay. Hattie lifted a hand to the right, and Raymond fired up the diesel. Once more, Hattie chose not to conceal the sound of the engine. This would be quick.

They sliced through the light chop of the bay water on an intercept course for the Crew vessel. Hattie kept the wedge of bent light taut around them as they closed the distance. Raymond eased up on the throttle, angling to come alongside their target before pulling the engine into reverse. The water behind them churned as the motor house groaned. The turbulence behind them slipped out of Hattie's illusion. It was time.

She released the light pinch.

The two Crew boatmen stood in frozen disbelief as Charley and Hattie leapt onto their craft. Hattie snatched a Tommy gun from the top of a crate nearest her chosen target, tossing it into the water. Charley wasn't as quick. His goon managed to lay a hand on his weapon before Charley clamped his hand over the stock. The two wrestled with the gun for a few seconds before Charley's face pulled into a horrific snarl. Enormous canines emerged from his mouth as his eyes shimmered into catlike slits. The gangster shrieked and released his gun, stumbling backward and tripping over his own feet.

Hattie gave Charley a nod as he ditched the second weapon into the drink. The partial transformation made him look like a true monster, a tiger wearing a human skin. Hattie wasn't the only one working on economical magics. As she watched, his face slid back into the familiar countenance.

Hattie cleared her throat and addressed the gangsters.

"If you have a brain between you, you'll remain still, and do as we say."

Charley's goon paused halfway into righting himself before freezing wide-eyed.

Raymond tossed several lengths of sisal twine onto the Crew boat and Charley began binding their wrists behind their backs.

Hattie added, "Here's the bit where I tell you the good news and the bad. The good, we have no intention of harming either of you. We're here for the hooch. Bad news is that these intentions only apply to your physical wellbeing. I'm afraid we're about to cost you your jobs."

Charley proceeded to gag both men, who were now in a state of simmering panic.

Hattie inspected the cargo, guided the men to the bow, then gave Raymond a whistle. He eased his craft away as Hattie took command of the Crew vessel, chugging it toward the shore where Blake and his company were waiting with gangplanks. They dropped the reinforced lumber over the side of the Crew boat and made quick work of the six barrels of white lightning quarry. A makeshift boardwalk led across the mud of the shore toward a truck with a canvas tarp pulled open. They loaded the men onto the truck ahead of the barrels, hiding them beneath the tarp, which they tied over the bed.

Blake gave Hattie a quick handshake as Charley gathered himself.

"You remember what to do?" Hattie asked Charley.

"A-yep. Controls are easy enough, as long as you don't mind scuttling the thing."

"That's the idea," she said with a nod. "I assume you know how to swim."

"I'll beat you to Baltimore," he said.

"I'm not going to Baltimore."

"Huh?"

"This shipment already has a buyer," she said, marching for the cab of the truck.

"Oh." Charley chuckled before turning back to the board-walk to scuttle the Crew vessel.

Blake stuffed his hands into his pockets. "You're not going alone, are you?"

"I'm picking up Raymond at Winnow's Slip, then we're driving straight on to Pittsburgh."

"You sound like a gangster." Blake laughed.

She laughed in response, but somehow it felt hollow. Somehow in fighting the gangsters she'd become one, and Hattie wasn't quite sure how she felt about that.

THREE HOURS of hard road travel hadn't done the men in the back of the truck any favors. Hattie did her best to avoid rough spots, but with every hard bump she'd hear groans behind her. For their part, they hadn't tried any monkey business. That was good, because she wasn't sure what she'd have done if they'd managed to find a way out from underneath that canvas.

Raymond polished a harmonica as they drove, angling it to the sunshine at his window.

"That's new," Hattie commented.

"Picked it up at Woolworth's. Figured I'd learn how to play."

"Any good yet?"

He lifted the harmonica to his lips and exhaled, producing a muddy, wheezing fistful of notes that made Hattie's skin crawl.

"Well. Don't expect to be making a livin' on the stage anytime soon."

"I don't get it," he grumbled. "Seen a fella at Maudite's play one like he was a one-man band."

"I'm sure there's a knack. With a few month's practice, you might be able to manage a goose call," she teased.

"Well, Nadine's put her foot down on playin' inside. So, it's here or…"

"Not here," Hattie stated with more force than she intended.

Raymond released a belly laugh and slipped the harmonica back into his pocket.

After a few more hours of driving, they pulled into a muddy patch of ground tucked between a filthy warehouse and the Monongahela River. A cadre of suited men in fedoras stepped out of the warehouse, hands tucked inside their jackets. Hattie eased the truck forward and put the gear into park before killing the engine.

"Stay in the truck," she whispered.

Raymond nodded, as she opened the door. One of the

Pittsburgh goons pulled a revolver from his jacket, keeping it aimed at the ground as she stepped forward.

"You Malloy?" one of them shouted.

"Aye. Got six barrels for you in the truck."

They stood silent for a moment, eyes searching one another for a sign that this was a bonafide transaction. Once a consensus was reached, two of the goons made their way to the truck to begin untying the canvas.

The tallest of the bunch approached Hattie, hands out and free of weapons.

"These are Masseria's?" he asked.

"I didn't say that."

He frowned. "On the phone, you said—"

"I said you'd best repackage and keep this clear of the New York traffic."

"Who'd you nick these barrels from, then?"

She smirked. "The less you know, the better. Unless you play a better poker face than what you're giving me now."

He shrugged.

"There's one more thing," she added. "Brought two men with us. They're competition, if you know what I mean. I intend to cut them loose and send them on their merry way. I'd appreciate it as a professional courtesy if you give them a running start?"

The goon smiled. "You are a little hellcat, aren't you? Fine. They have twenty-four hours."

He reached into his pocket to produce a roll of bills. He counted out the arranged payment, adjusting for the extra barrels, then walked away.

Once the last of the barrels had been unloaded, Hattie hopped up onto the truck bed and crouched in front of her hostages.

"Now, gents. You're in the territory of the Pittsburgh family. They don't want you. Nor will Vito Corbi, when he hears you stole the shipment of moonshine and sold it up north. If you return to Baltimore, there will be no judge or jury for you. Consider yourselves retired. If you leave the city, the local muscle has agreed to offer you twenty-four hours to make yourselves scarce. Nod if you understand your situation."

Both nodded.

"Right."

She pounded on the back of the cab. Raymond handed back an oyster knife, which she used to cut their bonds. Each of the Baltimore gangsters removed their gags, working their jaws as they climbed out of the truck.

"Best of luck, gents," she stated.

They trotted up to the river, then hooked north and out of sight.

Hattie shook her head. These were low level minions. And that moonshine she'd just stolen and resold was a drop in the ocean. How likely was it that Corbi would even notice? How many more strikes like this would it take to really make him feel the pinch?

She slipped her hands into the pockets of her overalls. Her fingers brushed against the envelope tucked in her pocket. And then there was *that* piece of business.

She returned to the truck with a worried frown.

Vincent passed two women in short dresses walking arm-in-arm as he made his way toward the Old Moravia hotel. They curtailed their conversation as he walked by, both peering at him with interest. Vincent didn't make a show of noticing, though he couldn't help but grin as the women giggled several steps behind him.

A wash of jazz and tobacco smoke poured from the front of the hotel, the electric lights snapping on to light up the darkening dusk. The brilliant glass-and-brass door glimmered as he stepped through. A jazz quartet pounded a bouncy tune and several besuited gentlemen nodded along near the front of the lobby.

The Baltimore Crew had taken over the hotel since the battle at the Havre de Grace vineyard which had left Vito's property in ruins. It was a poorly-kept secret that the hotel had become the headquarters for the Crew, rather than simply their preferred haunt. Even the city police had given the entire block a wide berth after Vito had moved into the penthouse.

But Vincent's purpose at the club that night had nothing

to do with the jazz, or jaw-wagging with his coworkers. He wasn't there for marching orders, he was there to wage war. Though the weapon he wielded as he stepped through the crowd in the lobby lounge was one he hadn't much experience with—a weapon far more delicate than the mindless chaos of a Tommy gun, far more subtle than a knife in an alley.

He was here to wage a war with whispers.

It wasn't long before Curley found him and gave him his first target to fire at.

"Vincent," Curley muttered as he corralled him into a corner by a potted palm. "You heard the latest?"

Vincent shook his head with well-practiced blasé.

Curley leaned yet closer. "Another boat crew turned coat."

"Turned coat?" Vincent repeated with the pretense of surprise.

"Yeah. Took the boat to land and rolled west with the whole damn shipment."

"You mean what happened last week?"

"No," Curley countered. "This was today. That's two in two weeks have run off with a shipment."

"Sure they weren't waylaid?"

"Word is they sold the hootch to Pittsburgh. Just like the others last week."

Vincent set his jaw. "I heard the one last week was sold to Atlantic City."

Hattie *had* sold both shipments to Pittsburgh, but the notion that all of Vito's men were jumping ship and running to any random family they could made for a more damaging story.

"Oh," Curley grunted. "What's going on? This kinda thing makes us look bad. It makes us look weak."

"I know." Vincent put a hand on Curley's shoulder. "We have to expect some of the Crew are gonna shake out after what happened in Havre de Grace. People are worried. Can't say I blame them either."

"But that's four men in two weeks," Curly protested. "It's embarrassing. There's talk Vito's lost control."

Vincent sighed. "The Capo is doing his best. If that's not good enough…" He let the statement drift into the ether.

Curley shook his head. "They wouldn't play like this in New York."

Vincent shrugged, then patted Curley on the arm. "I'm getting a drink."

And, shot fired. This was the plan he'd hammered out with Hattie, a slow game chipping away at the Crew's confidence in Vito's leadership. The hauls netted some coin for Hattie and the Charge, but the real payday was right here in this lounge. Of course, Vincent had to take care with how hard he pressed.

Vincent reached the bar and ordered an egg cream, choosing to keep his wits about him rather than fuming them up with liquor. The men at the bar beside him grumbled to themselves.

At length, one declared, "Trust the Capo."

Vincent lifted his glass. "Here, here."

They nodded with muted enthusiasm.

Vincent added, "May he reign as long as Jim D'urso."

One of the men cocked a brow. "Huh?"

His compatriot tossed a light punch into his chest. "Oh, come on. You wet behind the ears?"

Vincent nodded. "You should know the Crew's history, friend."

The two engaged in a lively conversation as Vincent stepped away. A conversation about the former leader of the Baltimore Crew, the founder—the one Vito had replaced. The man was a legend among the old guard. Drumming up a conversation about Vito's predecessor, the very man who had forged the Baltimore Crew out of pig iron…it would remind everyone how good it was before Vito took over.

A few words, and already the conversation in the room was folding itself into a castigation of Corbi's ability to lead.

The plan was going well.

The only man in the Crew who might see through Vincent's war of whispers hadn't spoken two words to Vincent since the vineyard. And until that moment as Vincent spotted Lefty boring a hole through Vincent's head from across the room, he didn't think it would become a factor.

Vincent sucked in a breath, muscled his shoulders square, then approached Lefty.

"Vincent," Lefty stated as if identifying a shrub.

"Lefty. It's been a hot second."

"You're well?"

Vincent nodded.

"And Miss Malloy?"

"Ship shape far as I know, Lefty."

"Good." Lefty reached for a Collins glass on the wall rail and gave it a quick pull. "She's keeping busy?"

Vincent squinted. "I wouldn't know."

"Wouldn't you?" Lefty asked through tight lips.

"We're not in regular contact." Vincent shrugged. "And when we are, we don't usually discuss business."

"Really?" Lefty set down his glass. "I heard someone talking about Atlantic City, and how we lost two shipments to them. Heard someone else say it was Pittsburgh. I wonder why are we losing shipments of booze and boatleggers all of a sudden?"

Vincent shrugged. "It's gossip."

"There's two or three men in this hotel who know exactly what happened to those two shipments." Lefty leaned in to lower his voice. "They both ended up in Pittsburgh."

Vincent forced his expression to remain nonchalant. "Take it up with Pittsburgh, then."

"I'm taking it up with you."

"If you think I had anything to do with those boys jumping ship—"

"They were shanghaied." He stepped closer. "And you know it as well as I do."

Vincent rolled his eyes. "If you think Hattie Malloy is capable of horse-collaring four Baltimore Crew boys and booting them off their boats—"

"I *know* she is." Lefty checked the nearby company to make sure his voice hadn't carried. "Because she's not alone. She has a whole gang of free pinchers, now. I know because I've seen them. And I know that you"—he poked Vincent in the chest—"are either in league with that ragged crew, or at least are throwing Vito's dogs off the scent."

"Would you listen to yourself?" Vincent scoffed. "You're acting like you don't know me."

"I *do* know you," Lefty snapped. "And jacking two boats of hooch then selling them out from underneath Vito's nose while poisoning the well here at home? That's exactly the sort of crack-skulled, cock-feathered scheme you'd sign up for."

He bit back a grin. Even if Lefty had essentially sniffed him out, and thereby became a direct threat to the plan, it was good to have someone know him that well. "And you're willing to risk embarrassing yourself in front of the Capo with this sort of wild-ass assumption?"

Lefty's face twisted with misery. "I'd rather save both of us a world of hurting and cut this off the branch before it turns into something deadly."

The man was clearly trying to save Vincent from himself —as usual. The task had grown more difficult as Vincent had put distance between him and Lefty, but that distance was important. When everything shook out, and when Vito Corbi found himself at the south end of Vincent's reckoning, Lefty would have to make a difficult decision.

"If I were that stupid, I'd thank you for getting my head square." Vincent gave Lefty a smile. "Lucky for both of us, I'm not that stupid."

Lefty searched Vincent's face, then turned away.

A pang shot through Vincent's guts as the other man slipped through the crowd without looking back. He'd shown too much of his hand at the vineyard. Lefty already knew he'd saved Hattie last year from the Capo. He knew Vincent had developed feelings for Hattie, and accepted that there was room in the Crew's demands for loyalty for romance. But the Charge was something wholly different. This was a cultivated, organized group of free pinchers acting in the very same city as Vito Corbi. And Lefty knew Vincent was involved.

He owed so much to Lefty. The man had taken him in after he was sold to the Crew. At first it was a begrudging obligation on Lefty's part. Vito had chosen him as Vincent's handler due to his past encounters with pinchers. It was the only qualification that seemed to matter at the time, though Lefty's demeanor had left plenty to be desired. The first year under Lefty's wing was abject misery. The curmudgeon hadn't had the time or patience for a sheltered pincher, unfamiliar with the mechanics of the world. But as the years passed and Vincent became more comfortable as a tool for the gang, Lefty had become more and more protective.

But Lefty's loyalty never wandered far from Vito Corbi. He was a company man, dyed in the wool. How long would that protective bent last if Vincent continued down the path he was on?

Cheers and salutations rippled through the crowd as Vito strode into the lounge, his broad forehead already speckled in perspiration, face flushed red. Ever since the vineyard, the Capo's health had seemed fragile, as if the strain of losing his home had drawn him taut. So, too, had the pressure that Vincent and Hattie were applying. Hattie grumbled endlessly about how meaningless these strikes on Vito's supply lines seemed to be, but she couldn't see the effect their plan was having.

Vito reached for a glass of water, gulping it like a man lost in the Sahara. Once he set the glass down, his lips lifted in an uncharacteristic smile. With a clap of his hands, he captured the room's attention.

"My friends. My brothers. These are times that test our resolve. They command our fullest measure of focus. Our dedication to the purpose. Our dedication to our dignity. We are men, and we do not shrink from this task."

A meager applause spattered through the lounge. Too many of the Crew were already convinced that Vito was more talk and bravado than real results and Vincent took satisfaction in that.

Vito continued, "The families wait and watch as we respond to this latest attack from New York. They expect us either to crumple, or to press our advance against Joe Masseria."

Sober nods around the room. That much was true.

"I suspect that many of you are waiting and watching as well." Vito's grin sharpened. "The time for waiting is over. Tomorrow I want everyone here. You get your boys pulled up from the water and the roads. I have an announcement that everyone will want to hear."

Vito withdrew back to the lobby, ascending the stairs to the upper levels as the rest of the Crew slowly resumed their conversations. This was unexpected, to be sure—so soon after the battle that had ravaged the vineyard, a battle that had taken down Masseria's lead pincher. Was Vito about to declare war on New York? Was this his last-ditch plan to regain the confidence of the Crew? If so, it would mean the death of the Crew and everyone he threw at Masseria.

How would that fit into Vincent and Hattie's plan? Vincent turned it over in his head but shook off the thoughts as he finished his egg cream. It was no good trying to get out in front of this when he didn't have all the information.

Besides, he had an important errand to run.

Vincent made a discreet exit and trotted up the street to catch the trolley. He hopped off in Hampden and walked the few blocks to his destination. Hattie's apartment building was well-lit from within, electric light pouring into the night sky from each window. Vincent reached into his pocket to caress the tiny felt box and crossed the street between chugging Model T's.

Rapping on the door to the Malloy residence, he stood with locked knees, trying to quell the nerves choking the breath out of his lungs. The door opened to reveal the silver-pated head of Alton Malloy.

"Vincent, me boy!" Alton bellowed. "Top of the evening to ya!"

"Good evening, Mister Malloy," Vincent replied.

"Oh, I'm afraid 'Attie's out and about."

"I know. I'm actually here to speak with you and your wife. If you don't mind?"

Alton stepped aside and ushered Vincent inside.

Branna stood from her chair, setting aside her knitting. "Why, Mister Calendo. What brings you about, then?"

"Missus Malloy. I wondered if I might have a word with the two of you?"

Branna's face drew tight. "What's happened?"

Alton stiffened in alarm. "Aye, has something happened to my girl?"

Vincent waved his hand. "Oh, no no. All's fine. I just... hell's bells this is awkward."

Alton screwed his white brows together. "Do you need a drink, son?"

"I'd, uh…rather get this out first. May we sit?"

Alton offered his own chair for Vincent and took a seat on the sofa. Branna withdrew to the corner of the room, remaining on her feet with arms crossed.

Vincent nodded. "Yeah, this isn't something I ever thought I'd be saying out loud. Not here. I mean, I suppose it would have to be here, but this wasn't—"

"Oh, spit it out ya daft man!" Branna snapped.

Alton lifted a hand to Branna. "Now, let the man speak, woman."

"I would if he could," she replied.

Vincent reached into his pocket to produce the felt-lined box. He popped it open to reveal a silver filigree band with a small diamond nestled in the middle.

Alton's eyes went wide.

Vincent said, "I…uh…I wanted to ask your permission for your daughter's hand in…well, you, know."

"The word is marriage," Branna looked toward the ceiling. "Matrimony, if you want to be an ass about't."

Alton eased back onto the sofa, wide eyes on the ring.

Vincent looked to Branna. "Your daughter means a lot to me. I think you know that. And I suspect there's no two people in this world who'd have a harder time finding someone they could share a life with. It's fate, maybe, that we found each other at all."

Branna stared at Vincent for a long moment, then looked to Alton. "Well, husband? What do you think? I know you like the boy enough. But do you have it in you to call him son-in-law?"

Alton closed his mouth, then finally blinked. "Well. I, ah…"

Branna chuckled. "Men can't keep their mouths shut when there's nothing to say, but when you need them to say something, they trip over their mouths."

Alton frowned at her. "I'm taking a moment here, woman. This is sudden."

"Honestly?" She laughed. "You didn't know this was coming? You should have your eyes checked."

Alton reached for Vincent's hand. "Well, m'boy. I'm not eager to see the girl leave. But you're right. I've thought about how she'd ever find a husband, with her life being what it is. You've been there for her. You've proven we can trust you. I can't see how I could say no to this."

Alton pulled Vincent off the chair into an embrace tight enough to make him grunt.

Vincent pulled away and looked to Branna. "And you, Missus Malloy?"

"What about me, then?"

"What do you say?"

Branna scowled. "I'm not her father."

"Perhaps not, but I want your approval just the same."

The woman eyed him long and hard. "You hurt her, and I'll slit your throat—pincher or not."

Vincent swallowed. "I'd never hurt her, ma'am. Never."

It seemed like forever that Hattie's mom stood there, her eyes boring into his.

"Then I guess I approve." She turned to cross the room, turning on the radio. As the tubes warmed and the tinny strains of the All-Star Orchestra poured from the speaker, Branna pointed to the kitchen.

"I'm thinking it might be time for that drink."

CHAPTER 3

Roscoe gave Vincent an accusatory meow as he stepped into the apartment.

"Oh, hush. You're not starving," Vincent grumbled, snatching the cat's food dish from the floor to set it on the counter.

As he opened a can of mackerel, the black cat wound figure eights around Vincent's ankles. He emptied the canned fish into the dish, then set the dinner on the ground.

Once he saw the cat pounce on the food bowl, Vincent pulled off his jacket and tie, rolling up his sleeves. As the cat ate, he began tidying up the apartment. After he was satisfied, he started a pot boiling on the stove.

There was a knock on the door, and Roscoe hopped over to rub his face on the casing.

Vincent shook his head. "How do you know that's not some goon looking to grease us both?"

The cat peered up at Vincent with a slow blink and a whisker-rattling meow.

"Yeah, I know," Vincent said as he opened the door.

Hattie smiled back at Vincent from the hallway, still dressed in her work clothes. "Who're you talking to in there?"

Vincent pointed to the cat, who was already rubbing the side of his face against Hattie's leg.

"Someone of equal intelligence, then?" she teased as she scooped up the cat in one hand, the other gripping a wine bottle.

Vincent held the door open and Hattie stepped inside to deposit Roscoe onto the dinner table alongside the wine.

"Not on the table," Vincent told her. "We eat there."

She laughed. "I think Roscoe's cleaner than either one of us."

"What, because he spends hours licking himself? Even more reason." Vincent shooed the cat off the table.

Hattie ran a hand along her overalls. "Sorry about this. I didn't have time to change. The day got away from me, and I…I couldn't wait to see you."

The last was said with a shy glance down at the floor that never ceased to melt him. Vincent leaned forward and kissed her, tousling her red hair to break the tension. "You're perfect, as always. Besides, I only just started dinner."

Hattie followed him into the kitchen, rummaging through his cabinets for a corkscrew. "Outstanding. I'm famished. What's on the menu, good sir?"

"Pierogis from the deli down the street."

"What's a pierogi?"

Vincent eyed the bundle on his countertop. "Not entirely sure. The owner's Polish, and I thought we'd try something different."

His chest tightened at the thought that he might have screwed up. The few times he'd cooked for Hattie, it had been his usual Italian fare. He knew it wasn't her sort of cuisine, and this seemed to be a good compromise. Hopefully they wouldn't discover they both hated Polish food tonight of all nights.

Hattie uncorked the bottle and poured two glasses.

Vincent nodded to his glass as she handed it over. "Who'd you steal this from?"

"Your boss, of course," she replied with a smirk.

They both took a sip. It was a dry red with fruit notes and a lingering essence of almond.

"The man *can* make wine," Vincent admitted as he turned back to the stove.

"Aye, true enough. Less so now."

Vincent grimaced, remembering the devastation at Harve de Grace. "I suppose so. How did it go today?"

Hattie wandered the few feet into the dining area and took a seat at the table, lifting her glass enough to allow Roscoe to jump into her lap. "Well enough."

"You don't sound enthused." Vincent dropped the pierogis into the water, sending up a rare prayer that they would be edible. "Anyone get hurt?"

"Not even your own goons," she replied. "Though I'm sure they won't be thanking me for it anytime soon."

"I appreciate that. I know it puts pressure on you."

She tilted her head. "Why Polish food tonight? Why aren't you making me pasta like you always do? You're Italian, after all."

Vincent shrugged. "I thought I'd do something different tonight—something new for both of us."

She chuckled and took a sip of her wine. "You're a bold man, Vincent Calendo."

"Truth be told, every meal I make is a gamble. It's not like I had an Italian mother to teach me my way around the kitchen."

Vincent winked at Hattie to assure her he wasn't taking a stroll down a dark alley of memories, though her face seemed to have wandered in that direction on its own.

"Not like you had a Polish mother, either," she replied softly.

He laughed and gestured to the pot of boiling perogies. "True. So, I can't vouch for any of this. It could be good. It could be terrible."

She wrinkled her nose. "Sure you don't want to go out?"

"I'm sure. I want a nice quiet evening," he said as he approached, "with a beautiful woman all to myself. That's what I want."

He reached down and took her hand, lifting it to his mouth to kiss in what felt like an appropriate romantic gesture.

Hattie smiled, eyes dropping to his lips as they lifted from her hand.

"You're a charmer," she whispered. "And who says you have me all to yourself?" She ran a hand over Roscoe, who purred and blinked at Vincent with satisfaction.

Vincent lifted a finger to the cat. "Paws off my girl, Roscoe."

The cat stared him down, and he laughed, returning to the kitchen to throw together what he assumed was an appropriate gravy for these perogies. It was hard to know, since the deli owner spoke very little English and his Polish was nonexistent.

As dinner came together, Vincent set the table while Hattie refreshed their wine glasses. She fidgeted with her pocket as he dished the food onto their plates.

"Well, here's hoping I don't poison us both," he announced as he sat at the table.

Hattie took a bite of a pierogi, then blinked.

Vincent followed suit.

They sat in silence for a moment, before Vincent muttered, "Well. This is different."

Hattie chewed thoughtfully. "I don't know. It kind of reminds me of that knocki you made me last week."

"Gnocchi," he corrected. "And no, this is not at all like gnocchi."

She looked down so quickly that he was sure she was hiding a smile. "Well, it's certainly not colcannon, that I know."

He laughed and took another bite. "I've no idea what that is. Will you make it for me sometime?"

She looked up under her lashes with that mischievous grin that always went straight to his heart. "Potatoes, cabbage, and leeks? Boy-o, expect it to be a weekly meal if you're stepping out with an Irish lass."

The thought warmed him. Well, the thought of potatoes, cabbage, and leeks didn't warm him, but the image of sharing meals with Hattie every evening, of going to sleep with her in his arms, of waking up next to her, of having her near him always. The box in his pocket felt heavy and he scraped his fork around the plate, undecided if this was the right moment or not. Probably not.

"Not an ounce of meat in these things," he commented instead

She speared a pierogi and lifted it in the air. "What is this, anyway? Potatoes?"

"I think so."

"Sounds like that gnocchi dish to me," Hattie teased. "I'm not complaining though. We Irish love potatoes. More onions and less garlic, maybe, but we love potatoes."

"Sacrilege," he countered with a smile. "Garlic is life."

They ate for a few more moments, then he broke the silence.

"Things going well for your parents?" The corner of the ring box was digging into his leg from inside his trousers pocket, making him nearly shake from nervousness. "I haven't seen them for a while."

"They're well enough," she replied.

"Have you seen them yet today?" he asked, sweating a bit at the thought that they might have said something to her.

"No. I came straight from the road." She smiled. "Why do you ask? You're quite the nosey one today."

He stared down at the pierogi, stabbing at one of them. "Just making conversation. I went to the hotel today. Everyone was a half-word from a fistfight."

"That's your doing?" she asked with a tilt of her head.

"I like to think so. I just wish…"

"What?"

He suddenly didn't feel like eating any more. "I wish Lefty didn't have to get swallowed up by all this."

She reached across the table for his hand. "Let's not talk about Lefty. Let's talk about us, instead."

"Agreed. I think the plan is working."

She released his hand with an odd look. "If you say so."

Vincent took another bite, eyeing Hattie as her mood darkened.

"You want to push harder, don't you?" he asked.

"Don't you?" she chased a pierogi around her plate. "This plan of ours may suit your speed, but at this rate Corbi will die of old age before we get anywhere."

"You're not hearing what I'm hearing at the hotel. One of these days you should light pinch your way in and see how thin Vito's wearing. We're winning this. We're wearing him down."

"I'd rather just put a gun to the man's head," she said with a sigh, dropping her fork onto her plate.

Vincent eyed her. "You don't really mean that."

"No, I suppose I don't." She ran a hand over her eyes, shoulders slumping.

"When's the last time you slept?" Vincent asked, his voice soft.

"Been a while."

"Still have the marble on you?"

She nodded.

"Is that what you've been thumbing in your pocket all night?"

She straightened in her chair and pulled her hand up from her lap. "No, I'm just… It's been a long day. I'm happy to see you, though. And dinner is good. I like this Polish stuff."

He frowned. "I'm worried about you, Hattie. You need sleep."

"It's just been a long day," she repeated, gathering their empty plates and taking them to the sink. "Truly, I'm fine. Truly."

Vincent watched her for a moment, worried that she was far from fine. "There's this Fritz Lang movie at the Odeon. It looks like a real noodle-bender. Let's go see that this weekend."

"What's it about?" she asked as she made her way to Vincent's couch.

"No idea. Looks like a fantasy, with buildings and machines."

"Sounds a bit like New York City."

Vincent went into the kitchen and rinsed the dishes. "Ever been?"

"Hmm?"

"To New York City?" He busied himself making coffee, staring out the window as he spoke, "I spent almost ten years there, mostly inside the walls of the school. I'd sit in the window and listen to the street sounds, and the smells. It seemed like the city was an entire world unto itself, like there could be nothing else outside the buildings and the side-walks, and the carriages."

Vincent pawed at his pocket and the box within. "When I came here, it was difficult. I'm glad I did, though. I'm glad because otherwise I never would have met you," he said as he took the box from his pocket. "There's something I wanted to ask you, by the way. Maybe it's not the most romantic moment I could've chosen, but I just can't wait any longer, and I need to do this before I completely lose my nerve. Christ, I'm babbling like a fool again."

He turned, box in hand, to face Hattie.

Who had fallen asleep on the couch, Roscoe purring on her chest.

Vincent exhaled and shook his head. So much for the moment. "I guess it can wait."

Slipping the box into his pocket, he took a blanket from a chair to drape it over Hattie as Roscoe hopped off with a *murr* of protest. Then he made himself some coffee and sat back at the table, ring box in his hand. He fiddled with it for a while, convincing himself this wasn't a bad sign. Hattie shifted on the couch, and he jerked the box under the table in reflex.

No, this wasn't a bad sign. This was good. Hattie had suffered from the effects of the demon trap in her pocket, wrecking her sleep and wearing her ragged. She needed sleep, and there was something oddly precious about her dozing off on his couch.

Vincent sat with his coffee until it had grown cold. He tossed it into the sink and returned to Hattie on the couch, crouching to brush a lock of her red hair away from her eyes. Hattie's face was eased, serene, no longer wrought with nightmares or dread. She was like a child slumbering in the safety of her bed. This was a blessing, but the hour was growing late. The bustling of his neighbors had subsided, and lights in the windows across the street had gone dark. The city was falling asleep, and Hattie had a ways to go before she got home.

He laid a hand on her shoulder to wake her and she sighed in her sleep and turned toward him.

No, there was no way he'd ruin this for her.

He whispered, "Well, if you're going to sleep here, we might as well do it right."

Reaching beneath her, Vincent scooped her off the couch. She rolled her face into his chest as he carried her to his bedroom, settling her on the bed with the blanket still covering her. Then he unlaced her boots and pulled them off, setting them beside the bed. As he reached to straighten the blanket over her, the fabric caught on something that crinkled as he pulled the blanket higher. Vincent eased the blanket back, looking her over to find the corner of an envelope sticking form the pocket of her overalls. He reached for the envelope, slipping it free of the pocket before settling the blanket up to her chin.

Vincent lifted the envelope to the light streaming in from the kitchen. The paper sported an official seal. State of New York, Office of Vital Records. He set the envelope on the nightstand with a curious cock of his brow. What was Hattie doing snooping around New York state?

Returning to the kitchen, he refreshed Roscoe's water and did the dishes. It was past midnight when Vincent turned off the light and retired to his bedroom. Hattie had rolled onto her side with the blanket up to her chin. Still asleep. Still at peace.

Vincent pulled off his shoes and suspenders, then settled onto the bed beside Hattie. He reached an arm over her shoulders. She gripped it through the blanket, muttering something unintelligible as she shifted back against his body.

As Vincent thought about the moment that had come and gone, the moment to ask Hattie the question he wasn't at all sure she would say yes to, he closed his eyes and fell asleep.

And dreamed of a future with the woman he loved.

CHAPTER 4

Sunlight flooded Hattie's eyelids, pulling her awake. She blinked several times as she stared at an unfamiliar wall. A thin blanket half-covered her. She shuffled it off as she rolled onto her back. An arm reached around her waist as she turned. Through the drowsy haze, Hattie remembered where she was.

Vincent's bed. And Vincent was lying asleep beside her.

Her heart thumped as she stared at the ceiling. What had happened? She ran a hand down her body, half-relieved/half-disappointed to find her clothing still on. Glancing over she saw Vincent beside her in his shirt and trousers. They'd slept, and that was all.

Hattie wiggled her toes, the joints popping as she wondered where her boots had gone. Indeed, where had the night gone? Here she was in the morning after a full night's sleep. She'd had no nightmares—not even dreams, really, at least none that she could remember. How long had it been since she'd slept like that?

Vincent stirred beside her, his eyes easing open.

"Good morning," she whispered.

"Hmm."

Hattie smiled at his unintelligible response, then sat up to stretch. "Can't believe I slept like that."

Vincent yawned, sitting up as well. "Yeah, you fell asleep on the couch. I figured you were too tired to drive home."

Hattie peered at him with a gentle glance. "You put me to bed. Slept beside me all night."

"I wasn't going to leave you sleeping on the couch." He rolled his shoulder loose.

She watched him stretch, watched the way his wrinkled shirt pulled tight over the muscles of his back and arms. He was always so carefully put together with his suits, his shoes, every dark hair in place, but sitting beside her in his bed… this was a Vincent she was privileged to see. This was Vincent with rumpled clothing, sleep-heavy eyes, his face relaxed and open, his tousled hair like a little boy's.

"You're impossibly sweet, you know that?"

He looked away with that humble bashfulness that she'd once thought contrived, then stood up with a smile. "What time is it anyway?"

She shrugged and he walked into the main room, returning with his jacket. With a grumble and a shake of his head, he checked his gold pocket watch. "Nearly nine o'clock."

Hattie's eyes shot open. "Mother of Jesus, already?" She hopped out of bed, kicking the boots on the floor. "I'm expected at the Charge."

"Have time for a quick breakfast first?" he asked. "Some coffee at least?"

Hattie pulled on her boots. Coffee. Yes, she definitely needed coffee, and from the hollow feeling in her stomach, a bit of food *would* be welcome. "If it's fast, I can stay."

Despite her need to hurry, once the bacon hit the skillet, she knew she'd wait for it to be done. As well as the coffee.

The two sat down and Hattie savored the smells and tastes as they ate.

"Glad you finally got some decent shuteye," Vincent commented.

"Aye, I needed it. I always seem to sleep better when I'm near you." She smiled, half teasing. "I think it's because of this soul twin business."

"See, I'm good for something." He saluted her with his coffee cup.

"You're good for lots of things. And I should sleep over here more often," she commented.

He smirked. "That can be arranged, you know."

His eyes shot open as he said it, and he shifted in his seat uncomfortably. The adorably daft bastard thought he'd pushed too hard, been too forward. *If only he'd be a little more forward*, Hattie thought.

She set her coffee down. "Well, that sounds like paradise to me. If only we could make that happen."

A frown knitted his brows together. Something was eating him, but she didn't have time to pry it loose. Not this morning, anyway.

"Right," Hattie declared after finishing the last bit of toast. "I need to hurry, or I'll be late. Thank you kindly for the hospitality both last night and tonight."

He smiled. "Give the others my regards."

"I will." Hattie searched the main room for a second. "I didn't bring a coat."

"A bit warm for a coat, huh?"

She put her hands on her hips. "Can't shake the feeling I'm forgetting something."

He stood, glancing around the room. "Well, if I see anything, I run it down."

Then he approached, setting his cup atop a sideboard. "You be careful."

"You, too." She reached for his shirt, pulling him in for a long kiss. What a warm, homey feeling this was, waking up beside this man she loved, sharing breakfast with him, kissing him goodbye as she left for work.

Reluctantly she pulled away. "Should I pinch light to be invisible?"

He gave her a puzzled look. "Why?"

"What will the neighbors think if they see me leaving? They'll know I've been here all night."

"Hang the neighbors." He smirked.

Well, if he didn't care, then she wouldn't either.

Hattie crouched down to give Roscoe a quick scratch behind the ears. "And you, mister. You keep him in line, eh?" The cat lifted himself as high as he could as she ran a hand along his spine before stepping into the hallway.

* * *

THE DRIVE in to the Charge was short from Vincent's neighborhood. Far shorter than winding her way through downtown during the morning. The Charge headquarters now sported an additional building off to the side, constructed out of half-rusted steel and tin panels. Hattie brought the car into the makeshift garage and pulled the sliding door shut.

She stepped through the front door, noting the improvements since the last time she'd been in the building. New rugs covered the worn floorboards. The chairs along the anteroom and main seating area had been reupholstered, the wood tables were oiled and shining. Curtains hung over the blacked-out windows, offering at least a semblance of livability. The free pinchers of the Charge had made this old abandoned warehouse feel more like a home. Indeed, more people lived in this building now than passed through. That gave Hattie hope and worried her as well.

Blake nodded at her from the kitchenette near the southeast corner of the first floor. "Hey, boss. You get those barrels to Pittsburgh okay?"

"Aye, we're all set," she replied.

Two young girls sprinted between Hattie and Blake, both regaled in Sunday dresses, giggling as both brandished sticks which passed as swords. A figure stepped out of the first bunk room, scooping one of the girls into her arms.

"Rawrrr, I've got you now." Maria laughed, then she snapped her jaw at the girl as if she were a monster.

The other girl shouted and gave Maria a *thwap* on the thigh with her stick-sword. Maria lifted a foot and held off the swordswoman as she tickled the one in her arms. The girl squealed, sending a shrill noise throughout the warehouse.

Charley bounded down the stairs. "Alright, you two. No shrieking."

Maria set the girl down and gave her bottom a tap as she sent them both off to play.

Charley crossed his arms, ducking his head a little as Hattie joined him. "Sorry about that. They wanted to spend the day with me. I couldn't say no."

"Nor should you," Hattie said. "It's fine. As long as they don't make too much noise, that is."

Maria nodded to the door. "Been a while since the Crew came sniffing around."

"Aye, but we're not about to take any chances."

Maria turned to Charley. "They're probably hungry. Shall I...?"

Charley smiled, "I think there's bread and cheese in the kitchen. Blake can put something together."

Maria lifted a hand. "No, let me. I'd like to."

She stepped over to the kitchenette as Charley watched.

Hattie poked an elbow into Charley's ribs. "Hmm, there. I do believe she's taken a shine to you."

He shrugged. "Thinking it's more like she's taken a shine to my daughters." As he walked off, Hattie noted how he kept casting quick, furtive glances at Maria when he thought she wasn't looking. With a shake of her head and a grin, Hattie marched up the stairs. She found Hassam al Ghasawi waiting for her at the top.

"Hassam," she greeted the man.

"We must speak," he stated, turning immediately for the office. Ghasawi held the office door for Hattie, closing it behind them as she took a seat at her desk. He stood in front of her in rigid formality.

"What's on your mind, then?" she asked.

"Do you remember what my mission here has been?"

"You're protecting me. And Vincent. The both of us."

"Though I have come to appreciate your company," he replied with an accented voice, "that is not my primary purpose."

"Yes, I know. You're here for the Hell Pincher." She moved two chairs forward and sat in one of them.

"Indeed. It was my assumption that he would find the Bright Soul and would make plans to capture the both of you, but it has been nearly six months, and there has been no sign of infernal magics or demon activity. Neither here nor anywhere within a day's journey."

Hattie blinked at him in surprise. "So, you're leaving?"

He nodded. "I must go in search of this Hell Pincher. He's clearly not coming to us."

"And leave us undefended?" she asked, incredulous.

Ghasawi smiled. "You are anything but defenseless. I've seen this firsthand. You and Mister Calendo share a powerful bond that will not prove to be such an easy target for a Hell Pincher were he to find you before I could arrive."

Hattie eased back in her chair. "I don't relish the thought of you leaving, Hassam."

"Nor do I. As I've said, I've grown accustomed to your company." He stared into the far corner of the office. "A Janissary's life is solitary, by and large. I was fortunate to have a companion for some time. Prior, however, I plied my trade alone." He smiled. "Perhaps I was at my best, then. No one ended up dead."

Hattie sighed, pressing her palms against the desk. "I understand. I do. If you must leave, then go with my blessing. Just know that I worry the Hell Pincher might just be waiting for you to leave."

"The thought had crossed my mind. However, I find I need to take action, to locate and pursue him rather than continue to wait."

Hattie stood and reached across the desk to shake the man's hand.

"Oh, I have something for you," he added with a lift of his chin. Reaching into his jacket pocket, he produced two silver-and-spangle earrings and dropped them into Hattie's hand.

"They're lovely," she said.

"They are more than simple accessories. I crafted these two nights ago during the new moon. They are charged with an obfuscation charm. These will bolster your powers, much like the talisman you employed in Ithaca."

Hattie examined them in the electric light of the office. "Thank you."

"They aren't strong charms," he warned. "So don't expect much. You'll be the force behind the magic, but these will help prolong the effect." Ghasawi bowed his head. "And now, it is time that I bid you farewell."

"You'll stay in touch, though?" she asked.

"As I am able."

"Right. Well, Godspeed, Hassam."

"Inshallah," Ghasawi replied with a folding of his hands into a prayer position.

Hattie remained behind her desk as Ghasawi turned to exit the office, and shortly thereafter the building.

Blake popped into the office, looking left and right. "Where'd the Arab fellow go?"

"His name is Hassam." Hattie rolled her eyes.

Blake shrugged. "He left for good?"

"I hope not," Hattie muttered.

"Alright. Well, that's bad news. He was good in a fight."

Hattie said nothing, simply rolling the earrings around in her palm.

Blake asked, "We got a job this week?"

"I haven't heard from Richmond. That's getting annoying, by the by."

"Yeah, we lost all our contacts down the bay."

Hattie sighed. Things in Charleston were heating up, and although there was no power structure in Richmond to hinder them, that unfortunately meant there was no power structure in Richmond to assist them either.

"We'll have to deal with that. Any rate, we have an open week unless something happens."

Blake nodded then blinked out of the room.

Hattie shouted, "What did I tell you about using doors?"

Blake's muffled voice called, "Sorry" from downstairs.

Hattie shook her head, then stood to drop the earrings into the pocket of her overalls, freezing as she realized her pocket was empty. She patted herself down, listening for the crinkle of paper. Nothing.

"Oh, for the love of…"

That was what she'd been forgetting this morning. The envelope. It had slipped out at some point. But where? She knew it was in her pocket when she had dinner with Vincent the night before. It had to have fallen out when he put her to bed.

Or worse…he'd taken it out.

Hattie leapt for the office door, flinging it open as she bounded for the stairs.

"Blake!"

"Yeah?" he asked, turning with a piece of cheese in his hand.

"Get the car!"

"What's up?"

She didn't answer. She just ran out the door for the garage. Blake had already popped into the shelter, crank in hand ready to fire up the vehicle. Hattie jumped into the driver side as Blake got the car running.

"Where to?" He hopped into the seat beside Hattie as the car began rolling.

"Vincent's."

"Okay. Something's going down?"

"I just… I need your abilities."

Blake leaned back, then harrumphed. "Oh, yeah. Okay. A little burglary, huh?"

"It's not like that," she said, swinging the car onto the street.

She made quick time, stopping the car on the street in a manner that wasn't exactly convenient for oncoming traffic. Horns burped at her as she and Blake left the car running, rushing for the building.

Hattie guided Blake to Vincent's door, then held up a hand. She gave the door several hard raps.

"Vincent? Are you still home?"

There was no answer so she gave the door several more knocks. Still nothing. She tried the knob, but the door was locked as she'd expected.

"Okay," she whispered. "He's already gone. I need you to blink inside and open the door."

"Is this kosher?"

"It's an emergency."

"I've never been inside that room. My powers are limited. If there's a couch or a sofa or something where I blink, I could lose a leg or worse."

"There's a clear space just on the other side of the door. About four feet by four feet. No furniture."

"It's risky, is all I'm saying."

Hattie reached for his arm. "This is important."

Blake sighed, shrugged, then faced the door. He ran a hand along its surface and closed his eyes.

"Here goes," he muttered before popping out of sight.

The door clicked and the knob twisted.

Hattie released a breath as Blake stared back at her from inside Vincent's apartment.

"You're okay?" she asked.

"Yeah."

Hattie brushed past him, searching the floor of the apartment for the envelope. Roscoe watched from the countertop, head darting back and forth as she wound her way through the apartment.

"What are we looking for?" Blake asked.

Hattie froze as she glanced at the dinner table. The envelope sat opened, its contents unfolded and resting beside the envelope.

CHAPTER 5

incent sat at his dinner table rolling the ring box around in his fingers. His lips pulled tight in a thin frown as he pondered the moment that had come and gone. She'd said she wanted to spend the night here more often, if they could find a way to make that happen. *That* had been his moment, but for the life of him, Vincent simply couldn't muster the courage to pull the box from his pocket. He'd slept on the damn thing all night with the sharp corners digging into his leg. The morning had been rushed, sure. But proposing had been on his mind constantly for months now, and Hattie had given him clear indications she wanted a future with him.

So why didn't he give her the ring? He shook his head as he set the box on the table. Everything inside him wanted to, but there was some phantom hand keeping him from actually asking her the question.

Was he frightened she'd say no? Or was it marriage itself that scared him stiff?

He stood up to shake off the self-torture and wash up for the big meeting at the hotel. Whatever Vito had in store, it would be a big announcement. Vincent hoped that Vito had been pushed into some half-brained declaration which would only serve to drive a wider wedge between him and his own *famiglia*, but he admitted to himself as he washed his face that Vito was skilled at adapting to change. He was a survivor. Wasn't that what Vincent had always admired about the man?

Clean, he changed his shirt in his bedroom. As he buttoned it up, he wondered if this plan of his and Hattie's was virtuous after all. Vito had caused Vincent so much suffering these past few years, but what would a Baltimore without Vito, what would *freedom* really look like? Without a strong leader Vincent and every other pincher in the Mid-Atlantic would fall prey to the strongmen lurking in the shadows. It would mean constant vigilance, a never-ending struggle just to keep themselves free.

But he wasn't doing this just for himself—this was for the Charge, for the families of pinchers yearning to stay together and not be torn apart and sold piecemeal to the mob, for the children born with gifts, these splinters of bright souls they never asked for.

Most of all, he was doing it for Hattie.

Vincent reached for his jacket and spotted the envelope on the nightstand. He sucked in a breath and reached for it, realizing this must have been what she'd forgotten. Hattie was long gone, but he knew where she was. Charge head-quarters. Vincent checked the time. It was close to eleven o'clock. He wanted to be at the hotel before most of the Crew arrived so that he could get a jump on the gossip, perhaps divining what Vito's big announcement was about ahead of schedule.

But the Charge wasn't all that far from his apartment. He could make a quick detour and drop off the envelope with

Hattie and still be early for the meeting. It would only take a few minutes.

On the other hand, Lefty was sniffing around Vincent more than usual. It was clear from the previous afternoon's conversation that Lefty was onto Vincent, at least on some level. He knew Lefty. The man would be watching Vincent's every move. It wasn't the best time for him to make casual visits to the Charge.

Stepping into the kitchen, Vincent held the envelope up to the sunlight. How important was this? If it was some simple water bill, then *that* wouldn't merit endangering Hattie's operation.

But this was no bill. New York State Vital Records. What the hell would Hattie have to do with Vital Records up in New York? He reached for a knife and slid it into the envelope, breaking the seal. It was better to apologize for snooping than potentially lead the Crew to discover the free pinchers.

Vincent opened the envelope and pulled a slip of paper free, unfolding it to the light. He searched for meaning in the jumble of paragraphs, sentences, names, and dates. It wasn't until he found one name in particular that the importance of this document dawned on him.

Vincenzo Giovanni Calendo. Born December 19th, 1899.

Parents Paolo and Chiara Calendo, late of Brooklyn, New York. Deceased May 7th, 1902.

Vincent reached for the chair at the table, but missed as he took a seat, knees failing him. He crashed to the floor, letter still in hand. Roscoe hopped up to him with a questioning mew.

Vincent shook his head as he read the names and dates over and over again.

Paolo and Chiara. Their faces wouldn't come into focus, but he remembered a faint smell of roses and tobacco.

Tears streamed from Vincent's eyes as he tried to remember their faces, their voices, the house they'd lived in. But nothing came. He'd been too young—he'd been too young when they'd died, too young when he was taken from them.

As he sucked in panicked breaths, a swirl of emotions pounded him in the guts.

This was it. This was the answer to the question he'd asked himself for as long as he could remember. What happened to his parents? Had the gangsters paid them a hefty sum for their child?

He'd always imagined them living in some well-appointed estate upstate, perhaps even in the Hamptons. They'd be wealthy, clothed in finery, driving fancy cars, perhaps even with children who had grown and attended private school. They might be sad from time to time thinking about the boy they'd sold to the mob. But that would fade as their lives marched on.

But their lives hadn't marched on. They'd been snuffed out the day the gangsters came for him. They hadn't paid his family, after all. Perhaps an offer was made, and they'd refused like the proper parents they were, and that refusal wasn't accepted.

That was that. Vincent had no family, now. No parents. No unmet siblings. He was truly alone. At length, he pulled himself together and stood, placing the envelope and letter neatly on the tabletop. This wasn't unexpected. It was always a possibility, a dark notion that nagged him. But now he knew.

He withdrew to the sink to splash cold water on his face. He had to push all of this down deep inside before the meeting. Show no weakness—especially in the face of the organization that had murdered his family.

Pulling on his jacket, Vincent adjusted his tie, staring hard at himself in the mirror. There was no longer any reason for him to feel guilty about what he was doing, no reason for him to have any loyalty at all to the *famiglia*. They were not his family; they'd snuffed out Vincent's family and raised him to be a weapon. Vito Corbi would go down. Alive, dead, it didn't matter anymore.

His time had come.

And maybe with that small bit of vengeance, he'd finally be free.

CHAPTER 6

By the time Vincent arrived at the Old Moravia lobby lounge, a staggering number of Crew members had already gathered. This was double the typical Friday night crowd, and it wasn't even a weekend. Unlike the day prior, Vincent felt compelled to grab a drink to even out his nerves. There was no way he could do anything productive with his current state of mind.

The barkeep poured Vincent some gin with a lime and stepped away without collecting a nickel. It seemed Vito had opened up the bar for the Crew. Well, that would explain the stellar attendance.

Vincent spotted Lefty near the broad masonry columns separating the lobby from the lounge. The man was deep in his thoughts, not even searching the crowd. Vincent was grateful he didn't have to weather another barrage of questions from Lefty since the man would have picked up on Vincent's rattled state.

The Capo came down the stairs just after noon. His face was considerably less flushed. His suit looked new, a shade of charcoal with pinstriping. He sported a fresh shave and his skin glowed. This newfound demeanor of healthy command worried Vincent.

Vito Corbi raised his arms, and soon the entire room was quiet.

With a clearing of his throat, the Capo announced, "We've struggled for some time now. All of us. The five families of New York have dominated our lives for far too long. We were targeted by Joe Masseria, not two months ago. A nightmare laid waste to my home. All in the name of keeping us beaten. In our place. No. This is not the way."

Vincent sipped his gin, interested to hear the rest. What wild scheme would Vito commit the Crew to now?

Corbi smiled. "Many asked how we would respond to this attack. Would we strike back? Would we curl up like a whipped dog? Everyone asked. They had their opinions. Yes, Capo. We strike back!" He shook his head. "What no one had suspected is that Masseria would reach out to us, that he would recognize the violence at Havre de Grace for what it was—a rogue element that had been goaded into foolish, brash action."

Vincent squinted and crossed his arms. Conflict with New York was vital to his and Hattie's plan. This conciliatory language twisted his chest into a knot.

Vito gestured for the lobby, where two men in light gray suits waited. Vincent peered around shoulders and heads for a glimpse of the newcomers.

"To make things right," Corbi declared, "a representative from Masseria has arrived with a peace offering."

Vincent finally pushed aside a beefy gangster to spot this representative and stifled a profanity under his breath. Angelo "Sparks" Floresta smiled at the room, eyes working hard to pinpoint someone in particular. As they landed on Vincent, they stopped.

The second man, a youth who looked to be barely out of

secondary school, stood stiff-armed, hat still on his head. He was lean, almost alarmingly so. His face was dappled with pimples, freckles, and razor nicks. He was bland to the eyes overall. Small frame. Stubby nose. But his eyes…his eyes were sharp, excited, almost hawklike.

Floresta offered a half bow to the room, though his eyes were planted firmly on Vincent.

Vito said, "Allow me to introduce Angelo Floresta. I think one or two of you know him by reputation."

Floresta lifted his hands and snapped his fingers in rapid fire, sending tiny blue sparks into the air to the applause of the room. Vincent, for his part, did not clap.

Vito wound around Floresta to lay meaty hands on the youth's shoulders. "And here…allow me to introduce you all to Joel Seiler." He leaned in. "They call you Buddy, yes?"

The youth nodded.

"I made arrangements late last year with the families of New York for new pinchers. Mister Floresta is here make good on that arrangement. Buddy is to be our newest pincher."

A wave of excitement rolled through the room.

Vito clapped his hands against Buddy's shoulders. "It has been my desire for some time to secure more *stregone* power. This couldn't have come at a better time. In addition, this gesture is only the first in a new spirit of cooperation with my counterpart in New York."

Vincent nearly rolled his eyes when Vito equated himself with Joe "the Boss" Masseria. It was as if a housecat declared itself equal to a lion.

"We stand at the gap, my brothers. A space we must cross, behind which we can never return. And I am gladdened by it. Baltimore will finally take its place at the table."

A cheer sprang from the Crew.

"We will be given our portion of honor."

Another cheer.

"And we have work to do."

As the announcement concluded, the gang swarmed Buddy.

"I asked him not to warn you we were coming," Floresta said from Vincent's side. "I wanted to see the look on your face."

Vincent turned to face him. "Hope you enjoyed the show, you prick."

"I did." Floresta eyed Buddy. "He's fresh from Ithaca, that one."

"I can tell."

"If you're wondering what the catch is, I'm here to tell you there is no catch."

Vincent lifted a brow at the other man.

"Well," Floresta amended, "there may be one tiny catch."

"Besides the fact that I'm gonna have to babysit this kid for a year or two?"

"That's right," Floresta chirped. "You're used to being the only child. This'll be a whole new world for you. I think you might enjoy having a counterpart, if you give the kid a chance."

"What's the wrinkle, Floresta?"

He waved his fingers at Vincent. "We'll discuss it in due time."

Clearly he wasn't going to get anything more out of Sparks. Vincent looked over to where Buddy was getting pummeled on the shoulders and back by all his well-wishers.

"So, what's the deal on this kid? What can he do?"

Floresta smiled. "He's what I've been calling a target pincher."

"What's that supposed to mean?" Vincent asked.

"Here," Floresta replied, grabbing Vincent's glass of gin. "I'll show you."

Floresta wound his way to Buddy, easing some of the crowd away from the kid while whispering into his ear. Buddy nodded once before reaching into his pocket to produce a nickel. He lifted it for all to see.

Floresta stepped through the crowd to the opposite end of the now silent lounge. He lifted the glass to Buddy, who nodded again. Floresta lifted the glass over his head.

Buddy turned around to face the lobby. With a casual flip of his thumb, he sent the nickel spinning into the air. It traced an unassuming arc over everyone's heads, flying across the lounge until it splashed into the glass with a tinkle and a spray of liquor onto Floresta's sleeve.

The lounge erupted in applause as Vito beamed. Floresta lowered the glass and wound his way back to Vincent.

"He hits his targets?" Vincent muttered.

"You should see what he can do with a revolver." Floresta closed in to whisper, "He's the real deal, and he's Ithaca trained. Don't waste him. Don't underestimate him."

Vincent scowled. "I'm more interested in why the hell you're dangling him in front of Vito."

Lefty approached them both. "The Capo wants us in the war room." He turned for the lobby before Vincent could respond.

They followed Lefty past the lobby desk and through the innocuous door that lead to Vito's de facto war room. It was the same four bare walls inside which he'd defended Hattie those months ago. Lefty stood midway along the far wall, arms crossed, eyes working the floor. Vito stood at the end of the table.

"And so," the Capo declared, "we have two *stregone*!"

Vincent turned to Buddy who had filed into the room just behind Floresta. The youth nodded to Vincent once, then gave Vito his full attention.

Vito turned to Lefty. "This young man is one of two we are owed, per my agreement last winter."

Lefty squinted at the Capo. "We *have* two, don't we?"

"Yes," Vito replied with a lift of his finger. "But Vincenzo was returned to us by Philadelphia. That does not count as one of our two."

"I see," Lefty turned to Buddy. "You're a target pincher, huh?"

Buddy nodded, his head bobbing enthusiastically.

Lefty eyed the boy, "You can speak. It'll make things easier."

Buddy drew in a breath, then said in a Brooklyn accent, "Yeah, I can hit pretty much anything, if I get a hair about it."

Floresta said, "He's a marvel, to be sure. Later we'll take him outside the city and we'll set up some targets."

Vito lifted his hands. "Unnecessary, and wasteful. Besides, we have business to attend to."

This must be the wrinkle, Vincent thought as Vito turned to him.

"This gesture of goodwill comes with an expectation of reciprocity."

Vincent set his jaw. No. He was *not* going back to Ithaca. And he wouldn't be traded away like some horse at auction either.

Floresta grinned. "Relax, Calendo. This is a business arrangement."

Vito nodded to Floresta, who stepped up to the table.

"As you know," he began, "Joe Masseria has engaged in a battle of wills with the rest of the five families. To date, he's come out on top of the pile. His greatest present threat is Salvatore Maranzano. Masseria's tried to take down Maranzano without going to war. No one wants guns out in the middle of New York. Not yet, anyways."

"So what's the arrangement?" Lefty asked.

Floresta gestured to the new pincher. "Capo Corbi has agreed to release Vincent and Buddy to my command until such a time as we can unseat Maranzano and put New York in the hands of Masseria."

Lefty muttered, "*Capo di tutti capi.*"

Floresta nodded. "Yes, exactly. Masseria aims to be the boss of the bosses."

"So, Buddy's just here on spec," Vincent pointed out. "That ain't exactly the gesture you had it out to be."

"Quiet," Vito snapped.

Vincent stiffened, then lowered his head.

"This business between Giuseppe and Salvatore makes it impossible to release the Ithaca *stregone,*" Vito added. "Giuseppe is being gracious. We will respond with respect."

Lefty asked, "Then we're throwing in with Masseria? What about the other families?"

Floresta shrugged. "Baltimore's too far from New York for that to be a problem for any of you. Once Masseria's free and clear the strongman in New York, he'll extend his protection to the Baltimore Crew. Plus, he'll deliver that second pincher to your Capo. That makes you the preeminent power south of New York. There's really no downside for Baltimore in this deal."

"Except that Buddy and I could end up with a lead cough," Vincent muttered.

"So, keep your head down and do what I say." Floresta chuckled. "This isn't a turf war. We're going to play this slick and quiet. If no one louses this up, Maranzano will go down before anyone knows he's under attack."

Lefty narrowed his eyes. "How many pinchers does Maranzano control?"

"Just a couple, at this point," Floresta replied. "O'Donnell hit them hard last summer, and they've lost some talent since, but the ones who remained are top shelf and dangerous."

Vincent turned to his Capo. "So it's just me and Buddy going to New York?"

Vito nodded to Lefty. "Alonzo will accompany you, of course. And as the man said," Vito added, "you will do as he says. Failure in this effort will not be forgiven."

Vincent held a breath, a fiery ball of hatred burning in his chest. Once there was a time when such a threat from the Capo would have sent a wave of terror through Vincent, but now, Vincent felt nothing but loathing.

"Yes, Capo," he replied in a careful tone.

The meeting adjourned, and Vincent followed Lefty into the lobby. Floresta and Buddy joined them, huddling together in a conspiratorial clutch.

Lefty extended his hand toward Buddy. "Welcome to the Crew."

Buddy blinked at his hand, then shook it briskly.

Lefty added, "You're wondering about the arm."

"Yes, sir," Buddy replied.

"Lost it in the War."

"You fought in France?" Buddy asked, his eyes wide.

"Sort of," Lefty replied. "It's complicated."

Vincent smirked. "You'll find everything about Lefty is complicated."

Floresta turned to Lefty. "I think the two of you should take some time. Get acquainted. I'll take Vincent, here. We'll get train tickets and meet you at the station?"

Lefty nodded and guided Buddy back toward the lounge while Vincent eyed Floresta.

"You got another wrinkle," Vincent accused the other man. "Don't you?"

"Maybe I do. And maybe it's the sort of wrinkle you and I should discuss somewhere private." Floresta marched for the hotel door as Vincent followed, wondering what sort of problem this was going to throw into his and Hattie's plans.

Hattie. Damn it all, he was most likely going to be stuffed onto a train in less than an hour, and he wasn't about to leave the city without letting her know what was going on.

"I'll meet you at the station," he told Floresta. "I've got a few things to do before we go."

"Calendo, there's something you need to know first."

"What?" Vincent eyed him impatiently. "That Luciano's making a move and this is all part of some convoluted plan?"

Floresta's jaw stiffened before it eased into a smile. "You're not half as dumb as you look, you know that?"

Vincent waved him away. "We'll talk on the train. I gotta grab a suit. Get my neighbors to feed the cat. That sort of thing."

"You have a *cat?*" Floresta shook his head. "Fine. Make it snappy, though. I'm getting the first train to New York, and no one wins if we're late."

Vincent nodded, then turned up the street for his car.

He had to move fast. And he had to find Hattie.

CHAPTER 7

*H*attie sat at Vincent's table stroking Roscoe as the cat purred in her lap. Blake had long gone, taking the car back to the Charge and leaving Hattie alone in her misery. She stared at the corner of the kitchen where the cabinets met the floor. Sounds from the street barely covered the sound of purring as she waited.

He'd opened the letter.

Hattie already knew what was inside. Her cousin had told her when she phoned him the second time about Vincent's family. And now, Vincent knew as well.

It was an hour before she heard footsteps in the hall outside the apartment. A key clinked in the lock, then spun free.

The air pulled tight in the time-pinched turbidity she'd grown used to inside Vincent's time bubbles. She forced her chest to draw in thick breaths as the door eased open. Vincent slipped inside his own apartment, gun drawn. When his eyes landed on Hattie, he lowered the gun and dropped the time pinch. The sounds from the street reemerged from the frozen moment, and his shoulders relaxed.

"Oh. It's you." He stepped toward her, then froze as he glanced to the tabletop, and the letter and envelope still resting there in neat order.

Hattie cleared her throat. "I wasn't ready to show you this yet."

"How long have you known?" He holstered his gun and reached down to pick up the letter. "Why didn't you tell me?"

"I got this a few weeks back, and…I…I couldn't make up my mind whether to tell you or not. Maybe you were happier not knowing. That and I was dreading bringing more sadness into your life."

He tossed the letter down on the table. "I'd been told they sold me. That's what I'd always believed."

Hattie got to her feet, swiping her face as tears stung her eyes. "Please don't hate me. Please don't."

Vincent froze. Cocking his head, he reached for Hattie's face to stroke her cheek, wiping a tear away with his thumb. "Oh, no. Don't think that. Don't ever think that. It's a shock, but I'm glad I know."

She leaned into his hand. "I… I sat here…thinking about all the ways you'd hate me for this. You yelling at me, kicking me out. Vowing never to see me again."

Vincent pulled her into his arms for a tight hug. "Never."

"I wanted to be here when you read it. I wanted to be here for you."

"Yeah," he said with a nervous chuckle, "I'm glad you weren't, to be honest." He released her and moved to put the letter back into the envelope. "I hate getting all weepy in front of women."

Hattie sniffled her way through a laugh. "You big burly tough man, you."

He flipped the envelope flap closed and pocketed the letter in his jacket. "I'm glad you're here, actually. A lot's happened in the past hour and I needed to see you. I have to go to New York City."

She shook her head. "What? Today?"

"We're leaving on the next train. I hope I'll only be gone for a few days, but it may be weeks. I'm not sure. Is there someone at the warehouse who can get a message to you if I call?"

"What happened? Is everything okay?" She reached out to touch his arm. "They're not…that toad of a man isn't trading you to another family?"

"No, as far as I know I'm still Vito's, but there's a dozen things in play right now." Vincent took off his hat and smoothed a hand over his hair. "For starters, there's a new pincher in town."

"Should I get my people—"

"For the Crew."

"Oh." Her eyes grew wide. "Corbi has a new pincher?"

"You remember Floresta? The one bidding on me at Ithaca? Well, he came rolling into town to meet with Vito. Brought him a pincher fresh out of the barn. An offering from Joe Masseria."

Hattie frowned. "Wait, I thought Floresta worked for Luciano."

"Yeah, they're all in bed together." Vincent folded his arms. "The deal is, me and this new pincher gotta take a train up to New York to help Masseria squeeze out his major competition. In exchange Vito gets to keep the new palooka, and he gets both a third pincher as well as the backing of Masseria's organization."

Hattie frowned. "That's the *last* thing we want."

"You bet your ass it is. Then, there's the *other* deal. Floresta. He's down the chain from Masseria, but Luciano's his real boss. I get the sense all this horse trading for pinchers is part of a double cross. Been thinking about it on the way over, and I'm not sure what the play is. But Floresta wants me away from Vito. Which means Vito might get shellacked in the end."

"Then, this is good?"

He shrugged. "Maybe. Problem is I don't trust Floresta. And I don't need some Ithaca kid breathing down my neck. Especially since…well, he's a target pincher. From the sound of it, anything he aims at, he hits. Gonna have to play it real smooth with that beanpole."

Hattie sighed. "Perfect."

"Still, I think I can make this work. Can you feed Roscoe while I'm out?"

Hattie stared down at the cat, then shook her head. "No. Because I'm coming, too."

Vincent's eyebrows shot up. "What?"

"Hear me out." She put out her hand to hold off any protest. "I won't be right alongside you, but I think it's best if I were nearby, maybe working another angle and gathering information on the sly. If there's as many pinchers in New York as I think there are, and you're playing two sides in a gang war, you're going to need backup you can trust."

Vincent nodded. "You're not wrong."

Hattie grinned. "I thought you'd fight me on this."

"No, you're right. Having you up there would absolutely take a load off. Besides, we have to be sure Corbi comes out of this cold in the ground or floating in the harbor. We've been playing a long game up until now, but if there's going to be changes in the power structure in New York, then we need to act fast down here in Baltimore. We'll have a tight window of opportunity, and I intend to take it."

Hattie tilted her head. "You've changed your tune on that."

Vincent unfolded his arms and turned to stare out the kitchen window. "I don't trust that Masseria or Luciano wouldn't replace Vito with someone who's got a team of pinchers loyal to him. We need New York busy with New York, and Vito replaced with…I don't know. Maybe nobody. The number of people I trust in the Crew is running low. I could count them on one hand, at this point. Part of me thinks we should burn it all to the ground."

Hattie stepped behind him, wrapping her arms around his midsection to pull him tight. "I don't know about that, but I agree that we've got to make be sure no one takes their place."

He turned to face her, kissing her forehead. "We'll figure it out. In the meantime, I've got to pack." Vincent eased away, moving for the bedroom. "And you need a plan for what you're going to do in New York."

"I'll rent a room in the city, not too far away from where you'll be. We can stay in touch and coordinate."

Vincent said from the bedroom, "Sounds thin."

"It'll come solid when we're in the city."

"You'll want to find Ghasawi. I'd feel better if you had someone watching your back when I'm not there," he called out.

"Right. Well, I have news about that."

Vincent peered at her from his bedroom, suit in hand. "What?"

"He's gone."

Vincent turned to put his suit down and stepped back into the kitchen. "What do you mean he's gone?"

"Left the city. The state, most likely."

Vincent winced. "The hell did we do to run him off like that?"

"Nothing. Hassam was here lying in wait of the Hell Pincher, and he hasn't shown. So now Hassam has gone hunting for the bastard."

Vincent nodded as he thought it over. "Well, okay then. Never appreciate what you got until it's gone, huh?"

"Something like that."

"You, uh…you got someone at the Charge you'd trust to bring with you? Charley, maybe?"

Hattie frowned. "Not with his girls here. He's spent enough time away from them. Besides, I'd like him to be close to help Raymond out with the business."

"Well, maybe think it over. I'm gonna be on a train for a day, and in the clutches of whoever Floresta's handing me over to. I have to figure out how I can run off without raising everyone's suspicion. Let's say we meet in two days at Union Station. There's a fish market in Red Hook. Meet me there at sunrise."

Hattie nodded. "I will."

Vincent reached for her, pulling her in for a kiss.

"I want you to be safe," he ordered.

"And you, boy-o. You get so much as a scratch, and we're having words."

Hattie left Vincent to his packing, regretting that she'd sent Blake back to the Charge with the car. She'd figured on needing a long walk to sort her misery once Vincent had given her the business. But that hadn't happened. Instead, they were possibly on the cusp of their endgame. The final stab at the mob. The first step toward freedom.

She took advantage of the walk to weigh her options for a traveling companion. Charley was good at getting in and out of spaces, though large forest creatures would draw a considerable amount of attention in the middle of New York City. He was the sort to take orders and fulfill them. But he wasn't all that good at thinking on his feet, or hooves, or whatever. Besides, there were the girls.

What of Blake? He had no family ties to worry about. And

Blake was decent with a rifle. His powers could come in handy in a crowded urban environment. But if anything, Blake was less able to make split-second decisions than Charley. And for all his virtues, Blake remained a country boy. The big city might rattle him to the point that he'd be more of a liability than an asset.

As Hattie stepped through the door of the Charge warehouse, her best option had become clear. She spotted Charley and Maria huddled over a tiny table, both sipping something warm. Hattie stopped abruptly, mouth agape as she took in Charley's freshly shaven jawline and short hair. He had to have gone to a barber in the city for a good cleanup, as this seemed far beyond his usual kitchen-shears self-done haircut. The look had taken two decades off the man, and a smile flickered over his face as he spoke with Maria.

"Eh, you two," Hattie called out as she moved for the stairs. "I need a word, please. In the office."

The two exchanged alarmed glances, then set down their mugs to rush after Hattie, who closed the door behind them.

"Right," Hattie said, sitting on the corner of the desk. "I'm leaving town for a space."

"Where to?" Maria asked with a worried frown.

"New York City. I'm not sure for how long, either."

"Is this Charge business?" Maria pressed.

"No," Hattie replied. "But depending on how things go, this could be the thing we've dreamt of. Our chance for a free state for pinchers. But it'll take work, and a lot of luck." Hattie looked to Charley. "I'm putting you in charge of the headquarters until I'm back."

Charley nodded.

"Have Blake with Raymond, and help him anytime he needs." Hattie then glanced at Maria. "And you... Do you fancy a trip to, oh what are they calling it now, the Big Apple?"

"Me?" Maria squeaked.

"Aye." Hattie hopped off the desk. "You're smart, strong, loyal, and you can think on your feet. You're used to coordinating and taking part in complex plans."

"So…you want me there as backup?"

Hattie shook her head. "As my right hand. This is the big league, Maria. I need someone I can trust at my side."

Maria peered at Hattie with a mix of confusion and amusement. "You trust me? Really?"

"I do."

"Not sure what I've done to deserve that. We were enemies not long ago."

"Well, you're one of us now, and you've proven yourself to be loyal so far."

Maria turned and glanced at the ceiling, eyes moving with thought.

Hattie pressed, "What do you say? Want to get your hands on these goons? Work side-by-side with me to bring about change?"

Maria straightened then turned to Hattie. "Yes."

"Right, brilliant. Go pack for a month, at least."

Charley moaned, "A month?"

"Could be a week. I honestly have no idea, Charley." Hattie patted his arm. "You got this in the meantime?"

"I'm not sure you got me figured square," he muttered. "But I've got it."

As she exited the office, Hattie turned to take in the surroundings. If things went well, they'd finally be able to strip the paint off the windows.

And if it went poorly, she'd never see this place again.

CHAPTER 8

Vincent steadied himself against the arm of one of the first-class railcar seats as the train took a bend somewhere north of Philadelphia. The seat was upholstered in a reddish-pink velvet, a wingback facing the aisle at an angle as it shared a table with its counterpart. Vincent tapped his fingers along the arm of the chair, balancing a napkin-wrapped pastry in his left hand.

"Hungry?" Vincent offered the pastry to Lefty with a half-shrug.

Lefty examined it with begrudging interest. "Is that almond crème?"

"Yeah."

"You remembered." Lefty reached for the pastry.

Vincent grinned. "After all the hell you gave me last time we made this trip? Sure, I remembered."

Buddy blinked at them with curiosity from the opposite chair.

Lefty took a bite, then mumbled around the pastry, "We had business a few years back up by Bensonhurst."

Vincent added, "He got this damn almond crème pastry

on the train and wouldn't shut up about it for a full year. I think he went to three different bakeries in Baltimore trying to see if they could make the same exact thing."

"That's an exaggeration," Lefty grumbled. "It was just the one."

Buddy's face twisted in confusion. "I don't understand. Why is this important?"

"Because it's a really good pastry," Left told him.

Vincent turned to the back of the car, giving Lefty's chair a light bump with the fat of his fist. Floresta sat in the back corner, consuming half of the long velvet bench. The window above his head revealed the track retreating behind them.

Vincent leaned against the table just in front of the bench. "You hungry?"

"Can't you make a four-hour train trip without eating?" Floresta grumbled.

"Sure, but it's bad luck not to eat on a train."

"That's bushwa."

"Yeah. Probably." Vincent took a seat next to Floresta and lowered his volume. "You ready to shoot straight with me about this trip?"

"Can they hear us?" Floresta asked with a nod to Lefty and Buddy.

Vincent shook his head. "Lefty's about to launch into one of his stories. I can tell. He's doing that thing with his hands."

"Good," Floresta replied. "How much have you pieced together on your own?"

"That you and Luciano are making a play on Masseria. Just can't figure out how, or why."

"The why should be obvious."

"I suppose," Vincent grumbled. "But it's the risk versus reward that don't make sense to me. This goes sideways, and we're all dead. Please tell me this isn't just Luciano gunning for glory."

Floresta shrugged. "If you ask him, that'll be about the long and short of it."

"But I didn't ask him; I asked you."

Floresta lifted his finger and thumb. A tiny blue line of electricity danced between fingertips. "Once was a time people like us were considered gods. Then witches. Now we're weapons. This used to be just lightning." He snapped his fingers, and a puff of ozone lifted from his palm. "Now, it's the future. We've wired our cities up to grids. Telephones and telegraphs. Radio waves. You're a time pincher, Vincent. Surely you can see how these times we live in have such potential."

Vincent stared at Floresta, waiting to find out where all this was going.

"No one's thought about where us pinchers are gonna fit into this new world that's being born right before our eyes." Floresta stared back through the window. "Everyone's just looking backwards."

"You and Luciano. You're looking forwards?"

"You think we'll see pinchers free in our lifetime?" Floresta asked him.

"I'd like to think so." Vincent leaned back into his seat.

"Then you're looking forwards, too."

"What's the play, Floresta? How are we supposed to take down Masseria?"

Floresta pulled his eyes away from the window, then leaned closer, "I have contacts inside Maranzano's organization. I've given them just enough to believe I'm double-dealing on the Boss. They don't trust our pinchers any farther than they can throw them. But you two? You're not from New York. You're riding in on a train with me. Not Catena."

"Who's Catena?" Vincent asked.

"Masseria's consigliere. He's basically his Number Two."

"That makes Luciano Number Three?"

"Something like that. Anyways, my people on Maranzano's side are expecting backup. You're it. You and the kid."

Vincent turned to look at Buddy, who appeared befuddled and a little bored at Lefty's story. "Is the kid one of your people?" he asked.

"Nah, he's fresh off the farm. Like I said."

"Surprises me. Figured you'd want an ace in the hole with this triple-cross."

"I couldn't use one of my people," Floresta stated. "Corbi would sniff it out."

Vincent snorted. "Fat chance of that."

"That right there's the difference between you and me, Calendo. You love to underestimate Vito Corbi. I'm completely unwilling to do that, especially when the stakes are this high."

"Fine. You sneak us into Maranzano's crew as backup. What then?"

"Maranzano's pincher has a plan. A quick game to knock over Masseria's money pot and his enforcement in one swoop."

Vincent squinted. "Then we go for the throat?"

"No. Then you lead them to Masseria, and they get slaughtered."

Vincent nodded, finally understanding. "Once Maranzano's down, you take out a weakened Masseria. And the last man standing is 'Lucky' Luciano."

Floresta grinned with satisfaction. "Now you see how delicate this has to be. Any of this airs out before the endgame, and it's curtains."

"So, here's the part where I ask you what I get outta this."

"What do you mean?"

Vincent looked out the window. "I ain't helping you out of the goodness of my goddamn heart, Sparks. Masseria can hang. It's Baltimore that I want."

"You might find Luciano open to negotiation." Floresta lifted a brow. "He's eager to shape the future for his empire. Get in early, and you can be part of that."

Vincent turned back to the other man, "It's time, Sparks. Time for Corbi to go away. That's what I want. If I make this happen for you, and by some miracle we don't all get ventilated doing it, I want Corbi retired and not replaced."

Floresta stared at him. "You got a preference for alive or dead?"

Vincent shook his head. "Either one."

"I can't make that sorta agreement," Floresta told him. "You'll have to talk to Luciano, himself."

"Fine. But until I do, I'm not signing onto this bag-of-cats scheme of yours."

Floresta sighed, then nodded. "I'll set up a meet when we get to the city. Meanwhile, we're putting you up at the Monarch."

"That's in Brooklyn?"

"That's Masseria's turf. Maranzano's held on to the Bronx and part of Harlem, but we're keeping the new guy well away from that."

"Suits me." Vincent stood up. "I need a drink."

He wound his way past Lefty and Buddy. Lefty was halfway through his art heist story, right about the part where the Serbian face man blew their cover. Vincent reached for the door, sliding it open as the rushing noise of the tracks filled his ears.

Could it work?

Maybe.

But first, he'd have to secure a promise of a free Baltimore.

*L*ong shadows stretched over Red Hook as the sun warmed the early morning sapphire. Hattie crossed her arms, stroking them in the early chill. It was mid-May, and she'd already grown accustomed to warm afternoons on the Chesapeake. But standing on a rocky pier jutting into the Upper Bay between a fish market and a grimy, soot-covered brick warehouse, Hattie wished she'd brought a jacket at the very least.

"Ain't that something?" a voice called behind her.

Hattie turned to smile at Vincent. "What?"

He nodded to the water. A tiny silhouette jutted from the horizon, the top third gleaming in bright green patina. It reached up with one hand declaring liberty for all, though at this distance it looked a bit like a child's soldier toy.

"Ever been to New York before?" Vincent asked.

"Once," Hattie replied. "When I was young. Twice, actually if you count when my parents came to America when I was two. I can't imagine trying to keep an eye on a toddler while working my way through Ellis Island."

Vincent put an arm around her and she leaned into him. "Give me that jacket of yours, will you."

He smirked. "What, not used to Atlantic wind?"

"Hand it over, boy-o."

He unbuttoned his jacket and held it for her. She wove her arms into the sleeves, feeling the leftover warmth from him, inhaling the scent of talc and aftershave on the collar.

"We have a room at the Monarch in Brooklyn," he told her. "What about you? Where are you staying?"

"We've rented a third-story room in Cobble Hill from a widow from the Old Country. Just up the way."

Vincent wrapped his arms around her, pulling her against his chest as she snuggled into him. "I think you're living finer than I am. Who'd you bring? I'm guessing it was Maria."

"Now, how'd you come to that conclusion?" She glanced up at his face.

"Probably the same way you did." He smirked down at her, then looked out over the bay. "I have a meeting with Masseria today. The big introduction. I got Floresta's plan out of him, by the way. He wants us to play the part of moles. Convince Maranzano we're setting Masseria up for a fall. Bring them all together and let the Boss's gang do the heavy lifting. Then Luciano greases Masseria, and we're back home to deal with Corbi."

"What's our take, then?"

"Luciano helps us with Corbi—at least, in theory. Floresta couldn't give me a bond on that. I'll have to go to Luciano myself to see what he says on the matter."

"So, you haven't met with Luciano yet?"

Vincent shook his head.

"Still feel this is a good idea?"

He shook his head again.

"Right. Well, we're committed now. If Luciano welshes, we can still come up with a plan. I intend on nosing around

Brooklyn today with Maria to see where the borders are between the families. I'll be just another Irish girl. I'm practically invisible already."

"I know the feeling," Vincent commented dryly. "I'm not sure when I can break away to meet with you again. We need a system of communication. In the meantime, mornings are best. These mooks don't seem to haul their carcasses out of bed before eleven."

"Shall we meet in two days, then?" She pulled a slip of paper with pencil scratches on it, handing it to Vincent. "Here's where we're staying. Come for breakfast and we'll compare notes."

He looked down at the paper and tucked it into his pants pocket. "What're you cooking me for breakfast?"

"Cook?" she laughed. "We'll be eating whatever you bring, boy-o!"

She shimmied out of his jacket, handing it back to him. Then she kissed him and turned to trot along the fish market on her way to the room she'd rented. The widow stood on the stoop of the red-stoned row house, running a broom over the steps. Hattie pinched light over her body, draping herself in an upper-middle class traveling ensemble, shading her hair brunette.

"Top o' the morning, Miss O'Toole," the old lady croaked in a tobacco-stained brogue.

"Morning, Mrs. Dunne."

Before Hattie could reach the top of the stoop, Mrs. Dunne called out, "You know…"

Hattie paused with her hand on the door latch, stifled a sigh, then turned to the old woman. She seemed nice. Harmless. She could barely open her eyes, and Hattie suspected there was very little interest in the old woman's mind for gangster intrigue, much less any predisposition to rat her out to the Sicilians should she see or hear too much. But what

Hattie and Maria had discovered shortly after handing over two weeks' worth of rent, was that the woman wasn't just talkative. Someone had beaten her with the Blarney Stone, knocking out all of her teeth and replacing them with tiny elves that never shut their gobs.

"Yes, Mrs. Dunne?" Hattie said with a magic-enforced smile.

The old woman leaned against her broom. "My sister never married. She'd tell me, Oh Margaret, men are good for two things, and I can get one of them from the vegetable stand."

Hattie snickered. "What's the other, then?"

"Their money, child. But she couldn't stand the sight or smell of them. She took her dowry and traveled with't, you know that? Went to Burma and India. Didn't hear from her for nigh on fifteen years. Postcards, though. My late husband and I would keep them in a book."

The old woman lifted a foot to climb the stairs. Hattie trotted down to offer an arm, guiding her up step by painful step.

"Well, come to find out, she didn't go it alone after all. She had a traveling companion. A spinster from Cork whom she'd met on the boat to Calais. Spent the better part of her life traveling with this woman, seeing the other side of the world. And no one thought twice about it, especially since there were no men to kick up a fuss. And no one talked about't. We let it be."

Hattie squinted at the woman as she gripped her arm.

"So, you and your companion are welcome to stay as long as you like. Thought you should know."

Hattie smiled. "Well, Mrs. Dunne, that's much appreciated."

The widow patted Hattie's arm then stepped inside.

Hattie followed into the building, climbing the stairs and keying open the door to the room.

Maria glanced up from a chair, a cup of coffee in her hand. "How'd it go?"

Hattie dropped her light pinch with a sigh. "He's meeting Masseria today. Also, Widow Dunne thinks we're a couple."

The other woman snickered. "I could do worse."

"You could do much better, as well." Hattie went over and sat in the other chair. "Once the goons are up and about, I want to get the lay of the land."

Maria set down her coffee. "Are we starting in Brooklyn?"

Hattie thought for a moment. "Either Brooklyn or the Bronx. We'll need to get the skinny on the speakeasies and do it quietly. This isn't Maryland. They enforce prohibition here."

Maria nodded. "I've been around the block a few times with Galloway. Maybe you should let me take the lead?"

"That suits me just fine. Let's start after lunch." Hattie pulled off her boots and jumped onto the bed, bouncing on the loud springs. "I'm lying right here until then."

"You don't want to go see the sights?" Maria teased.

"I'd rather catch up on sleep."

Hattie did her best, but sleep couldn't find her. Her insomnia had returned along with the nightmares that plagued her once she managed to close her eyes. And although she knew it was the proximity of the demon trap in her pocket that disturbed her sleep, she was terrified to let the thing out of her grasp.

What if it fell into the wrong hands? If someone set the demon loose and it killed people, she'd never forgiver herself. And if the Hell Pincher managed to find it…that would be the worst nightmare of all.

After a couple hours of tossing and turning, Hattie gave up. She and Maria dressed in city wear and stepped out around noon. Maria guided them north to the Bronx, where they found a handful of Irish delivery boys whose information was easily pried loose with a few coins. They pointed the women to a basement room speakeasy near Belmont.

Once they reached the alley and the stairs leading below the street, Maria turned to Hattie. "Okay, now. You're going to have to decide who you are."

"What do you mean?"

"Do you want to be the red-head? Or the brunette? Because once we step down those stairs, we're in the open."

Hattie nodded, then glanced to Maria. "You're right. And you should stay on the street."

Maria scowled. "You're not thinking of going down there alone?"

Hattie pinched Brigid O'Toole back over herself. "Not me. Brigid."

"That's fine and all, but what happens when someone gets handsy? Or if your magic starts pulling too hard?"

Hattie gave one of her earrings a tap with her fingernail. "I've got a little help. You're of greater value as an unknown in all this. Watch the street. If it looks like a gang is coming with their business faces on, give the ground a couple good thumps. I'll pinch myself invisible and come running."

Maria nodded. "Okay. Be careful."

Hattie gathered herself, double-checked her illusion, then descended to the speakeasy door. Per the delivery boys' instructions, which she hoped were bonafide, she gave the door three knocks, one, then three again.

A voice boomed from inside, "We're closed."

"Delivery for Chester," Hattie replied with the code phrase for entry.

"Chester ain't here."

"I'll leave it on the counter."

The bolt slid with a snap and the door slipped open just

enough for Hattie to squeeze through. Inside she found an innocuous room with a pegboard wall behind a counter. Various hair creams and pomades sat in neat rows. For a half-second, she wondered if she hadn't been put on.

The man guarding the door, a gentleman with shoulders as wide as a Ford, stepped up to the counter. "You from outta town?"

"You could say that," Hattie replied. "What gave me away?"

"You're a little early for the crowd." He reached for the peg board, fingers slipping behind the display to trigger a latch. Half the display wall hinged open to reveal a pair of heavy curtains. "Ain't no music yet."

"That's fine," she said. "I'm here on business."

The man chuckled, a sound that was more like a hacking cough than mirth. "Then you're right on time."

She stepped through the curtains and into a squat room cloaked in tobacco smoke. The lights were so dim she had to pause a moment for her eyes to adjust. A bandstand of sorts, more like lengths of sheet tin held a few inches off the ground by construction lumber, sat direct ahead against a grimy brick wall. Tables ran left and right, still littered with glassware and cigarette butts from the previous evening.

One man stood behind a rail, a series of amber bottles behind him. He held a bottle in one hand, carefully pouring its contents into another. As Hattie approached, he jerked with a start, spilling a splash of gin onto the rail.

"Jesus! You scared me."

"Sorry about that." She nodded at the bottles. "Giving the inventory a good watering down?"

He scowled. "Nah. Nothing like that. Just combining half-empties. You want weak gin, you go to Jersey. Here we take care of the customers." He finished and straightened up, extending a hand. "I'm Pauly."

"O'Toole," she replied, shaking his hand carefully. "Brigid O'Toole."

"Yeah, okay. Nice. I think they'll like you here. You got some spit-polish to you, so that's good. A word of advice, though?"

She cocked a brow at him.

"See what you can do about that Irish jangle you got." He gestured at his mouth. "Most of the fellas here are either old school white bread or paisans in business suits."

"I don't follow," she said.

"How long you been in America?"

"Most of my life, if that matters."

Pauly held up his hands. "Hey, I got no beef. I got a girl I see on the regular who's off the boat. I'm just saying you'll get more business if you get your way around the white bread accent. Just tryin' to help, is all."

"Who do you think I am?" she asked with a tilt of her head.

"You a new girl? Or..."

"I'm not a call girl. I'm a customer."

Pauly stiffened, then pulled the bottles off the rail. "Oh. Oh! Oh, Jesus. I'm sorry. Sorry about that, lady!" he blurted. "It's just you comin' in so early, I figured you was one of Salvatore's girls."

"Who's Salvatore, again?"

Pauly clamped his jaw shut, a bead of sweat popping up on his forehead. "Uh, yeah. Can I get you a drink? First is on the house on account of me bein' rude and all."

Hattie smiled. "Some of that gin. Fresh bottle, if you please."

Pauly smiled. "Yeah, I suppose that's fair."

"On ice, if you have any."

He chuckled. "Hey, this is a fine establishment here. We got ice. We got bourbon. We got jazz after nine."

He poured Hattie's drink and set it in front of her.

"And, you have working girls as well?"

"Yeah, we do. But if that's your thing, you'll have to go somewhere else. Owners are upstanding Christians, so they don't square with lavenders."

"Well, it's good to hear I'm in the hands of Christians." She sipped her gin. "Salvatore…he owns this place?"

Pauly shrugged.

"It's a secret, then?"

"Not much of a secret. Just not polite to discuss it, is all."

"Does he ever come around?"

Pauly chuckled. "Yeah, you're off the boat. No, lady. They don't ever come to bars or speakeasies."

"Who?"

He leaned in. "The *famiglia*. You know. Italians?"

Hattie feigned ignorance. "I don't follow."

"Jesus, lady. Yeah, the gangsters own everything 'round here. They're tight like family. And they got rules. One of which, you never go drinkin' in a speakeasy."

"That a fact?"

"Least that's what I heard. Ain't never seen one of them who weren't here to collect. Suits me, too. I'd rather the customers not get spooked off." He stepped around the rail and began gathering glasses from the tables. "So, because I've been at this a while and I'm no spring chicken myself, might I ask you a question?"

"If you like."

"You in the business? What I mean is, you in with the Irish gang?"

Hattie turned, leaned against the rail, and lifted the glass to her face. "Now, whatever led you to that conclusion?"

"You're a dame. You're here at one in the afternoon. You're sizing up the joint like you're planning to move in. And you're asking about Salvatore Maranzano like you didn't have a care in the world. I figure either you're loopy on poppies, or you're in the business."

"And if I were?"

He paused over a stack of glasses, glancing over to Hattie. "Then I'd encourage you to get lost. Maranzano ain't no friend of Killer Madden." He held his gaze. "And I'm sure you're about to tell me you ain't never heard of him, either."

"I'm new to town."

"Boston?"

"Baltimore."

Pauly laughed. "Well, ain't that a peach? You're fightin' an uphill battle, lady. Dwyer's in the poke and his boys are dukin' it out over in Hell's Kitchen. These boroughs here belong to Maranzano. I suggest you turn around and go back to Baltimore, if you know what's good for you."

"I have some experience with these matters." She took a sip of the gin. "I've no intentions of either running, or hiding. I'm in the city to do some business." She set her glass on the rail, and walked around the table.

He shrugged. "Okay, but you don't want to mess with these guys. They've got weapons, and I'm not just talking about Tommy guns, if you know what I mean."

Hattie smirked, knowing exactly what he meant.

"Pinchers? Yeah, I know pinchers. You know what happened to Jonas O'Donnell down in Baltimore?"

Pauly looked around, then whispered, "I heard Corbi's men took him down."

"Don't believe everything you hear." She sat on the corner of the table. "I'm no dame. I am motivated, and I have resources. Pincher resources."

Pauly stepped away and moved for the rails. "Okay, lady. Your funeral. Step on down to Piscatori's. It's on Westchester. You get there right before dinner, or right after. Look for a fella by the name of Polizzi. 'Pockets' Polizzi."

Hattie smiled. "Thanks for the drink." Then she turned diving through the curtains and giving the secret door a knock.

Maria nodded to Hattie once she reached street level. "That was fast."

"It was empty, short of one bartender." Hattie told her. "Happily, he was a well-informed bartender. We should have dinner out tonight. Do you like Italian food?"

* * *

THE RUSH of the Bronx during the change in work shifts was both alarming and awe-inspiring. Hattie and Maria pressed against a wall beside a stoop of concrete steps as a river of men with five o'clock shadows filed past, hats pulled tight over weary eyes. Cars weaved past one another in an ordered chaos. The din from the street was oppressive, as was the sooty fume that filled the air.

Hattie leaned in to shout, "I think that's it." She nodded to a red awning across the avenue and two doors down.

Maria nodded. "Good. But how are we getting across this street?"

They found a clump of grimy men ready to muscle their way between Fords. The women slipped into their wake as drivers gave them the business. Once they were clear on the other side, Hattie checked her shoes.

"Does this damned city ever dry out?"

"It's a filthy mess, isn't it?" Maria stared at the restaurant. "How will you know which one is him?"

"Not sure. I'll go on intuition."

"You mean we'll go."

Hattie winced. "Well, about that."

Maria crossed her arms. "I skipped lunch getting ready for this."

"Sorry. I've been piecing together my plan of attack, and I'll need you out of sight again."

"Are you serious? I'm starving."

"It's not like I'll be eating, either. We'll grab something after."

Maria huffed.

"Look," Hattie said, giving Maria's arm a pat, "I need you to keep an eye on me. I need these bastards to think I'm the next Vito Corbi. Brigid O'Toole has her sights on Baltimore, and she'll need support from New York."

"What?"

"I realized back at that speakeasy that these people are prepared to accept anything if I sell it well enough."

Maria's eyebrows shot up. "But you're a woman."

"I've noticed."

Maria rolled her eyes. "You really think they'll buy that a woman is edging Vito Corbi out of his own territory?"

"I know enough of the Crew and their business to sell it. If I tell them I've come to town with one of my pinchers? That'll get me an audience at the least."

Maria shook her head. "You're insane."

"The thought's crossed my mind. I'll give you a signal. When I do, give the table a good thump from below."

Maria glanced at the ground. "There's basements and sewers under our feet. I can't be so precise."

"Right. Well, give the building a rattle, then. Just so I prove my point. It's all in the theatrics."

Maria nodded. "You sure about going in alone again? If I'm your pincher, then why am I not at your elbow?"

"On one hand," Hattie said, pulling her out of the way of another rush of workers on their way home, "Brigid is here to start a conversation. Not a fight. It'd be indelicate to bring her muscle before she's even met the first gangster. A second, well…I don't have enough magic to cover us both in illusion while we're in there."

Maria examined her clothes. "What's wrong with this?"

"It's fine for Baltimore. These New York City mobsters expect women to be in their Sunday best."

"Fine. What's the signal I should be looking for?"

Hattie stared into the sky for a second. "I'll light a cigarette."

"You smoke?"

"No, but men love to share their tobacco with strange women."

Maria grinned. "Alright, then. Good luck."

She gave Hattie's arms a quick shake, then wandered toward the corner of the restaurant's masonry front.

Hattie reached out with her powers to knit the illusion of Brigid back over herself. The smell of garlic hammered her in the face. Tiny square tables covered in red-and-white gingham ran at odd angles across the smoke-filled room. An elderly couple sat at one table. The woman was still slowly working at a bowl of pasta, while the old man seemed to have fallen asleep in his chair. A short space near the kitchen housed a longer table, bare wood exposed, covered in the remains of someone's lunch. A squat man with a full, black mustache sat cross-armed as he leaned against the wall. His eyes bobbed in slow jerks. The man looked drunk, though there was no evidence of booze on the table.

A thin boy with a towel over his shoulder stepped up to Hattie.

"One for dinner?" he asked with a cracking voice.

"Aye," Hattie replied. "Near the back, if possible."

"Sure." He led her to a table beside the mustachioed gentleman and held the chair for her.

"Ya want some water and bread?" the boy asked.

"I'm waiting for someone. If you could give me a few minutes?"

The boy shrugged and disappeared into the kitchen.

Hattie sat with full, regal posture, making a demonstration of not looking at the man at the table beside her.

After a space of pregnant silence, the man asked, "Who ya waitin' for?"

She glanced slowly over, putting on the air of only having just noticed him. "Beg your pardon?"

The man pulled himself off the wall, leaning over the table with a grunt.

"You, uh…you one of Dwyer's girls?"

"I'm afraid I don't quite follow. I'm waiting for a business acquaintance."

He grinned. "Sorry."

After a pause, she added, "His name is Polizzi."

The man's eyes narrowed. "That so?"

"Aye. I'm here to discuss certain opportunities that may prove advantageous for his employer." She turned to give him a coy smirk. "If you see him, you'll let me know?"

He stared for a long moment before his eyes wrinkled at the edges, his mustache fluttered, and he released a roaring laugh. With considerable effort, he lifted himself off his chair. Once he was standing upright, Hattie realized he wasn't so much portly as he was brawny. His forearms were almost as thick as his biceps. The man wound around the long table to pull a chair across from Hattie. As he dropped into the seat, she worried it would crash into pieces under the strain.

"You got a way of talking, miss…" He bobbed his head for her to fill in the blank.

"O'Toole. Brigid O'Toole."

"Sure you're not part of Dwyer's old gang? I mean, not that there's much left."

Hattie searched her recent memory for a name Pauly had dropped. "I'm not in league with Madden, if that's what you're worried about."

Polizzi shook his head. "No one's worried about Madden save for Madden himself."

He reached for his jacket pocket to produce a flask. With a single flip of his thumb, the cap unscrewed and flew away at its hinge. He took a swig, then offered it to Hattie across the table.

She held up a hand and shook her head once.

"You keeping your wits about you. This must be business." He took another hit, then settled the flask back into his pocket. "You a pincher?"

Hattie fought the impulse to set her jaw. "No, I'm on the other side of that dynamic."

"Huh?"

"I'm no pincher, Mr. Polizzi."

"Call me Pockets," he mumbled. "Mr. Polizzi was my father."

"If this is, as I suspect, a safe space…might we speak directly?"

He nodded.

"Do you have access to Salvatore Maranzano?"

Polizzi laughed again. "Lady, you don't know who I am? You come looking for me, and you don't know who I am?"

She shook her head, wishing she had a better answer.

Polizzi reached into his jacket to pull a revolver. Hattie stiffened for a second, then eased as he set it onto the table like a pile of lint. He reached into the pocket again to produce one flask, then a second. Then an adjustable wrench.

She squinted at the wrench.

"I was working on the boss's jalopy last night. Forgot to put it away." Polizzi continued reaching in the liner pocket of his jacket, producing a deck of cards, and then a roll of dollars. He eyed Hattie as she stared impassively.

"Well, if that don't impress you," he grumbled, lifting the first third of a baseball bat from the liner of his jacket.

Hattie held up a hand. "No need for that. And I can see why they call you Pockets. You're a pincher, I take it."

He grinned, then began replacing all his bric-a-brac. "My point being… I have access."

She let him clean up his belongings before asking, "Might it be possible to arrange a meeting with Mr. Maranzano?"

"Depends on what you're meeting him for. He's getting on in years, so I don't think he'll be interested in womanly attention."

"That's not the sort of attention I'd like to give him."

"More business? What're you so hot to trot over?"

She shifted in her chair to cross her legs, twisting a little at the waist to put him at an angle. "You got a smoke in that magic pocket, big boy?" she asked.

He smiled, then produced a cigarette case from his jacket. It was a shiny brass thing embossed with an ornate P. He flipped the case open and extended it to Hattie.

She fished out a cigarette, keeping it between her fingers unlit as she gestured to him. "I hail from the Baltimore area. Are you familiar with any of the families south of New York?"

He nodded. "I hear that used to be D'urso's turf."

"It's been in the hands of Vito Corbi for about eight years, now."

"You in his crew?"

"No. His crew, for what it's worth, is due for retirement."

Polizzi laughed again. "That's not what I hear. I hear they took down Masseria's nightmare boy."

"O'Donnell?" Hattie shook her head, looking heavenward. "Do you *really* think a fatuous bastard like Corbi with his feeble crew of rum-runners could possibly take down Jonas O'Donnell? The man's only got one pincher to speak of. A bit of a joke, at that."

Polizzi squinted. "Word 'round the campfire is there was a dust up. Pinchers coming outta the woodwork."

"Aye," she said with a sizzling grin. "And where do you think those pinchers came from?"

Polizzi's squint narrowed yet further.

She leaned back in her chair. "For a woman to operate at this level, she must plan ahead. She must be careful. And she must be very, very good at what she does."

Polizzi nodded. "I suppose."

"So, as I said, Corbi's time has come to a close. I intend to be the one to draw the curtain. I have the magical muscle to do it. What I lack is the hardware. And a woman cannot keep a city in line without gunpowder."

He crossed his arms, sizing her up. "Where'd you get all these pinchers, anyhow?"

"Not to be impolite, Mr. Polizzi, but that's the sort of conversation I'd rather have with Maranzano."

"Yeah, well if you don't convince me, that ain't happening."

"Am I not convincing?"

"I think you went to grammar school. You know how to use your words well enough. But I'm more of a see it to believe it type."

Hattie nodded with a smile. "Got a light?"

He paused for a second, then slowly reached into his jacket to produce a box of safety matches. Polizzi pulled one and struck it against the side of the box. Hattie leaned forward with the cigarette between her lips. She puffed the cigarette in quick bursts, just enough to light the end.

As she leaned back, the dishes on the long table began to

rattle. Polizzi turned to peer at the plates. The table began to clatter.

The boy with the towel rushed out of the kitchen. "You two feel that?"

Polizzi stood cautiously as the floor trembled. Hattie crossed her elbows, holding the cigarette close to her cheek as she kept a razor-sharp look on Polizzi.

He noticed her look, then nodded. "Yeah, alright. I get it."

Hattie stabbed the cigarette out in the glass ashtray, and the trembling subsided.

The boy stood slack jawed, staring at the walls.

Polizzi gestured at him with a wave of his hand. "Get lost, Carlo."

The boy disappeared back into the kitchen.

Polizzi remained standing. "And you're saying that wasn't you?"

"It was one of mine. They're watching us, now."

He spun on his heel, staring out the window. Hattie peered around him, hoping Maria knew enough not to stand in front of the window.

Polizzi's shoulders tensed. He turned back to Hattie with a weary expression. "Wish you'd pulled this before I had two flasks."

"So, you'll arrange a meeting?"

He nodded. "Yeah. You want hardware? He's got hardware. You'd just better have some cabbage to go with those pinchers. It's a seller's market in this city."

Hattie stood. "I didn't come to New York hat-in-hand, Mr. Polizzi. I'm here to do business. Now, can you give me a place and a time?"

Polizzi glanced at the kitchen, then sighed. "I gotta make a call. Give me a minute, huh?"

"Thank you, Mr. Polizzi."

He grumbled as he turned for the back, "Call me Pockets."

CHAPTER 10

*L*efty stepped into a deli, leaving Vincent and Buddy alone on the street. It was the first time they'd shared a private moment since Buddy had arrived and Vincent didn't know what to do with it. He nodded to Buddy, who nodded back, neither saying a word. A car clattered by, backfiring as the driver mismanaged the clutch. Buddy's eyes shot wide and he reached in his coat in instinct.

Vincent pinched time, pulling the other pincher's gun from his holster and pocketing it. He returned to his position on the sidewalk, then snapped his fingers.

"Easy, kid," Vincent told him. "It was just a backfire."

Buddy froze, then patted his empty holster before easing his hand out of his jacket. "Neat trick."

"Saved my bacon more than once."

The boy held out a hand. When the street was clear, Vincent handed it back.

"Were you showing off, or trying to save someone from getting popped?" Buddy asked.

Vincent shrugged. "A little of both, maybe."

"You don't need to show me nothing," Buddy grumbled, his face red as he holstered his gun. "I know who you are."

"I got a reputation up in Ithaca?"

"More out of the farm than in. Floresta thinks you're underutilized."

"That's a good word."

"You like it?" Buddy frowned. "From what I can tell, it ain't Vito who's leaving you in the barn."

Vincent rolled his eyes. "I'm here, aren't I?"

Lefty emerged from the deli with a paper-wrapped package.

"You two playing nice?" he asked.

"We're peas and carrots, Lefty," Vincent replied.

"Good. Masseria don't exactly have a sense of humor. You need to keep this professional."

Vincent lifted his hands. "I'm always professional."

"Says you. I'm serious, Vincent. Don't get cute with Joe the Boss."

Vincent nodded as Lefty glared at him. "That goes for you too, Buddy," he added, turning to the other pincher.

Buddy didn't reply.

"I don't think he has it in him to be cute," Vincent drawled.

Buddy reached down to pick up a bottle cap left on the sidewalk. He gripped it in the curve of his index finger, slinging it against the side of the building. The cap bounced off, angling back to smack Vincent on the chest.

"Alright," Lefty grumbled. "Knock it off. We got business."

They began their march from the deli toward the center of Brooklyn and Vincent nodded to Lefty. "What's in the kit?"

"Mortadella. Some salami. Can't get decent meat in Baltimore."

"Taste of the Old World?"

Lefty sighed. "You don't gotta make small talk, you know."

"What else am I gonna do? I'm about to clam up for God knows how long while Floresta monologues for the next two hours."

"This is important, Vincent." Lefty stopped at the corner to let another car pass before crossing. "Important for the Capo."

"It's the job," Buddy chimed in. "Whatever is important to the Capo is important to us."

They continued up the street until they reached the front of a four-story brown bricked building overlooking a grocer on one side and a suit shop on the other.

Floresta stepped out of the building with a nod. "Gentlemen," he announced. "You're on time. I'm amazed."

None of them dignified the statement with comment.

"Spirits are high, I see," Floresta said. "Let's step inside."

"What is this place?" Vincent asked as Floresta held open a glass door.

"It's one of three buildings Masseria owns in this part of Brooklyn. We use them for business, mostly."

"Mostly?"

"Got another down in Bensonhurst where we keep the cabbage."

Lefty eyed him. "No banks?"

"They get knocked over."

"So do buildings in Bensonhurst."

Floresta snickered. "Yeah, and anyone who tries better hope they ain't got family."

They stepped through a short hall into an open space surrounded by a mezzanine. The center of the space housed an arrangement of chairs and desks with tiny teller's lamps. One old man sat hunched over a desk, his fingers tapping away at an adding machine.

"I don't know, Lefty," Vincent mumbled. "Looks like a bank to me."

"It's business," Floresta declared with a wide gesture. "The business of the family is business."

Lefty leaned in to Vincent. "Tony usually takes care of the books for Vito."

"I'm thinking Masseria moves more merchandise than we do."

Floresta gestured toward a clutch of sofas underneath an open staircase. "You fellas have a seat. I'm gonna see if Catena's home."

"What about Masseria?" Vincent asked.

"You gotta see Catena first. That's the deal. No one sees the Boss without Catena sayin' it's all good. You boys hold tight. Smoke 'em if you got 'em."

Floresta wound around the sofas to climb the stairs to the mezzanine. Buddy remained standing, arms crossed behind his back as he took in the space. Vincent sat next to Lefty, who shifted away a few inches.

"What's he doing, you think?" Vincent whispered, nodding toward Buddy.

"Checking exits. Blind corners. Doors and windows," Lefty replied.

"For what?"

Buddy answered without turning, "Angles of attack."

Lefty shot Vincent a challenging smirk that bordered on smug. "That's professional, you mook."

"I can do that."

"So why don't you?"

Vincent chuckled, knowing that he'd proven over and over throughout the years how valuable quick reflexes and a time pinch could be.

After a while, Floresta returned with a second pair of footsteps clacking down the stairs behind him. A willowy gentleman with salt-and-pepper hair greased straight back from a receding forehead peered at the men. His eyes were dark brown orbs that danced back and forth without stopping. Vincent shook his head a little, wondering if the man had a condition.

"You're Corbi's men?" Catena asked with a quick, disapproving tone.

Lefty and Vincent stood.

"Vito sends his regards," Lefty replied.

"And you are?" Catena asked.

"Alonzo Mancuso. I'm responsible for Vito's assets."

Catena nodded, then glanced at Buddy and Vincent as he fidgeted with the ring on his left hand. "Sparks gave you the full picture?"

"He has," Lefty replied.

Catena stepped past Lefty, looming just an inch closer than Vincent felt comfortable. He stood a couple inches taller than Vincent, glaring down at him like one of the priests at the old school. Finally, Catena moved on to Buddy. The kid nearly wilted under the man's stare, which he kept short.

"Right," Catena said with a brisk turn. "Come on."

He set a ferocious pace up the stairs. The others bustled after him trying to keep up. At the top of the stairs a double door led to a business suite. Catena opened the doors and stepped inside, leaving the other to follow. The room sported dark wood paneling in the style of a Victorian parlor. Thick emerald carpeting ran from wall to wall. A gathering of men lingered near the walls, all decked in well-tailored suits, most carrying lit cigars. They spoke in hushed conversation with one another, tiny islands of conspiracy crammed shoulder-to-shoulder in the room.

Floresta tapped Vincent on the shoulder and pointed across the room to a man in a gray three-piece. His dark brows lifted in severe angles, his eyes drooped in continual disinterest. His nose was sharp, thrusting from his bronzed skin like a cast sculpture. The man didn't look a day older than Vincent.

"That Luciano?" Vincent whispered.

Floresta nodded. "We'll grab him later."

A man of average height and hefty girth stood in the midst of a clutch of gangsters. The man was broad-faced, jowls forming at the edges of his jawline. His visage possessed the same sort of blasé that Vito tended to cultivate, a sort of droopy-eyed disdain for everyone and everything in the room.

Joe "the Boss" Masseria.

He spotted Catena from the corner of his eye and turned, lifting a hand to silence the volume of the room. Catena spoke several quick sentences in Italian, less than a quarter of which Vincent could follow. Then he gestured to Lefty, who picked up the parlance in return. It was rapid fire, a manner of pronouncement or etiquette which seemed strange to Vincent. It was the native quality the words held in Lefty's mouth. This was his birth language. He was born in Italy, even though around Vincent and the Baltimore Crew, he predominantly spoke in English.

Lefty concluded his greeting, standing with arms at his sides.

Masseria nodded, then spoke in deliberate, clumsy English. "Alonzo Mancuso. My father…knew your father." The corners of his mouth dropped into a facial shrug. "He was a powerful man. A good man."

Lefty nodded. "Too good for this world."

Masseria peered over Lefty's shoulder. "Who have you brought?"

Lefty turned to Buddy and Vincent. "May I present Vincent Calendo and Joel Seiler? *Stregone* from Baltimore."

Masseria stepped forward, all eyes in the room planted directly onto the two of them. "You are here to help?"

Lefty responded, "We are."

"This is good. This kindness will be remembered.

Lefty continued, "Vito sends his regards and hopes that cooperation between our families—"

Masseria released a single dry chuckle. "Enough of that. We know why you are here."

He nodded to Catena with a grunt, a sort of verbal stamp of approval. With that cue, Catena reached for Lefty's shoulder, guiding him into the others, corralling them back to the door.

They all made their exit, lingering as Catena whispered something to Floresta. Floresta remained inside the room as Catena closed the doors behind them.

"That went well," Catena said.

"You were expecting otherwise?" Lefty asked.

"Seldom is the rival family who doesn't create a problem when they visit, either by impudence or hostility. Then again, the Baltimore Crew presents little in the way of a threat. You have only to gain by this, and very little to contribute."

Lefty stood with a casual lean, allowing the insult to sail by without comment.

Catena grinned. "Not so easily goaded, then?"

"Is there anything else you'd like us to do before we get to business?" Lefty asked.

"You have accommodations, yes?"

Lefty nodded.

"Then we shall meet in the evening. Return at nine."

Lefty checked his pocket watch, then nodded. "Nine."

Catena withdrew back into the room, leaving the three alone.

"Come on," Lefty grumbled as he turned for the stairs.

Vincent lingered, staring at the door. Floresta and Luciano were still inside that room. Without the two of them, Vincent wasn't sure what his play was. At the moment, he was in the employ of both Vito and Masseria. Gauging the energy in the room, Vincent figured there was very little room for unexpected gestures.

"Vincent?" Lefty called from below.

Vincent shook it off and trotted down the steps after the others.

"You okay?" Lefty muttered.

"Was I professional enough for you?"

"You were a peach. Keep it up."

"We'll see how easy it is when we get our hands dirty," Vincent said.

"You don't think they're dirty just for being in this building?"

"Yeah, but we're only up to our knuckles. I figure we'll be elbow-deep before this is over."

Buddy grumbled as they exited onto the street, "You two always talk this much?"

"That's what normal people do, Buddy," Vincent said to him over his shoulder. "We don't run on diesel and axle grease."

They returned to the Monarch, each with their own single-bed rooms. Lefty excused himself to make a sandwich with his deli haul. Buddy remained in the hallway, staring at Vincent.

"What?" Vincent asked him.

"I don't know what to do."

"Yeah, that makes two of us."

Buddy's face betrayed a flicker of panic.

Vincent sighed, then gestured for his door. "You know how to play Gin?"

Within a few minutes, Vincent had pulled a side table to

the center of the room and had cards dealt. Buddy sat on the edge of the bed while Vincent took a seat in a chair near the window. He peered out to the street below as Buddy arranged the cards in his hands.

"You barely had any time to see Baltimore before we left," Vincent said as Buddy drew and discarded. "This must feel a little overwhelming."

"I'm here to serve."

"You gotta shake that off, Buddy." Vincent drew and discarded. "Ain't gonna make no friends with that Ithaca bushwa."

Buddy sucked in an alarmed breath. "It's not bushwa."

"It's not normal. People don't go around saying 'I'm here to serve.' Makes you sound like a butler."

"You serve Corbi. So does Lefty."

Vincent nodded. "Yeah, but you don't see me acting like a marionette. Right? I have thoughts. Opinions."

Buddy drew and discarded. "Opinions get in the way. They're dangerous."

"You think you're gonna serve Vito by spitting out what he spoon-feeds you? He needs you to think. Use your noodle. Evaluation situations and speak your mind."

Buddy shook his head. "It's not my place."

Vincent set his cards into his lap, staring at Buddy. "Here's an extra edition for you, Buddy. Vito ain't God. He's a human being. And yeah, he owns you. But just because someone bought and paid for you, don't mean they're not capable of making mistakes. Vito's a mook like me and you. What makes him more powerful than me and you is that he's got me and you to catch him when he's about to blow it."

Buddy lifted his chin, eyes narrow.

Vincent continued, "I know you think I'm some smart-mouthed cart pusher, doing the bare minimum. But I've been at this for a long time, now. I feel like I've aged in dog years, like I'm older than Lefty sometimes."

Buddy grinned, ducking his head away.

"You gotta be a man, is what I'm saying. Not a machine. And let Vito be a man, bad breath and everything. The quicker you thaw out, the easier it'll be to work with all the rest of the boys." Vincent lifted his cards and focused on his hand. "Not for nothin'. I don't really care, either way."

Buddy cocked a brow. "If you didn't care, you wouldn't be playing cards."

"I'm bored."

"You're waiting for something."

Vincent peered at Buddy over his hand. "What?"

"You keep looking out the window."

Vincent hesitated a moment. "I was born in New York. Been here a couple times, but never had time to... Never mind."

Buddy lowered his cards. "Time to what?"

"So, I came into the system before Ithaca. Got picked up young and educated in a Catholic school up just outside of Queens."

"Sounds inefficient."

Vincent laughed. "Yeah, I suppose."

"And you've never gone back?"

"Never had time. Don't know what the point would be. I just wonder sometimes."

Buddy set his cards down on the table. "You never had time before. But we got nothing but time, now."

Vincent shook his head. "Nah, I'm keeping you entertained."

Buddy scowled. "I'm not a toddler."

"I noticed." Vincent peered at him. "You sure?"

"Unless you want me to come with you? Would that make you feel safer?"

Vincent set down his cards face up. "Had a shit hand, anyway."

Buddy nodded. "I'll go bother Lefty instead. Maybe he'll let me have some of that salami."

"Don't count on it." Vincent stood and went for the door, pausing as he twisted the knob. "Thanks. I appreciate it."

Buddy almost grinned. "No problem."

Vincent left the door open, strolling for the stairs. Once he was out of earshot, he upped his pace. Finally, he'd found a way to get free of Buddy and Lefty. Now, the only trick would be finding Floresta.

As he stepped out of the door and back out onto the street, Vincent found a car waiting for him. Floresta grinned at him from behind the steering wheel. "Going my way?"

Vincent slipped into the car. "How long you been here?"

"Just arrived. You made quick work breaking free."

"Luciano waiting for me?"

"Yes." Floresta's smile faded. "I didn't realize that the Old Man knew Mancuso."

"Me neither."

"That makes things more complicated."

Vincent shrugged. "Don't see how. If Luciano signs on, then we'll take them all down."

Floresta shot him an incredulous look. "And you don't see how that'll complicate things between you and your handler?"

"Things are already complicated. Besides, you really think I'll be able to salvage anything when we take down Corbi?"

"Let's not put the cart before the horse, shall we?"

Floresta drove to a restaurant not far from the Monarch, parking on the street. The pair walked into the restaurant, finding Luciano seated in the center of the room facing the door. Floresta urged Vincent forward, staying near the entrance with his gun tucked into his jacket at the ready.

As Vincent approached the young man, his eyes followed Vincent like a predator.

"Luciano?" Vincent said.

"You Calendo?" Luciano said in a thick Mediterranean cadence.

"Yes, I am."

"I hear you have some requests," Luciano purred as he pulled a cigarette case from his jacket to light a smoke.

Vincent nodded. "I'm hoping that if I help you and Sparks, then you help me."

Luciano lit the cigarette. "Why should I trust a *stregone*? Hmm?"

"You trust Floresta, don't you?"

"I wouldn't rush to conclusions."

Vincent bit back a smile. "He tells me you're forward-thinking."

Luciano's face pulled into the barest of grins. "*Si.* But are you?"

"I'd like to think I am."

Luciano nodded. "I am told you are one of the many *stregone* ripped from their families as *bambini*. I've heard this story many times before. Would it surprise you to hear that these stories move me?"

Vincent squinted. "It would, actually."

Luciano grinned. "Then my reputation precedes me. Fine. I shall stop trying to play the wise man. *Stregone* are wasted in the old ways. Such power left to waste and wither. It is tragic."

"You think we pinchers aren't getting worked hard enough?"

Luciano wagged his cigarette. "You misunderstand. My only concern is business. The way things are? This is bad business. Slavery is bad business. Now incentive? That is good business."

Vincent shook his head, not sure if he believed this man or not. "You want to put pinchers on a payroll, then?"

Luciano gave Vincent a noncommittal shrug.

"Will you agree to help me topple Vito Corbi if I help you?"

Luciano took another long drag off his cigarette as his sharp eyes took Vincent in. Finally, he exhaled a plume of smoke and replied, "I cannot involve myself so directly. I can, however, turn a blind eye."

"That's not much," Vincent informed him.

"That is business."

Vincent sighed, then nodded. "Then I'll take it."

"Any other requests?"

Vincent suddenly had an idea—a wild crazy idea that surely wouldn't fly, but was worth throwing out anyway.

"Ithaca," he replied. "I want it shut down."

Luciano grinned as he cocked his head. "The pincher farm?"

"You know what it does. You know the sort of pinchers it creates. Mindless drones. If you're serious about giving pinchers the latitude and incentive to do what we do best, then you'll understand why I'm asking for this."

"*Bene.* Ithaca will be dismantled. Masseria and Maranzano both go down. When I am *Capo di tutti Capi*, you can have Baltimore. I will not interfere. And, if I'm feeling generous, I may encourage the others to follow suit."

Vincent reached a hand across the table.

Luciano gripped it in a surprisingly vicious grip.

"Then we have an agreement," Vincent said.

"*Si.*"

Vincent stepped back out onto the street, Floresta beside him. "We're on. What's next?"

"Next you meet Maranzano's people. This is the tricky bit. We have to keep quiet. Any of our people catch a whiff of this, it's over. I'll pick you up from the Monarch at midnight. Be sure you're alone."

Vincent sighed. Twice in one day he'd have to shake his entourage. At least it would be late into the night hours. He knew Lefty was the "early to bed, early to rise" sort. But what about Buddy?

At this point, he didn't have a choice. He'd have to risk it. Because now he finally had a plan.

CHAPTER 11

True to form, Lefty retired after a late dinner, leaving Vincent and Buddy to sort themselves out. Buddy took a moment to grill Vincent over whether he'd found the school in which he'd spent a childhood of imprisonment. Vincent brushed the question off with a display of emotion. It was enough to sell that he had, in fact, confronted some demon of his past.

It was the demons of his present that Vincent ruminated on as Buddy withdrew to his own room. Luciano was playing a high stakes game with this scheme. It was too easy for this to go wrong. Granted, there were degrees of separation between Vincent and Luciano. And Vincent was sure Floresta had some manner of trap door in case things went terribly wrong.

Floresta pulled up to the front of the Monarch promptly at midnight, rolling half a block east before stopping. Vincent slipped into the car, checking the front of the building for prying eyes.

"Let's go," he muttered, confident that neither Buddy nor Lefty were spying.

Floresta drove to the Bronx, a painfully slow journey as he wove around jaywalkers and crept behind horse carriages. Vincent marveled at the sheer number of people streaming through the city after midnight.

"Maranzano's turf is the Bronx?" Vincent asked.

"And Queens. A bit of Brooklyn. That's where the dust-ups go down, usually."

"What about the other families?"

"Too small to matter," Floresta replied. "It's a two-sided war."

"Bet we tipped the scales when O'Donnell went down."

"You'd be surprised how quick Masseria adapted. It's Maranzano who's on the ropes. He lost some talent in the last brouhaha. He's basically down to two pinchers at this point. Which is why I came to rattle your cage. The time's right. We're meeting with those pinchers tonight."

Vincent's back straightened. "How much do they know?"

"They know I grabbed you from outta town. They know you're inside Masseria's operation, and that you're here to help wheedle him down."

"That's it?"

"That's it."

Vincent nodded. "They gonna play nice?"

"Depends on you, I suppose." Floresta's eyes searched the street, his grip tightening on the wheel. "Just...remember the long view. Right? Don't get punchy. We'll be okay."

"Yeah, sure."

Floresta pulled alongside a series of U-shaped tenements rising about six stories. The courtyards tucked between the buildings were well manicured—almost gardens. The boughs of elm and maple that hung over hedge rows cast dark shadows along the pathway. The lights from the city barely penetrated these islands of silence. It was the perfect place for a secret meeting.

Or the perfect place to be murdered without a fuss.

Floresta stepped through the hedges, a blue light emanating from a ball of electricity rushing between his fingers. He fanned his hand in front of him like a torch as they proceeded deeper into the courtyard.

A shadow rose from a bench beneath a maple, and Floresta held his position. As a man stepped into the blue light, Vincent cocked his head for a better look. He was barrel-shaped, with thick forearms and a neck that rose from his meaty shoulders like the trunk of an oak tree. A bushy black mustache covered his lip, drooping at the sides. It gave his earthy countenance an air of mirth, though the man's eyes were sharp, moving back and forth between them.

Floresta nodded. "Pockets."

The man replied in a velvety baritone, "Heya, Sparks."

Floresta released the electricity from his hand, gesturing to Vincent in the darkness. "Pockets Polizzi, this here's Vincent Calendo."

The man reached out with a bear paw of a hand, his mustache lifting in a grin. "Good to meet ya."

Vincent shook his hand, bracing for a bone-crushing grip, but Polizzi shook Vincent's hand with a quick, courteous toss.

"You, uh, you're here to pull some shit with us?" he asked.

"I'm here to help," Vincent replied.

"Is Maranzano in the city?" Floresta inquired.

"Yeah. Just got back last night."

"We'll need a meet. I know he won't sign off on this until he meets Vincent."

Polizzi shrugged. "Get in line. He's already got a meet tomorrow."

Floresta stiffened. "That a fact? With who?"

"Some broad from Baltimore. Here to drum up some muscle. Looks like Corbi's got a problem coming his way."

Floresta glanced to Vincent, who simply shrugged. He scowled for a second, then turned back to Polizzi. "A *woman?*"

"Yeah, I know what you're thinking." Polizzi chuckled. "But trust me. She's got talent on her side. Anyways, I can see what we can do about getting you two together. He's not a spring chicken no more, so he keeps these things short."

Vincent nodded. "That'll be fine. I suspect there—"

"What's her name?" Floresta snapped.

"O'Toole," Polizzi replied. "Brigid O'Toole."

Floresta scowled turning to Vincent. "What do you know about this woman?"

Vincent shook his head. "Nothing. Never heard of her."

"So, she's lying about being from Baltimore," Floresta pressed.

Polizzi lifted his chin. "Wait. You're from Baltimore?"

Vincent said, "I am. I'm Corbi's pincher."

Polizzi frowned. "Well, if Corbi's game to help Maranzano, then I'm brooming her off. Don't want trouble if we can afford it."

Vincent stepped forward. "I wouldn't worry. Corbi's not here to help Maranzano." Floresta reached for Vincent's arm, but Vincent pulled away. "Truth is, Corbi's thrown in with Masseria."

Polizzi stepped back.

Vincent continued, "Now if this dame's what she says she is, then you'd do best to roll out the red carpet for her because Vito's looking for an alliance with Masseria."

"Then what're you doing here?" Polizzi asked.

"I'm here because Corbi is weak. Why do you think he wants to shake hands with Masseria in the first place? If this jumped-up dame with a pincher or two has a shot at taking Corbi down, that oughta show you how severe the situation is."

Polizzi chuckled. "I guess. She's taking credit for offing O'Donnell. You know that?"

Floresta grumbled, "Bushwa. That was my man, here."

Vincent stiffened as Floresta thumped his arm. Clearly Hattie had already taken enormous strides to set up her con with Maranzano. And here he and Floresta had nearly dismantled it. He had to keep her relevant and in the game.

"Actually," Vincent muttered, "there's a thing or two you don't know about how that went down."

Floresta scowled. "That a fact?"

"Truth is we were pinned down at Vito's vineyard. They were pressing in hard, and I was damn near tapped out of magic. Then outta nowhere come these pinchers." Vincent rolled the dice on how Hattie had sold her bill of goods to Polizzi. "They had this earth pincher with them. Shook the ground. Sent cars flying."

Polizzi bobbed up and down on his feet. "Yessir! That's the one!"

Floresta glared at Polizzi. "The one what?"

"That O'Toole broad had a pincher with her. Somewhere. Watching. I take it she's the cautious type. Her pincher shook the whole city block. It was a thing to see."

Vincent shrugged. "Vito's got me so close these days, I can't sniff around like I used to. I know there used to be a woman who was running Richmond. Maybe it's the same one?"

Floresta cocked a brow at Polizzi. "Speaking of which, where's your partner? I thought this was all hands on deck?"

Polizzi shook his head. "You know her, Sparks. No one can control her. She's just as likely to blow this off as she is to make it."

A woman's voice slithered from behind Polizzi. "I figured I'd show up tonight."

Vincent stiffened, stepping to the side to peer through the

shadows at Maranzano's second pincher. That voice. He knew that voice.

"Just had a waiter for dessert. He was…gifted."

Finally she stepped close enough for Vincent to see. "Now. Who's this pigeon you brought in for us, Sparks?"

Vincent caught his breath, hands balling into fists as he turned to face the woman who'd become his nemesis.

Betty Sharp's eyes narrowed. With a snap, she thrust her hands upward. The sound of snapping glass filled the court-yard. Window panes cracked from their lintels, flying through the air like flocks of martins. The glass spiraled into a cone of jagged death as Betty snarled.

Vincent pinched time. The darkness eased inside the time bubble, sending his vision into the bleak monotone of frozen night. The glass shards hung in the air, their sides gleaming in the captured light of the time bubble, all twisting together into elegant spirals of death.

He stepped aside, fists still clenched. Polizzi's face was frozen in a moment of slack-jawed disbelief. Vincent eyed Floresta. His face betrayed no surprise. Of course it wouldn't. He knew exactly who Betty Sharp was, and what she meant to Vincent. That would be a conversation for another time. For now, this entire scheme was in danger of evaporating. Betty was a madwoman, hell bent on taking Vincent's life. There was no way this could work.

Vincent stepped around Betty, pulling his revolver and slipping the barrel under her chin. Then he released the time pinch.

The flying daggers crashed into the spot where he had stood, filling the air with a cacophony of tortured glass. Floresta hopped to the side, covering his face as shards smashed into a pile beside him. Vincent lifted the gun, digging it into the soft skin of Betty's jaw.

"You want to play nice?" Vincent asked her as he cocked his gun. "Or are we going to make this messy?"

Betty froze, her hands still stretched out in front of her.

A gun clicked next to Vincent's ear.

Polizzi held a Colt up to Vincent's temple. "Easy, Baltimore."

Vincent grumbled, "She just tried to cut me into a million pieces. Or did you miss that?"

"No," he grumbled. "I didn't miss that. And I want some answers right now."

Floresta stood cross-armed, staring at the ground.

"Betty and I have a history," Vincent said.

Polizzi smirked. "What, did she love you then leave you?"

"Nothing like that," Vincent replied. "She tried to kill me pretty much the first time we met."

Polizzi glanced at Betty. "What's your take on this?"

Her lips tightened, then she relaxed, dropping her clutched hands. "He murdered my husband," she replied with a quavering note of false grief.

"Oh, please," Vincent spat. "I don't think you're going to fool this man with mawkish sentiment."

Betty glared. "Fine. Let's talk. But take the iron out of my face."

Polizzi said, "That's a good idea all around."

Vincent eased the gun from underneath Betty's chin, stepping away. She turned slowly to face him, and Polizzi lowered his weapon.

"You had about as much love for Capstein as I did," Vincent said. "The man damn near killed me twice over. If anything, I did you a favor. I handed you Richmond on a platter."

Betty sneered. "Then you kidnapped me and brought me to your boss. And the two of us get shipped up to Ithaca, where you got the four-star treatment while I was tortured and humiliated."

Polizzi shook his head. "So this is just a grudge?"

"It's more than that," Betty spat.

Polizzi holstered his piece. "Don't sound that way to me. If this is personal, then you're gonna have to let it go, Betty. We got business."

"Not with him!" she shouted, turning to Polizzi.

Sirens sounded in the distance as residents began filing into the courtyard.

Floresta stepped forward, crunching over the glass. "I think our time's up, folks. What say we continue this tomorrow? At which point, Betty, I hope you find a way to play ball. For your sake. And Maranzano's."

Polizzi stepped between them. "I'll see you for breakfast, Sparks. We got some details to iron out before we mix these two in the same pot again." Then he turned to Betty. "Come on, you hellcat. Let's get scarce."

Betty glared once more at Vincent. He watched her with caution as she backed away, finally turning to follow Polizzi.

Vincent and Floresta hurried up the pathway and out of the courtyard before the cops arrived. Once they were in the car and several blocks away, Vincent finally spoke up

"What the hell are you pulling?"

"It was a gamble," Floresta replied.

"Gambling with my life."

"Oh please. I knew you were a time pincher. I knew you'd see her and defend yourself."

"That's supposed to make me feel better?" Vincent tossed his hands in the air. "Fine, then!"

"She's all we have to work with."

"She's vowed to kill me, Floresta! You know what they did to her. You were there. You were at the Ithaca auction. Didn't it ever occur to you to warn me?"

"I figured you knew where she ended up. Maranzano's men were at that auction, too."

Vincent scowled. "I was too busy trying to save my own hide to think about who bought Betty."

Floresta snorted. "DeBarre was the one who saved your hide. Fat lotta good it did him in the end."

"You seriously expect me to go along with this now? Even if I was willing to work with Betty Sharp, there's no way in hell she'd work with me."

Floresta pulled over and put the car in park. "Now you listen to me, Betty Sharp is Maranzano's problem. He wants this. He needs this. That's all that matters."

"You think *he* can control her?" Vincent snapped.

"He has so far."

"Now that he's down to two, though? I can tell you from experience. She doesn't do well with power. She's getting more and more important. Once she sniffs out that Maranzano's leaning on her to make this happen, that's when she'll become the most volatile."

Floresta lifted a hand to silence him. "This is the play, Calendo. We work with those two to take Masseria's knees out from under him. There's no backing out now."

"Is that a threat?"

"You really want me to go back to Corbi and tell him you're making his funeral arrangements?"

"And do you want me to go to Masseria and tell him that you and Luciano are doing the same?"

The two sat silent for a moment.

Floresta squinted. "Don't get so righteous about this. I'm not the only one holding back, here."

"What're you talking about?"

"Who the hell is this O'Toole dame?"

Caution slipped into Vincent's anger, softening him enough to let him think.

"I told you."

"No," Floresta snapped with a lift of his finger. "First you said you never heard of her. Then you came up with this cockamamy story about some strangers descending from Heaven and saving your bacon. So, which is it?"

"Maybe I don't feel like airing out all my laundry for you."

"Maybe there's more to this story than you want me to know."

Vincent shook his head. "Now you're being paranoid."

"Am I? You got no love for the Baltimore Crew. I know that. If some broad with an army of pinchers comes sweeping into the city with her sights set on Vito Corbi, I figure you'd find a way to approach her. And if she is what she says she is, there's no chance she'd let an insider slip outta her grasp."

"Nice story."

"You like it? Because it sounds good enough to be true."

"It's not."

"What kills me about this is how Mancuso ain't said a word about her. And that's the giveaway."

Floresta drove on while Vincent played out his next move. How would he spin this so Floresta would believe him? The man wasn't simply paranoid. He was cautious. To play a triple cross the way he'd planned, he would have to be.

As they parked in front of the Monarch, Floresta turned to Vincent. "Look. Do you want our help taking down Corbi, or not?"

Vincent nodded.

"Then we gotta trust each other. There's no way this'll work if we don't. No more secrets."

"Secrets like Betty Sharp?" Vincent asked.

Floresta looked down to the wheel, then muttered, "Yeah. Like that."

"I get the feeling you're not ready to believe me, no

matter what I tell you about O'Toole. How're we gonna get over this?"

Floresta killed the engine and stepped out. Vincent followed suit, panic washing through his stomach as Floresta moved for the entrance.

"Wait," Vincent urged as he grabbed Floresta by the elbow. "Where do you think you're going?"

"Here's the deal. I'm gonna go up there and knock on Mancuso's door. And you're gonna stand there with your trap shut while I ask him exactly what went down at that vineyard. If your stories don't line up, then I know you're playing your own angle. And we're done. That sound reasonable to you?"

Vincent took slow, even breaths, trying to calm himself. "What if our stories do line up? Where do we go from there?"

"Then I have eggs with Pockets tomorrow and iron it out. First things first."

Floresta pulled the door open and bustled up the stairs. Vincent followed, his brain racing for a way out of this. Lefty had been there. He knew it was the Charge who'd come to their aid, although Vincent was sure the other man didn't know exactly what the Charge was. This might cut the entire scheme off at the base. Vincent would have to come clean to Lefty and probably to Buddy. Lefty would be disappointed, to be sure. It would most likely be the end of their relationship, but he wouldn't sell Vincent out to Corbi.

Buddy, on the other hand...

Floresta paused at the trio of doors. "Which one is it?"

Vincent knocked on Lefty's door himself, then stepped back behind Floresta.

It took a full minute before Lefty opened the door. He peered at the two with slow-blinking eyes.

"The hell the two of you want?" he mumbled. "You drunk?"

"We gotta talk. Won't take but a minute," Floresta stated in a clear, calm tone.

Lefty nodded for them to enter. Vincent glanced around Lefty's room. It was immaculate. No clothes lying around. Everything was clean and orderly…almost Spartan. He'd even stopped to make the bed before he'd opened the door.

Lefty turned to face the others as Vincent closed the door behind him. "Alright, let's talk. What's the beef?"

Floresta glanced at Vincent with a warning lift of his brow, then replied, "I need to ask you about the day Jonas O'Donnell got scratched."

Lefty shrugged. "Yeah?"

"Where was it?"

Lefty eyed Vincent, his brow creasing just a little in the middle. "Havre de Grace. Vito's villa."

"A villa, huh?"

"Yeah," Lefty said, his patience already rubbing thin. "He's got a vineyard on the hills up that direction."

Floresta released a breath. "So, it was a vineyard."

"What's this about?" Lefty asked Vincent.

Vincent shook his head and kept his mouth shut.

Floresta said, "Everyone this direction heard it was the Crew who took down O'Donnell. Now, I'm gonna ask you a question. I'll keep it simple, because I'm not trying to stick my nose into your business. Was it one of your people who killed Jonas O'Donnell?"

Lefty looked to Vincent, his eyes now wide awake. Vincent could tell Lefty was piecing together the nature of this conversation. Only, Lefty didn't have enough information to get to the heart of it.

"No," Lefty finally replied. "It wasn't one of ours."

Floresta lifted his chin. "That so?"

"It was a woman. A pincher."

Floresta prodded, "A pincher working for that Irish dame?"

Lefty shot Vincent a semi-panicked look. "You told him about her?"

Floresta shook his head at Vincent with a laugh. "Well, son of a bitch. I guess you was shootin' straight with me after all, Calendo." Then he looked over to Lefty. "Would it surprise you to learn this O'Toole broad is in the city right now playing Maranzano for guns and foot soldiers?"

Lefty glared at Vincent. "I suppose nothing would surprise me, at this point."

Floresta turned to Vincent with an outstretched hand. "Alright. We're square. I'll get my end sorted. You guys get ready for Maranzano."

Floresta saluted them with his fingers and stepped into the hallway.

Buddy peered in through the open door as Floresta took his exit. "Everything okay?"

"Go to bed," Lefty grumbled.

Buddy nodded, wide-eyed, then stepped away.

Vincent shut the door, slipped his hands into his pockets and leaned against the wall. "I should explain."

"What the hell are you doing?" Lefty snapped. "You brought Malloy along on this little outing? For what purpose? And what were you doing out on the town with Floresta?"

"I'll tell you what we were doing," Vincent said, once more gambling with a half portion of the truth. "First, we ran into Betty Sharp."

Lefty scowled. "That lunatic? She's here?"

"Maranzano bought her from Ithaca. I was there when it happened. Just didn't piece it together until she nearly ripped me into chum."

"Sounds like her. That makes this job a bit tougher than I'd like. Does she know you're in town?"

Vincent nodded.

"Shit." Lefty turned for the window. "What about Miss Malloy?"

"Okay, yeah. I brought her along."

"Why in God's name—?"

Vincent lifted his hands. "Because I got a farm-fresh pincher hanging around my neck. And I don't trust him. I don't trust Masseria. Floresta. None of them. These are the same goons who run the damn farm like their own personal pincher factory. You don't think it stinks that they suddenly made good on their IOU to Corbi, just in time to march us back up to the city?"

Lefty smirked. "The thought had crossed my mind."

"Right? You want to know what I was doing out and about with Floresta? I was getting the real megillah from the man before we got in too deep. Before we couldn't get out."

"And you ran into Sharp?"

"Yeah. Her and about a million shards of glass."

"So, this O'Toole story. That was yours?"

"Hattie's. She's sniffing around Maranzano for us. Looks like she cooked up this Brigid O'Toole business to needle her way inside." Vincent added with a shake of his head, "Knowing her, the story got bigger than she'd planned."

Lefty smiled. "Sounds about right. Fine. Miss Malloy's in play. I assume you want this on the down-low?"

"From Floresta, Masseria…and Buddy."

Lefty turned to face Vincent. "For what it's worth, I think you're wrong about Buddy. He's a bit stiff, but he's too bright-eyed to be playing two sides. Boy's got a shit poker face."

"Well, we got a deck of cards if you want to put that to the test."

Lefty clapped Vincent's arm. "You keep hiding these things from me, son. It's gonna be a problem soon. Just remember something," Lefty added as he moved for the door. "I've been at this longer than you. You get a notion, you'd do better to bring me in. I could've told you Floresta was a double-dealer."

Vincent stiffened.

Lefty added, "And he's angling to take out Masseria as well as Maranzano. I can't work out if his true loyalty is with Catena or Luciano, but it's one of them."

"Luciano," Vincent told him.

"Then I'm right?"

Vincent nodded.

"And your take from all this? The reason you're scurrying around, ducking me and Buddy?"

"Luciano…he becomes Capo di tutti Capi."

Lefty paused, hand on the door knob. "Why do you care about him?"

Vincent searched for the correct answer. It would have to be convincing. It would have to satisfy Lefty's finely-honed suspicions. But it couldn't be the truth.

"Ithaca," Vincent replied. "Luciano's pledged to close it up."

Lefty released the door knob, returning to Vincent. "Why in all Hell would he do that?"

"Because he's young," Vincent replied. "He's looking to the future. I think he knows there's a day coming when the gangsters can't control us pinchers anymore. He and Floresta have in mind a future that uses pinchers less like slaves and more like employees. It's the only way he'll keep the rogue pinchers out there from rising up. And as long as Ithaca's open for business, there won't be a pincher alive who'll back him."

Lefty sighed. "You've always been a dreamer."

"Is that such a bad thing?"

Lefty returned to the door, opening it and holding it for Vincent. "Only when those dreams cloud your vision. Get some sleep. We got a big day tomorrow."

Vincent nodded and left the room.

As he retired to his own bed, pulling off his shoes and trousers and hanging his jacket up on the wardrobe door, Vincent wondered if he'd managed to navigate the evening without completely screwing up. Floresta was off his back. Lefty was off his back. Sure, he had a psychotic glass pincher to deal with, but if he wasn't looking over his shoulder every other minute, that might work.

As Vincent stretched out over the covers of his bed, he grinned. Hattie had been busy. He looked forward to the next time they compared notes. With the swell of anticipation rising in his chest, he closed his eyes and drifted to sleep.

CHAPTER 12

"**Y**-you want Carlo Catena," the trembling man in grimy overalls sputtered.

Hattie smiled up at the man as he peered from the open door of his Ford, which was teetering on a column of basalt that had suddenly risen from the alleyway.

"Who's he, then?" Hattie asked from behind her O'Toole illusion.

"Masseria's consigliere," he wheezed, reaching to balance himself as the car shifted on the stone pillar. "No one talks to Joe the Boss without going through him."

"And I'd find him where?"

The man gave Hattie directions to Masseria's business office. Satisfied he was frightened enough that he wouldn't bother trying to lie, Hattie turned to Maria with a nod.

Maria swept her hand toward her hip, easing the column back into the earth a few feet before dropping it entirely. The Ford bounced on its front suspension as the man whimpered in relief.

Hattie marched back to the main street alongside Maria,

peering over her shoulder at the Ford as it spun its wheels trying to escape the brash and indefatigable Brigid O'Toole.

"Consigliere, huh?" Maria muttered as they stepped into the evening pedestrian traffic. "What the hell does that even mean?"

"Heck if I know." Hattie held up her hands. "It's probably an Italian thing, although I've never heard that word around the Crew."

Maria snorted. "Vito might have had a vineyard, but I doubt he's important enough to have a Consigliere, whatever that is."

"It must be an advisor, or the second in charge." Hattie giggled. "Maybe it's the man who scrubs the floors."

"Or the one who meets with troublesome females," Maria teased. "Either way, this Masseria seems more organized than Maranzano."

"That's for certain," Hattie replied, dropping her illusion. "You're not sitting this one out, I'll tell you that for nothing."

"About time. As you pointed out, I'll need a dress if I'm going to be rubbing elbows with the muckety-mucks."

They stopped on a street corner and Hattie peered between buildings to the west. Rows of tall buildings sparkled in the balmy late-spring evening air. "We ought to do this properly."

Maria followed her gaze toward Manhattan. "Fifth Avenue?"

Hattie shrugged. "Might as well see the sights while we're here. We might both end up dead tomorrow."

The two took a long stroll across the promenade of the Brooklyn Bridge, pausing beneath its colossal gothic arches to admire the view. A beat cop urged them on as they lingered, and at length they found themselves in the thick of Manhattan.

Hattie had spent most of her childhood wondering what

shopping in a fine clothing store might be like. It was only ever a fantasy, though. Their family was poor, barely able to buy food. And she'd never assumed she would need that sort of outfit. But times had changed. She'd packed a healthy bankroll from the recent Pittsburgh runs, and Hattie decided it was time to indulge a fantasy.

They stepped through a gleaming storefront, marveling at the enormous interior space bright with electric light. The dresses were a touch more daring than she could find in Baltimore. The hemlines were higher. The fringe longer. The spangles brighter.

Hattie nudged Maria, wide-eyed with awe. "Here, then. What's your style?"

Maria ran her hands over the sides of her thighs. "I'm not sure I have the legs for these dresses."

Hattie nodded at the men's section. "If you like, we could dress you in trousers and a jacket. You'd look fine in a bowtie."

Maria laughed. "I don't think so."

After an hour of shopping, they left with a dress each, a cloche for Maria, and new shoes. The store closed shortly after they'd paid, and they found themselves in Manhattan well into the entertainment hours. Unlike Baltimore, however, the Volstead Act had been enforced to the point that jazz clubs and dives weren't open. The streets, though busy, were devoid of music and mirth.

They walked back to their room, a chill in the night air finally descending over the East River.

"Where are we going first?" Maria asked as they reached their rented room. "Masseria or Maranzano?"

Hattie hung the garment bag on the back of the wardrobe door. "Has to be Masseria. I don't know how to play Maranzano until we know what the competition expects."

Maria dropped onto her side of the bed. "Tomorrow, though? My feet are killing me."

"Aye. We've had enough excitement for one day."

Maria fell asleep almost instantly. Hattie, however, lingered by the window while Maria snored lightly. Her body was heavy with fatigue. Her feet ached. Her mind hummed with colliding thoughts while her stomach twisted with anxiety over the task at hand.

Pinching light helped Hattie feel a little more invincible —perhaps even invisible at times. But this wasn't a matter of hoodwinking some two-bit rum-runners on the Bay, or side-stepping Corbi's oblivious muscle in the streets of Baltimore. This was big league ball. The stakes here were higher than she'd ever dared to gamble. And with every-thing running around in her head, Hattie couldn't escape her thoughts for even a few hours of sleep. She closed her eyes, slouching in her chair as the street noises persisted throughout the night, managing to find that twilight between waking and sleeping, a sort of trance state where the buzz in her head dulled to a hum, and the nightmares of flames and demons simmered just beneath an inky surface.

The sun rose eventually, and Hattie pulled herself out of her chair, stretching her neck. She stepped into slippers and shuffled down the hall to the bath, where she ran some water over a cloth to clean herself up. When she returned to the room, she found Maria awake, regarding the dress they'd bought her the night before.

"We should make an effort to find an audience with Cate-na," Maria said without looking at Hattie.

"Aye. After lunch, though."

"I think we should go in the morning." She turned to Hattie, the dress held over her front. "The man's a consigliere, not an enforcer. Unless that word actually means he cleans the floors, then I'm thinking his business is morning business."

Hattie nodded. "You know more about't than I."

"It's why you brought me, right?"

"That and keeping me from getting killed."

"A man in Catena's position would respond to etiquette more than that bruiser we thumbed last night. Are you ready for that?"

Hattie shuffled off her robe, stepping half-naked across the room to reach for her new dress.

Maria squinted at her as she unzipped the garment bag.

"I'll have to be," Hattie replied.

* * *

THEY STOPPED by a corner bakery for rolls. Maria munched on hers as they made their way for the streetcar. Hattie pocketed hers.

The building their source described was a square three-story chunk of masonry. Arched windows adorned the front of the edifice, with iron bars covering the glass. It looked more like a bank than a gangster's hideout. Hattie pinched Brigid O'Toole over herself, then marched for the front door. A bronze plaque set into the stone just before the wide double doors confirmed her suspicion. First Empire Bank and Trust. Did Masseria truly operate out of a bank building?

Maria held the door for Hattie, adopting equal air of a valet and an enforcer. It was crisp and professional, the sort of etiquette this Catena fellow would expect for a nascent kingpin.

They stepped inside an anteroom set before a wide open-air atrium. Hattie paused to take in the view. Rows of accountants' desks ran in a grid along the center axis of the room. What had been a series of tellers' windows had been renovated to create a lounge area just beneath a sweeping marble staircase leading to a mezzanine. Gentlemen in suits stood watch on the railing, peering down on the handful of men in long-brimmed visors tapping away at adding machines and scribbling with pencils.

A clutch of men stepped through the doors behind them. Hattie stepped aside as they brushed past. Her eyes widened, and she held her breath as familiar faces peered back at her.

Vincent!

He peered at her with alarm. She nodded him on discreetly, and he stepped into the atrium. Lefty followed with a thin boy who looked to be in his late teens trailing behind. Lefty offered her a gentile nod, but otherwise seemed not to notice her. The last was a man Hattie recognized, but couldn't place.

They proceeded up the stairs, winding around the first corner of the mezzanine to another set of double-doors. Vincent shot her another quick glance just before heading into the mystery office.

A man stepped from a side office, nodding to Hattie and Maria. He was tall and lean, a pate of silver hair greased away from a scalloping hairline. His face bore the wear and tear of decades, though nothing about his movement seemed aged. He slid through the desks, the tips of his fingers tucked into his front panel pockets.

"Can I help you, ladies?" He asked as he approached.

Hattie dug deep to unearth the finest Brigid O'Toole condescension.

"I'm here to speak to Carlo Catena," she declared. "Would you be a dear and let him know Brigid O'Toole would like a moment of his precious time?"

The corner of his mouth lifted. "You must be this Brigid O'Toole I've heard about."

"And how have you divined that?" Hattie asked.

"One of my men came back last night warning you'd be paying us a call. Along with your earth pincher." His eyes shifted to Maria, narrowing a hair. Then he gestured for her to follow, adding as they reached the far end of the atrium, "Your pincher will have to wait outside."

Hattie turned to Maria with a steady gaze. "Very well."

The man gestured to the couches beneath the stairs. Maria lingered a second, then nodded, taking a seat as the man held the side office door open for Hattie, closing it behind her. An ornate desk sat before a series of floor-to-ceiling bookcases filled with leather-bound volumes. He gestured for one of two seats as he rounded the desk.

"You're Catena, I gather?" she muttered.

"And you're sniffing around New York for muscle, I gather." He took a seat, gesturing again for Hattie to do the same.

She took her seat. "You're well informed."

"We haven't risen to the top of the New York families by burying our heads in the sand."

She nodded to the bookcases. "Have you read all those?"

He turned with an amused smirk. "Most. Not word for word, naturally. New York Consolidated Civil Code. United States Federal Regulations. Some law reviews, though I tend not to keep those here."

"You're a lawyer?"

"Harvard."

"Impressive."

His eyes dipped as he fingered his ring. Hattie took heart in his nervous tic.

"One does one's best," he declared, folding his hands on the desktop. "What is it you want, Miss O'Toole? Specifically. I gather you're interested in unseating Vito Corbi, and that you've already acquired magical assets toward that end. And you're looking for…what would you call it? Hardware?"

"Guns, Mister Catena. And men to use them."

"Why New York?" he asked, his demeanor completely businesslike. "Of all the places to drum up foot soldiers, you've chosen the most competitive market on this continent."

"Is that a fact?" she said, leaning back in her chair and crossing her legs at the ankle.

"Five families are vying for dominance in the boroughs. After three long years, one family is ready to emerge. Three years of quiet, back-alley fire fights and entrenched loyalties. Fatigue has set in. The greatest challenge will be in maintaining morale as the final silent bullets are fired." He leaned forward. "And this is the climate you've chosen to enter and do business in? That tells me you're not here for men. Not *only* men, anyway. This isn't about hardware. It's a calculated move. You're coming out. Presenting yourself as an option to Vito Corbi. Presenting…to the New York families." He leaned back in his seat with a wave of his hand. "You were seen speaking to Pockets Polizzi yesterday."

Hattie plastered a scowl on her face, suddenly feeling very outmatched in this game she was playing.

"Oh," he chuckled. "Don't take it personally. Precious little happens in this city that I don't know about. I'd be a poor second if it were any other way."

"Yes, I met with Polizzi yesterday. Maranzano is interested in doing business, and it's in my best interests to see what he has to offer," she said.

"I'll save you some time, Miss O'Toole. He doesn't have much to offer. He's poised to lose the Bronx. He's already lost most of his territory in Brooklyn. Next will be Queens, and he'll be on a boat back to Sicily by Christmas."

Hattie shrugged. "Then he has little to lose in doing business with an upstart such as myself and everything to gain."

Catena smiled. "An upstart. Indeed, that's how he sees you."

Hattie leaned back in her chair, getting an odd notion about that smile. "And how do *you* see me, if you don't mind my being direct?"

He stood and wandered over to a sideboard. "Brandy?"

"Isn't that illegal?" she quipped.

The smile turned charmingly conspiratorial. "Only if we get caught."

"Then I graciously accept."

He poured two tiny glasses, handing one to Hattie as he sat on the corner of his desk.

"How do *I* see you, Miss O'Toole? I see a woman with abilities and promise."

Hattie paused over her brandy before taking a sip, eyeing him from the rim of her glass.

He continued, "But you're a name, and nothing more—at least, at the moment."

She lowered the glass. "I seem to have impressed Maranzano a degree more than I have you."

"Let's ignore Maranzano for the time being." He sipped his drink. "What you want, he can't provide."

"And what is it that you think I want, if not the guns and men I came here for?"

"You want recognition," Catena replied. "I'm about to say something that will likely upset you. Please understand that I don't mean this as an insult. But the truth is, this is a man's game. Women can't succeed with us Old World fossils."

She tilted her head, acknowledging his point. "Yes, but perhaps you haven't met the right woman."

"Perhaps." He set his glass down on the desk and leaned forward. "If you want to supplant Vito Corbi in Baltimore, you'll have to find a way to earn the respect of your peers. And none of your peers will accept a woman as…well…"

"As a peer?" she finished.

He shrugged his way into a nod.

Hattie eyed him over the rim of her glass. "Jonas O'Donnell didn't see me as a peer, either. Look where that got him."

Catena slid off his desk with a nod. "O'Donnell was a poorly-conditioned weapon of destruction. A bomb waiting to go off." He added with a lift of his brow, "And don't think I missed your suggestion that you had anything to do with O'Donnell's death. We both know better."

"I was there. It was my people who took him down, with Corbi cowering in his wine cellar." She set the brandy snifter on the desk and regarded him boldly.

Catena stared at her, then sat back down into his chair. "If I were to grant you that, that you were behind our Iron Pincher's downfall, wouldn't that make me *less* predisposed to do business with you?"

"Not if it meant I was something more than just a name."

Catena considered her for a moment. "There's a meeting I should be in, but I feel as if I'm shorting you the attention you deserve. Might I be so forward as to request dinner tomorrow evening?"

"You may be so forward," she replied.

He stood up again, motioning for her to join. "Tomorrow night, then. The Julietta Social Club on Thirty-First Street, at say…six o'clock?"

She strolled for the door as he held it open. "Until then, Mister Catena."

He offered her a gracious bow as she took her leave and went to collect Maria. The two filed back between the desks toward the front doors. Hattie glanced over her shoulder to the double-doors atop the mezzanine, brow furrowed.

Outside, Maria asked, "What did you learn?"

Hattie exhaled, trying to shake off the spike of adrenaline from playing verbal chess with the consigliere. "I learned that I'll need to watch my step around Mister Carlo Catena."

"What does that mean?"

"He's smart, sharp, and dangerous. I've got to be careful. This will be work. I have a follow-up with him tomorrow night. With luck, that'll give us time to work Maranzano."

They made their way down the street, pausing at a delicatessen for sandwiches. As they ate their lunch, Hattie considered the scheme at hand. Maranzano's man seemed easily pressed by a pincher, almost desperate to get her in the room with his boss. Catena, on the other hand, seemed far more cautious and circumspect.

"I want to speak with Vincent before we meet with Maranzano," she leaned over the table and whispered to Maria.

"Why?"

"He was there. At Masseria's. You didn't see him?"

Maria shook her head. "I was trying to keep my spine straight."

"He and Lefty. And I suppose their new blood." She shook her head. "Vincent seemed panicked that I was there."

"Okay," Maria mumbled around a bite of pastrami. "Then we wait."

Hattie nodded with a sigh.

"Will you do me a favor, though?" Maria asked.

"What?"

She pointed down to Hattie's plate. "Stop worrying and eat!"

CHAPTER 13

*V*incent unbuttoned his jacket, slinging it over his shoulder in the morning sunlight of the Red Hook pier. A warm breeze blew off the Upper Bay, swirling through the fish market. Summer was coming. He wondered if he'd be back in Baltimore before the solstice. Baltimore had only a few tolerable weeks of weather in the year, and he didn't treasure the notion of whiling them away in New York doing the bidding of two masters.

"For the love of Mary, Vincent," Hattie grumbled a few feet away. "Could you find a warmer place for us to meet?"

He cocked his head at her. "Are you cold?"

"Aye, I'm freezing my kneecaps off."

He shook his head. "I thought it was nice out." As he reached out to embrace her, he noticed a tension around her eyes. "Are you okay?"

"I'm quite well, boy-o." She smiled up at him, the tension easing. "I feel I'm treading on very thin ice with some of these gangsters, that I'm playing a game I where I don't know all the rules."

"Yeah, me, too." He sighed. "And speaking of which, how is Brigid O'Toole feeling today?"

She jabbed him in the ribs. "She's tired of doing the heavy lifting."

Vincent chuckled and gathered her under an arm to stroll back away from the wharf. "I had to think fast and cover for you with Polizzi. If I'd known you were pulling out some alter ego, I would've been prepared."

"It was a bit of an improvisation. But it's working."

"I'll say. Catena wouldn't shut up about you."

Hattie paused. "What, now?"

"I think you've made an impression."

She relaxed a bit under his arm. "Good to hear. I was really worried I'd blown it with him. So, what have you found out so far?"

"Luciano's behind all of this," Vincent told her. "He's behind Vito getting a new pincher, us being summoned to Masseria. It's all been orchestrated by Luciano through Sparks Floresta."

Hattie winced. "He's a real bastard."

"No argument here."

"I saw him with you at Masseria's."

"You'll remember him from the Ithaca auction." He stopped and swiveled to face Hattie. "Speaking of which, do you remember the glass pincher at that same auction?"

She nodded. "Capstein's wife? The one who nearly cut your leg off in front of everyone?"

"She's sworn to kill me, if that paints a more colorful picture."

"You seem to have that effect on women," Hattie teased. "So what about her?"

"Do you remember who bought her at that auction?"

"Just some goons from New York." Hattie's eyes grew wide. "Oh, no. She's with Masseria?"

"Maranzano."

"Well, isn't that just a handful of shite?"

Vincent chuckled. "She nearly cut me to ribbons the other night. Polizzi reined her in, but this won't be easy."

"Wait," Hattie tilted her head to look up him. "Why were you talking to Polizzi?"

"That's Luciano's play. Double-deal on Masseria. Give Maranzano a hand destabilizing their power base. Then get them both in a weak position. Bang, bang. Luciano's the last man standing. If we help make that happen, he'll give us carte blanche to go after Corbi."

Hattie scowled. "Why would he do that?"

Vincent stared back to the fish market and the water beyond. "He got to talking about the future of pinchers and doing business. Talking about progress. I don't know if he was shining sunlight up my trousers, or if he's ready for the sort of future you and I've been talking about."

She eyed him askance. "Sounds a bit too good to be true."

He shrugged. "At the very least, he's sympathetic to pinchers in some way. At least Floresta's sold. Might be why they were hot to trot trying to land me at that Ithaca auction."

Hattie crossed her arms. "I'm not about to trust another gangster. They do this, boy-o. They devour each other like lions."

Vincent wrinkled his nose. "Lions *eat* each other?"

Hattie laughed, then shook her head. "Don't call me out on my metaphors. I have enough problems."

"Right now, Luciano is the one in play. We let Masseria's people take down Maranzano. Then when they're softened up, we go for the kill. Both houses are toppled. Luciano is the Capo di tutti Capi. Then we can turn our full attention on the Baltimore Crew."

Hattie sighed. "Ever get the feeling we could just do it

ourselves and save some trouble? I mean, we're playing in the devil's sandbox already."

"The worry has always been that we take down Corbi only to find him replaced by some New York goons with more smarts and firepower," he countered. "Getting a commitment that the New York families will ignore what we're doing in Baltimore, that they'll keep their noses out of our business, is key."

"You're right." The tension returned to her face once more. "I'm going to meet Maranzano today."

Vincent nodded. "I'm meeting with his pinchers again tonight. Any advice?"

"He's losing the war. He knows it and Masseria knows it. That silver-mopped lawyer of his drove that much home. Shouldn't be too much of a chore convincing him you're on his side. I suspect he wants to believe it, anyhow. What I'm worried about is Sharp."

"Yeah," Vincent said. "Me, too."

A voice barked from between buildings, "Then you'll need backup."

Vincent nearly jumped out of his skin as he turned to spot Maria peering at them from an alley. "Well. That's just unsettling."

Hattie looked over at the earth pincher. "What're you doing here?"

Maria stepped up beside them. "My job. Watching your back."

Vincent chuckled. "You think I'm that dangerous?"

Maria shrugged. "Maybe. Maybe not. Either way, I work for her. Not you."

"But you want to back me up with Maranzano's pinchers?" he asked.

Maria nodded. "It's why we're here, right? If this glass

pincher is so damn dangerous, you'll want someone watching over you from the shadows."

Hattie nodded. "It's a good thought."

Vincent scowled. "Yeah, if I wanted a babysitter—"

Hattie punched him in the arm. "This was your idea, you turnip. You brought us here to help.

He lifted his hands in surrender. "Alright, alright. I have an escort, so you'll have to find your own way there, though."

"She'll have been there all day," Hattie told him. "Remember?"

"Oh. Right."

They reached Mrs. Dunne's house. The old woman was sweeping the stoop, pausing to lift a brow as the trio approached.

"Top o' the morning," she declared in a scratchy brogue.

"Good morning," Vincent replied with a grin, placing a kiss on Hattie's cheek before turning to Maria. "The meet's at nine p.m."

He strolled up the street, a vigorous conversation taking place behind him. He just kept walking, leaving Hattie to whatever issue her temporary landlady might have taken with that kiss.

* * *

NIGHT FELL at some point that day. He'd spent most of it indoors with Buddy, discussing the finer points of their magical limits. Buddy, as it turned out, could easily kill himself by attempting to hit a target too far away. Vincent kept the descriptions of his own powers general, and suspected Buddy had done the same. It was common among pinchers to understate their own abilities.

The trick would be finding yet another way of brushing off Buddy tonight, before his intrigues with Floresta could commence. Though Lefty seemed resigned to Vincent's evasion, he took delight in making it difficult. So, Vincent feigned a stomach ache and made his exit through the window, scaling the fire escape to the street where Floresta was waiting.

"Took you long enough," Floresta grumbled.

"You have the luxury to come and go as you please, you mook. Don't start."

Floresta drove to some tenements on the border of Queens and the Bronx, where Polizzi and Betty were waiting. As Vincent stepped out of the car, Betty turned her back to him.

Polizzi stepped forward to shake Vincent's hand. "She's in a mood."

"When isn't she?"

"Good point. Alright, the big man won't be joining us tonight."

Floresta scowled. "I was told he'd be here."

"Yeah, well, plans change."

Vincent asked, "What changed?"

"He had a meet today with some broad from Baltimore. Got him in a twiffle."

Vincent lifted a brow. "A *twiffle*?"

"The closest thing the old man gets to excited. He ran off to Atlantic City to press some flesh and pull some strings. He put this in my hands."

Betty marched away.

"Is she gonna be a problem?" Floresta asked Polizzi.

"Nah. She knows better than to thumb her nose at the boss. She'll get it done."

Vincent shook his head, feeling as if they'd completely lost control of the situation. "What is it we're getting done, anyways?"

Polizzi gathered them into a huddle. "So, Masseria owns

four or five buildings in and around Brooklyn. We're too low in manpower to scout them all out, but we know that he keeps most of his treasury in one of these apartments."

"He keeps his money in an *apartment?*" Vincent asked.

"Safer than a bank."

"How do you figure?"

"Banks don't got as many choppers guarding the vault."

Vincent nodded. "I suppose so."

Floresta cleared his throat. "I know which one."

"I figured as much," Polizzi said.

"The one on Bergen," Floresta added. "In Prospect Heights."

Polizzi turned to Betty, who watched from several yards away. "Bergen."

She grinned at him. "I told you."

"Yeah, yeah…" Polizzi turned back to the others. "The plan is to hit their treasury at night. We do it clean, quick and quiet."

"No guns blazing?" Vincent asked.

The pocket pincher shook his head. "We can't afford to light the fuse just yet. We're down on manpower, and the other families are about ready to back Masseria as it is. If we pop off the firecracker, it'll be curtains for all of us."

Floresta nodded toward Vincent. "Our man, here, has a way with getting in and out quiet-like."

"Yeah. Time pincher, huh? That'll be useful."

Vincent frowned, feeling completely lost and not liking it one bit. "So, this is a *robbery?*"

"The old man's ready to buy some guns for this Baltimore connection. He'll need cash, and every cent Masseria don't got is as good as a dollar in our pockets. You just get me inside their money room. I'll get it out."

Vincent smirked. "How much cash can you stuff into those magic pockets of yours?"

Polizzi shrugged. "I'd love to find out!"

"Alright," Vincent sighed. "When?"

"Has to be tomorrow night," Polizzi replied. "We got a window, what with the baby and all."

Once more Vincent was completely lost. "What baby?"

Polizzi gestured to Floresta, who answered, "Two of Masseria's pinchers had a baby last month. The parents got greased in a dust-up a few weeks ago, so Masseria has a good dozen or so of his best men guarding the tadpole. They're thin on skilled manpower right now."

"That's convenient," Vincent drawled

Floresta shrugged. "Yeah. It's almost like I planned for this."

"How many pinchers does Masseria have in total?"

"Four," Floresta answered. "The baby obviously won't be of any use for at least a decade. That leaves three. You're looking at one of them now. Which leaves Lenny and Augustus."

Vincent squinted. "I haven't seen hide or hair of these pinchers since we got here."

"There's a reason for that. Lenny's got a problem." Floresta made a glass-tipping gesture. "He likes to bend the elbow. Only got worse since O'Donnell took the dirt nap."

"And the other?"

"Augustus," Floresta reminded him. "That's the one you gotta keep your eyes peeled for. He's a colored man from Texas. He's all smiles and southern charm and likes to hang back in the shadows, but when Masseria needs someone taken care of quietly, he's like the grim reaper."

"What's his power?"

"He's a Squeeze Pincher. You give him a crack under a locked door, he'll press himself flat and slip through that crack before he slips a knife between your ribs."

Vincent frowned. "How will we know if he'll be at this money room?"

Floresta said, "Leave that to me. The three of you just get the cash without being seen. I'm serious about that. Masseria can't know Maranzano's people were behind this." He pointed to Vincent. "And even worse, that you're involved."

"I got it," Vincent muttered. "Alright. Tomorrow night, then."

Polizzi shook his hand.

Vincent turned to Betty, then lifted a hand. "Give me a second, gents."

He stepped up the walk toward Betty, who crossed her arms with a sneer.

"What?" she snapped as Vincent stood in front of her.

"We're gonna be working together, Betty. Like it or not. This is delicate. You understand glass, so let me get metaphorical. This whole plan to take down Masseria is a glass figure with tiny, thin pieces. You and I? We're putting strain on those pieces. Too much strain, and the whole thing'll snap. And then we bleed."

Betty glared. "You don't have to talk to me like I'm a child. I understand the situation."

"I'm just saying, let's ease up on the pressure. Huh?"

"Look. You do your part. I'll do my part. We don't have to talk. We don't have to look each other in the eye. And when it's all done and Masseria goes down, then I'll kill you."

"And in the meantime?" Vincent asked.

"In the meantime, I'll do my best to keep pointed objects away from your throat."

Vincent shrugged. "What is your part in this, anyway?"

Betty uncrossed her arms and stepped past him. "Someone's gotta pick the lock."

As Vincent followed her back to the others, he scanned

the surrounding alleys and rooftops for Maria, hoping he hadn't just wasted her evening.

Floresta drove him back to the Monarch, dropping him off three doors down for Vincent to find a way to make a discreet entrance. Instead, Vincent lingered in an alley between a grocer and a haberdashery. He pressed his back against the bricks and waited.

In time, a woman swept around the corner, breathless.

"I was too far away to hear. Anything you need me to tell Hattie?" Maria asked, panting.

He grinned at her. "I'll talk to her tomorrow. Are you okay?"

She shook her head. "Couldn't…get a car. Had to run."

"Appreciate you being there," Vincent said. "Sorry, you ran all that way, though. I'll let Hattie know what went down in person."

Maria's face drew long. "It's just… Does she not trust me?"

Vincent frowned. "What makes you think that?"

Maria turned to lean against the wall alongside Vincent. "She keeps taking these meetings without me. I'm not included in what you both talk about. And now you won't even tell me what went down back there."

"She wants you to guard her back. Hard to do that when both of you are in the room. And I know she updates you on everything that's going on, including what I tell her. The reason we meet alone is…" He grinned sheepishly. "Well, we don't have a lot of time for romance lately, you know."

Maria snorted, then covered up the laugh with her hand. "Okay. Fair enough, I guess."

"Listen, I probably shouldn't tell you this," Vincent added. "Hattie invited you on this trip for one specific reason. She wanted to prove to the rest of the Charge that you were someone she could trust, someone she can rely upon to pick up the reins when needed, to be a leader. She's not waiting for you to screw up. She's waiting for you to deliver."

Maria blinked at him in surprise. "I don't know what I'm supposed to deliver? She's here and there and everywhere, and I feel like I'm in a whirl just trying to keep up with what she's planning and doing."

"That's Hattie." Vincent smiled. "I feel the same way most of the time. I can't even manage to find a way to ask…" He didn't finish the sentence. Hell, it almost slipped out.

Unfortunately, Maria was sharp enough to piece it together. She spun around and gripped both of his arms. "Are you serious?" she squealed.

He squirmed away from her. "It's nothing. Never mind."

Maria pressed, "You're popping the question?" Her face broadened into a delirious smile. "When? When are you gonna—?"

"I don't know, dammit." He stepped in to lower his voice. "It's harder than it looks."

"Do you have a ring?"

He nodded.

"Okay. Alright. She wants me to deliver? I'll deliver. And so will you." Maria reached for his head, tousling his hair.

"Hey," he grumbled, pulling away to smooth it back down.

"We *both* got work to do." She stepped for the street, pausing to turn back to face him. "Thanks, though."

"For what?"

"Understanding."

He shrugged, then nodded.

Maria trotted away, rounding the corner of the alley and out of sight while Vincent stood stiff, straightening his hair. Well, he was going to have to trust Maria eventually. Might as well have been tonight.

CHAPTER 14

"C'mon, boys. You're leaving a girl to drink alone?"

A round of faces wreathed in sweat and five o'clock shadows grinned bashfully back at Hattie. She lifted her empty glass to give it a waggle at Pauly.

He shook a quick martini for Hattie, or rather for Brigid, reaching underneath the bar for the good stuff. None of the boys gathered around her seemed eager to press her for conversation, much less anything untoward. They hovered in a cloud of expectant silence, cowed at this point by the legend of Brigid O'Toole and her new association with Salvatore Maranzano.

"Well, if you're all to be so ungallant, then I suppose there's nothing for it but to buy you lot a round."

Pauly lifted his chin as the young bucks finally responded with a cheer. He grabbed a mismatched assortment of shot glasses, pouring from the watered-down bottles. As the bargain basement gin was passed around and pounded by the patrons, Pauly gave Brigid a discreet nod. There was no way he would actually charge her for the drinks. Especially not with Maria looming in the corner like a panther poised to strike. No, Hattie knew she was robbing him blind by giving away his liquor like that. She'd make it up to him somehow.

"Hey, uh… Miss?" one of the men ventured. "Where ya from, anyways?"

"Old Dublin Town, boy-o," she replied. "Where we know a thing or two about having your hard work trodden on by fat men who never leave their desks."

A few nods and contemplative grins.

She continued, "It's what I love about America, you know. You work hard, and it's maybe only a fifty-fifty chance they'll put the screws to you."

This generated a few chuckles and a lift of a glass as a salute. The cheer faded as face after face turned to the far corner, the one the light never seemed to reach. A figure stepped from the shadows, a gaunt man with dark skin that glistened in the flickering candlelight. He wore a wide-brimmed hat of black felt and a bolo tie with a single triangle of turquoise suspended just below his throat. The man's eyes were slits, gauging the postures of everyone in the room.

Those postures were largely stiff and motionless.

Hattie pivoted on her stool as Maria jumped to her feet. She held out a hand for Maria to hold her position. This man had made an entrance with some drama, and the men in this speakeasy were close to pissing themselves. He was clearly a pincher.

As he approached, those gathered parted like the Red Sea before Moses. Hattie kept her illusion tightly knit so as not to betray the panic flooding her face.

He removed his hat to reveal a smooth, bald head. With a lift of his brow and a clearing of his throat, he spoke. "Ma'am?"

Hattie blinked at the thunderous bass of this fellow's voice. "How can I help you, um…"

"Henry," he replied with a Texan twang. "Augustus Henry."

Pauly whispered over her shoulder, "You know this is Maranzano's turf, Augustus. What're you trying to start over here?"

Augustus' eyes shifted toward Pauly. "Let's not get all impolite. I'm here on business."

Hattie shrugged. "I am, after all, a businesswoman. So, Augustus is your name then?" She extended a hand. "Brigid O'Toole. It's a pleasure."

He took her hand then reached into his jacket to produce a slip of paper. "Mister Catena begs your forgiveness, but he must reschedule your meeting this evenin'."

She lifted the note to read it in the dim light. An address and a time.

"Well, then," she replied with guarded tone. "What time would be more convenient for Mister Catena?"

"Nine o'clock, if that's alright with yourself?"

Hattie cocked a brow. "Nine o'clock it is. Thank you, and tell your boss I'll be looking forward to some quality brandy when I see him."

Augustus took a step back and placed his hat back onto his head, giving Hattie a polite nod. "Miss O'Toole."

With a tip of his finger to its brim, he turned to the others. "Y'all be good, now."

As he turned back to the dark corner he slipped from, he glanced to the near corner of the room. "Pleasure to see you again, Maria," he said with a nod before stepping into the shadows and disappearing through the wall boards.

Hattie turned to Maria with a lift of both brows. The mood of the room had dropped like a wet rag, so Hattie quickly wrapped up her business and left with Maria. On the street, she glanced back and forth for the mysterious man.

Maria grabbed her arm and pulled her farther down the

block. "Don't," she whispered. "He might be following us. He could be anywhere."

"Who is he, then?" Hattie asked, struggling to keep her illusion intact after so long.

"Later."

They continued down the street until they hailed a street-car. Maria didn't break the silence until they were back in Brooklyn and up inside their room.

Hattie pulled off her earrings, setting them on the vanity as she rubbed her earlobes. "So?"

Maria paced on the far side of the room. "His name is Augustus Henry."

"I caught that much. Is he a shadow pincher? Like Bolton?"

"No. Not like Bolton. He's a squeeze pincher. He can get into damn near anywhere."

"And he knows you?"

Maria nodded. "Before Galloway. We stared each other down from opposite sides of a turf war in Cleveland. He was legendary. Ice water in his veins. He could slip into a room without anyone knowing, then cut your throat before you knew he was there. It was a short turf war."

Hattie crossed her arms. "Yet you're still standing."

"I am. My owner, on the other hand…"

"I see."

"I escaped in the collapse of my organization. Ran south to Cincinnati where Galloway found me."

Hattie sighed. "See, this is precisely why."

Maria stopped pacing, cocking her head. "Why what?"

"Why I want you on the outside during these meetings. So that they don't see you coming." Hattie added with a softer tone, "Not because I don't trust you, but specifically because I do."

Maria nodded. "I don't know what this does to our cover, now."

Hattie lifted her chin. "To be honest, I do believe it plays into our hand."

"How so?"

"You say he knows you from a war his side won. Well, where would he assume you went, then?"

Maria shrugged.

"One way or another, you'd end up in the hands of someone else. And what is the good Miss O'Toole's first step in world domination?"

"Scooping up pinchers on the cheap." Maria nodded. "Yes."

"Let's just keep calm and press on." Hattie lifted the note. "Catena pushed back the appointment at the social club."

"Should that worry us?"

"That is the question," Hattie replied as she took a seat on the bed. "Whatever the reason, let's hope it plays in our favor."

THE JULIETTA SOCIAL Club was everything Hattie had expected from New York nightlife. An open space of tables spread before a cramped stage, smoke hanging near the ceiling like a carpet. A four-piece jazz band throbbed in syncopation, a muted trumpet squeaking over the bassist as he thumbed a walking beat. All that was missing was the gin. This was no speakeasy. Rather, it was a lounge that had elected to abide by prohibition, serving coffee and other innocuous beverages in lieu of the hard stuff. Pursuant to this business decision, most of the club was empty, save for the band, Hattie, and Carlo Catena.

Maria was somewhere outside, out of sight. The

reminder that Masseria still had professional pinchers in hand had sent Hattie's forward press into something of a stall. Her gamble was predicated on being twice again as cocky as the men in suits. And despite her brandishing Maria's powers for Maranzano's people, in a fight she was still catastrophically outnumbered and outgunned.

Hattie stepped toward Catena's table with a calmness she was far from feeling. "I do hope your unexpected business hasn't ruined your mood."

With a polite smile, he reached to take her wrap. She was glad she'd actually bothered to wear a wrap rather than knitting one out of pure light.

"It could not be helped. I do apologize."

He held her chair for her. As she took a seat, he guided it closer to the table, the tips of his fingers brushing her shoulder as he swept back around to his seat. A crackle of panic swept through her as he penetrated what she'd economically cast as a purely visual illusion. Any discrepancy between what she he was seeing and what his fingers sensed could jeopardize everything.

Catena settled across the table from Hattie, laying a napkin over his lap.

"No brandy, then?" she asked as a waiter filled a glass with water.

"The face we put forward in public is well manicured, Miss O'Toole. Our men do not partake openly."

"Is that why you lot are so fain to haunt restaurants?"

He released a quick, genuine belly laugh. "That has as much to do with the Sicilian appetite as anything."

"So, may I ask a question? Are we here to discuss business, or is this purely social?"

"Business. And curiosity." He watched her over the rim of his glass as he took a sip of water. "I wonder how you came upon the notion of challenging Vito Corbi in the first place."

With a smirk, she replied, "Truth of the matter is that I'm tired of watching those bandits play crooks and keystone cops, tripping over one another and leaving money on the table."

"That's a very particular frustration for a woman in your position."

"I find incompetence grating."

He shook his head. "But how is it your concern in the first place?"

"I believe I could do better."

"It seems to me you've skipped the first two acts of your story."

"I'm sorry?"

"How does a lady from Dublin develop an interest in organized crime in America? How does she learn the ins and outs, develop relationships with those in control, and culti-vate a herd of pinchers all on her own?"

"A herd?" She wrinkled her nose. "You take a poor view of pinchers, I think."

He waved his hand. "They are what they are."

"Human beings?"

"I suppose. But being human does not necessarily impart any particular significance."

She leaned back. "You don't believe all life has value?"

He chuckled. "You can't be serious. In this profession you seem so eager to break into, one must recognize that people exist in varying degrees of value. The greatest value reigns over the lesser. The lowest find themselves to be...disposable."

She raised her eyebrows. "And here I thought America was the land of opportunity. All men are created equal?"

"Thomas Jefferson was a slave owner, Miss O'Toole. When a man such as himself declares all men to be equal, there are assumptions at play. What he meant to say, I'm sure, was that all white men with land should pretend they are equal in order to preserve the farce of democracy they intended to inflict upon the world."

"A dismal view of the Founding Fathers, if every I heard one."

Catena squinted. "I was born in Palermo, Sicily. These were not *my* Founding Fathers."

"Does that make you more valuable than Joe Masseria, then?" She smirked. "Because he's barely made any effort at all."

Catena snickered, a noise that rumbled into a laugh. "I do enjoy a good conversation outside of the office. But I recognize that you've deflected from my question."

Hattie nodded, her face twisting in concentration behind the illusion of the unflappable Brigid O'Toole. This was it. She'd have to invent a story to satisfy this man's curiosity. She was acutely aware this was a feeler meeting, probing her out for lapses in her story. Looking for a reason to have her killed.

Keep it simple. A lie that was close to the truth would be harder to sniff out.

"My father," she began, "taught me how to read and write and do my sums, about business and efficiency. He felt I had certain potential that would be wasted in a conventional woman's life." Here was the gamble. "Did I mention he worked for Michael Collins and the Free State?"

Catena leaned back with a nod. "That would explain things."

"So you can see, I grew up with the life. My father worked for one of the most notorious free pinchers in modern history."

"And that man's legacy bears out the myth of free pinchers."

"Myth? Surely you mean value? The good they can accomplish?"

"Or the damage they can inflict?" he scoffed.

Hattie watched the other man carefully from behind her illusion. Michael Collins's use of magic against the British sparked the violence in Dublin—violence which ended with the weakening of British rule, and a clamp-down on pinchers throughout Ireland. Collins, for his part, used his freedom to rally the Free State Army around Irish home rule until he was gunned down by anti-treaty fighters. His body had been displayed in the city as a warning to other pinchers.

"You'll pardon me if I feel otherwise," she told him. "Our family was close to the cause."

"Of that I have no doubt. Let me fill in the rest. Your family fled Ireland for America, where your father was recruited by former IRA cronies. He was killed shortly after, leaving you and whatever was left of your family to find a new direction. After wasting years of your life in menial labor, you decided to employ the education your father afforded you and make a name for yourself." He smiled. "How close am I?"

Hattie exhaled in relief. Catena had given her a way out of concocting an entire biography on the fly.

"Close, but my father died before we left Ireland."

"I see." He knitted his hands together in front of him. "Then this is about legacy."

"If you like."

"It certainly fills me with more confidence in your resolve. You're not some silly girl with a misplaced sense of glamor in the life of a bootlegger. And it helps to know that you won't underestimate the powers of your pinchers."

Hattie unwound her arms, draping herself casually over her own chair. "Oh, I'm very familiar with how dangerous a pincher can be when pressed."

"And it would do well for you to keep that in mind." He frowned as he reached for his water. "There will come a day when another Michael Collins will rise—perhaps even in America. And people like you and me will be responsible to clean up the mess."

"You're so certain the pinchers are waiting to rise up and overthrow the lot of you?"

"Any student of history recognizes the threat, Miss O'Toole. A powerful underclass kept beneath the heel of oligarchs. Revolution is inevitable."

Hattie stifled a grin. The man was correct. Here she was, a free pincher, taking advantage of the in-fighting between the mob families. And revolution was most certainly her aim.

Aware that Catena was still sizing her up, Hattie went on the offensive.

"Your man, Augustus, then."

"What about him?"

"He makes an impression."

Catena laughed. "His powers are as useful as his charm."

"Is he the only pincher you have left? Now that O'Donnell is out of the picture."

"No," Catena grumbled as he set down his espresso cup. "I have more."

Hattie eyed him. "But not as many as you'd like?"

"I didn't say that."

"You didn't have to. I suspect you've grown impatient with Ithaca?"

His eyes narrowed. "Your grasp of the intimate details of our organization is as surprising as it is alarming."

"Best not to underestimate me, then. Don't you think?"

He glanced at the table, eyes working through a thought before he said, "I'm *am* down a few. We lost O'Donnell earlier this year."

She nodded.

"In the wake, Maranzano went on the offensive," he continued. "Both sides suffered losses. Now the assets have dwindled."

Hattie nodded. "A shame, especially since your pipeline for new talent seems to have dwindled."

"True, but there is a baby in the wings. We'll see if the child has powers in good time. With these things, the odds are in our favor, but it doesn't always take. Like any sort of animal husbandry, it's a numbers game."

"There you go again." She struggled to keep the tone of her voice cool and disinterested. "Referring to them as animals."

"It helps to dehumanize them," he stated matter-of-factly. "Some advice for a nascent gang leader, Miss O'Toole. Avoid the habit of seeing pinchers as people."

"And how, good sir, do you see me?"

He sipped his espresso. "I see a woman who's looking for someone to recognize her."

She grinned. "Recognition is nice when you can get it."

Catena's smile sharpened. "Sometimes it's the last thing you want."

"Do I take it, given your situation, that your boss's offer of available talent to Vito Corbi has rubbed you raw?"

"An investment," he replied through tight lips.

"And if this investment becomes a boondoggle, might you find yourself in the market for veteran talent?"

He stiffened, jaw working back and forth. "You are full of surprises, Miss O'Toole."

They both finished their coffee in silence, then Catena rose to help Hattie with her wrap. He remained as she left and headed down the street. Maria joined her several blocks away, and the pair walked for several more blocks before speaking.

"How'd it go?" Maria finally asked.

Hattie looked around before replying. "I get the impression that Masseria's more desperate than he wants anyone to know. They're low on pincher power. He sees me as a possible source, but I'm not sure how we can use that yet."

"So, a wasted evening?"

"On the contrary. If I read the man correctly, he's taking O'Toole seriously. That can only help."

Maria nodded. "I'll bet Augustus reported back that you had a genuine pincher on the payroll."

"He wouldn't enjoy the thought of me paying you, that much is certain. He hates us. If I've learned anything, it's that. The man is secretly terrified of pinchers."

"Strange that he's in charge of so many."

"He's convinced this country's on the verge of a pincher revolt." She looked around at the buildings towering above them. "And God willing, he's right."

CHAPTER 15

Vincent and Buddy leaned against the brick wall of a corner deli while they waited for Masseria's pincher to emerge. Just as Buddy began to fidget, a disheveled fellow in his forties with a leathered face and bloodshot eyes staggered free of the door with a tin mug in his hand.

Vincent eyed the mug, spotting steam rising in the morning air.

"You must be Lenny."

The man jerked, halting his droop-eyed shamble. "Yeah? Who the hell are you?"

Vincent extended a hand to the man. "Name's Vincent Calendo. I'm here on behalf of—"

"I know who you are," he grumbled before sipping what for all rights looked to be coffee, though Vincent picked up a whiff of booze on the man's breath.

"A little hair of the dog?" Vincent asked with a nod to the cup.

"Tied one on last night," Lenny said. "Who's the kid?"

"That's Buddy Seiler."

"Another one of you Baltimore gremlins?"

Vincent smiled. "Yes."

"What'd you want?"

"Sparks sent us," Vincent replied. "There's a meet at the cash room."

Lenny scowled. "Someone's gonna pop that smug little shit right in the puss one of these days."

"Who, Floresta?"

Lenny plodded forward after Buddy, who had started walking. "Gets his nose halfway up Luciano's can, and now he thinks he's the new prime."

Vincent squinted. "Prime?"

"Prime pincher."

"Like Jonas O'Donnell?"

Lenny crossed himself. "God rest his fucking soul."

Vincent thought it over as they proceeded up the street. "I was under the impression that O'Donnell wasn't the personable sort."

"Yeah," Lenny replied. "And that suited me just fine. Do your damn job. Go home. The higher-ups leave you alone and you get on with gettin' on. Tongue-waggers like Sparks just get you volunteered into one hare-assed plan after another hare-assed plan. Early morning meetings so they can hear their own voices. Hell with him."

"So, who *is* the prime pincher if not Floresta?" Vincent ventured.

"Sure as hell ain't me," Lenny replied.

Buddy called from half a block up, "Which building is it?"

Lenny pointed to a beige-stoned three-story just two doors down and across the street. "Top floor. We own the building, but we let out the bottom floor to keep up appearances."

They crossed the street, ducking between cars. As Vincent reached the far side, Lenny paused, glancing back at the ground. Without checking the traffic, he doubled back, bending over for a nickel lying flat on the road.

A driver pumped the horn as he tried to steer free of the man. As the tires angled to the side, the entire vehicle fishtailed, sending half a ton of Ford engineering into Lenny. The front fender struck him in the shoulder, crumpling in on itself as the tire popped with a long hiss. The car's rear end lifted several feet, dropping back onto the ground as the driver bloodied his nose on the steering wheel.

Lenny stood up to examine the nickel, giving it a polish on his lapel before turning and shuffling back to the sidewalk without so much as a scratch.

Vincent stared at the wreckage of the car, then again at Lenny.

"You bulletproof, too?" Vincent asked.

"When it counts," he said as he pocketed the nickel and moved for the building.

* * *

LATER THAT NIGHT, Vincent stood outside the building, Pockets and Betty beside him. He had a plan for getting all three of them inside, but it had some significant risks. If this didn't go off seamlessly, then he might end up Masseria's number-one suspect in this robbery.

"What's the layout?" Polizzi asked.

"Everything's on the third floor," Vincent replied as he watched Betty for sudden moves. "They got two apartments connected. Knocked a door into the adjoining wall. The safe's in the second apartment. That hall door's barred up good and tight. Be easier to punch through a wall than try it."

"So we go through the first apartment."

Vincent nodded, buttoning his jacket as the three huddled

beneath a street lamp. A cold breeze flowed through the city, bringing a last gasp of the passing winter with it.

Polizzi eyed the beige-stoned building from the corner. "I'm guessing they got a small army inside, loaded for bear?"

"Something like that."

"Passwords?"

"I think they got people watching from the first two floors. They'll know if an uninvited guest shows up."

Betty crossed her arms. "Then how do we get in and out without them seeing us?"

Vincent pinched time, walked around the back of Betty, then released the bubble again. "I have my means."

She jumped, twisted on her heel, then sent a fist into his jaw.

Vincent's head snapped to the side. He rubbed his jaw with a wince. "Remind me never to do that again."

Betty breathed hard through her nose, hands still clenched into fists.

Polizzi chuckled. "You two are chicken and dumplings."

"More like chicken and a lit stick of dynamite," Vincent muttered as they moved across the street.

"Alright," Vincent whispered as they reached the corner of the building. "They know me. I can get most of the way up. That's all I'll need. When I have a clear path, I'll pull the two of you inside. Get ready for it, and if you pop into a room out of nowhere try not to gasp or shout or anything." He peered at Betty. "Like taking a swing at the nearest mook."

Betty scowled. "No promises."

Vincent pulled open the door and entered the building. The hall lamps flickered from flimsy wiring, giving the front stairs the appearance of motion. He paused for a couple seconds in case one of the Masseria guards had staked out the first floor. No response.

He proceeded up the stairs to the narrow halls of the second floor, allowing his shoes to clack against the floor boards and treads of the stairs to announce his presence.

The moment he cleared the second landing, a door opened. A broad-shouldered thug in a suit stepped out of the door with a pistol in his hand.

"Alright, hold it," the man grunted.

Vincent lifted his hands. "Take it easy, fella. I was here this morning."

The thug eyed him. "Don't remember you."

A second door opened behind Vincent. This time a thin man in spectacles stepped into the hall.

"It's okay, Chuck," the spectacled man declared. "He's one of the Baltimore pinchers. He's on the up and up."

Chuck with the Shoulders stepped back through his door, closing it gently behind him.

Vincent peered at Spectacles. "Thanks. I lost my wallet today. Trying to retrace my steps."

The man nodded upstairs. "Most of the boys are into their cards. Go on up. It's three knocks, then one, then two."

Vincent nodded, then took several steps toward the stairs. When the door closed behind him, he pinched time and pulled himself back down the stairs before releasing his time bubble.

Betty jumped when he popped back into the flow of time in front of her.

He held up his hands, bracing for her to take another swing. "Hey, easy."

Polizzi asked, "What's the lay of the land?"

"No one on the first floor that I can tell. Second floor, they have two lookouts."

Betty sneered. "We can take them out easily enough."

Polizzi groaned. "No, no, no. We're in and out. No trace we were ever here."

Betty huffed and turned away.

Vincent said, "I can pinch time and get us past the second-floor landing, but it'll be work. I'll have to dead-carry both of you up a flight of stairs."

Betty shook her head, still facing away. "You're not laying a hand on me."

"Oh, shut up," Polizzi snapped.

Vincent rubbed his chin. "Unless…"

"Unless what?" Polizzi prodded.

"I haven't tried it in a long while. It's tricky. Takes concentration."

Betty turned to face him. "You'll have to use your brain? We're doomed."

Vincent ignored her. "When I pinch time, I create a bubble in the normal flow of the cosmos. Like a big rock in a fast-moving river. The spot right behind it turns into a whirlpool."

"Yeah?"

"The bigger the rock, the more power it takes. Which means I try not to overextend the size of the bubble."

Polizzi shrugged. "Yeah, and?"

"Well, I usually pinch the bubble of frozen time right over top of myself. It's easier, and it's how I'm used to doing it."

Betty narrowed her eyes. "But you can freeze time over someone else with you."

Vincent nodded. "Exactly. I did it…maybe twice before. Long time ago."

Polizzi asked, "What are the downsides?"

"Takes more energy. Plus, the time bubble pops easy if I get distracted."

Polizzi said, "But the upside is we can march up those stairs without them being the wiser. It's clean."

"The cash room is on the top floor. If we get you two up

the stairs, you can wait while I give the daily knock." Vincent peered at Polizzi. "Is it worth the risk?"

"It's up to you."

With a nod, Vincent turned back to the front of the building. He led them through the front door. Once they reached the top of the first flight of stairs, he held out a hand for them to wait. Vincent focused on the doors which the lookouts had popped out of. He closed his eyes and visualized the space of apartments across the hall one from the other. This would take not one, but two remote bubbles of frozen time.

Vincent fanned out his fingers, tuning out his thoughts enough to feel the flow of time streaming past him. This subtle rush of seconds upon minutes tingled against his fingertips. He reached out with his consciousness to feel the rhythms and rushings inside and around his targets. With a gentle urging, he began to slow the flow of time around each apartment.

"How long is this going to take?" Betty whispered.

Vincent's magic dropped. He opened his eyes to glare at Betty.

Polizzi gave Betty a quick thump on the arm and Vincent started over, reaching out to create two bubbles of frozen time around each of the lookout rooms. The strain was considerable, and he found the two bubbles impossible for him to maintain. With a cock of his head Vincent laced the two bubbles together. The chaotic energies cascaded one into the other, finally settling into one humming pulse. Vincent eased that pulse into a slow beat, and then finally into a muddy stillness.

He moved forward, the others behind him. Motioning for them to continue up to the next landing and hold still, he positioned himself in the spot he'd left when he fetched the others. Then Vincent released the time pinch.

The energy crashed back into the normal flow of time.

The first door opened, and the broad-shouldered lookout nearly leapt into the hall.

Vincent glanced up at him impassively. The man muttered something under his breath, stepped back into the room and closed the door.

First obstacle passed. On to the next.

Vincent climbed to the others at the top of the next landing, pointed to the second door on the right and gave them a gesture to wait. He walked up to the door and did the secret knock. A bolt threw open, and a short man with a greasy comb-over stared up at Vincent.

"Yeah, what?"

"I was here earlier today. I think I dropped my wallet when I reached for a—"

The man opened the door, cutting off Vincent's practiced alibi. "Yeah, alright."

The short man turned back to a table with three of his coworkers, all with cards fanned out in front of their chests. Piles of cash and coin sat on the table, ready for the next wager.

Vincent wandered into the room, searching around for the mythical lost wallet. The cover story gave him a good excuse to take in the room and the men inside. The cash room door was on the far side of the room, which would be easier on Vincent.

He crouched down next to a sofa, pretending to look underneath for his wallet. He balled fists near his knees, clamped his eyes shut, then extended another bubble of frozen time over the card table. This was easier than two entire apartments. Confined space, limited radius. The bubble snapped into place, immobilizing the four men at their game.

Vincent eased back up to his feet, finding it easier to

move and maintain focus. He opened the hall door and gestured for Betty and Polizzi to approach.

When Polizzi entered the room, he stopped to take in the scene before him.

"Well, ain't that a thing?" he whispered, eying four men frozen in time.

Betty brushed past him. "It's overrated"

Vincent sighed. "This one's easier than the last floor, but let's not take any more time than is necessary."

Polizzi strode for the cash room door, pointing to it with a questioning look to Vincent. Vincent nodded. Polizzi reached for a padlock barring the door shut with a solid iron hasp, giving it a tug to test.

"Okay, Betty," he muttered. "Time for your voodoo."

"So, you picked up lock-picking since Ithaca?" Vincent asked her.

Betty peered at the card table. With a quick jab, she thrust her arm into Vincent's time bubble.

He released a guttural breath as if someone punched him in the gut. With a redoubling of his willpower, he steadied the time bubble as Betty snatched a glass ashtray from the table, dumping the contents onto the lap of one of the card players.

She strolled toward the padlock as Vincent released a long, whistling breath.

"Please don't do that again," he huffed.

Polizzi glared at the ash covering the gangster's trousers. "What part of 'leave no trace' confused you?"

Betty pressed the ashtray against the padlock. The chunk of steel sank into the glass like a hot knife through ice. Once the entire bottom of the padlock was immersed in a solid sphere of glass, Betty closed her eyes and gripped it with her fingertips. Tiny cracking noises filled the air as the glass filled the interior of the locks, manipulating the tumblers.

Finally, with an exhale, Betty opened her eyes and pulled the lock open, slipping it from the hasp.

"Neat trick," Vincent said.

Betty glanced at him over her shoulder, her brow lifted, mouth pulled into a triumphant grin.

"The safe's gonna be the hard part. Keep the time bubble up," Polizzi told Vincent. "We'll crack the vault and grab the stash as fast as we can."

Vincent nodded as Polizzi pulled the door open.

The man stopped at the threshold, lifting his chin. "Damn…"

Vincent peered over his shoulder into a room bare of furniture save for a single desk in the center of the room. The rest of the space was full of paper boxes loaded with dollar bills, a few stashes of jewelry, and no safe to speak of.

"That's a lot of loot," Vincent said. "How many trips, do you think we'll need? I don't know if I can hold these mooks and the rooms downstairs at the same time, or manage this twice. I'm already feeling queasy."

Polizzi winced. "Just one trip. Give me a minute."

Polizzi entered the room, closing the door behind him.

Betty stood next to Vincent, crossing her arms, hate radiating from the woman.

"Can you tell me something?" Vincent asked her. "Why do you have it out for me? I mean, I know what they did to you at Ithaca. They did it to us both."

Betty glared. "You had it easy, you horse's ass."

"There was nothing easy about it."

"Ten times easier than what I went through, and you know it."

He shook his head. "But that wasn't my fault, and you know that."

"Who says this is about Ithaca, anyways?" She turned to

face him. "You kidnapped me. Strolled right into my bar and took me to Vito Corbi."

"After you glassed my hands to the bar."

"After you threatened me."

"After you tried to kill me last year."

"After you killed my husband!"

Vincent squinted. "Did Capstein really mean that much to you?"

"How would you know what he meant to me?" she spat. "You killed him, then tried to sweet talk me into your little cult before his body was cold."

Vincent shook his head. "I seem to remember you trying to seduce me into sneaking you away from Capstein and up to Baltimore behind his back. Besides, the man was a lunatic. He was trying to scoop up or murder as many free pinchers as he could."

"And what were you doing?" she snarled. "Haven't you been on the hunt for years, now?"

"That's...that was different."

"How?" she demanded. "Because you're supposed to be the good guy? You're forgiven for everything you've done, every life you've taken? Just because you're you and I'm me?"

Vincent felt a trickle on his upper lip. He turned to find a hand inside the time bubble reaching slowly for cards. He balled his fists and refocused with a quick swear under his breath.

"I hate you," she declared. "It's just that simple."

"Ain't nothing simple in this life, Betty."

She snorted. "That's what they want you to believe."

Vincent glanced at her. "They?"

"Shut up."

"Unhappy with your situation? Maranzano not paying you enough?"

Betty turned away, pacing toward the hallway door. "I told you to shut up."

"You want to know what I think?" he ventured.

"You do love the sound of your own voice, don't you?"

"I think your hatred keeps you going. It got you through Ithaca. It's getting you through Maranzano and certain defeat at the hands of Masseria's gang. It's the one constant in your life, and now that you're working with me, you're starting to see me as a human being. And that's upsetting the one solid thing in your life. And I reckon that's got you feeling rattled."

Betty leaned against the wall, her face twisting in fury. Before she could reply, the cash room door opened. Polizzi staggered out, face pale and clammy, a drop of blood running from his nostril. He turned and closed the door, taking a moment to catch his breath as he reached for the lock.

Betty held out a hand, the remains of the ashtray lifting as a blob into midair, sliding to her palm.

"We…should move," Polizzi wheezed. As he replaced the padlock.

Vincent eyed him in concern. He looked fine, otherwise. No cash stuffed into his trousers or jacket. No jewelry dangling from his lapel. But the man was clearly at the end of his magical reserve.

Betty opened the hall door, guiding Polizzi through as he steadied himself against the door jamb.

Vincent told them, "Wait at the top of the stairs. I have to play this out."

They closed the door behind themselves as Vincent crouched by the sofa once again. He released the time bubble, the weight of the persistent effect lifting like a Ford off his chest.

The sounds of gambling and merriment resumed. One of the gangsters swore loudly as he brushed ash off his lap.

Vincent stood up with a shake of his head. "Sorry boys. Looks like I wasted your time."

Only one of them looked up in response. The comb-over goon squinted.

"You okay, fella?"

Vincent shrugged.

The man pointed to his own nose.

Vincent lifted a finger, wiping some blood from his nostril.

"Oh, yeah. Smog gets to me sometimes."

The man nodded. "Yeah, it's been hell this year."

He returned his attention to his own cards as Vincent took his leave of the room.

The others huddled at the top of the stairs. Polizzi looked even paler.

"You gonna make it?" Vincent whispered.

"Less talk," Polizzi replied. "More beating of feet."

Vincent slipped down the next flight of stairs, giving his nose another wipe with his finger. He clamped his fists closed, focusing on the two apartments. The load on his system was almost too much. But they were so close. It was almost done. He had to pinch those apartments one more time.

Just one more time.

He gripped the handrail to the stairs and threw all of his power into it, bridging the two bubbles to lighten the load.

"Go. Now."

The others bustled down the stairs as his grip on the time bubbles thinned. As they reached the landing, Polizzi's footing weakened. He stumbled and Betty tried to catch him. Flailing, Polizzi's arm slammed into Betty's chest, knocking her several steps down the hall.

And right into the bridge of frozen time between the two apartments.

A surge of pressure hit Vincent in the chest, sending his guts into a twist. The room spun, and he nearly fell down the last few steps as the load jerked the very life out of him. The bridge between the two bubbles snapped. Vincent's spinning head could only grab hold of one of the two bubbles.

One guard frozen in time. One not.

Betty yelped as she fell backward onto the hall floor. Footsteps pounded behind the first door, which swung open to reveal the broad-shouldered lookout.

"The hell?" he grunted, surveying the scene before him. One pale-faced man with a bloody nose, and a woman sprawled on the floor.

"Pockets!" the thug grunted, lifting his piece and giving it a cock.

Betty reached for the chunk of glass that had fallen from her hand as she fell. The glass snaked into the air in a savage arc, wrapping around the lookout's gun arm.

He wheezed as a wet, slicing noise filled the air. The gun dropped to the floor, along with the rest of the arm below the elbow.

The thug stared at his arm in shock.

Betty whipped the line of glass back behind her head, sending it around the man's neck.

Vincent closed his eyes, focusing his attention on the last remaining time bubble rather than the sound of a pop and something heavy hitting the floor.

A hand landed on Vincent's shoulder. He opened his eyes to find Betty staring at him. "Are you good?" she asked.

Vincent nodded.

"Then let's go."

They made it down the last flight of stairs, and the last of Vincent's power failed, dropping the time bubble overhead.

As they staggered out onto the street, Polizzi pulled a white handkerchief from his pocket, waving it three times in the air. A car down the block swung onto the street, pulling to a stop beside them. Betty opened the back door, shoving Polizzi inside. She nodded for Vincent to join him. Once they were all loaded, the driver pressed his foot down.

They made it to a train yard outside Queens as a light rain began to fall. Polizzi was barely hanging on to consciousness as both Vincent and Betty helped him through the mud of the yard and into a storehouse. Three men had gathered with oil lamps, a bare table set in the center of the building.

Polizzi chuckled. "Gonna need…a bigger table."

He unbuttoned his jacket and reached inside to produce a wrapped stack of ten-dollar bills. And another. Then another. He continued, pulling handfuls of cash from inside his jacket until the entire surface of the table was covered with a single pile of cash. As the money poured from Polizzi's jacket, Vincent watched in wonder.

"So, that's why they call you Pockets?" Vincent asked.

Polizzi looked up at Vincent, some color returning to his face. "Sorry, pal. Thought you knew."

Soon the table was covered with stacks of cash high enough to wobble. Polizzi then turned to his trousers pockets to unload the jewelry, dropping them in neat piles onto the ground. Vincent left Polizzi to unload the haul, turning back to the open door and the falling rain. Betty lingered by the door, arms wrapped around herself.

"You saved our bacon back there," Vincent muttered.

"I saved myself." She shifted her weight. "They'll know it was me. Arm and head cut clean off. Only one glass pincher in town. Masseria's going to know it was us. I'm a dead woman."

"Maybe. Maybe not. His goons don't look that smart."

Betty shook her head. "Catena is. He'll put it together.

And Maranzana doesn't care enough about me to save my neck either."

"Sparks will run interference for us. Let's not worry until it's a problem." He turned back to take in the loot they'd robbed. "Think this'll put Masseria back at all?"

She shrugged. "That's big picture stuff. I'm just here to kill."

"Are you, though? Or are you just biding your time?"

She glanced at him with a puzzled expression. "Biding time for what, exactly?"

"I don't know. Something better to live for?"

"Have you found anything better?" she asked, her lip curled in a sneer.

Vincent nodded, feeling a sappy smile curl his lips upward. "Yeah. Matter of fact, I have."

Betty stared at him for a moment before looking away. "Yeah, well…you're an imbecile."

A grunt behind them captured Vincent's attention. Polizzi staggered for the table, reaching to steady himself. His hand slapped the side of the cash, sending it and himself spilling onto the ground.

Vincent rushed over to check on him.

Polizzi coughed, spitting up some blood.

"You gonna make it?" Vincent asked.

Polizzi caught his breath. "Remind me never to do that again."

He gestured for one of the goons standing over him. The man produced a flask and handed it to Polizzi who unscrewed it to take a sip.

"A little white lightning?" Vincent asked.

"Curative. One of the boys who used to work for us made some before he got stitched last fall."

"Water pincher?" Vincent prodded.

Polizzi nodded, his breath returning in deep heaves.

Vincent guided Polizzi to a sitting position as his health returned. Polizzi stood, steadying himself as he handed back the flask.

Vincent patted his chest. "Good work."

"You, too. Learned a new trick tonight, huh?"

Vincent shrugged. "Maybe I'm not such an old dog. Speaking of good work, I think Betty deserves…"

They turned for the open door, but Betty was gone.

Polizzi grumbled, "Now, where'd she run off to this time?"

Vincent trotted for the door, staring out into the dark nighttime rain. No sign of Betty.

"She was worried Masseria's people would link her to that surgical butchering she pulled off," Vincent said. "Maybe she's gone to clean up?"

Polizzi shook his head. "That woman's a bag of cats. There's no figuring her out."

Vincent continued staring into the rain, wondering if that was true.

CHAPTER 16

"Whoever did this thing, I want him dead!" Joe Masseria paced around the meeting room, shoulders hunched. Words continued to pour from his mouth with spits and snarls as he mixed Italian with English.

Vincent watched Catena from his position in the room. The consigliere stood vigil in the corner, arms bent, hands in his pockets.

Masseria waved a fist in the air. "There will be blood! I will return this attack tenfold!"

Everyone in the room stood stiff, bracing for an order to go to war. Floresta stood alongside Vincent in an equally stiff posture, though he seemed pleased enough before the meeting with their accomplishment. Luciano, for his part, seemed as uninterested in Masseria's bluster as Catena.

Once Masseria had expended his anger and his saliva, he spun on a heel to exit the room, slamming the door behind him. After a few seconds of silence, Catena eased himself away from the corner to address the rest of the room.

"Alright, gentlemen," he began, "we have work to do. The damage is about thirty thousand in cash, and five thousand worth of gold and gems. We got the worthless sons of bitches who decided playing cards was more important than guarding the cash locked up downstairs. So far, they seem to know nothing."

Catena's eyes shifted toward Vincent, then away again.

"There was one body at the scene. Lou. Some of you knew him."

A few nods in the room.

"He was cut to pieces by whoever did this. Floresta? We have the body downstairs. I want you to take a look. See if you can sniff out whether there are any pinchers in town with that sort of talent. The usual suspects…and newcomers."

Floresta nodded once more, glancing to Vincent as Catena dismissed the meeting. The two huddled together by the front door as the rest of Masseria's crew received marching orders.

Vincent whispered, "Masseria seriously doesn't know who's behind this?"

"Catena sure as hell knows," Floresta replied. "Which means he'll bring the talent into this." He nodded in warning as Lefty approached around the desks with Buddy in tow.

"I think we came at the right time, Floresta," Lefty said. "Your pals in Queens decided to make this trip interesting."

Floresta shrugged. "If it's Maranzano's people, then they've just decided on an early retirement."

Buddy stepped forward. "Is this normal? No one knows anything?"

Lefty patted him on the shoulder. "Oh, they know. This is pageantry. Bluster meant to get the blood up with the foot soldiers."

They all fell silent as a figure approached. Luciano pulled his hands from his pockets and gestured with a single finger for them to follow him onto the street. The group filed through the front doors, gathering around Luciano as he squinted in the sunlight.

"No war," the man said. "Not yet. We find the glass pincher."

"What glass pincher?" Buddy asked.

"What about your pinchers?" Lefty asked, ignoring Buddy's question. "Is this on us contractors, or are your boys getting in the game?"

"You meet with them today. Behave yourselves." Luciano turned and walked up the street.

Floresta sighed. "Well, folks. We have ourselves a ballgame. You'll meet with Lenny and Augustus today."

"Are those all the pinchers you got?" Lefty asked.

"Unfortunately. It's been a bloody month."

"What about Maranzano?" Lefty prodded. "What does he have in terms of magical power?"

"A glass pincher by the name of Betty Sharp. And then there's Pockets."

Lefty nodded. "Betty, I know. What about this Pockets fella?"

Vincent muttered, "I'm familiar with him. He's a pocket pincher. If he can hold it, he can stuff it in his coat."

Lefty chuckled. "Seriously? What use is that?"

"You'd be surprised," Vincent muttered.

The Baltimore delegation withdrew for a light lunch, waiting for word from Luciano where to meet the others. Word came late afternoon. They were to meet at a closed-up theater on the south side of Queens near Harlem.

The rain from the previous night had swept the streets clean, and a warm front from the south kicked enough humidity into the air to make the city feel uncomfortable. As they waited at the theater for Floresta to arrive, Vincent shuffled over next to Lefty.

"Things are about to pop off," Lefty grumbled. "Hope you're ready."

"I'm ready."

Lefty checked Buddy's location. The youth had his back turned to the two, inspecting a leaflet that was discarded from a show several months before the theater was shuttered.

Lefty whispered, "Tell me you had nothing to do with this robbery."

"I had nothing to do with this robbery," Vincent replied matter-of-factly.

"Then why is it I don't believe you?"

"When would I have time or resources to knock over Masseria's cash room? Besides, you heard the man. If Betty Sharp is in the city, do you really think I'd be in line to help her butcher the people we're here to help?"

Lefty lifted his chin, then nodded. "Good point. Though that might prove problematic for us later."

"Trust me, I know."

Lefty peered at Buddy again. "He's loosening up. I don't know what you told him, but he's been talking you up."

Vincent blinked. "What?"

"Yeah. Asking me when the two of you can put your heads together. He's trying." Lefty jabbed a finger into Vincent's chest. "You have a chance to keep this boy from making all the mistakes you made. So, consider that. Will ya?"

Vincent gave Lefty a sober nod.

A figure approached from the south, a lean black man in a wide-brimmed Stetson and a long coat. His face was lean, as was the rest of his frame.

"Heads up," Vincent called to Buddy.

The stranger stood in front of the group, hands on his hips. "Why, there y'all are," he boomed. "Punctual. I like that."

Vincent stepped forward, a hand extended. "Vincent Calendo."

The man eyed his hand. He gave Vincent's hand a shake. "Augustus Henry."

Lefty gave the man a nod. "Call me Lefty. And that one's Buddy Seiler."

Augustus turned to glance up the street. "So, Sparks and Lennie are late as usual?"

Vincent shrugged.

"Yep." Augustus eyed the doors. "Still locked up?"

Buddy reached out to test the doors, which rattled but remained closed.

Augustus pulled off his hat to reveal a shining, bald head. He held the hat out for Buddy. "Hold that for me, Buster."

Buddy squinted at the man as he pressed a hand against the crack between the doors.

Augustus nodded, then turned to the side, pressing his shoulder against the crack. He inched into the doors, his body easing onto the brass stiles as if melting into them. He gave Buddy a wink as his face disappeared between the doors as easily as a slip of paper. And then he was gone.

Vincent muttered, "Well, that's gonna sit in my head."

After a while, a clatter from the side alley caught their attention. Augustus rounded the side of the building with a smile. He reached for his hat, snatching it from Buddy's hands and setting it back onto his head.

"Y'all follow me."

They entered the theater building from a side entrance which Augustus had unbolted from the inside. The building was dark and musty. Dust hung in the air, dancing like krill through the air vaulting above rows of velvet cushioned seats facing an art deco proscenium.

"Guess they cut off the power," Lefty grumbled.

Vincent nodded to a row of windows above the mezzanine, all battened shut with sliding shutters.

Buddy reached into his pocket to pull four nickels.

"Give me a little room," he said.

Vincent eased away as Buddy rotated his shoulder, loosening the joint. He bent his knees to shift his weight back and forth, then whipped a nickel into the air as if skipping it across a pond. The nickel sailed across the room, flipping sideways as it curved up over the balcony rail. The slug of metal smacked a lever beside the shutters, and the slats dropped open to send a shaft of dusty light pouring into the space. He continued three more times, each nickel slicing an impossible arc through the air and dropping the shutters open with unearthly precision.

When the last shutter had opened and the space was well lit, the others offered Buddy a hearty clap.

Vincent nodded as Buddy reached to wipe a trickle of blood from his nostril. "Was it the distance?"

Buddy grinned at him. "Trick shots aren't easy."

"You'd rather just shoot a bastard in the street, huh?"

"Better I shoot him than the other way around."

The front doors rattled as someone attempted to pull them open. A spate of profanity muffled against the locked doors as the rattling subsided.

Augustus cupped hands over his mouth to shout, "Side door, Lennie!"

After a minute, Lennie entered through the side, squinting as his eyes adjusted to the dim light inside.

"Ain't no one got a damn key to this place?" the man grumbled.

Floresta entered behind Lennie, reaching for a wall switch with a handful of purple light. The bulbs along the proscenium flickered to life with angry buzzing.

Augustus tipped his hat to his compatriots. "Got a plan

for us, Sparks? Or is Lucky leaving us to kick up our own mischief?"

Floresta took a seat in one of the chairs, crossing his legs. "Everyone with a brain knows Maranzano's behind the hit on the cash room. Poor Lou had an arm and his head nicked off his body clean."

"That hellcat bitch of his, huh?" Lennie grumbled.

Floresta sighed. "Time's not right to bring this into the streets. Maranzano hit us on the sly. Lou probably stepped out at the wrong time. Otherwise, this was supposed to be bloodless. Least, that's how I size it up."

Augustus chuckled. "Well, it weren't."

"Where does that leave us?" Vincent pressed.

"Masseria put Luciano in charge of this. Lucky's word on this is to keep it quick and quiet."

Buddy asked, "Why don't we just clean house? I don't understand."

Floresta uncrossed his legs and leaned forward. "There are political considerations. We have the other families in line. We might lose their cooperation if we make this fight… vulgar. Whichever families go full-war end up weaker once the dust settles."

Lefty added, "Basically, it's smooth sailing as long as we don't make waves."

"Any of you fine gents ever met Betty Sharp?" Augustus asked the three from Baltimore.

"As a matter of fact," Lefty answered, "we have. No love lost with that one."

Floresta stood up. "Speaking of which, it's Luciano's opinion that an eye for an eye would be a proportional response. We find the cash, or most of it. And we relieve Maranzano of one of his soldiers."

"Hell with that," Lennie spat. "We don't have a money problem. We have a lunatic problem."

Augustus nodded. "Yeah, I'm with Lennie on this one."

Vincent glanced to Lefty, who seemed troubled by the turn in conversation.

Floresta held up his hands. "It's Lucky's call."

"Then we'll take it up with him," Lennie pressed. "She's the one who put Lou down. You want an eye for an eye? I say we drop that crazy hag and they can keep the money."

Augustus nodded once.

Floresta peered at Vincent. "Where do you stand on this?"

"Since when do they get a vote?" Lennie blustered.

"Since when do you?" Floresta snapped.

Vincent said, "Look, fellas. I've been tangling with Betty Sharp since she was Betty Capstein. I know she has reasons to be the way she is, but all those reasons alone don't add up to the sack of crazy she's turned into. Proportional response aside, we'd be doing all the families a favor by putting her down. It'd do more to keep the peace than anything Maranzano or Masseria would do."

Augustus gave Vincent's comment a quick applause. "That, right there."

Floresta glanced to Lefty, who remained silent. "Right, I'll take it to Luciano."

CHAPTER 17

*H*attie slumped in the chair and stared out the third story window at the neighboring Brooklyn rooftops. The pall of night covered the city, and a haze of humid air created a halo from the streetlights running east to west from the building. Drowsiness filled her head, easing her eyelids lower. Her thoughts dulled to a hum as she stared through the glass pane.

The halo of streetlamps darkened to a hungry red, flickering like the pulse of a heartbeat. Her heartbeat. The sky was no longer a simple, starless night. It was the vast, unblinking pupil of an eye glaring through her soul. She was suddenly small, a mote of dust before a titan. Flames lifted in the corners of her vision, but she was too terrified to shift her gaze. Transfixed. Harrowed.

"Hattie!" Maria's voice thundered through the dream.

Hattie blinked her eyes open. The fog around the streetlights was just fog. The night was a cloud-covered shroud over New York. She sucked in a breath and turned to Maria, who stood in the middle of the room.

"I've been calling your name for a minute," Maria said, eyes wide with concern.

Hattie ran a hand over her forehead, pulling it back dripping with sweat. "Sorry. Dozed off there for a moment."

"What's going on?" Maria prodded, crouching in front of her. "You're not sleeping. And when you do, you toss and turn with dreams."

Hattie lifted a hand to calm her, but noticed it was trembling. She stuffed it back into her lap. "I'm alright. Just tired."

"You look like you have a fever." Maria reached for her forehead. Hattie tried to dodge her hand, but Maria managed to pull the back of her fingers against her cheek. "No, you're cold."

"I'm fine," she insisted.

Maria stood with a scowl. "You brought me here to help you. I'm trying to help. Why won't you let me?"

"Because it's nothing you can help with." Hattie stood up, grateful her legs didn't give. She pulled her sweat-soaked shirt away from her chest. "I'm going to wash up,"

Grabbing a towel from the cabinet by the foot of the bed, Hattie stepped into the hallway, leaving Maria behind. She regretted the curt exit, but it was more to keep from having an emotional breakdown in front of the other woman than to be rude.

As Hattie peeled off her clothes and stepped into the tub to rinse the sweat and grime off, she resolved to treat Maria with more consideration. This damned soul trap could steal her sleep, but it wouldn't take her kindness.

She finished and toweled herself dry. As she reached for her clothes, she gave them a sniff. Her nose wrinkled. They needed a good washing. Hattie turned and ran more water, giving her working clothes a good soak and scrub. As she twisted her trousers beneath the running water, she heard a loud *clack* in the tub. The tiny obsidian marble had fallen free of her pocket. It sat wobbling in the water, a spark of red sweeping across its surface. The soul trap rolled an inch toward the drain.

Hattie watched it, her body rigid.

If it washed down those pipes and down the drain, it'd be lost. Flushed down into the city sewers. Maybe buried forever in filth. Maybe swept out to the river. It would be gone. The Deltaville Demon, and the grip it had on her body and mind, would vanish forever.

No.

Hattie slapped her hand over the drain, catching the marble before it fell away. Just a hair away from the pipes. She pressed it against the floor of the tub. Just a wiggle one direction, and it could still disappear.

An urge swept through her chest. Almost a plea. *Don't do this! Save me.*

Hattie lifted the soul trap from the tub. Its surface pulsed a brilliant red, dulling slowly to a shiny black once more. The demon didn't want to control her. It didn't want to damn her soul, or haunt her dreams.

It just wanted to be free.

Hattie set the soul trap onto the floor as she returned to her clothes. She wrung them out as well as she could, slipping the marble back into the pocket of her trousers before she wrapped a towel around herself and lugged the damp clothes down the hall back to her room.

Hattie stepped inside and walked over to the wardrobe, slinging her trousers, shirt and undergarments over the edge of the door to dry. "So, listen. Now that I'm me again, I owe you an apology. I've been in a twist all week, and you've tried everything to break through. For that, I'm sorry."

Hattie reached for her towel, unwrapping the cinch near her collarbone as Maria turned. "I'm not sleeping well. Not at all. But it's nothing you can help, which is why I've tried not to burden you with't."

Maria's eyes widened and she lifted a hand, but Hattie cut her off.

"No, let me finish. I've thought about this in the bath, and I think it's time—"

As Hattie pulled open her towel to let the air cool her skin, Maria pointed to the corner of the room and shouted, "Hattie!"

She froze, turning to find Vincent sitting in a chair.

Hattie yelped and scrambled to pull the towel closed.

Vincent jumped out of his chair, turning to face the corner.

Hattie stammered, "What…you're…eh, boy-o!"

"Sorry! I didn't think you'd—"

"You better turn your skinny arse around, there!"

"It's turned! It's turned!"

Hattie twisted the towel tight around her armpit, glaring at Maria.

"You were just going to let him sit there?"

"I tried to warn you," Maria chuckled.

Hattie thrust a finger at the door. "Give us a moment, then?"

Maria nodded and laughed as she moved for the door. "Gladly. I think you need it."

"Oh, don't get too excited girly."

Maria gave them both a wink as she dipped out into the hallway.

Hattie turned to find Vincent still dutifully examining the corner.

"It's alright," she said. "I'm wrapped up tight again."

He turned to catch a glimpse. "I wasn't expecting that."

She took a seat on the corner of the bed, keeping her legs tight in front of her. "Did you enjoy the show, at least?"

A dopey smile crept across his face.

She nodded. "Well, that's good to hear. I thought we weren't meeting until tomorrow morning."

"That was the plan, but there've been developments."

"Go on."

"So, Maranzano's pinchers and I knocked over Masseria's cash room."

Hattie nodded with satisfaction. "Impressive."

"It wasn't easy. And there was a problem. Betty killed one of Masseria's men on the way out."

"The woman can't help herself."

Vincent squinted. "It wasn't entirely her fault. We were blown. Something had to happen. Anyways, her sort of violence is easy to identify. Masseria still doesn't want open warfare, so he's sent his pinchers in deal with Betty."

Hattie nodded with a frown. "Does that include you, then?"

"Me and Buddy."

"Doesn't that make things easier on us, though?" she asked.

"Not really. In a way, killing Betty would probably bring everything to a peaceful conclusion. The other families would accept the act because she's developed a bit of a reputation as crazy and unstable. Maranzano would be left with Pockets as his only pincher. He'd be forced to return the cash and bow out gracefully. Or else, it'd be a quick stab in a dark alley, and the war would be over."

"You're saying we have to protect Maranzano?"

"I'm saying we have to protect Betty."

She winced. "Right, then."

"And that won't be easy, because I think I put some thoughts in her head. She's run off."

Hattie sighed. "What thoughts?"

"I don't know," he said, strolling toward the window. "The

more she tries to kill me, the more I understand her. She's as much a victim of the system as we are."

Hattie swiveled to face him. "I'm lost. When did our mission here become helping Betty keep her head?"

"We're here to secure a future for pinchers. All pinchers." Vincent rubbed the back of his head. "I'd say I feel responsible, but there's probably a dozen ways you could talk me out of that."

Hattie stood, walking over to reach for his arm. "I could, but I know better. Your problem is that you care too much."

He smiled at her. "Is that a problem?"

"It is when you're trying to take down the two largest crime families in New York City."

Vincent laughed. "Let's just call Capone and put him on the case."

She smiled at him, rubbing his arm. The feel of him, the nearness of him put her at ease.

"How are you feeling?" he asked.

"Hmm?"

"You were telling Maria you aren't well."

She pulled away with another sigh. "It's the damned soul trap."

"How much longer do you think you can keep that thing?"

She shook her head. "I've no way of knowing. But I think we have a duty to this demon."

He cocked a brow. "What sort of duty?"

"It's part of us. Connected to us. Our dark twin. Isn't it?"

Vincent shrugged.

Hattie continued, "It's been imprisoned inside this marble for half a year, now. I think… I don't know. I get the sense that it's panicked. Lonely. Or rather, just caged. It's in misery."

Vincent nodded. "So, all of this leakage is—?"

"It needs help. Somehow it knows I have it. Maybe it's part of the connection." She turned away. "I almost dropped it down the drain tonight."

Vincent lifted his chin with a grimace. "Really?"

"It would've been cruel of me."

"Would it?"

"We call it a demon, but what does that mean? Is it necessarily evil? A lieutenant of Lucifer? Or is it just a different sort of creature than we are? I don't know. I just feel it should be where it belongs. And that's not at the bottom of East River. Nor in my pocket."

Vincent asked, "What do you want to do with it, then? If we let it out, the Hell Pincher might find it and trap it again."

"At least it would have a fighting chance. Like this?" She shook her head. "It's helpless."

Vincent reached for her shoulders, giving them a rub. "Do you even know how to release it if you wanted to?"

"Hassam does. I'm sure of it."

"I thought he was gone."

She turned to find herself in Vincent's arms. Closing her eyes she listened to his heartbeat. It hammered quicker as she gripped him tighter. "I wish you could stay. I can't feel the demon when you're with me."

He whispered, "I wish I could stay, too."

She pulled her head up to meet his, kissing him with a desperate passion. His hands slipped lower down the back of the towel, pulling her tightly against him. When she broke the kiss, they continued to hold each other for a while, settling into the peace of the moment.

"You should try to sleep," he murmured into her hair. "Let me take the soul trap tonight."

Hattie stiffened at the offer. They were soul twins, equal partners in the universal balance against this demon. Why had she carried the weight of it on her own shoulders for so long? As she struggled to find a way to rationally deny his request, she finally understood her reluctance.

"I've gotten used to it, used to the lack of sleep. We're playing a dangerous game here, and I don't want to risk you being distracted or tired."

"Is that the only reason?" he asked.

She bit her lip, burying her face against his shirt. "No. I feel like it's asking *me* to protect it, that it trusts me."

"It's a demon, Hattie." His voice was gentle as he caressed her back.

"It's a living being, though."

Vincent pulled back a bit to look her in the eye. Finally, he nodded. "Then we'll protect it together."

Taking her hand, he led her to the bed. He began unbuttoning his vest, but she brushed his hands away to tend to it herself. She pulled his vest off his shoulders, tossing it onto the ground. Fully clothed, he lay on top of the bed, gathering one of the pillows under his arm. Hattie crawled onto the bed, curling up in her towel as he draped an arm around her. She placed her hand on his chest, feeling it rise and fall.

And they remained there, silent. At peace.

Hattie's mind filled with thoughts of Vincent's family as his breathing evened out in sleep. She thought of what his parents had gone through, what fate they'd suffered at the hands of these gangs. No parents. No siblings. He'd been a young child, completely alone.

Sorrow gripped Hattie as she pondered his life. She wanted more than ever to be his family. The desire for it filled everything inside her. Gripping him tight, tears fell from her eyes.

And just like that, sleep found her.

Hattie awoke to the sound of the room's door scraping against the floor boards. She'd rolled over at some point during the night, her towel splayed open up to her waist. She reached to straighten it lazily as she blinked awake.

The realization that she'd actually fallen asleep dropped into her brain, and she sat upright. Vincent was still there, lying on his back, eyes closed.

Hattie glanced toward the door, finding Maria entering with two mugs. The aroma of coffee filled the room.

"Alright, you two," Maria announced loud enough to wake Vincent. "Coffee and sunshine. Everyone up and at 'em. Clothed, preferably."

Hattie pulled herself to the side of the bed, re-tucking her towel as Maria handed her one of the mugs.

Vincent grumbled awake, shaking his head. "The hell?"

Maria held his coffee in front of him until he was coherent enough to take it.

"Rude awakening," Hattie muttered.

"I spent the night wandering the streets," Maria said. "Drank too much. Sobered up. Got my own coffee, then decided the two of you needed to cut this short."

"What time is it?" Vincent asked.

"Nearly nine."

He straightened, then pounded some of the coffee as he stood up.

Hattie gestured for the two to turn their backs as she dropped the towel and pulled on her dried clothes.

"You late for a meeting?" Maria asked Vincent.

"As a matter of fact…"

"Things went…well?" she prodded.

Hattie watched Vincent as he gave Maria the tiniest of glances. Sure, the woman would be eager for gossip. Due to the awkward housing arrangement, Hattie couldn't blame her. But why plug him for the details?

Vincent searched for his vest. Hattie reached to the floor and tossed it to him.

"I better get to Queens," Vincent grumbled. "Before Lefty starts nosing around."

Hattie buttoned her shirt, adjusting her trousers.

"Can you give us a minute?" she asked Maria.

Maria sneered. "I gave you ten hours. I'm exhausted."

Vincent urged, "It's fine. I really have to run."

Hattie said, "We're tailing Masseria's people today. With any luck, we'll find Betty before they do."

"Okay." He turned back to the corner chair to gather his jacket and hat. "You'll be right behind me. Keep an eye out for that thin black fellow with the hat. He's a crafty one, I can tell."

Maria made an amused noise with her nose. "He is. I know firsthand."

Vincent buttoned his jacket and slipped his hat back onto his head. He gave Hattie one more kiss, this one sweet and affectionate.

"I'm never far away," he said.

"It doesn't feel that way, sometimes."

His smile filled with misery. "We'll fix this. We'll fix all of this."

Vincent left the room, pinching time to take his exit. She noted the sensation as his time bubble proceeded down the stairs, and she slipped free of its confines as he made his way to the street.

Maria emerged from the bubble none the wiser, shaking her head at his disappearance. "Doesn't that bother you?"

"It doesn't affect me," Hattie replied as she moved to the window.

Glancing down at the walk, she watched as he turned to give her one more look, pausing as if fighting a battle within himself. He turned and walked away.

"You look better," Maria said to break the silence. "Did you sleep?"

"I did. Miraculously."

"He's good for you."

Hattie smiled, feeling a little giddy with happiness at her words. "Ready for a busy day?"

Maria nodded. "You said we're tailing Masseria's people?"

"How well do you know Betty Sharp? The glass pincher?"

"Reputation only."

"Then you know how difficult this will be."

"How does she figure in all of this?"

Hattie stepped away from the window to face Maria. "She's suddenly, annoyingly, the lynchpin of our entire scheme. Come on. I'll explain on the way."

CHAPTER 18

Vincent pulled open the window to his room at the Monarch, slipping in from the fire escape while the morning rush stood frozen on the street below him. Once inside, he released the flow of time and pulled off his shirt to change before running a comb over his head. Looking in the mirror, he decided he didn't have time to deal with the stubble rising on his jawline. Snatching his hat and jacket, he stepped into the hallway to check on Lefty and Buddy.

As he passed Lefty's room, he found the door open.

"Vincent?" Lefty called from inside the room.

"You ready?" He peered inside.

Lefty stood at the window staring down at the street. "Almost."

"Where's Buddy?" Vincent asked.

"I sent him on ahead." Lefty turned to Vincent. "Step inside and close the door."

Vincent felt a twinge in his gut. This was Lefty's business face. Something was wrong. He complied, stepping into the room and closing the door.

"There's been a development you need to know about before we go to Masseria's," Lefty informed him.

Vincent released a slow breath. "Yeah?"

"This O'Toole thing you and Hattie have cooked up is about ready to blow up in your faces. Catena knows she brokered a deal with Maranzano."

Vincent leaned against the door. None of this was news to him. He could work with this. "Yeah. So she's got Maranzano distracted. It'll be easier for us to reel him in this way."

Lefty scowled. "You know that cash haul Maranzano's people nicked from Masseria two nights ago? Word broke… every cent of it was spent last night. Thirty-five-some-odd boys from Cleveland and Rochester are on their way along with three crates from an Army surplus store on the Hudson. Thompson repeaters and old army issue Colt revolvers, and enough ammo to melt their barrels."

"That was a quick turnaround," Vincent admitted, suddenly worried that Hattie was going to be put on the spot to pay for triggers and fingers when he knew she didn't have enough to afford all that.

"You and I both know Malloy doesn't make enough scratch from Crew business on the bay and her little side gig knocking off shipments—and don't think I don't know about all that—to pay for that sort of muscle. And when she welshes on Maranzano, she's going to be in a bag in the river. That also leaves him with a standing army in New York City."

Lefty took a step forward. "Which brings me to my next worry. You sneaking out every single night."

The floor dropped out from underneath Vincent. His heart leapt into his throat as waves of panic washed through him. "Um…"

Lefty scowled. "That window in your room isn't as quiet as you seem to think it is," Lefty said. "You've been sneaking out every night since we checked into the Monarch. At first, I figured you were visiting Miss Malloy, getting rid of the kid so you could meet with your gal."

Vincent attempted to deflect, but Lefty lifted a hand to silence him.

"I paid a delivery boy to follow you a couple days. He had trouble staying with you. I'm guessing you used your powers once or twice. That shook him. But not last night. He followed you all the way to Brooklyn Heights. Said you spent the night there." Lefty took another step forward, lowering his voice. "If my boy can follow you, so can others. You're putting her in danger. You're putting yourself in danger. You're putting all of us in danger."

Vincent's heart sank back into his chest, his hand balling into fists. He clamped his jaw shut and said nothing.

Lefty turned away with a shake of his head. "I knew O'Toole was Malloy since she bought the boatlegging business from Lizzie Saddler. I mean, an Irish woman playing the part of an Irish woman? I get it. Easier to keep the accents straight, but it's a bit on the nose. And you know, I didn't mind. She was getting the job done. At first. Then we start losing barrels. And crew. And now…this."

Vincent stared at his own shoes.

"What kills me, though? What eats my guts? You kept me in the cold when I coulda told you this wouldn't work. You didn't trust me enough to at least…at the very least…keep you from getting yourself killed." Lefty took a breath. "I would've told you Maranzano saw right through you, and that Masseria is at the very least suspicious."

Vincent snapped his head up to glare at Lefty.

Lefty continued, "You don't think Maranzano agreed to O'Toole's proposition just a little too quick? With no negotiation? You don't think this cash room heist wasn't already planned out? That it wasn't meant to purchase those guns from the start? He has no intention of letting her have those men or those guns."

A new wave of panic flooded through Vincent's stomach. The clarity of Lefty's words filled him with dread.

"You think maybe you got Maranzano where you want him, armed to the teeth and ready for war? It never occurred to you that's where he wanted to be all along? He just needed a pretext. And the two of you gave it to him."

Vincent swallowed hard.

"I know you were involved when everything got swiped from the cash room. It's how they got in and out." He turned and smacked the flat of his fist against the wall. "Damn it, Vincent! If you'd... I could've explained it all to you. Kept it from getting this far. I might have saved you. Luciano's gonna get you killed, Vincent. And he'll get Miss Malloy killed as well."

Vincent cleared his throat, trying to speak a couple times before he gave up.

Lefty wiped his hand over his face, rubbing the back of his head with a sigh. "Why, Vincent? Why would you cut me out like this?"

Vincent didn't answer.

"Are you angry with me? Did I do anything at all to deserve this?"

"It's not that."

"What's your end game, here? I don't understand it. Even if Masseria and Maranzano end up six feet under, and Luciano's in charge...where does that leave you? Where does that leave Vito? Is this for the Crew?"

Vincent's eyes hardened.

Lefty shook his head. "Or, are you ready to lead a revolution. Is that it? Is this about pincher freedom?" He stood up again. "Is that why you shut me out? You see me as your slave master with my hand on the whip."

Vincent stared into Lefty's eyes. "Lefty, *you* are the whip."

Lefty blinked at the words and turned away. "Vincent, you really don't know me, do you? And you have no idea how deep you are in this."

"You really think I don't know? You think I didn't know going in that this might end up with both me and Hattie killed?"

"You're okay with that?"

Vincent walked forward and reached for Lefty, clamping a hand onto his good shoulder. "Things have to change. And there are some things worth dying for."

Lefty peered over his shoulder at Vincent. "When? When did you turn? Was it Ithaca?"

"It was a lot of things."

Lefty shrugged off his hand and withdrew to the window. "Things have to change, huh? How many centuries have pinchers been right where they are now? How many times have they risen up, only to start the cycle over again? Nothing changes, Vincent."

"Nothing changes because people like you keep insisting that they don't."

Lefty nodded. "You know, I've been around pinchers most of my life. I loved one, once. I still love her, although I've got no idea where she is, or if she's alive or dead."

Vincent blinked, straightening a little.

Lefty pressed his forehead against the pane of glass. "The things we did together, the things we saw. I went to hell for her, and she took me to heaven. And after all of that, do you know where we both ended up? Right where we began." He turned to face Vincent. "This isn't some theory for me. I've seen more of this world than you. That's not a rebuke, you need to understand."

Vincent stuffed his hands into his pockets. "I didn't know that about you. I didn't know you and a pincher…"

"There's a lot you don't know. Which is why I'm trying to help you."

Vincent stared at the other man, feeling like a complete chump. Had he gotten Lefty wrong? The man had always been there for him, but if it came to a choice between his vow to Vito and Vincent, which direction would he stand?"

"Yeah, okay. What do we do now?" Vincent finally said, wanting to know what Lefty had on his mind as far as a plan.

"Well, you obviously can't leave town." Lefty began to pace. "Corbi would feed you to the dogs, and Masseria would use it as an excuse to strike at Maranzano before his army arrived. Best thing you can do now is to break off whatever you got going on with Maranzano. Then, become useless. Polite. Cordial. But useless. Your only exit is for Masseria to kick you out of the city. And Miss Malloy needs to leave right now and head back to Baltimore."

Vincent scowled. "I have no interest in being useless."

"Yeah, well you're about to put Maranzano on top of the New York families. He'll take controlling interest of Ithaca, and with his forces depleted he'll farm pinchers harder than ever before."

"Then I stick with Luciano's plan. Both houses fall."

Lefty shook his head. "You're still not reading me. Luciano's a patsy. I've seen the man in action. He thinks he's smarter than he is, but he's a follower by nature. There's no way this doesn't end with Luciano dead and Masseria or Maranzano squeezing the life out of the entire East Coast."

"I disagree. You said it yourself. They want a war. They just need an excuse."

"Vito wins if Masseria wins."

"Maybe I don't want Vito to win."

Lefty crossed his arms. "Yeah, I see that now."

"I know you're a man who values loyalty, Lefty. But as

long as he's in charge of Baltimore, there can be no life for me," Vincent told him.

Lefty eyed him. "You mean for you and Miss Malloy."

Vincent's eyes stung as tears threatened to well up.

Lefty shook his head. "You can't take these men down."

Vincent wiped his eyes, then wagged a finger in the air. "Masseria has a blind spot."

"What blind spot?"

"Catena."

Lefty chuckled. "He's no blind spot."

Vincent urged, "But he is. O'Toole has impressed him, and he's hedging his bets. Hattie's good at this. Better than any of us thought. She can play that old man. And the more we know about Maranzano, the easier her job becomes. Plus, Maranzano's got his own blind spot."

Lefty thought it over. "Betty Sharp?"

Vincent nodded. "Betty Sharp. I have Hattie on the hunt for her today. We keep her from Luciano's pinchers, and Maranzano has the pincher power to keep Masseria cautious."

"You really think that woman can be controlled?"

"No. But, God help me I can't believe I'm about to say this, I think she can be reasoned with."

Lefty grinned. "Well, I'm out of my depth on that one." He reached for Vincent's arm. "I do value loyalty. Which is why this stings. I don't betray my oaths. You know that. But I've also vowed to keep you alive. If I can't sway you from this path, then you'll have to tell me how I can help you."

Vincent grinned as the tears he was fighting slipped free of his eyes. "Just keep the rookie out of my way."

Lefty nodded. "Come on. They'll be waiting for us."

CHAPTER 19

*H*attie slipped with ease between the shoulders of the lunchtime crowd as she followed the two pinchers. There was no need to even conceal herself from their notice with magic. The cloud of humanity did all the work. Besides, she didn't need to be Brigid today.

The taller one, the lanky black man with the hat who had crept up on her in Maranzano's speakeasy, was easier to follow. He stood head and shoulders above the rest of the New Yorkers. Not to mention the cowboy hat really stood out among the derbies and bowlers.

His companion, the shorter, red-faced bruiser with a permanent scowl, faded into the dull gray press of jackets and working clothes on the street. Of the two, he moved with more suspicion, continually peering over his shoulders. August only ever looked forward, his confidence unshakable.

They'd taken a car into the Bronx, moving north to the outside edge of town. Maria nicked a car for them to follow the pinchers. Hattie didn't bother asking where she found it, or how she planned to return it. Maria dropped Hattie off, then took the car around the block, circling in case they needed a quick exit. Hattie wasn't entirely sold on the need for that much caution, but she deferred to Maria's experience with gangsters.

The pinchers led Hattie to a grotto on the border of Queens, a complex of run-down masonry flats, some with laundry hanging from the windows. Power lines crisscrossed the open space between buildings, the walks below covered in pigeon droppings. Following at a safe distance, she crept up the stairwell as the two men tread down the second-floor hall. As soon as they vanished from sight, she peered around the corner of the corridor, watching as the men counted down doors, stopping at the third room on the right.

The shorter of the two gave the door a good knock while Augustus lingered by the side, taking cover from whatever Betty decided to send at them. The other pincher didn't seem overly concerned about flying glass.

They stood for a moment without a response. The short pincher knocked again, and finally shrugged at Augustus.

"I'm gonna check," Augustus muttered as he pulled off his hat, handing it to his compatriot.

Running a hand along the seam between the door and its frame, Augustus stepped sideways as his body slipped inch by inch through the crack. Hattie squinted, her stomach twisting a little from the bizarre sight. Augustus disappeared inside the apartment, and his partner leaned against the wall, arms crossed.

After a long wait, Augustus slipped back through the crack.

"Place is empty," he declared. "She's probably outta town."

His partner grumbled, "Or she's just waiting for us to leave."

Augustus smirked. "She don't got that sorta patience, hoss."

"Yeah. You got a point."

The two turned to approach the stairs. Hattie pinched light around her, disappearing into the corner of the stairwell.

"You think that time pincher from Baltimore's gonna kick up a fuss with our dear Madame Sharp?" Augustus asked his partner as they rounded the landing.

"They definitely got some history," his partner replied. "Boy's got skills, though. Luciano says we should use him any chance we get."

Augustus nodded. "What're the odds we can poach that boy from Baltimore, you think?"

"Dunno. Don't care."

They stepped out of the building, the door slamming shut behind them.

Hattie crept down the stairs, watching as they returned to the street, then released her pinch of invisibility.

Maria trotted across the courtyard after a few minutes, ducking inside the stairwell with Hattie. "No one's home?" she asked.

"They say she's out of town," Hattie replied.

"Then why are we still here, and not following them?"

Hattie glanced up the stairs. "Instinct, perhaps?"

"You think she's actually there?"

Hattie shook her head. "I suspect our counterparts wouldn't have left if they weren't thorough. But I don't think she's skipped town."

"You want to wait?" Maria prodded. "It might take a while. No way of telling when or if Betty will show up."

Hattie nodded. "True. If you have a better idea, then I'm interested."

Maria sighed. "Right. Well, come on."

"Where are we going?" Hattie asked as Maria pushed open the exit doors.

She led Hattie around the corner of the building, running her fingertips along the outside masonry. "Which one is it?"

Hattie eyed the length of the building, counting windows. "Here, I think."

Maria closed her eyes and curled her fingers into the stone of the building. "Yeah. Empty."

Hattie smiled. "You can tell from touch? That's brilliant."

"Vibrations. It's not exactly like tuning a radio, but if it's quiet in the other apartments I can tell." She opened her eyes. "It'll be easier at night."

"Then we come back at night," Hattie declared.

They did return after sunset, both decked out in their new dresses. Maria led them around the rear of the building, stepping through the shadows to a spot below Betty's window. Maria checked the wall, slipping her fingertips into the masonry.

"There's still a lot of noise. Radios. Kitchen racket."

Hattie nodded. "It should quiet down as it gets later."

"This is home for a while, then."

They huddled up shoulder-to-shoulder, backs against the building. "If only we had a deck of bloody playing cards."

Maria snickered. "I suppose we could talk."

Hattie shook her head. "I think I've had enough talking."

After a few minutes, Maria gave it another shot. "You look a lot healthier today."

"Remarkable, the powers of sleep."

"It was Vincent, wasn't it?"

Hattie looked into the distance, a sappy smile curling her lips upward. "Aye. It was him."

"You know, if you ever needed God to tell you who to marry, this would be the next best thing to a burning bush."

Hattie felt her face go hot and jabbed the other pincher in the ribs. "I'm not thinking about marriage. Not right now."

Maria squinted an eye at her. "That's a load of bull feathers."

"You know what these gangs do to their pinchers, yes? They breed them like rabbits in a warren."

"But you're a free pincher."

"Vincent's not. And there's a few in the Crew that know what I am. We marry and they talk, then I'm no longer free. And any children we have will be slaves."

"You think Vincent won't protect you and his children?" Maria snorted. "You've seen that man in action. He may act like a well-dressed goon, but he's smart and he's ruthless when it comes to what he cares about. And you? You've kept a whole lot of pinchers free, including yourself."

Hattie squirmed "Until every pincher has the same freedom to choose a life, I'd be a hypocrite looking for my happily ever after."

Maria rolled her eyes. "You deserve some happiness of your own, Hattie. Besides, have you ever asked what Vincent wants? Because I'm thinking he wants a happily ever after with you."

"Then what in the hell is he waiting for," Hattie snapped. "He won't do more than kiss me, because of some old-fashioned ideas of gentlemanly behavior, but he's not made any move to take what we have any further in terms of commitment."

Maria made an odd noise, as if she were holding back a laugh. "That so?"

"I've slept in a bed with him twice, and both times he's kept all his clothes on." She sniffed. "Last time I'm naked in a towel and he doesn't even get a wandering hand."

That did make Maria laugh. The woman put her hand on Hattie's shoulder. "He's a chivalrous man, like some kind of knight in a book about King Arthur or something. He respects you, and this is his way of showing it. Plus he knew that you needed sleep more than you needed any tossing in the sheets."

Hattie glared at the ground. "Well, he's wrong."

Maria patted her shoulder. "Give the man time. There's a lot's been going on these past few weeks. I can tell he loves you, and I'm sure he's working up to something."

Hattie rolled her eyes, thinking that Maria was being overly optimistic. "I was happier without the talking."

"We could be here for hours. What else do you want to do?"

Hattie slid down the wall, resting on her heels as she crouched against the stone. "Think happy thoughts?"

Maria abandoned conversation as they waited. She ended up on the ground beside Hattie, staring across the back lot at the rear of another building almost identical to this one. Gray stones. Power lines. Fuzzy nighttime light hanging in haloes over streetlamps.

An hour passed, then a portion of another. Maria's head slipped off the stones, nudging Hattie's shoulder.

"Oy," Hattie grumbled with a sharp shrug. "You're drifting off."

Maria sniffled and sat upright. "Sorry."

"Anything?" Hattie grumbled.

Maria pulled herself to her feet, cracking her knuckles before resting her fingertips against the smooth stone blocks lining the exterior of the building. Her fingers pressed into the stone, pushing to the first knuckle as Maria closed her eyes.

"Quiet, now. Some buffalo down the hall is snoring enough to shake my fingernails." She lifted a brow as she drew in a breath. "Wait."

Hattie scrambled to her feet.

Maria whispered, "Footsteps."

"In her apartment?"

Maria squeezed her eyes tight in concentration. "I think so."

"Good enough to take a shot, then."

Maria pulled her fingers out of the stone, opening her eyes as she shook out her hand. "What's the play?"

"I think it's high time Miss Sharp met Brigid O'Toole."

They marched around the front of the building, climbing the stairs to the second floor.

Maria eyed Hattie as she pinched light around herself to don Brigid's face. "How dangerous will it be knocking on that door?"

"Fair point," Hattie replied. "Give it some space, perhaps?"

Maria scowled as she turned to walk up the hall, while Hattie waited in the stairwell. She adjusted the straps of her dress, then faced the door, stepping away a full pace before giving it a brisk knock. Then they waited. Just as Maria began to turn back toward Hattie, the knob twisted and the door opened a crack to reveal sharp, savage eyes glaring at her from beneath a disorderly mane of blonde hair.

Maria set her jaw. "You Betty? Betty Sharp?"

"Who the hell wants to know?"

"You can call me Maria."

"You one of Masseria's people?"

Maria eyed the stairs, then replied, "No. I work for Brigid O'Toole."

Betty shook her head. "Never heard of her."

"I think you have," Maria said.

"Alright, I don't like you already."

She closed the door and Maria shrugged at Hattie.

The door opened again. Betty peered at Maria with narrow eyes. "Wait. You said who, now?"

"Brigid O'Toole," Hattie declared in full Irish brogue as she marched down the hallway. She pinched light around her to brighten the colors of her dress, pulling as much majesty around her as possible.

Betty eased the door open, eyes on this mysterious woman.

Hattie stood in front of her door, hands on hips. "It's a pleasure meeting you."

Betty nodded slowly. "You're the one who's buying the guns from Maranzano."

"The same. May we come in?"

Hattie marched for the door before Betty could respond. She pressed the door open, stepping past Betty and into a scene from a jewelry store. Shelves upon shelves of tiny glass figurines glistened in the flickering candle light from Betty's kitchen. Her table was a solid glass sculpture, a flat surface scalloping out of a clear base shaped with lion's feet.

Hattie took in the room with wide eyes. "This is absolutely brilliant. You're an artist, then?"

Betty stood rigid at the door.

Maria consumed the door frame, waiting for Betty to move inside.

Betty picked up the hint and shuffled back into her own apartment as Maria closed the door behind them.

"You're a gangster or something?" Betty mumbled.

"Gangster?" Hattie snickered. "That's such a masculine word, isn't it?"

"What do you call yourself, then?" Betty asked.

"An entrepreneur. It's a French word. It means 'one who seizes life by the testes and squeezes until it gives you want you want.'"

Betty grinned. "All that, huh?"

"You work for Maranzano. That was an observation, not a question."

Betty said, "And you're ready to go to war with Vito Corbi. Also an observation."

"Assuming your boss has the means to secure the material I require."

Betty dropped onto a sofa, crossing her legs beneath her. "I think the question is whether you really have the money."

"Is there any doubt?" Hattie retorted as she sat in a chair across from Betty.

"More than a little." Betty eyed Maria. "Who's your goon?"

Maria stiffened as Betty smirked at her.

Hattie nodded. "She's been called worse, I assure you. She's my pincher, naturally."

"Then you are a gangster."

"If you insist. Though I feel the time has come not only to retire that term, but the entire group as it stands."

Betty pursed her lips.

Hattie added, "The gangs, I mean."

"You're one of those types." She uncrossed her legs and moved for the door, brushing Maria aside. "I've heard this before. Not interested."

As Betty held the door open for the two, Hattie remained seated.

"Your life is in jeopardy," Hattie declared.

"What's new?"

"They were here, Betty. Today. Masseria's pinchers were here inside your apartment."

Betty eased the door closed. "Here?"

"That tall Texan lad? He slipped right through the crack of your door. Good thing you weren't home."

"Good thing for him," Betty spat with a frown.

Maria smirked. "But the short one…you can't hurt him, can you?"

Betty glared at Maria, then nodded. "Lenny. He's got some tough skin."

Hattie said, "They've made you the scapegoat. One tiny

robbery, and they're ready to sacrifice a woman on the altar of keeping the peace."

Betty crossed her arms. "They had me figured out, huh?"

"Wasn't hard," Hattie replied. "Glass cuts clean. Masseria isn't ready to go to war over this heist of yours, which is the good news. The bad news is that he's put a hit out on your head, and Maranzano is ready to sacrifice you to keep the proceeds. You don't matter to them," Hattie said as she stood up. "You're an inconvenience, for Masseria *and* Maranzano. The other families won't call for blood if they spill yours. It'll be another day, another entry in the ledger."

Betty's sucked in a harsh breath, her eyes lighting up with fury.

Hattie lifted a hand. "I haven't come to get you stirred into a tussle."

"Then why are you here?" Betty snapped.

"Well, not to put too fine a point on it, I want you."

"For what?"

Hattie grinned at Maria. "To survive. To join us. To help me create something that's been a long time coming."

Betty shook her head. "You're adding me to the bill of goods? I cost more than all the guns in New York City."

"Who said anything about buying? Maranzano doesn't want you. He needs you, but he doesn't want you. I think you know that. You've created more problems than you've solved. You're impossible to control. What use does he have for a woman like you?" Hattie stepped toward Betty. "At least, that's what he's asking himself. You should be asking the same question. What use do you have for these gangs?"

Betty's lips lifted into a smile. "You're serious?"

"What is it that you want, Betty? Do you really want to play the role of a pawn for these men? Or do you want your freedom, once and for all?"

"Freedom?" Betty laughed. "What woman do you know could call herself free?"

Hattie curled her brow as she thought the question over. "Myself, for starters."

Betty sighed. "No, you're in a cage just like the rest of us. You just can't see the bars. I know what my prison is. I think I prefer it that way."

"Sounds to me like the sort of thing your keepers trained you to think."

Betty's smile melted. "Alright, now you're really annoying me. It's time you left."

Hattie shook her head. "You don't have to accept things the way they are now."

"You made me laugh, which is why I'm giving you one more chance. Get out. Now."

One of the sculptures behind Betty, a coiled serpent wrapped around a pyramid, began to writhe. The serpent uncoiled itself, extending away from the pyramid toward Hattie.

Hattie nodded. "Right." She turned for the door, gesturing for Maria to go on ahead.

Outside, Maria leaned in to whisper, "That went nowhere."

"Give her time."

"How much of that do we have?"

Hattie scowled. "You were where she is, once. You found a way out. Not everyone's as resourceful as you. Some people need a leg up."

Maria nodded. "You're committed to this, aren't you?"

"Committed to what?"

"Rescuing every pincher you run into," Maria replied as they marched back toward Brooklyn.

CHAPTER 20

A thunderous pounding on Vincent's door jarred him awake. He threw off his top sheet and jumped out of bed, pinching time to check the commotion in the hall. As he eased the door open, pistol at the ready, he found Floresta standing hands on hips. Vincent released the time bubble and glared at the man.

"What the hell?"

Floresta blustered, "Get dressed. It's going down."

"What's going down?"

The doors to Lefty's and Buddy's rooms opened, each stepping into the hall with guns in hand.

"Masseria's mobilizing," Floresta answered.

Lefty muttered profanities under his breath before returning to his room.

Buddy nodded twice. "Finally, some action."

When Buddy ducked into his room to get dressed, leaving Vincent alone with Floresta, Vincent whispered, "It's too soon."

"No choice," Floresta whispered back. "Betty Sharp's gone

to ground. Catena had a closed-doors meeting with the Boss, and now it's war drums."

"Then we have to tip off Maranzano. Get some guns in their hands."

"I can't do it," Floresta grumbled. "Luciano's sticking close to Masseria, and it's all hands on deck. I can buy you some time, but you boys need to be at the Bank sharpish."

Vincent nodded. "I might have a way. Give me fifteen minutes."

"How in hell are you going to make it to the Bronx and back in fifteen minutes?"

Vincent shook his head. "Just buy me fifteen minutes."

Vincent threw on clothes in a fury, double-checking his gun before stepping into Lefty's room. Lefty was already dressed, working his way into his tailored one-sleeve jacket.

"I'm running up the road. I'll be back in fifteen."

Lefty scowled. "Now?"

"Won't be long."

"Take the kid, then," Lefty urged.

"Not an option."

Vincent gave Lefty a long look, one that Lefty deciphered with a squint and a nod. "Fifteen, then we're in the fight."

Vincent hustled down the stairs and out onto the street, flagging down a yellow cab. After a short ride, and a time pinch to bypass Widow Dunne, Vincent found himself knocking on the door to Hattie's rented room.

The door swung open, Maria brandishing a length of pipe in one hand and a fist in the other.

"Easy," Vincent gasped as he stepped back.

Maria lowered the pipe with a frown.

"It's your man," she called as she turned to let Vincent inside.

Hattie stood from her chair by the window, overalls still on. It looked like she hadn't even tried to sleep yet.

"What's the hubbub?" she asked.

"I need you to go to the Bronx."

"Aye, for what?"

"Masseria's about to march on Maranzano."

Maria shook her head with a snicker. "That was quick."

"What's happened?" Hattie wondered aloud.

"Not sure," Vincent said. "But they couldn't locate Betty Sharp. Seems his consigliere talked him into taking the fight to the street."

Hattie and Maria exchanged glances.

"What's the play?" Maria asked.

"Our only chance is to get Maranzano's people armed and ready. If they can take each other out—"

"What about the rest of New York?" Hattie asked. "Isn't this likely to kill bystanders?"

Vincent sucked in a long breath, heart pounding as he played out the notion in his mind.

"Bridge," Maria stated.

Hattie turned to face her. "Hmm?"

"Steer both of them to a bridge. Let them send each other to Hell there."

Vincent shook his head. "Masseria's loading up now. They'll be across the East River by the time you even get to the Bronx."

Maria scowled. "Then find a way to stall them." She nodded to Hattie. "You get to the Bronx. I'll see what I can do to create a funnel. What say, Brooklyn Bridge?"

"Doesn't give me much time," Vincent grumbled.

"Then you'd better move your ass," Maria barked before shooing him back into the hall.

* * *

THE BANK WAS CRAWLING with activity. Men in suits lugged

Tommy guns over their shoulders as they loaded up four cars. Men hung on to the sides of the doors, arms gripping for dear life.

Vincent and Lefty sat shoulder-to-shoulder in the back of a Ford as Buddy half-stood with his torso hanging out the side of the car. As the motorcade steered onto 31st, Buddy released a yip-yip and banged excitedly on the top of the car. Vincent and Lefty exchanged bemused glances. This was Buddy's first big fight, and his Ithaca-infused decorum had surrendered to his youthful enthusiasm.

The parade moved north rather than west. As Vincent eyed the spires of the Brooklyn Bridge fading behind him, he asked, "Where are we crossing?"

The driver, a grizzled man with a white beard, replied, "Queensboro Bridge."

Vincent fidgeted, looking back toward the southwest.

Lefty lifted a brow at Vincent but said nothing.

After several minutes, the line of cars slowed to a halt. Vincent peered through the windscreen at what appeared to be an otherwise cleared street.

"What's the holdup?" Lefty asked.

Buddy climbed higher onto the car, then slipped back inside. "Looks like a sewer gave, or something. Big trench in the road."

Vincent closed his eyes and released a long breath. Maria had made good use of her time. "What's the nearest bridge besides Queensboro?"

The driver shrugged. "We could try the Manhattan."

Vincent leaned back against the seat as the motorcade turned to the south. More road ruts created diversions, each sending a new spate of profanities from the front seat. By the time they'd reached the Manhattan Bridge, and discovered its access ramp was blocked, the congestion of morning traffic choked their progress to a crawl. After waiting for ten minutes, the driver waved the group to turn around, and they headed back.

Buddy's excitement had long since faded, and he sulked in the seat beside Lefty as Vincent watched the Brooklyn Bridge rise in front of them.

"Good news, boys," the driver declared. "Road's clear."

Vincent pulled his gun and held it in his lap. Buddy watched, then followed suit.

The hour of the fight was upon them. Could this work? Would each side pepper one another down to such low numbers that Vincent could draw a curtain on the entire apparatus? Maria had certainly bought them enough time to get Maranzano to the bridge. With any luck, he'd have spent the heist money on more muscle by now.

Vincent could do it easily enough. With enough bullets flying, he could pinch time, squeeze off a shot, then slip back into the fray without anyone noticing. Except maybe for Lefty.

The cars turned onto the bridge, rising the great arc over the East River. Oncoming traffic dwindled to nothing, and pedestrians ran past their cars in a panic. Their driver slanted the car into a herringbone formation behind the other three. Doors swung open. Men dove out of cars, taking cover behind steel doors.

Vincent and Lefty wove around the rear of their car as the driver rushed forward to join the rest of Masseria's goons.

Buddy climbed to the top of the car again, shielding his eyes against the morning sunlight as gunshots rang out in the distance. He hopped back to the bridge's concrete surface as the Masseria line returned fire.

"What's it look like?" Lefty asked.

"They're at the center of the bridge. About a hundred yards out."

Vincent shook his head as he lifted his Colt revolver. "Not much point popping shots with something like this."

"How about it?" Lefty asked Buddy. "How's your accuracy from this far out?"

Buddy shook his head. "I can do it, but I'll only get two shots, tops, before it'll put me down. We gotta close the distance if I'm going to do any good."

Augustus Henry sprinted around the side of the nearest car, pulling off his Stetson as he gave them a nod. "You boys ready for a dust-up?"

Buddy released a quick shout, which drew a smile from Augustus.

Vincent scowled, "How're we supposed to do any good at this distance? Can't exactly see the whites of their eyes."

Augustus nodded to the front line. "We was hoping you could give us a hand with that."

Vincent clenched his jaw, then nodded. "I can spirit two or three at least halfway."

"We'll just need three," Augustus replied.

Lennie strolled around the cars, well wide of the cover the others were taking. A stray bullet sprayed off his shoulder without so much as a wince.

"Right," Vincent muttered. "Bullets aren't exactly a problem for Lennie."

Augustus pointed to Buddy. "You get Lennie and the kid, here, to about forty yards or so. Lennie will cover him as he does some real damage. Sound good to you, kid?"

Buddy nodded with a grin. "Let me at 'em."

Lennie pulled off his hat and checked it for holes. "Let's get this done, if we're gonna. Had to skip breakfast for this."

Vincent tapped Lefty's shoulder, then ducked down to creep to the front of the Masseria line. "Alright, kid. I need you to tense up. Sounds ridiculous, I know. But it makes it easier to drag you when we're inside a time pinch."

Buddy's brows screwed together in confusion.

Lennie stood up, turning to snarl at the Maranzano line. "Let me get to the middle. Then do what you have to do." He nodded to Buddy. "You poke your head too far out from behind me, and it'll get blown off. I ain't your nanny, so get it right."

Buddy nodded and Lennie popped his hat back onto his head, turning to march directly up the center of the Brooklyn Bridge. The Maranzano line opened fire like a Union regiment, sending lead flying as Lennie closed the gap with a nonchalant stride. His hat flew off his head when he reached the accurate range of the incoming bullets, and soon his chest and head began to spray from slugs smashing against his impenetrable skin.

Vincent shook his head. "That's a sight."

Buddy lifted his revolver. "Now?"

"Wait. Give him another twenty yards."

Lennie continued, pausing to wipe shrapnel from his eyelashes before reaching the midpoint of the bridge.

He turned with a lift of his fingers to his lips and gave them a whistle that Vincent could barely hear over the gunfire.

"Alright, Buddy," Vincent shouted. "Let's go!"

Buddy pulled his arms close to his ribs and tightened his legs.

Vincent pinched time. The gunfire dropped into a slurry of muffled pounds, dropping finally into silence. He reached for the back of Buddy's jacket, giving it a tug. The youth was slight of frame, and much lighter than some others Vincent had pulled through a time bubble. The kid did a fine job of setting his muscles. He dragged Buddy heels-on-pavement toward Lennie, who had turned and spread his arms in a taunting gesture to the Maranzano line.

Dodging the hail of suspended bullets took tremendous

effort, and by the time Vincent had settled Buddy into the void behind Lennie, he knew he didn't have enough power left to make the return trip. He shook his head in frustration, then did his best to crouch behind both Lennie and Buddy before releasing the time pinch.

Gunfire filled his ears, now with almost deafening clamor.

Buddy dropped to his rear, jerking from what seemed to his point of view to be a jarring moment.

Vincent reached to steady him, guiding him back to his feet. "You good?" he shouted.

Buddy trembled for a second, eyes wide as he oriented himself.

Vincent pointed toward Lennie's back. "That way."

Buddy released several breaths, then twisted at the waist. Bullets buzzed past Lennie's frame, and Vincent was glad for the man's ample girth.

Buddy pulled back the hammer on his pistol, set himself, then reached around Lennie to squeeze off a shot.

"Did you get him?" Vincent asked.

Buddy lifted a brow.

"Right," Vincent grumbled. "Forget I asked."

Buddy checked his targets again, then aimed at angle, firing a shot against one of the thick suspension cables. The bullet ricocheted off the cable with a spark. Vincent made out a barely-audible yelp over the gunfire.

Buddy reeled back behind Lennie, lifting a hand to the side of his face.

"You hit?" Vincent asked.

"Nah. Trick shots are murder."

Vincent regarded his young counterpart. Three shots in, and he'd already grown pale. A trickle of blood had seeped from his nostril. This was not a long-term plan. Buddy would kill himself before they'd laid out a significant number of Maranzano's people.

He glanced back down the bridge to the row of Masseria men just standing and watching. Though Vincent appreciated the spectacle they had created, this was in fact their job. They were supposed to be doing the shooting, and more importantly, the dying.

"Pace yourself, kid," Vincent urged.

Lennie turned his head. "You boys gonna wrap this up, or what?"

"What do you want us to do, Lennie?" Vincent shouted. "There's two dozen of them and two of us."

"Hey, I'm not the brains of this outfit. I'm just sayin' if I take many more bullets, I'm gonna give these fine gentlemen shooting at me quite a show."

Buddy squeezed off three more shots, then doubled over to wretch onto the pavement.

"I said pace yourself. Take it easy," Vincent snapped.

Buddy composed himself, then reached for a quick-loader in his pocket. "Can't you…time jump…or whatever you do?"

Vincent considered it. He could, in fact, use the same tactic he'd employed against Galloway. Get behind the line and cause chaos. The problem wasn't doing it. The problem was doing it too well and leaving Masseria's people untouched. He needed to get them in the fight. But how?

Just as despair crept into Vincent's brain, the gunfire stopped.

Vincent turned to check on the firing line, but Lennie swatted him back with a meaty palm.

"Down!"

Vincent and Buddy huddled against the pavement as an eerie rushing noise filled the air. Instead of the spatter and spray of bullets slamming into Lennie's frame, Vincent's ears were tormented by a shrill, hellish twist of cacophony. Debris rained onto his back as he clenched his eyes shut. When the noise abated, Vincent shook his head and opened his eyes to find shards of glass raining down from his hat.

Buddy lifted a tiny, jagged shard of glass with a curl of his brow. "What is this?"

"Trouble," Vincent grunted.

Lennie rolled his shoulders and dusted off more glass shards from what was left of his suit. "Oh, you bitch."

The voice of Betty Sharp rose from behind the Maranzano firing line with a cackle. "Nice suit, Leonard!"

"Thought you'd run off," he shouted.

"And miss a fight? Doesn't sound like me."

Vincent craned his neck to catch a glimpse of the glass pincher. She stepped between two cars, hands on hips, a knee-high dress of fringe dancing in the breeze.

Her eyes narrowed as she spotted Vincent. "Looks like you have a couple rats hiding in your shadow."

Lennie sighed. "You know you can't cut me, woman. Why even bother?"

"Maybe," she replied. "But I can cut them."

Buddy lifted his gun and gave Vincent a nod. "I can thin them out, right now."

Several shards of glass lifted off Buddy's clothes, joining the rest as they hovered in mid-air. The sharpest points turned to face the two of them.

Vincent considered the situation. This could be it, the moment Betty made good on her threat. He hadn't expected to lose to Betty Sharp today. He wasn't even thinking about her. But now, as the thousand glass daggers pointed at his throat made it clear he should have thought about Betty Sharp, Vincent wondered if he shouldn't just let the kid take the shot.

Before he could decide, Buddy rolled onto his back, took aim between Lennie's legs, and pulled the trigger.

The report shook Vincent.

The thousands of tiny glass daggers dropped to the pavement with a clatter.

Vincent spun around Lennie's legs to find Betty simply standing there, eyes wide. Betty ran a hand over her chest, abdomen, then forehead. She was unharmed.

Several feet to her left, one of the thugs slumped against a car before pitching to the pavement with a tidy hole in the center of his forehead.

Buddy shook his head. "That's…not possible."

"You missed?" Vincent asked.

"I can't. I literally can't miss."

Vincent hopped to his feet as the glass fragments surrounding them slithered along the bridge surface back toward the Maranzano firing line. They marched like ants back to Betty, pouring into a sheet of thick glass in front of the Marazano goons.

"She's walling up," Vincent shouted.

As Lennie turned to face him, Vincent finally caught a glimpse of the ruins of the man's clothing. Lennie whistled to the Masseria crew, whipping his hand over his head. Cars rumbled to life, and soon their own muscle began marching up the bridge on both sides of the vehicles.

Vincent crouched next to Buddy, still lying on his back, staring at the sky.

"You okay, kid?"

Buddy blinked. "How did I miss?"

"You look like a dog chewed you up. Maybe you just ran dry?"

"No. That's not it. I…hit her. I hit something."

Vincent patted him on the shoulder. "Yeah. Some poor bastard whose number came up."

"I always hit what I aim at. Always. It's not possible. I shot at her. She should be dead. She should be dead." Buddy sat pale-faced, a sheen of sweat rising on his forehead. He seemed on the verge of an apoplexy, and Vincent knew this was the toll of his powers. The boy seemed panicked over this impossible circumstance.

But Vincent had an inkling of what had happened. He'd felt a familiar tingle in the small of his back, one that lifted his spirits. He knew exactly what Buddy had aimed for—an illusion of Betty Sharp.

Hattie was here.

Augustus trotted up along with a handful of gunmen. "How thick is that, anyways?" he asked, nodding to the glass bulwark.

Lennie walked up and gave it a rap with his knuckles. "Well, it ain't champagne glass."

Vincent asked Augustus, "If we get a crack in that, do you think you can slip through?"

"Son, getting through ain't no problem. But I ain't sticking my head over that ways to get it shot off!"

Lefty came forward to collect Buddy, speaking to him as the youth sat bleary-eyed. The older man gave him a few exhortations with his typical lack of decorum, and it seemed to jar Buddy out of his paralysis.

Vincent eyed Lennie as he wiped a streak of blood from his cheek. "What, you get a scratch from all that?"

Lennie scowled. "Go to hell. I'd like to see you keep your magic up for a couple thousand rounds of bullets."

Vincent nodded. The man was, in fact, a pincher. Every impact he absorbed was a decision to use magic, and each time it cost him.

Floresta approached with a chopper in his hands. "Let's simplify the equation, shall we?"

The other pinchers parted to give him a clear shot,

Vincent ushering Buddy and Lefty toward the center of the bridge while Augustus and Lennie swept closer to the edge.

Floresta cranked the gun and sent a single strafe of bullets against the glass, rising from road to top. A line of tiny craters erupted along the bulwark's surface, millions of spiderweb cracks sweeping side-to-side. Floresta lowered his weapon, then turned to whistle at one of the Fords idling behind him.

The driver gunned the engine as Floresta hopped aside.

The Ford slammed into the glass wall right at the cracks. The wall shattered into fragments from the size of a window to a fine spray of sand. The car lurched past the glass wall, taking immediate gunfire as its radiator belched steam.

The Masseria army released a war cry as they funneled through the breach, guns blazing. Vincent watched in slack-jawed dread as cries of pain rose above the gunfire.

Lennie wiped the blood from his nostrils and sucked in several breaths, raising the will to plunge through a thinned portion of the wall to create a second breach. Augustus hung back, firing potshots over Lennie's shoulder.

Buddy braced his shoulders, but before he could plunge into the fray, Vincent gripped him by the arm. "Easy on the trick shots. Don't kill yourself with your own magic, right?"

Buddy nodded, then crossed the ruined glass bulwark.

Vincent leaned in to Lefty. "You ready for this, old man?"

Lefty rotated the barrel of his revolver against his thigh, checking his chambers, then pulled the hammer back.

"Reminds me of San Matteo," Lefty replied.

"How'd that go for you boys?"

"Just fine. Until it didn't."

Vincent shook his head. "I had to ask."

The two stepped through the breach beside the car, nearly slipping over two fallen Masseria men before joining Buddy near the front of the ruined Ford. The driver's blood coated the interior of the windscreen—the bits that hadn't been shot clear of the frame.

Lennie pressed forward with Augustus behind. The man was growing pale, and a stream of blood ran from his nostril. He wouldn't take much more of this punishment. But they were almost to the Maranzano car line.

Buddy took shots at the opposite line, emptying his revolver before pulling another quick-loader out. He didn't appear to be using his powers. Vincent wondered if he'd lost his nerve, or if he simply didn't bother with them at this range. The boy had a good aim even without his magic.

"Where's Betty?" Vincent shouted.

Lefty shook his head as he squeezed off a couple shots with his army issue Colt. "Haven't seen her."

"Think she took off?"

"Possible. She's not the frontal attack sort."

Vincent peered over the heads of the Maranzano people, searching for Hattie. He couldn't find her. Either she'd found a solid hiding place, or she'd withdrawn like Betty. For that matter, where was Maria? He peered over the railing at the East River below. No earth underfoot for her to pinch. This battlefield removed Maria from the equation.

Lennie reached the car line, and Augustus took a diving slide beneath the nearest car while his companion held himself up to catch his breath. Arterial spray shot into the air behind the car as Augustus went to work with his Bowie knife.

Buddy fired six more shots, then lowered his revolver. "I'm empty."

Vincent handed the youth his gun. "Here."

Lefty eyed Vincent. "What're you planning?"

"Need to take a quick head count."

Vincent pinched time, stepping out from behind his cover. Bullets hung midair, still twisting in their high-powered trajectories that Vincent's time bubble couldn't fully stop. He ducked beneath them, making sure not to make contact and send all of their force into his body. Near the middle of the bridge, he took a quick count. Despite the bold move by Masseria's people, they'd taken far more casualties than Maranzano's. The breach had funneled them into a kill zone. At this rate, Maranzano would prevail in this fight, even with Augustus going to work behind their line.

Vincent took in the bridge, and its steel suspension cables running from the granite towers.

Steel.

Vincent withdrew, searching for Floresta among the Masseria men huddled around the breach, then released the time pinch.

Floresta shook his head as Vincent materialized beside him. "Good way to get shot."

"How much power are you packing?" Vincent shouted over the gunfire.

"Come again?"

"Your electricity. How much can you create?"

Floresta gritted his teeth. "Depends on how sick I wanna get. Why?"

Vincent pointed to the arcs of cables beside them. "Think those'll carry a charge?"

Floresta grinned. "They might. That's steel."

"So are their cars," Vincent added.

"I like the way you think, Calendo."

Floresta holstered his gun and sidestepped through the firing line toward the edge of the bridge. He stretched his hand toward the cabling, closing his eyes as he felt the charge in the air. "Better step clear of metal, boys!" Floresta shouted.

Vincent released several whistles, trying to capture the attention of the Masseria men nearby. Those still able to move eased away from the wrecked Ford as violet arcs of energy slashed from Floresta's hand, wrapping its forked fingers around the bridge cables.

Floresta's eyes clamped tighter as he released a long bellow. His body quivered. The air stank of ozone. And with a jerking spasm that rocked his body, a bolt of lightning flew from Floresta's hand into the bridge.

The air hammered with a clap of thunder. Vincent covered his eyes as his ears rang. When he blinked away the spots floating in his vision from the arc of electric fury, he found most of the Maranzano line twitching on the ground.

A cheer rose from the Masseria line as the rear guard on the opposite side of the bridge began a slow retreat. Two of the Fords they'd used as cover were licking fire, fuel spilled from bullets ignited by Floresta's lightning.

Floresta slumped to his knees, sucking in ragged breaths. Vincent tapped his shoulder, testing for sparks, before wrapping an arm around Floresta to help him back to his feet.

"You okay?" Vincent asked.

Floresta nodded, his eyes still clamped shut.

An explosion boomed from the Maranzano line as one of the cars went up from the flames. The slow retreat became a panicked frenzy as flames spread to the other cars.

Vincent left Floresta to catch his breath, rushing forward to find Lefty and Buddy.

"That was something!" Buddy shouted with a wide grin.

Lefty shook his head. "Remind me never to underestimate that creep again."

Vincent squinted through the black smoke rising from the bridge, searching the far side for Lennie and Augustus. "Where are the others?"

He spotted Lennie, patting the tatters of his clothes to put out tiny flames. He wobbled on his feet, punch drunk from the toll the magic had exacted on him.

A line of spilled fuel took fire near his feet. He danced

away from the flames to the edge of the bridge, stomping his feet as his trousers caught.

"Lennie!" Vincent shouted. "Pull back!"

Lennie turned to face Vincent and the others. The man was obviously spent magic-wise. His face was crisscrossed with red slashes. A full blossom of blood from a gunshot wound spread near his shoulder. Nodding, Lennie plodded back toward the Masseria people just as the car behind him exploded.

The ball of flame knocked Lennie off his feet, sending him tumbling over the steel railing. He clawed for purchase, his hand grabbing the railing before he went over the edge.

Augustus emerged from the choke of black fumes, sprinting toward Lennie with enough speed to blow the hat off his head. "Lennie!" he shouted, reaching for the other man's hand. Before Augustus could reach him, Lennie's eyes rolled back, his hand went limp and he slipped over the edge.

Vincent rushed for the railing, peering down at the water in time to see Lennie's body smack against the waves of the East River.

A queasy shock ran through his chest at the sight. The man was tough. He was bulletproof. But even if he was still conscious from the blood loss, even if he'd managed to pull his powers up enough to absorb the impact, the cost of the magic, as spent as he was, would have killed the man. Even if he'd miraculously survived, he'd be unconscious and would drown by the time they managed to get off the bridge and to him.

Buddy walked up beside Vincent, his face pale as he stared at the river below with wide eyes. Augustus slumped over the edge of the railing, knees weak. Floresta staggered toward them, breathing in short, rapid bursts. "We…gotta run."

Vincent turned, searching the Masseria men for some

sort of leadership and finding none. Finally Lefty began barking at the foot soldiers, whipping them into motion as they withdrew past the wrecked glass wall and the ruined car, back to the remaining vehicles. There would be plenty of room left in those cars for the return trip, as they were leaving behind quite a few dead on the bridge.

Floresta cleared his throat and approached Augustus. The two exchanged heated words as Augustus finally pulled himself away from the edge. Vincent collected the man's Stetson from the middle of the bridge, offering it to Augustus as they made their way back to the cars and back to the hotel.

From the other side of the stand-off, the violence seemed almost tame. Two lines of cars had blocked off an entire lane of the Brooklyn Bridge. Two or three shots had sung out over the East River, but otherwise the two gangs appeared to have stopped short of one another's range. Hattie glanced over her shoulder at the crowd gathering along the street to gawk. To these New York City residents, it was yet another flare-up between gangs. To Hattie, it could mean the end of an era. Assuming they got close enough to actually shoot one another.

A car whisked around the nearest corner, and Hattie stepped aside as its wheels locked, sliding to a halt several paces in front of her. She'd conjured the Brigid O'Toole illusion when she found Polizzi at Maranzano's rail yard hideout and warned him about the incoming war party. The fact that the foot soldiers had made it to the bridge before Masseria could even get out of Brooklyn was indication that Maria had done a stellar job grinding them to a halt. But they had pinchers on their side, and without magic firepower, Maranzano was doomed on that bridge.

Polizzi stepped out of the car, tipping his hat to Hattie.

"I hope you've brought some motivation," Hattie declared. "They've all got their hands in their pockets."

A second individual stepped out of the car, shooting Hattie a jagged smirk.

"Betty," Hattie stated. "I suppose that'll motivate them."

Betty Sharp stepped past Hattie, glaring at the bridge. "Is that Lennie?"

Polizzi nodded to the man marching to the center of the bridge, arms outstretched. His frame sparked with lead bullets spraying off his impenetrable skin.

"He'll have one or two behind him," Polizzi replied. "Whoever's brave or dumb enough to follow."

Hattie's stomach twisted as she spotted the two men who were both brave and dumb enough. Vincent and Buddy.

Betty turned to Polizzi. "Did you bring my glass?"

He nodded and unbuttoned his jacket, fanning it open to expose his interior pockets.

Betty reached for Polizzi and a stream of glass poured up and out of his pocket, sending shivers through his body. Hattie stared with wide-eyed interest. A veritable river of glass emerged from his endless pocket, surrounding Betty in several haloes. When the last had slipped free of Polizzi's pocket space, he released a long sigh and shook his head.

Betty twisted the levitating glass into a figurine the size of a car. Enormous glass wheels turned on axles as the glass block followed Betty onto the bridge.

"How long can she keep that up?" Hattie asked.

Polizzi shook his head. "Long enough to do some damage."

"Will it make a difference?"

"Why do you think she and I are the last ones standing?" he replied.

As he turned back for the car, Hattie asked, "Where are you going?"

"Maranzano. I'm moving him to a safe location."

"You're not helping?"

He closed the door and spoke to her through the window. "Only a stupid man would commit all his pinchers to one fight."

Hattie nodded to herself as he pulled away. It was true. Masseria had lost his numbers in pitch skirmishes like this one. Perhaps Maranzano was winning the war of attrition after all.

The view of the fight became obscured by gunsmoke, and Hattie trotted onto the bridge, sticking close to the side railing in order to catch a glimpse of Vincent. Betty's glass sledge ground against the pavement behind her as she sauntered up to the rear of the Maranzano line. Hattie broke into a jog in order to close more distance, ducking her head as Buddy fired off three shots, dropping three men in the process.

Buddy. The one who never misses.

The glass sledge melted into a thick puddle against the pavement stones as Betty shoved men aside. The puddle splintered into several thousand daggers, all lifting into the air. Hattie's ears filled with a thunderous rushing sound, like a waterfall of glass, as her weapons sliced out overtop the Maranzano line to plunge into Lennie's chest. They shattered into dust and shards as they hammered into the man's body, ruining his clothing.

Hattie caught a glimpse of Vincent peering from behind Lennie just as Betty's glass shard congealed into fresh blades, rising from the halo of dust surrounding Lennie, Vincent and Buddy. The jagged glass daggers hovered at throat level, advancing by inches toward Vincent.

Hattie balled her fists.

No.

She couldn't allow him to die like this.

A wave of dizziness swept through Hattie's brain, like an avalanche of fatigue overtaking her entire body. With a blink, the sky over the East River fell into darkness. Infernal clouds swept over the rooftops of Manhattan, all bearing a blood-red hue. Sulphur filled Hattie's nostrils. The soul trap in her pocket blazed with sudden heat. The demon. It was lashing out. Enraged. It wanted to protect Vincent as much as she did.

Hattie shook her head, and the image faded. Morning sunlight returned to her vision, as did the sight of a new face peering from behind Lennie. Buddy had his revolver cocked in hand, eyes searching for his target.

If he fired at Betty, she would die. It was impossible for him to miss. Hattie struggled in a panicked second. Her heart pounded. A pincher was about to die at the hands of another. It would save Vincent, but...

Hattie reached out with her powers, knitting an illusion over Betty. Light pinched around her, rendering her invisible. But that wouldn't be enough.

With a quick glance, she chose a gunman standing six feet to Betty's left. It wasn't a decision as much as a reflex. Hattie cast an illusion over him. He became Betty Sharp.

And that was all Buddy needed.

One shot.

One bullet.

And the thug dropped to the ground as Betty stood dumbfounded.

Her daggers fell to the pavement in a rain of cracking glass.

She needed to know what had almost happened. Hattie dug deep, pulling on as much of her personal power as she could muster. Both the charms dangling from her ear lobes and the soul trap in her pocket thrummed with magical heat. Hattie poured a vision into Betty's eyes, drawing her into a single moment, fully immersed in the death she'd avoided. One shot. One bullet. Betty falling to Buddy's gun.

The drain overtook Hattie, and she fell to her knees. The Brigid O'Toole illusion melted away, rendering Hattie as she was. A red-haired woman, huddled against the side of the bridge railing.

Betty turned and withdrew, first marching away from the front line. Then, running. She sprinted past Hattie with ragged breaths, her eyes wide and wild.

Tears fell from Hattie's eyes as blood ran from her nose. She killed that gunman to save Betty. She'd taken a gamble on Vincent's life to save a woman she barely knew—one who she didn't even like. Or had she? There's no saying that if Buddy had aimed at Betty, she wouldn't have slit Vincent's throat before the bullet hit.

Hattie shook her head. She couldn't make sense of anything through the pounding headache and swells of nausea overtaking her. Pulling herself to her feet, she fought back a gag as she glanced toward the fight. A wall of glass separated the two warring parties. Betty's last act before running off.

She had to leave. As much as she wanted to stay and make sure Vincent was okay, she would be of no use to him physically and magically drained.

Leaving the carnage on the bridge, she made her way back to the Manhattan side, hand over hand as she gripped the rail. Her legs found some strength by the time she reached the street. The crowd had tripled in size, and two men rushed to her side to help her to a curb. One pulled a handkerchief, offering it to Hattie. She took it and cleaned her face.

"Are you hurt, Miss?" the other asked.

She shook her head but didn't attempt to speak.

A rush of gasps swept through the crowd. Hattie twisted to glance back at the bridge. A brilliant violet bolt of light filled her vision. She blinked away the spots burned into her eyes as a clap of thunder sounded over the city. A second explosion rocked the bridge. Onlookers stumbled backward into the street as cars slid to a halt.

A body fell from the center of the bridge, plummeting for several long seconds before smashing into the river. Hattie's heart stuttered in panic.

"Vincent!" she screamed as her vision swam, darkening into a murky black.

CHAPTER 22

Everyone inside the bank stood silent as Joe Masseria railed and ranted behind the double doors to his office on the second floor. Their eyes exchanged glances, filled with equal parts fatigue and trepidation. They'd just lost a pincher and a friend. Now, the math was equal for both sides. They were down to two pinchers, and casualties from the battle on the bridge which bled them to dangerous levels.

Lefty hovered over Buddy, who had huddled up on one of the sofas beneath the stairway. He was pale and wide-eyed. Dread had overtaken his youthful excitement, and Vincent felt for the boy. He'd just seen a pincher die, he was fearing that his powers had failed him at a crucial moment in the battle, and a gangster leader, one of the very men Ithaca had taught him to unquestionably obey and serve, was furious and bound to make someone pay for the day's losses.

As for the boy's fears about his powers, Vincent knew better. Buddy had hit his target. He just didn't realize he'd been firing at an illusion and not the real thing. As Masseria's voice continued in its muffled thunder, Vincent wondered what had possessed Hattie to save Betty Sharp's life. Not that he begrudged her that. This fight for freedom wasn't strictly personal. It was for all pinchers, even psychopaths like Betty. Whatever Hattie had done, it had clearly rocked Betty to the core.

But there would be fallout from this, and Vincent hoped Hattie had thought it through.

The double doors opened, and Catena emerged from Masseria's office. The man was a pillar of calm despite the tongue lashing he'd endured. Luciano followed, less comported than Catena. Luciano rushed down the stairs, snapping his fingers at several attendees, including Floresta, to follow.

When Catena reached the base of the stairs, he nodded to Lefty. "I wonder if we might have a word in my office?" He turned to Vincent and Buddy. "All of you."

The Baltimore boys followed Catena into his first-floor office. Catena motioned for Buddy to close the door behind them.

Vincent pulled the single chair for Lefty, who took it. The formality of the moment felt natural to Vincent. This was Old World etiquette, and Lefty was the senior.

Catena poured himself a finger of hooch, pounded it, then chased it with another. With a loud exhale and a tremble of the shoulders, he turned for his desk and calmly took a seat.

"Well, this was a disaster," Catena stated as he reorganized the papers on his desk from one neat stack to another.

Lefty watched the other man with a steady calm. "It was a war party. No one expected it to be tidy."

"Regardless, we've lost an asset."

Vincent set his jaw at the comment. He'd come to despise these sorts of dehumanizing epithets for pinchers.

"Have they found the body?" Lefty asked.

"Not yet," Catena replied. "We might never. From what I hear, we should expect the worst."

"My condolences," Lefty offered. "Seems Luciano has marching orders."

"Yes." Catena sighed. "Masseria's put out an official hit on Maranzano."

Lefty leaned back in his chair. "It's come to that, has it?"

"He's angry. It's not often he's goaded into extreme measures, but once he's there he commits. Luciano has the lead on that, happily enough. I won't be bothered with it."

Vincent asked, "Where does that leave us?"

"In an even heat with Maranzano, regrettably. When it comes to magic, at any rate."

Buddy cleared his throat, then asked, "What about Ithaca? Can't you get more talent?"

Catena sighed, leaning back in his chair to rub the bridge of his nose. "Ithaca is understaffed and underfunded."

"Underfunded?" Lefty prodded.

"Last year they fell victim to a burglary. Most suspect it was an inside job. One of their proctors is being…sought after."

Vincent bit back a grin.

"In any event," Catena continued, "with recent events shedding light on our weakened position, the other families are exerting their contractual claims. All of this to say, no. Ithaca is not the salvation we seek."

"Which brings me back to my original question," Vincent stated.

Catena shot Vincent a warning glance. "I am not without options, Mister Calendo. Which is why I've asked you here." He leaned forward with a nod to Lefty. "I believe Vito Corbi is familiar with a contractor by the name of Brigid O'Toole."

Lefty tensed. "She's a rum-runner. Works bay traffic for

us shipping product in and out of the Chesapeake. What about her?"

Catena shook his head. "She's more than a simple trafficker."

Lefty shook his head. "Why are you asking about O'Toole?"

"When our man, O'Donnell, suffered his moment of weakness and came to your city with guns blazing, she was the one who saved Corbi and the rest of you from certain death."

Lefty glanced over his shoulder at Vincent, who simply shrugged.

"I don't follow," Lefty stated.

Catena squinted. "If you're protecting her, you needn't bother. I know what she is. And I know what she's after."

Vincent swallowed hard. "And what, might I ask, is she?"

"She's a power player," Catena replied as he knitted his fingers together beneath his chin. "The woman's been in this office, plying me for material support against Vito Corbi. I suspect she's done the same with Maranzano. She has her eyes set on Baltimore, I'm afraid."

Lefty sighed. "Is everyone on this Earth a simple bastard?"

"Believe her or not," Catena added, "she claims to have a passel of assets that she's poached from other gangs."

"Are you inclined to believe her?" Lefty asked.

"At this point, I don't see that I have any choice. We'll never survive that rabid glass pincher unless we secure O'Toole's cooperation."

Buddy leaned forward eagerly. "Well, you have us."

Catena chuckled. "Indeed? And what happens when O'Toole goes to Maranzano? Do you think he won't press his advantage?"

Vincent asked, "What if Luciano succeeds in greasing Maranzano?"

"That would take an act of God, I feel. It's my place to plan for his inevitable failure."

"Then what do you want from us?" Vincent pressed.

Catena stood. "O'Toole. Masseria wants to meet her face-to-face. I suggest the Julietta to avoid cries of indignance from the other families. Find her and bring her to the club."

Lefty sneered. "We're supposed to trust her now that we know she's campaigning to take over Baltimore?"

"I expect you to abide by your Capo's agreement to assist mine."

Lefty maintained a steel-sharp glare. "And when my Capo hears that yours is conspiring with our enemies?"

"He'll decide whether it's worth angering Joe Masseria," Catena snapped. "Do you think he cares whether it's Vito Corbi or Brigid O'Toole running liquor in and out of Baltimore? Whatever it takes to secure the New York families is paramount. Now, the Baltimore Crew can attend with good faith in our agreement, or we will find alternatives."

Lefty stood, pausing to brush off the front of his jacket. "My apologies. I hadn't realized you were quite that desperate."

Catena glared at Lefty as he turned to his men.

"We'll find O'Toole," Lefty declared as he led them to the door. "Julietta Social Club. Tonight work for you?"

Catena lingered for a moment, then answered, "Give Luciano a day, at least. He might get lucky."

"Tomorrow, then." Lefty tipped a finger to his hat.

Buddy opened the door for Lefty, and the two followed him out past the tellers' desks and to the street.

Buddy half jogged beside them. "I don't understand what's happening."

"Catena's putting his money on pincher power," Vincent told him. "That's what's happening. We have to wrangle more pinchers before he's satisfied. Same old song, different verse."

Lefty sighed as he waited to cross an intersection. "One of these days, someone's going to tell me exactly where this Brigid O'Toole came from."

"Ireland, I think," Vincent replied with a smirk.

"Don't be a smart-ass."

"So, now what?" Buddy asked.

Lefty nodded to the youth. "I need you at the Julietta. Talk to the manager, the maître d'. Whoever can get us a private room. I want to know where the exits are. How big the kitchen is. Is there a cellar access? Any way this could go sideways on us. Understand?"

Buddy stared at the ground, mouth twisted in disappointment.

Vincent put a hand on his shoulder. "Listen, kid. If this O'Toole has these pinchers like they say she does, it's possible one of them is..." He lowered his voice to a dramatic whisper. "One could be a light pincher."

Lefty squinted at Vincent.

"A light pincher?" Buddy gasped.

"An illusionist. Don't get rattled about missing that shot on Betty Sharp. Could be, you were aiming at an illusion the whole time and never knew."

Buddy's eyes grew wide and he shivered. "Really?"

With a nod, Vincent added, "Welcome to the big leagues, kid. We got ways of working around each other's witchcraft. It's a bag of nuts, and you gotta get over it and keep pressing forward." He gave Buddy's shoulder a squeeze. "Right?"

Buddy nodded, eyes still wide. "Right."

"Go on," Lefty urged.

Buddy took a cleansing breath, straightened his spine, then trotted back down the street to hail a cab.

Vincent turned to find Lefty staring at him.

"Light pincher, huh?" Lefty grumbled.

"Maybe."

"There's no maybe about this. I need to know what Miss Malloy is planning here."

Vincent sighed. "You know how she is. Half the time I'm in the dark as much as you are."

"Catch you boys at a bad time?" a voice called from the street.

Floresta trotted through the intersection to join them.

"I hear you're on a snipe hunt," Lefty called out.

Floresta waved him off. "Luciano's sitting on it."

"Right," Vincent said. "Wouldn't do to whack Maranzano before Masseria's in the crosshairs."

Floresta pulled him aside. "Lower your voice, ass."

"Well, Catena's got us playing matchmaker. Putting Masseria together with O'Toole."

Floresta nodded. "He's looking to fill a Lennie-shaped gap."

Vincent sneered. "I can see you're real choked up about him."

"Don't be a child. He was half here, to begin with. Drunk most of the time. Pissed at the world the rest of the time. We're better off."

"Catena doesn't see it that way," Vincent said.

Floresta shrugged. "Let him waste his time with O'Toole. If she's really got a coterie of pinchers to make deals with, it'll only help our plan."

"You want Masseria loaded with magic?" Vincent asked. "Won't that make it more difficult for Luciano when things go down?"

"Listen," Floresta whispered. "Whatever deal Masseria hammers out with O'Toole, you can bet the bank he has no intention of following through. She may be a legitimate player, but as far as the Boss is concerned, she's still just a dame. Let's not get in a lather over this. It's temporary."

Lefty shook his head. "You might find this dame has more muscle than you do. Things aren't always what they seem."

Floresta smirked. "You might do well to remember that."

He nodded to both before stepping up the block toward the bank.

They watched him for a moment before Lefty turned to Vincent. "Get the feeling we're being dangled at the end of a hook?"

"Yep," Vincent replied. "Getting tired of it, too. I'd rather *be* the hook."

CHAPTER 23

Floresta and Vincent sidestepped between box cars to enter Maranzano's rail yard. A recent rain had muddied up the ground, creating puddles of varying depth in the craters. As Vincent tread carefully toward the abandoned port authority warehouse, he kept an eye out for Betty Sharp.

Pockets Polizzi stepped out of the warehouse with a nod. "Thought you two would show up sooner or later."

"Is he here?" Floresta called.

Two gunmen emerged from the warehouse entrance, choppers in hand but pointed to the ground. As they took positions on either side of Polizzi, Vincent held a hand out for Floresta to hold up.

"What's going on?" Vincent asked.

Betty Sharp's voice rang from the front of the rail yard, "Trying to figure out which side you're on."

He glanced over his shoulder to find Betty lounging atop a box car, flanked by more gunmen.

"Looks like we stepped right into a murder hole," Vincent muttered.

Floresta lifted a hand. "Everyone, stay calm."

Polizzi squinted. "We *are* calm. It's been a good week. Masseria lost 'bout twice the men we did in his thunder-assed bluster. And he's lost a pincher, to boot. The only thing to sour this fine affair is one question. Are the pinchers who were supposed to be on our side still on our side?"

"Is Maranzano here?" Floresta pressed. "We have news."

"Answer his damned question," Betty shouted.

"We're on your side," Vincent replied. "We had to march with Masseria to keep our cover."

Betty sat up, pressing with fists against the boxcar roof. "And your little Ithaca cur? He dropped seven men by himself." She slid off the train, landing with a hard splash of mud. "And nearly put one into my forehead."

Vincent turned to face her. "You're alive, aren't you?"

Her face, though twisted with anger, held something new. A flicker of uncertainty. A pang of fear that Vincent hadn't seen in her since Ithaca.

Floresta shook his head. "You know how this sort of game works, Pockets. You want us on the inside? We gotta make nice with the enemy. Don't get your shorts in a lather. You know better."

Betty marched toward Vincent, scowling. "What made him miss? He's a target pincher. How did he miss me?"

Before Vincent could reply, Floresta stepped toward Polizzi.

"How about you answer my question, now? Is Salvatore here?"

A voice called from the warehouse. "No *stregone* ever speaks to me that way."

A thin man emerged from the darkened doorway. He wore a light gray suit with a white coat draped over his shoulders, to match his wide-brimmed hat. His face was cratered and aged, puckered near the corners of his eyes. A cigarette burned at the end of an ivory stem as he stepped carefully around a puddle.

Floresta bowed. "My apologies."

Salvatore Maranzano nodded to the gunmen, and they slung their weapons over their shoulders.

"I *do* understand this game," the old man declared. "And if you are truly with us, Floresta, then my adversary has but one *stregone* left."

"I'm with you," Floresta replied. "And I've come with a warning. Masseria has put out a hit on you. A personal hit. He's suspended courtesy."

Maranzano's face cracked into a feeble grin. He gripped the cigarette holder between his teeth and reached for his lapel to slip a bright red flower from a button eye.

"A red dahlia," he stated through clenched teeth before tossing it into the mud at Floresta's feet. "He has made his intentions clear."

Vincent turned to spy the flower on the ground.

Floresta leaned in to explain. "Red dahlia. It's a formal language, like a code. Masseria has suspended the code of conduct by declaring a hit on Maranzano personally. This is his way of maintaining etiquette."

Vincent peered at Maranzano. "Then you need to move to a safe location."

The gunmen snickered as Maranzano's grin broadened. "Dear boy, I'm not afraid of a beaten and desperate hound."

"Masseria's not the one you should be afraid of," Floresta told him. "He'll send Augustus Henry to do the deed. Right now, no one knows where he is. Even Luciano. The man lost his friend yesterday. He might be looking for some payback." Floresta added with a squint, "You might wish he was the one who went over the side of the bridge. You'll never see Henry coming, and I don't think there's a pincher here who's equipped to stop him."

Polizzi shrugged. "The gloves are off, Sparks. Masseria's open game, now. If Henry wants to take his sweet time, then let him. Meanwhile, we're coming for his boss."

Betty slapped a hand against Vincent's arm. "How did he miss? How did that kid miss killing me?"

"Quiet, woman! This is not your place to speak," Maranzano snapped. With a gesture to one of his gunmen, he added, "Get her out of here!"

Vincent took in Betty's expression…rage mixed with resignation. They had her cowed, thanks to Ithaca and Sebastian. But this could be an opportunity.

Vincent turned to Maranzano, "You should be thanking her, you know."

Maranzano's eyes crinkled into hard squints. "What?"

"She marched right onto that bridge," Vincent explained. "Her glass wall meant Masseria's men had to funnel through a small space to get to you, presenting themselves as easy targets. If it weren't for Betty, you wouldn't be in the position you are today."

Maranzano made a quick gesture with his cigarette holder, and the gunmen returned to his side.

"It's true, though," Vincent continued. "Masseria crossed the line, and you can take him out. And since he's the one who suspended courtesy, you'll have the families behind you. But you can't dismiss Augustus Henry. He's motivated and dangerous. Not to mention, you'll have to think past Masseria. What happens to his apparatus when he goes down? You'll need talent to consolidate your power. Magical talent."

"Your point?" Maranzano spat.

"Ithaca's hamstrung. Getting pinchers from the farm is an agony and gets the families in a frenzy. There's an option." Vincent stepped forward. "Brigid O'Toole."

Polizzi turned to explain, "The Irish woman I told you about."

Maranzano nodded thoughtfully. "She is the one threatening the power in your city, no?"

"We're not worried," Vincent replied. "But she claims to have pinchers to spare. Whoever steps up to secure her partnership stands to inherit a windfall."

Maranzano grinned. "And why would you volunteer this information? Is this not a betrayal of Vito Corbi?"

Vincent shook his head. "Oh, I have no delusions that you will actually follow through with any agreement you reach with O'Toole. She's a cult of personality, but she is no leader."

Floresta quickly picked up Vincent's line of reasoning. "Secure her pinchers, take down Masseria, then eliminate O'Toole. You will, in one swift stroke, become the *Capo di tutti Capi*."

Maranzano stared at the ground, eyes darting back and forth in thought.

Polizzi offered, "I've met the woman. She has the assets. But she's a clever one, and I don't think she's satisfied with intermediaries."

Maranzano declared, "I should meet with this woman personally?"

Floresta snickered. "Pockets isn't exactly spit-polish. You'll need a diplomatic touch."

Maranzano mulled the thought over, then nodded. "Let us not rest on Masseria. We acquire *stregone* and kick the man while he's down."

Vincent bowed. "I'll set up a meet with your glass pincher."

He turned to Betty, who narrowed her eyes as Vincent ushered her back through the rail yard.

"What are you doing?" she snapped.

"Take it easy. The meet's tomorrow night. Julietta Club," Vincent whispered.

"Why do I care?"

He leaned as close as she would let him. "You want to know why my pincher missed you on the bridge? Brigid O'Toole, is why."

Betty stiffened. "What?"

"You take a moment and think about that. She has people you'll want to talk to. You're only alive and standing here because of O'Toole."

Her eyes searched his face with a wary intensity. "Whose side are you on, anyway?"

"Believe it or not, I'm on your side." He stopped and added with a nod, "Do us both a favor, and keep that to yourself. Huh? If you find both Maranzano and Masseria in the same room?"

She laughed. "That'll never happen."

"But if it does?"

"What are you—?"

Vincent leaned down to whisper. "We have people ready to take down your boss. You'll have to be the one to take down Masseria. Do you understand what I'm saying?"

Vincent stepped away, straightening his sleeve as Betty stood bewildered.

"Tomorrow night," he added, then gave Floresta a nod as he approached.

The two exited the rail yard, heading back to Floresta's car.

"Quick thinking," Floresta said as they got in.

"Your plan's back on track," Vincent declared. "Both bosses will be at the Julietta tomorrow night."

"You're sure about that?"

"As sure as anyone can be. Listen, can you drop me off in Brooklyn Heights?"

Floresta eyed him with interest. "Why?"

"I've just volunteered someone for something and I think they ought to know."

CHAPTER 24

Hattie watched as Maria paced. She would have been up and pacing too, if she wasn't still completely worn out. Keeping the illusion of Bridget O'Toole up for hours had been draining, even with the earrings to help, but when she'd cast an illusion of Betty over a gangster, made the original Betty invisible, *and* kept the O'Toole illusion up, it had been too much.

When that bullet had slammed through her illusion of Betty, killing the gangster, it had nearly killed her as well. She still wasn't sure how she'd managed to make it off the bridge, but the one thing she did remember was that figure falling to his death from those heights.

"I went to the hotel, I asked as discretely as I could. I even snuck up and knocked on the door. He hasn't been there. None of them have been there. Then I went to the bank where we met Catena, but I couldn't get close because of all the activity, and I didn't seem him there. Then I stopped by a speakeasy, and everybody was all abuzz about what happened on the bridge, but no one seemed to know exactly who died, or who it was that fell into the river."

Hattie clamped her jaw tight to keep from crying. She could find out. She could get up and use an illusion to sneak into the bank and listen in on conversations. But she needed to recover from this morning's exertions. It wouldn't do anyone any good if she ran out still exhausted and barely able to hold an illusion for five minutes. She just had to hope Vincent was okay.

"But I did manage to pick this up." She extended a cup with steaming tea inside. Hattie couldn't help but smile, transported instantly back to her parents' house. They always drank tea, and she'd forever associate the beverage with her childhood and comfort, even though she'd become Americanized enough to prefer coffee.

"Chamomile," Maria told her. "Relaxing and soothing. My mother always made it for us at nights when we couldn't sleep. It won't make you groggy or anything, just help you relax a little. You drink this and rest, and I'll go back out and look for Vincent. I swear I won't be back until I hear what happened."

Hattie took the tea. It warmed her hands as Maria's words warmed her heart. When she'd passed out at the bridge, Maria had been there, rushing through the crowd to gather her up and take care of her. She'd coordinated the concerned onlookers like a general organizing troops, and when Hattie had regained consciousness, she'd found smelling salts under her nose, a woman urging chocolate on her, and a car waiting to take her back to their room.

She had been grateful for the car—and the chocolate—but most of all she'd been grateful for Maria who'd proven that she not only had Hattie's back, but that she was a true friend. On their ride back, Hattie had tearfully poured out as many details as she could given the big ears of the cabbie driving them. As soon as Maria had gotten her settled, she'd gone out in search of news about Vincent, with a promise to return promptly.

And the news was no news. A knot of worry settled in Hattie's stomach as she sipped the tea. No one but Vincent knew she was here. If he'd died, Lefty would, no doubt, have sent a message to her back in Baltimore, but she wasn't in Baltimore. Her only hope was that the death of a pincher would be big enough news that it would soon be on the streets. In a way, the lack of information was reassuring. One gangster falling to his death in the river among so many who'd been gunned down in the violence wouldn't have drawn much notice.

Maria left and Hattie finished her tea, falling into a fitful doze. When she woke it was after noon, and she was feeling much better, although she knew it would be a while before she'd be able to pull off any more than the briefest of illusions.

Getting up, she bathed and dressed, then sat in the room wondering whether she should wait for Maria's return or head out to see what she could hear on her own. If the woman didn't come back soon, Hattie was determined to leave her a note and go out on her own, at the very least because she was hungry for lunch.

Lunch came and went and she was just getting ready to write that note and get dinner, when there was a knock on her door. Hattie stood, bracing in case Maria's news wasn't good, only to see Vincent peek his head through the doorway.

"Glad you're hear. We need to talk."

Hattie heard nothing from the rushing in her ears. The man had barely stepped a foot into the room before she'd barreled into him, wrapping arms and legs around him as she sobbed into his chest.

He stumbled against the wall from her onslaught. "Whoa! What…? Hattie, what happened?"

She felt his hands smoothing her hair then wrapping around her shoulders and waist to pull her tightly against him.

"I saw…I though…I…" she stuttered, trying to get enough control of her crying to speak coherently. "If you'd died, I don't know what I'd do. None of this would mean anything without you—the Charge, my fight against Vito and the Crew, life. Nothing. I know how Sadie felt, because nothing is worth it without you."

He squeezed her tight and she felt his breath in her hair. "Hattie, what are you talking about? I'm fine. I saw what you did with Betty and that illusion, and I can't believe you pulled that off. You saved all of us—me, Buddy, *and* Betty. Why are you so upset?"

"I saw…" she gulped, reliving the memory. "I saw someone fall of the bridge and I thought…I worried…"

He held her tight. "Oh, God. Hattie, if I'd have known that you though…I would have sent a message or something. It was another pincher—one of Masseria's. Not me."

She remained in his arms as he rocked her, making soothing comments and kissing her hair and face as his hands rubbed her back. Then when she finally felt like herself again, she eased away and gave him a watery smile.

"That took a lot out of me, you know—the Betty illusion."

He ran his hands along her face, his smile warm and loving. "I know. And when I met with her this afternoon, I made sure to put a bee in her bonnet, that O'Toole was the only reason she was still alive. I'd expect a visit from her, although who knows what the nut-case might do."

Hattie stood on tiptoe and kissed him. "I had a split second to decide, and I felt horrible risking your life to save Betty. If it had failed…"

"It didn't fail. In fact, because of you, we're in an excellent position. You saved a pincher, put Maranzana and Masseria both in a position where they need to reach out to O'Toole for help, and managed to get all the pieces on the chessboard where we want them." He smiled, cupping her face in his hands. "Can I say how much I love you? How much I think you walk on water, that the world revolves because of you?"

Warmth poured through her. "Well, I feel the same, boy-o."

His dark eyes grew serious, tentatively searching hers for...something. "There's something I want to talk to you about. The timing's not ideal, but I'm not sure it ever will be, and I really need to do this while I still have the courage. Hattie, I want—"

The door opened and Maria edged in. "I found out it was a pincher—"

The woman caught sight of Vincent and froze. Then screamed. Suddenly Hattie found both Vincent and herself being enveloped in a huge hug."

"I'm so glad it wasn't you!" Maria told him. "I heard that Masseria lost a pincher in the fight, and while some people said it was one of his, others said it was another pincher from out-of-town. I couldn't manage to get close enough to the bank without Hattie's illusions to get the real scoop."

Vincent squirmed in Maria's embrace, and Hattie hid a smile, knowing he was uncomfortable with having the other woman hug him. Silly man.

He shrugged Maria off and Hattie stepped back as well.

Vincent straightened his jacket and took off his hat. "It was one of Masseria's pinchers that went over the bridge, which puts him in a difficult position. He's down to one, not counting Luciano's pincher Floresta. He's also down quite a lot of manpower. Suddenly this isn't such an uneven fight, and Masseria's worried. He knows he needs pincher power to finish this off—and he wants to finish it off. He's put a hit out on Maranzano, and he's let him know this is war."

Hattie caught her breath. "Pincher power. I've made it known that I've got pinchers on my team."

Vincent nodded. "And Maranzano is worried about that. Suddenly you, or rather O'Toole, is the winning ticket in all this. Masseria suddenly needs you to get the upper hand on Maranzano, and Maranzano needs you because he can't risk having your resources go to Masseria."

Hattie exchanged a glance with Maria. "How do you want me to play this?"

"Schedule a meeting with both of them at the same time two nights from now at the Juliette Social Club."

"Both of them?" Hattie knew where he was going with this, but after all that had happened today, she felt this was all coming to a head faster than she'd anticipated.

Vincent nodded. "That's the plan. Get them all in one room, and let the pair of them die, leaving Luciano to pick up the pieces. And if he keeps his agreement, he'll be hands-off to anything we do in Baltimore."

Hattie scowled at Vincent. "And how likely is it that he'll keep his word?"

Maria snorted. "Next to none."

"That all depends on how impressive we are in this," Vincent told her. "You show him that you're a force to be reckoned with, and he'll leave us alone. He'll be busy enough dealing with all the families in New York to want to do much down in Baltimore, anyway."

Hattie thought for a moment, then shook her head. "Tomorrow night? That doesn't give us much time to plan, or for me to get myself back in order."

He winced. "Sorry for the short notice, but I had to think fast. Augustus Henry was given the task of assassinating

Maranzano. This has to go down before he gets a chance. And he's motivated. I think Lennie was a friend of his."

Hattie rubbed her temples. "Was he *really* that close to the bulletproof fellow?"

Vincent shrugged. "I don't know, but I get that impression. All I can tell you is Henry disappeared after what happened on the bridge, and his specialty is sneaking in and out of places to knife people in the back."

Maria nodded. "He's quick to latch on to people, and when he counts someone as his friend, that's important. He doesn't take that sort of thing lightly."

Vincent and Hattie pivoted to stare at Maria.

She continued, "Before things fell apart, he and I exchanged a few pot shots. Nothing serious. It was a gentle war in Cleveland, compared to all this. But he had friends who died at the very end. It rattled him. Hard. He's not as stoic as he lets on. These things get to him."

Vincent smoothed a hand over his hair. "How much danger is Maranzano in?"

Maria tilted her head. "A lot. If Henry can find him, that is."

Hattie turned to stare at the window. "And what about Betty? Do you think she's game to unleash her fury on Masseria?"

"I think she's got a lot going on emotionally. She's conflicted," Vincent replied. "Whatever you did on the bridge, it got to her."

Hattie grimaced. "I showed her how close she came to the grave. Put an illusion of herself getting plugged with your young pincher's bullet into her head and made her live it. Might be the first time she ever really thought about that."

Maria blinked. "She's powerful. What she did on the bridge? That took a lot of effort."

"I think it's her anger that fuels her," Vincent said. "It gives her an edge—a razor edge."

Hattie continued staring through the window. "I think she's lost."

Vincent and Maria exchanged glances.

Hattie added, "I'll have a word with her."

Vincent stretched his neck. "I should get going before Lefty gets antsy."

Hattie stood up and approached Vincent with a smirk. "By the by, boy-o… I think I wasn't the only one who took exception to your reckless ways. Our friend from Deltaville was noticeably upset at you being close to death this morning."

Vincent shook his head in confusion.

She planted a peck on his cheek. "You go dying on us, and I'll let him loose to give you a what-for."

"Then I'll try to avoid that," Vincent said with a grin.

* * *

MARIA SIGHED as they rounded the last flight of stairs to the floor of Betty Sharp's apartment.

"What're you on about?" Hattie whispered.

"They say that insanity is doing the same thing the same way and expecting a different outcome."

"Who says that?"

"Read it on a train station wall." Maria crossed her arms at the top of the stairs. "You know, not everyone needs saving."

Hattie frowned. "I suppose. But is it so dreadful a thought that some of us might?"

"It is when it's an addled glass-pinching hellcat," Maria grumbled as Hattie marched down the hall.

Stitching Brigid O'Toole's persona over herself, Hattie

knocked on Betty's door. The door opened quickly, with Betty Sharp eyeing Hattie with incredulity.

"You?"

"Aye. In the flesh."

"What are you doing here?" Betty asked, easing the door almost shut, so that only her eye was visible.

"I wanted a word with you."

"I thought I told you to piss off."

Betty shut the door and threw the bolt closed.

Hattie glared at Maria who smirked with infinite self-absorption.

She turned to the door and called, "And if I had listened to you, that target pincher on the Brooklyn Bridge would've ventilated your skull. But I didn't listen, did I?"

The bolt threw again, and the door eased open.

Betty muttered, "So it *was* you?"

"May we come in?" Hattie asked.

Betty peered into the hallway. "Is your guard dog with you?"

Maria stepped into the open and Betty grinned as she opened the door for the two of them.

Hattie walked in and glanced over the shelves of glass figurines, pausing when she spotted Betty lingering by her stove clad only in her underwear. Hattie looked away out of reflex, and Betty snickered.

"You're the ones barging in on me. What, you want me to go put on a dress for you?"

Maria closed the door. "Do you enjoy being this unpleasant?"

"It suits me," Betty replied as she snatched a glass of illicit hooch and draped herself over her sofa. "And I see no reason to stop."

"You can act as tough as you like. I prefer it that way, to be honest," Hattie told her.

"Who says it's an act?" Betty asked.

Hattie crouched directly in front of Betty, meeting her gaze with determination. "I do."

Betty lingered for a second before taking a distracted sip of her drink.

Hattie pressed, "You nearly died yesterday."

"Occupational hazard."

"You can make light of it if you like, but you're here because of me."

Betty sneered. "Oh, so now you think I owe you? Is that how it works?"

"Not at all," Hattie replied. "But perhaps it affords me the right to ask you a single question?"

Betty squinted, then lowered her glass. "Okay, I'll bite. What's the question?"

"What do you want?" Hattie asked.

"What do I want?"

"Yes. What's your win? Your best-case scenario?"

Hattie held her gaze for a long moment as Betty's face twisted through a gamut of emotions.

Finally, Betty replied, "For you to leave me alone."

"I don't buy that for a second."

"Then why not tell me what it is you want me to say, so that we can end this, and you can go home?"

Hattie stood up. "You want your freedom, is what you want. You want to go back to that clear, sweet memory between the death of Elmer Capstein and the day the Baltimore Crew delivered you to Ithaca."

Betty's face puckered into a vicious scowl.

Hattie headed her off. "Don't deny it. You asked for none of this. That was the only time you felt freedom. Ruling over Richmond like a Dowager Queen. But it wasn't the power you wielded that your soul clings to. Is it? It was the sheer, unshackled freedom. You had no one to answer to. No one to tell you no. That you couldn't go here or there. Couldn't drink this or that."

Betty squirmed for a second.

Hattie continued, "But those days were short, and they are in the past. Or, are they?"

"I want you to leave," Betty muttered.

"And I want you to open your eyes."

Hattie put her hands on her hips, lording over Betty with just a little pinch of illusion-driven theater.

Betty set her glass onto the table behind the sofa and closed her eyes. "Did Calendo get to you?"

"The question you should be asking is did I get to Calendo?"

Betty shook her head. "You're no better than the rest."

"Are you so sure? I saved your life on that bridge for one reason, and one reason alone. Would you like to know what that reason is?"

Betty opened her eyes. "Okay, fine. Why?"

Hattie turned to Maria with a grin. "Maria, do I own you?"

Maria smirked, then laughed. "That'd be the day."

"Then why in the name of the Virgin Mother are you still hanging about?"

Maria sighed. "Because you're the best chance I've seen for…"

Maria didn't finish her statement, and Hattie turned to face her.

"Seen for what?"

The two exchanged meaningful glances, Maria probing Hattie for the play. But there was no play. Hattie was putting Maria on the spot, and Betty was watching with intensity.

Finally, Maria answered, "Freedom."

"Is that all?"

"Real freedom," Maria added. "Not just escape. A place to live. To be equal."

Hattie turned back to Betty. "Equality. That's why I saved your life."

Betty shook her head. "You plan on making sense any time soon?"

Hattie took a seat beside Betty on her sofa, shoving her leg aside to make room. "How many gang lords have you met who were women?"

Betty chuckled. "Are you serious?"

"Precisely."

"What, are you some sorta suffragette? We got the vote seven years ago."

"Did we really?" Hattie countered. "As a woman, sure. But as a pincher?"

Betty recoiled just a bit. "Hold on. There's no way to—"

"You were a free pincher in Richmond. You were free of any accountability beyond what the laws of nature demanded of you."

Betty shook her head. "That was never gonna last."

"But what if it could?"

Betty withdrew into her corner of the sofa with a silent scowl.

Frustration overtook Hattie, and she released a long exhale. "What is it with you, then? It's like talking to a brick wall."

Betty shrugged. "I don't care."

"But you should," Hattie implored.

Betty set her glass down and leaned into Hattie close enough to force her away.

"Maybe I just don't trust gangsters."

"That's what I am, is it?" Hattie whispered.

"You're liars. All of you. All you want is to own people. This crock you're dishing about freedom?" She shook her head. "Just another lie. You want power, and I have it. All us pinchers have it. It scares you that we're stronger than you."

Hattie lifted her chin. "You think I'm a liar."

"You're worse. You're a liar who wants me to like you. At least Elmer, and Calendo, and Maranzano…they don't care what I think. I'd rather a bald-faced deception than getting stabbed in the back."

Hattie nodded, then stood up. "You know something? You're right."

Betty blinked rapidly. "I…am?"

"Aye. I have been lying to you. And no, you shouldn't trust me. There's something I need to show you."

Maria stepped forward. "Don't."

Hattie held her off with a palm. "I have to, Maria. I have to come clean."

"She's not worth it," Maria muttered.

Betty's eyes were wide. "Your guard dog is probably right. Whatever you're dangling, here…keep it to yourself."

Hattie stared at Betty. Her words feigned disinterest, but the woman's eyes were hungry for whatever secret Hattie had in store.

"I do want a free pincher state," Hattie said. "A place to live not just free, but equal. I'll never get that done without the trust of my fellow pinchers."

Hattie waved a hand over the front of her body, disassembling the Brigid O'Toole illusion. The light snapped back into clear focus around Hattie to reveal her true form. Grimy overalls snapped over a working shirt. Boots. Shoulder-bobbed hair of straight red. Freckles. No glamor, just Hattie.

Betty's jaw slackened a little as she took in the woman suddenly standing before her.

"This is who I really am," Hattie said with her softer, American-toned accent. "My name is Hattie Malloy, and I'm a light pincher."

Betty's eyes drifted from Hattie's chin to her boots and back again.

Maria balled a fist, ready for Betty to snap.

"I'm no gangster," Hattie added. "I'm one of you."

The glass pincher nodded to herself as she looked away, staring at one of her figurines on display. The silence hung like a lead blanket for a full minute.

Finally, Hattie muttered, "Say something, will you?"

"I knew," Betty whispered. "I knew there was something wrong with you." She looked back at Hattie. "Something about the way you held yourself. I couldn't figure it out until now."

"Held myself?" Hattie asked.

Betty reached for her glass, pounded it, then stood to refresh her drink.

"I've been around bloodthirsty bastards my whole life, Miss O'Toole." She winced. "Wait, what was it?"

"Malloy."

"Men absolutely stand in line to treat me like garbage. I'm a collector. Connoisseur, maybe?" She poured a finger of clear hooch, then lifted it to stare at it. "You didn't have that look. Even with your…whatever you do. You never pulled it off. You're not a killer."

Hattie glanced at Maria, who simply shrugged.

Betty huffed, then set down the glass. "This rotgut won't do. Come on."

"Come on…where?" Hattie asked.

"There's a speakeasy just a few blocks from here. They keep some Canadian liquor under the deck and they're all terrified of me."

"You want to go drinking?" Maria grumbled.

"Hey," Betty asked with a whip of her head. "Can you pinch up some good steppin' out dresses?"

* * *

THE SPEAKEASY WAS dark and humid, a hole carved out of the dirt beneath a tenement. The door was little more than a few sheets of corrugated tin held together with screws. When Betty showed up, the doorman stepped aside instantly. It was clear she was a regular, and that the proprietor wasn't too happy about that.

Betty marched into the dank space, flourishing the illusionary gown Hattie had pinched around her. She was owning the illusion like a Long Island heiress, lifting her nose specifically to look down it.

"Three whiskeys, Klaus," Betty shouted to the thin, elderly man standing behind two barrels in the corner. "The reserve."

The man eyed the women, frozen in disbelief.

Betty snapped her fingers. "Schnell!"

The old man hopped to, reaching for the bottom of the barrel to produce a labeled bottle of Canadian whiskey.

Betty muttered, "Most of the clientele are German immigrants. They're accustomed to a certain quality of booze, but they don't have two pennies to rub together. So, you get this little diamond in the rough."

The man poured whiskey into three shot glasses, handing them over before withdrawing like a whipped dog.

Betty cackled at the old man before lifting her glass. "To three boozy broads on a bender!"

Hattie and Maria exchanged patient glances before shooting the whiskey with Betty.

"You're in high spirits," Hattie muttered. "Or is it just the spirits talking?"

"Oh," Betty harrumphed as she reached for the bottle on the barrel to carry it to the rear of the speakeasy. She dusted off the top of a shipping crate and sat cross-legged as she poured herself more whiskey.

Maria held out her glass, glancing at Hattie as Betty filled it. "What? She's buying."

"We're here on business," Hattie declared.

"This is how I do business," Betty replied. "So. Getting both of the big bosses in one room. That was you?"

"It was a group effort," Hattie admitted.

With a squint, Betty muttered, "Yeah. You got your mitts on Calendo?"

Maria nearly choked on her sip of whisky. She rubbed her nose with a wince as she avoided Hattie's glare.

Hattie grumbled, "He's on the team."

Maria added, "Is he on top or bottom?"

Betty blinked rapidly as Hattie gave Maria a shot to the ribs.

"We have an arrangement," Hattie said, "with Luciano."

"That snake?" Betty chuckled. "Don't hold your breath."

"What does that mean?" Hattie asked.

"He's a shifty one. Likes to pitch people against each other, let them hack each other off at the knees while he ends up on top."

Hattie nodded. "That's the general plan, here."

"Well, that's fine and good if you don't give a rat's ass about New York City. But whatever you get out of this deal, you'd better be ready for disappointment."

Hattie and Maria exchanged glances, then Hattie replied, "We'll be ready, then."

Betty nodded and sighed wistfully. "I've been looking forward to killing Maranzano ever since he snatched me out of Ithaca."

"Well," Hattie muttered, "I hope you don't have your heart too set on that. I'll need you on Masseria."

"Why can't I kill Maranzano?"

"We have to think long-term. When Luciano takes over, he'll inherit whatever mess we leave him. If it's true what you say and getting him to support us after this is over is a long shot at best, we'll need to cinch up those odds best we can."

Betty scowled. "Then who's greasing Maranzano?"

Maria leaned back with a weary sniffle. "I think you know."

Hattie nodded. "Vincent."

Betty crossed her arms. "See, that right there's the catch to this whole thing."

Hattie shook her head. "I've heard all about you and Vincent, and what they did to the two of you in Ithaca."

"Two of us? He got off easy. They practically gave him breakfast in bed while they—"

"It's possible your memory of the events has become clouded," Hattie pressed. "Besides, the inequity of your suffering was their way of manipulating the two of you. Don't saddle Vincent with the blame, here. You want to murder someone, then when we have our free pincher state, you can go find this bastard Sebastian yourself. Hell, I'll even help."

Maria nodded. "We'll all help."

Hattie pressed her finger into the top of the barrel. "But for right here, and right now? I need you. And I need to trust you around Vincent."

Betty eyed the two women with simmering resentment. She finally reached for the bottle and refreshed their glasses. "I could lie to you and tell you sure. Peachy keen. I'll be a good little girl and play nice. But you came clean with me, so I'm going to come clean with you. There's no world in which I'll forgive Vincent Calendo. And I know myself. I'm in a chatty mood right now but come tomorrow I'll be just as likely to get the storm clouds."

Hattie peered at Betty as she finished pouring and popped the cork back into the bottle.

Betty concluded, "But, you did save my life on the bridge. That deserves something. So, best I can do? I'll try. That's a pledge, not a promise. Because I want these sad sacks to pay for what they've done." She lifted her glass. "If you can live with that, then I'm in."

Hattie sighed, staring at the glass.

Maria lifted her glass. "That's all I gave you, Hattie. And it's all you've needed."

Hattie nodded, reached for her glass, then lifted it to clink against the others.

"Right, then. To us gangster girls."

There was far more traffic on the street in front of the Julietta Club than Vincent felt comfortable with. The meeting was set late at night, partially to help sidestep the fuzz, but also to minimize any bystander injuries. Bullets would be flying and keeping the fight inside the club was a best-case scenario. But for a Thursday night closing in on the witching hour, there was a solid stream of cars and sporadic foot traffic flowing past the venue.

"What is this, rush hour?" Vincent grumbled as Lefty shifted in the car seat beside him.

"We're close enough to downtown," Lefty said. "This is gonna keep up."

Buddy peered between the two from the rear seat. "What's the problem? This is just some meet, right?"

Vincent held his tongue. Buddy was still under the impression that they were there as backup for the Masseria-O'Toole meeting, keeping an eye out for trouble. Unlike Vincent, Buddy was unaware that trouble was already on the way.

"Can't be too careful, kid," Vincent muttered.

"Is that her?" Buddy asked, pointing to a figure strolling up the lane for the front door of the social club.

Vincent spotted Hattie. He wondered as she glanced up and down the street, what it was the others saw. A second figure joined her. Maria. She wore an evening gown, and her sinewy shoulders and arms seemed poised for a fight.

"That's the one," Lefty answered. "And probably one of her pinchers to boot."

"Earth pincher," Vincent muttered. "Keep your feet underneath you."

"You know her?" Buddy asked.

"I do." Vincent turned to scowl at Buddy. "She's not trouble, so don't get trigger-happy."

Buddy nodded. "I'm never trigger happy. Can't afford to be."

"I hear you," Vincent replied, turning back to the club.

The two women entered, glancing over their shoulders as they filed inside.

"And here we go," Vincent declared, leaning back in his seat.

Buddy eased back as well, shifting as he sighed. "I hate waiting."

Lefty offered, "If we're lucky, that squeeze pincher with the hat will have found Maranzano by now. It's just politics, now."

Buddy sniffled. "Even worse."

"Which means," Lefty added, "we're almost done here, and we can get back to Baltimore."

Vincent considered that notion as he kept an eye out for Maranzano's troops. Going back to Baltimore. What would that be like? What would become of the Crew when Luciano took over? Would he follow through on his end of the deal? Or was this yet another scheme of Floresta's?

They sat for a while. Vincent checked his pocket watch

for the time, giving it a wind to make sure he kept his bearings. Buddy became increasingly restless, as did Vincent as the midnight hour had passed without Maranzano. Something was wrong.

Lefty lifted his chin. "You boys feel that?"

Vincent glanced at Lefty, then to Buddy. "Feel what?"

The suspension of the car began to rock. Vincent pressed his hands against the steering wheel.

Buddy whispered, "Did you say earth pincher?"

Vincent pushed open the car door. "Come on!"

* * *

"YOU SEE THEM?" Hattie asked, keeping her eyes discreetly forward.

"Vincent and his handler?" Maria replied. "I do. Alley across the street."

Hattie approached the storefront door for the Julietta Social Club, her Brigid O'Toole illusion firmly stitched around herself. "If they're still staking the joint, that means Maranzano hasn't shown his hand yet."

Maria lingered by the door. "You want me inside or out?"

"Best come in," Hattie said. "We want to show a greater force than we have."

"We're faking it, is what you're saying."

"Welcome to the last twenty years of my life." Hattie took another look up the road for Maranzano's men before stepping into the social club.

The interior was nothing like her last visit when she'd plied Catena for interest. There was no music. Not even a puff of tobacco smoke. The tables had been cleared, most of which were pushed aside to create a space in the middle of the room. A single table remained, with Joe "the Boss" Masseria seated. A throng of guards stood along the perimeter of the room, hands crossed in front of them, jackets unbuttoned for easy access to weapons. Catena stood behind Masseria like a buzzard, watching with interest as Hattie approached.

"Gentlemen," she declared as she stepped into the room, offering a half-bow to Masseria. "Mister Masseria, I presume?"

Masseria glared at her, his pudgy cheeks pushing his eyes into a squint.

Catena cleared his throat. "Miss O'Toole." He gestured for a seat at the table. "If you would? Your pincher may remain by the door."

Hattie nodded to Maria, then willed her feet forward to approach the table. Masseria shifted uncomfortably as she took a seat.

"I understand you're in need of my pincher assets?" she began.

Masseria's face soured as she spoke. He turned to nod over his shoulder at Catena.

Catena replied, "An opportunity has presented itself, one which may benefit our organization."

Hattie nodded. "I'm aware of the state of things after your dust-up on the Brooklyn Bridge. More than half the city's been on about't."

Masseria cleared his throat. "Do you have *stregone*?"

She straightened a little, validated now that Masseria had deigned to actually speak to her. "I do."

"How many? What is their witchcraft?"

Hattie allowed herself a smile inside her illusion. The man was irrepressibly Old World. "Four in the city now, with access to four more if needed. For a price, of course."

Masseria waved a hand in front of his chest with a single swipe. "Money is no issue."

"And," Hattie added, "this is not a sale of assets. This is a temporary loan, a limited partnership, yes?"

Masseria nodded once more.

"We've spoken at length regarding your plans in Baltimore," Catena said. "Beyond the current deal, I wondered if we might open up the conversation to discuss a possible role you might have within our organization. That is, should you be dissuaded from wasting your talents in Baltimore."

"My assets, you mean?" Hattie said.

"No. *You.* Your talent for misdirection, for weaving, as it were, a semblance of what you'd like us to see."

Hattie struggled to keep her breathing even. He couldn't…there was no way he could know. Holding her illusion of O'Toole tight, she shook her head. "I don't follow."

"Your abilities, my dear," Catena added with a smirk. "Your…magical abilities."

Hattie eased back in her seat, desperately hoping he was fishing and that she could somehow bluff her way out of this.

"I'm afraid you've taken a wild notion, Mister Catena," she drawled.

"Have I?" His smirk turned into a sneer, his eyes hard.

Maria edged closer to the table, but four nearby gunmen drew weapons on her. Hattie lifted a hand behind her, keeping her eyes square on Catena. Out of the corner of her vision, she saw Maria lift her hands and step backward to press her back against the wall.

Catena nodded toward Maria. "You'll keep your ground-pounder on a leash, now?"

Hattie clenched her teeth. "What are you on about?"

Masseria spoke, "You are *stregone.*"

"No," she declared with a vigorous shake of her head. "You're mistaken."

Catena snickered, walking around the table. He pulled a

red blossom from his own lapel, giving it a sniff as he paused in front of her. "Am I?"

He reached down with the flower, slipping its stem directly through the button hole of her blouse. As he stepped away, the realization sank in. He'd seen through Hattie's illusion to land the flower so perfectly. He had to, because Bridget O'Toole was wearing a fringed dress, with no buttons or buttonholes.

"Why not show us your true face, Miss O'Toole. And your lovely red hair," Catena said as he returned to the other side of the table.

Hattie sucked in panicked breaths. He knew! How long could he see through her illusions? How had he done it?

She peered over her shoulder at Maria, whose face was calm. Almost meditative. The woman's fingers tapped against the wall behind her in tiny rhythms.

Hattie set her jaw, turned back to face Catena and his master, and dropped her illusion. "Right, then," she grumbled. "I suppose the jig's up."

* * *

VINCENT AND BUDDY rushed across the street. Lefty lingered behind, eyes to the north. A line of cars approached, swerving recklessly as they skidded to a halt in front of the Julietta. Lefty lunged for the street, dropping into a roll as gunmen poured out of the cars. Maranzano had arrived.

Vincent braced, pulling Buddy behind him as guns whipped into the air. One gunman lifted a pistol at Lefty, pulling back the hammer.

Vincent pinched time, plowing through the time bubble for the gunman. He snatched the gun from his hand, twisting him around to face the others as he pressed the pistol against the back of his head and released the time pinch.

The gunman staggered, then stiffened as he got his bearings.

Vincent shouted, "You boys need to take a breath."

A lean figure stepped from the last car, white coat draped over his shoulders, crepe-paper eyes wrinkled in a disapproving squint.

Maranzano.

Polizzi stepped up alongside him, shoving arms down. "Easy, now."

Vincent took a breath, then released his grip of his hostage as guns began to drift to the ground.

The sound of a gunshot echoed across the street. Red blossomed over the cream-ivory vest covering Maranzano's chest. The old man staggered backward, caught by his closest thug. His face drained of all color, leaving him slack-jawed and pallid as his arms dropped to his sides and his weight fell dead into his enforcer's grip.

The entire street went silent. Vincent turned to spot Buddy, with his revolver lifted and still smoking.

"Shit!" Vincent pushed his hostage in front of him as the space in front of the Julietta erupted in gunfire. He pinched time once again, still staring at Buddy's enthusiastic face, the ends of his mouth lifting in triumph. Slugs hung suspended midair, some only inches away from Buddy's head. Vincent gripped the youth's arm, dragging him toward the pavement to avoid the crossfire.

As Vincent secured him close to the ground, he glanced up to find Lefty frozen in the time pinch halfway to his feet. Bullets were a mere hair's width from his midsection. Vincent dove through the murky air, snatching Lefty by the leg to fold him backward away from the bullets.

As Vincent coasted through the time-frozen space, he misjudged the angle he had taken, and as Lefty fell clear of the salvo, Vincent's sleeve made contact with one of the slugs hanging in its slow, rifled spiral. The full force of the gunshot translated instantly into Vincent's arm, pulling him out of the time pinch. Vincent twisted sideways as time restored its flow.

Bullets whizzed by his head as he hurtled through the air. Heart racing, he managed to get a grip of his wits and pinched time once again.

Reaching out, Vincent pushed himself upright, then grabbed Buddy and Lefty by the collars to haul them back toward the Julietta's front door. The effort of his time pinch tugged heavily on his chest. He had to get them out of the line of fire and into the building.

Although he was fairly certain what they were going to face inside wouldn't be any better.

CHAPTER 26

"When you sauntered into my office," Catena announced with a grin that oozed smug self-importance, "we were in need of additional magical assets. And now, through your interference I suspect, we are in yet greater need. How appropriate, then, that you should fill that need."

Hattie stood up. More guns trained on her.

Catena lifted both hands. "Stand down, boys. No damaging the merchandise."

Masseria stood, straightening his clothes as he turned with disinterest for the back of the club. "Deal with this. Report when it's done."

Catena nodded, then turned to face Hattie. "For what it's worth, my dear…your talent is considerable."

Hattie glared. "Refer to me as your dear one more time. Please."

"Or what?" Catena countered, taking a step forward. "You'll disappear? Turn into one of my soldiers in an attempt to confuse? Or will you somehow pull a gun on me, though I can obviously tell you are unarmed?" He glanced up to

Maria. "Or are you relying on your sole compatriot to save the day? An earthquake, perhaps? Please."

He was right. She'd grown accustomed to the safety of her illusions. Now that she had been laid bare as if her powers didn't even exist, Hattie felt so very small. So impotent. Unable to save herself, and worse…unable to save Maria.

She gauged her situation carefully. Surrounded by guns. Her illusions didn't work. Maranzano hadn't arrived to open Pandora's box with Masseria…the latter of which was about to make his escape through the kitchen.

This was a desperate moment. She had to do something. For Maria. For Vincent.

Just as she prepared to dig into the floor and lunge for a gun nearby, the air turned suddenly turbid. Hattie paused, glancing back and forth. No one reacted. She was alone inside a time bubble.

Vincent!

Even Catena seemed trapped in the time pinch. However it was that he'd seen through her illusion, it didn't seem to be working on Vincent.

She took advantage of the moment, moving back toward Maria. Unfortunately, the time bubble dropped before she could reach her earth pincher. The gunmen jumped as she materialized in front of them. Guns lifted.

Maria started. Then, a gunshot echoed through the air—outside the building.

Time pinched again. Whatever had happened outside, Vincent was in trouble. She felt this deep within her chest. He needed help. But then, so did she.

Hattie plowed forward, snatching guns out of the grips of nearby thugs, leaving them to hang suspended midair as she cleared Maria from imminent danger. She heaved against her friend, pulling her toward the center of the room.

Time restored its normal flow, sending the woman tumbling into the center of the Julietta, just as a pandemonium erupted outside the front doors.

The Masseria people ducked in response, twisting toward the front of the club and grabbing the guns that had clattered to the floor. Hattie peered up toward the kitchen, and the doors that swung on their hinges. Masseria had escaped. It was over before it started. She reached back to Maria, who gripped her hand with rapid breath.

"What's…happening?" Maria gasped.

Hattie grabbed her and dove to the floor. Some of the gunmen were hugging the wall, peering at the windows to see what was going on and gauge the threat, but others had turned their weapons toward Maria and Hattie. Just as she tensed for what seemed to be an inevitable death, the kitchen door opened.

Masseria eased backward, toe-to-heel, arms lifted in the air. As he cleared the far column by the kitchen, Hattie could make out the figure of Betty Sharp following him with a particularly savage length of glass arcing from her grip, its razor edge against Masseria's throat.

"Oh, where are you going?" Betty purred with a tight smile. "Running off like a rat? Did you ever think in a hundred years that it'd end like this? Some crazy pincher in a closed-up bar?"

Hattie got to her feet, she and Maria edging out of the line of fire. Glancing to her left, she noticed that Catena had disappeared.

Betty laughed. "There's literally no way you're clawing your way out of this today. This is the day you die. How does that feel, knowing that?"

Masseria glared at her. "You'll die, too."

Betty shrugged. "Oh, that's a given. And I don't care. You want to know why? Because right here, right now, there isn't a man or woman alive who can stop your death. It's inevitable. I hold it in my hand." She eased the glass blade up to touch the bottom of Masseria's chin. "I have all the power, and you are powerless to stop it."

Masseria sputtered for a second and Betty's eyes shifted toward Hattie, lifting in triumph—triumph that immediately dissolved into alarm.

There was a *thunk* and Hattie saw Maria pitch forward onto the floor, landing hard at the same time a hand slipped around Hattie's throat, and she sucked in a gasp just as a gun barrel pressed against her right temple.

Catena's voice boomed from behind her, so loud she could feel his breath. "Drop the glass!"

Betty halted, as did Masseria. Hattie struggled for breath, choking a little as Catena's fingers tightened over her throat.

"Drop it!" Catena repeated.

The gun pressed harder against Hattie's head. What illusion could save this? Would it work? Clearly, no. Hattie was utterly prone and helpless. There was nothing she could do.

Betty eased her blade a little higher, forcing Masseria to lift his chin. "You drop yours, big boy."

"You want this bitch to die?" Catena snarled.

Betty snorted. "You think I care about her?"

The pressure eased on Hattie's temple as Catena sucked in a breath.

Betty added, "I don't know her. All I know is that your boss is a dead man."

Catena pulled back the hammer, dropping the gun to the middle of Hattie's back. "I've done the math. You're a pincher whom no one can collar. This illusionist is gathering an army of pinchers. And now you show up...and I'm supposing that's Maranzano's men outside. You may be able to bend glass to your will, but you'll never outthink a man like me."

Hattie's face grew red as a ball of anger swelled inside her stomach. For a second, she wished Betty would simply kill Catena, even if that meant she would die.

But then, where would that leave Vincent? Or Maria? Or everyone else in the Charge?

Or her parents?

Tears threatened to blur Hattie's vision as Catena dug the gun into her spine. Betty's face, on the other hand, betrayed nothing but her usual confidence.

Slowly, Betty lowered the glass blade, her face darkening.

The pressure on Hattie's spine eased.

"Drop it!" Catena barked.

Masseria took that moment to slip behind three of his gunmen who formed a human shield.

Maria slapped her hand against the ground and Hattie braced for some seismic event—a spike of granite or a crevasse opening up to swallow the Julietta Social Club. But no. Nothing happened.

Catena chuckled. "Drop that blade," he said. "And I'll make this quick."

Betty glanced at Hattie and the two locked eyes.

Masseria was there, the thickness of one man's chest away from death. Betty could cut the guard in half easily and still slice Masseria's throat. Hattie knew that. Betty knew that. Every man gathered there, including Masseria's bodyguard, knew that.

But Betty's eyes were planted hard on Hattie.

Catena shook his head. "You women. Make up your mind, already."

Betty set her jaw. And with a deft motion, swung the glass blade into the air in an underarm pitch. The glass split into three dozen smaller blades, all slicing through the air in a cloud descending onto Catena.

Hattie wanted to close her eyes and brace for the

inevitable. But she couldn't. There was something in Betty's glance that communicated a sentiment that was…human.

The glass blades arced through the air in a giant cone, all coalescing onto Hattie and Catena. Even Maria rolled aside to duck the impending doom.

As the glass reached a space roughly two feet away from the two of them, it pulverized into dust. Simply…disintegrated. Each blade slapped against a sort of barrier, the resulting sand splashing and falling along an invisible sphere before creating tiny dunes on the Julietta floor.

Betty's eyes widened, and she took a step back.

Masseria bowled past his human shield, knocking Betty Sharp to the ground as he dove through the kitchen doors. Catena released Hattie, sending her pitching to the sand on the floor alongside Maria as he stood up with a grin.

"Now," he declared. "It's my turn."

He lifted his gun.

* * *

VINCENT RELEASED HIS TIME BUBBLE, tumbling over Lefty. The three scrambled for cover as Maranzano fell limp atop the thug trying to catch him.

Buddy crawled alongside Vincent as they took shelter beside the Julietta doors. "I got 'im!" he shouted over the gunfire. "Got the rat bastard!"

Vincent clenched every muscle in his body, trying not to panic. The youth had dropped Maranzano ahead of schedule. It was supposed to be Vincent, but that had been a maybe. The biggest problem was that the act had happened ahead of schedule. Right now, the entire apparatus of the New York gangster community hinged on whether Masseria was still alive.

Lefty pulled on the doors to the Julietta. They clunked against a deadbolt.

"It's locked!" he shouted over the gunfire.

Vincent groaned in frustration. The last time pinch had drained him. He could pull one more out, if need be, but once that was done, there would be nothing left and he wanted to reserve that last-ditch pinch for when he laid eyes on Hattie.

The ground pounded, lifting each of the Baltimore boys into the air only to send them hurtling to the ground in a jolt. Vincent shook his head as he caught his breath. He glanced up to find the doors to the Julietta hanging askew.

"Go!" he yelled.

Lefty kicked one door open with his heel and Buddy tumbled over him, rolling into the space with Vincent diving after him. The gunfire on the street continued, muffled as Vincent pulled the door closed behind them. He spun on his knee to find the Masseria crew with guns lifted at him.

"Whoa!" he shouted.

Catena stood, visibly trembling as he gripped a gun at arm's length. A pile of sand surrounded the man in a queer style of dune.

That's when Vincent spotted Hattie. She eyed him with panicked eyes, clearly in trouble. Then Vincent followed Catena's gaze to Betty Sharp. The glass pincher stood unarmed, completely wilted save for the flicker of anger shining in her eyes as she stared down the barrel of Catena's gun.

Damn it to hell. He'd been saving this last reserve of time pinching for Hattie. But what could that accomplish now? Without a second thought, Vincent paused time as Catena's finger pulled back on the trigger.

Time froze around the pistol as the plume of muzzle flare billowed like silk from the weapon. Hattie turned on her knee and plunging through the time bubble for Maria, jerking the other woman off the ground with effort.

Vincent's guts twisted as Hattie struggled to haul Maria across the time-frozen room. He couldn't move. Any stutter in his posture would reveal his complicity with Hattie and Betty Sharp. Now that Maranzano was dead, that was no longer an option.

Hattie cradled an arm around Betty Sharp, grimacing as she lugged her two compatriots through the double doors into the kitchen and out of sight. Vincent gave them as long as he could before releasing his time pinch.

The retort from the gun echoed in the room, and the bullet struck the far wall. Catena lowered his gun, eyes searching the room as something heavy pounded on the doors.

Vincent staggered into the room toward Lefty and Buddy. "He's dead," he gasped at Catena. "Maranzano."

Buddy lifted his gun, his mouth wide in an excited grin. "Went down like a sack of apples, boys!"

Another slam against the front door and Masseria's men turned to train their weapons at the commotion.

Lefty eased alongside Catena. "What about Masseria?"

Catena cleared his throat, holstered his weapon, then straightened his suit. "Safe."

"And O'Toole?" Lefty pressed.

Vincent watched with interest as Catena ran a finger beneath his nose with a sniffle.

"She no longer matters."

* * *

HATTIE TENDED to Maria as Betty stood next to her in the alley behind the Julietta. Gunfire sounded from within the building, but the end result had already been determined. Maranzano was dead and Masseria had escaped.

And Catena had seen through Hattie's illusions since day one.

"What the hell happened?" Betty asked, wiping the blood from her nose. "And how did Catena do that to my glass?"

"I don't know," Hattie replied. "But it's all gone wrong. Everything. Horribly wrong. And I'm not sure there's any way we can fix it."

CHAPTER 27

$\mathcal{A}$ weary celebration filled the Bank as men lifted flasks to Joe Masseria, the *Capo di tutti Capi*. Bandages adorned arms, still bloody from gunshot wounds. Their numbers were thinner now—even thinner than after the Brooklyn Bridge fight. But Maranzano had fallen and Masseria remained. Victory, costly though it was, belonged to them.

Floresta wove through the throng, eyes set and narrow. He swept up to Vincent who leaned against a desk.

"A word?" Floresta demanded.

Vincent nodded, pausing to give Lefty a warning glance as Floresta led him out the rear door into the trashcan alley.

Floresta spun on a heel, thrusting a finger into Vincent's face. "Well, you've all gone and cocked this up!"

"Blame Catena," Vincent snapped. "We did our part. Catena had an ace up his sleeve. That's what caused all this."

"Yeah. And that's what I'm talking about. Don't tell me for a second that O'Toole isn't one of your people."

Vincent sighed. "She was part of the plan. Backup."

Floresta shook his head in bewilderment. "It was damned

stupid, is what it was. Now Masseria has absolute rule, and Luciano's still third in line."

"We can salvage this," Vincent muttered, exhaustion overtaking him.

Floresta waved his hands in the air. "Forget it. Catena has focus, now. The window has closed."

"Nothing has closed. Masseria's still down to one pincher. We outnumber—"

"You don't get it, Calendo! This had to go down a specific way. Now, if we gun down Masseria, the rest of the families will point the finger at Luciano and pop off a whole new war for the city."

Vincent shrugged. "This was a long shot to start with. You knew that."

"Yeah," Floresta snapped. "I did. But it's over now. You people will get your marching orders soon enough."

Floresta turned to leave, but Vincent grabbed his arm. As he pulled on the man to halt his exit, Floresta spun and slammed a fist into Vincent's jaw, sending him spinning to the pavement.

"Don't touch me," Floresta growled.

Vincent got to hands and knees, rubbing his jaw. "What about us?"

"What about you?"

"What happens to Baltimore?"

Floresta sneered. "Fuck Baltimore. Deal's off." Floresta paced a circle, taking breaths until he calmed a little. "Listen, your boy dropped Maranzano. That's going to smooth things out between Masseria and Corbi. He did you boys a favor. But…if you got any play in mind against the Crew, you can kiss that goodbye. Corbi's as good as in Masseria's pocket."

Vincent pulled himself to his feet, dusting off his trousers. "So that's it, then? Our asses are in the wind?"

Floresta glared at Vincent. "You'll land on your feet."

Floresta turned and tipped his hat. "I'll see you in the papers, Calendo."

Vincent stood hunched over, rubbing his face as Floresta made a brisk exit back to the front street. After taking a moment to will himself to walk, Vincent returned to the bank.

Lefty smirked at Vincent, pointing to Vincent's cheek. "You gonna need a steak on that?"

"You're a real comedian." Vincent looked around for Buddy. "Where's the kid?"

"Up in the office. He's getting a medal, or something. Pat on the back."

"He'll eat that up," Vincent muttered.

Lefty leaned in. "Miss Malloy is fine."

"I know."

"Wasn't sure if you were distracted by it."

Vincent peered at Lefty, then nodded once. "Thanks."

After a moment of foot-shuffling, Lefty added, "You need to go check on her?"

A wave of emotion swelled up through Vincent's throat, nearly bringing him to tears. "Didn't think it'd be a good time for me to be absent."

"Go," Lefty urged. "I'll cover for you. Wouldn't be the first time."

Vincent sucked in a breath, nodded again, then turned for the exit.

* * *

WIDOW DUNNE STOOD cross-armed at the top of the stoop, glaring at Vincent as he plodded up the stairs. He was drained of magic and couldn't pinch time to side-step the old woman.

"And what're you doing out at this obscene hour, then?" she asked with a frown.

Vincent sighed. "Is Miss Malloy in?"

"If she is, young man, I'm sure she's sound asleep by now. So, why don't you turn your arse back around and—"

A voice called from the door, "It's fine, Mrs. Dunne."

The widow turned to find Hattie haunting the doorframe, eyes heavy, skin pale.

"Fine, is it?" Mrs. Dunne squawked. "It's past two in the morning. I can't have boarders waking me up all hours like this. It's indecent."

Hattie stepped forward, resting a hand on the widow's shoulder. "Please, let my brother come up. We'll be quiet."

Dunne's eyes shot wide. "Brother?"

"Aye," Hattie sniffled.

"But…he's a guinea, isn't he?"

Hattie grimaced, then looked up at Vincent. "He's…he's my half-brother. He's been in America for the past ten years."

Dunne eased away from Hattie. "You listen to me, girl. I took you and your friend in because I felt sorry for ya. But I'm not here running no bordello. I won't have men visiting all hours, and I won't be lied to. I know a bloody gangster when I see one. And I have no patience for that sort of violence here. You go on up and pack your things. I'll have you out. Tonight."

Hattie sucked in a breath to make her case, but thought better of it, choosing simply to agree.

Vincent waited on the street for almost a half hour until Hattie and Maria emerged with their suitcases, followed to Vincent's surprise by Betty Sharp.

Dunne closed and locked the door behind them, leaving the quartet on the street.

"Well," Vincent declared. "I suppose we'll need a cab."

"Where are we supposed to go?" Maria grumbled. "It's three in the morning."

"Come to the Monarch. The doormen there don't care if you're women."

Hattie shook her head. "That's Masseria's property, isn't it? Wouldn't that be the last place we'd want to be?"

Betty snickered. "Right. Which means it's the last place they'd look. Honestly, you people need to start thinking like gangsters if you want to play at being gangsters."

Vincent shrugged. "She's right. I'll put you up in my room."

"What about Lefty?" Hattie whispered.

"He'll be fine."

Maria asked, "And your sharpshooter?"

"Well, that's a different story," Vincent admitted. "But he's had an exciting day. I think he'll have put himself to bed before we even get there."

They managed a cab back to the Monarch, where Vincent escorted them through the front doors while keeping an eye on the street. Satisfied they'd avoided the notice of the Masseria crew, he led them to his room, unlocking his door and holding it open for the women. Hattie led the way, but halted directly in the door, causing Maria to nearly bowl her over.

"What?" Maria grumbled.

Hattie cleared her throat and said, "Good evening, Lefty."

Lefty nodded to her from the window. "Miss Malloy. You've been busy, I see."

The women shuffled into the room, now crowded with the extra company as Lefty leaned against the window sill.

Hattie and Maria set down their suitcases as Betty fished a cigarette out of her clutch. The glass pincher tossed herself onto the bed, leaning against the headboard as she motioned to Lefty.

"You got a light?"

Lefty reached into his pocket to produce his army lighter, tossing it to Betty.

Vincent shut the door, leaning against it with crossed arms. "The gang's all here, I suppose."

Hattie approached Lefty with head hung low. "I suppose I have some explaining to do."

"Don't bother with that." Lefty reached out to pat her on the shoulder. "I've pieced it together on my own. All except the part where your scheme flew to pieces."

Betty sighed. "It's obvious, isn't it? Catena played you people all along. All of you were supposed to die in that club. Me too, I suppose."

Hattie shook her head. "But how did that bastard see through my magic? Was it from the beginning?"

"Definitely," Betty replied with disinterest as she took a drag from her cigarette.

"Is it possible the man's a null?" Hattie asked. "Like that Scandinavian battle-axe at Ithaca?"

Vincent shook his head. "Catena froze up with the rest of the room when I pinched time. Whatever went wrong with your magic, it didn't save him from that."

Betty blew a thin stream of smoke into the air. "It's a pity I didn't get the chance to kill Gertha."

Vincent smirked. "She's taking a permanent nap at the bottom of a lake."

"Good for you," Betty quipped.

Lefty lifted his hand. "Once Masseria's people sober up, they'll realize they let two pinchers slip through their fingers. Then they'll turn the city inside-out looking for you. It's time we got you ladies back to Baltimore."

"What about Betty?" Hattie asked.

All eyes turned to the glass pincher, still lounging on the bed.

Betty rolled her eyes. "What? You want me to beg to come with you? Forget it."

Hattie said, "Now that Maranzano's dead, you'll be in trouble."

Vincent turned to Lefty, "In this whole stuffed-shirt system, what happens to pinchers when their gang falls to hell?"

Lefty replied, "Usually the assets are redistributed locally per family agreements. In a case like this, however, the spoils go to the victors."

"So, Polizzi's going to get rolled into Masseria's crew?" Vincent asked.

"That's likely," Lefty replied before turning to Betty. "You, on the other hand?"

Betty waved him off. "Suits me. I'd rather kill them all."

Hattie looked to Maria. "Your old Cleveland gang was massacred. Both sides, right?"

Maria nodded. "That's how Augustus ended up in New York. I took advantage of the confusion and made a run for it." She nodded to Betty. "That's always an option."

Betty sneered. "Run? Just when it's getting fun?"

"This is no joke," Hattie scolded. "They're going to hunt you down, Betty. And we need you."

"You don't get it! There's no hit on me. Not anymore." She eyed Maria and Hattie, then turned away. "I cut a deal."

"With whom?" Lefty asked.

"Catena. Who do you think?"

Hattie shook her head. "I don't believe you."

"Well, you should. Catena knew about you all along. Don't ask me how, but he knew." Betty wound around Lefty to stare out the window. "Henry found me two nights ago. Coulda had me, too. It would've been the end for Betty Sharp, but he had something to offer. A deal with Catena—a deal to serve you up on a platter. I do that, and he lets me walk."

"But you didn't serve me up," Hattie said. "You chose to save me, instead. Didn't you?"

Betty frowned, slipping her cigarette between her lips and looking away.

"That was a decision, Betty," Hattie pressed. "You chose me over freedom. You're part of something, now."

The glass pincher pulled the cigarette out of her mouth, sat up, then blew a line of smoke into Hattie's face. "I just got bored."

Maria reached out and knocked the cigarette out of Betty's hand. "Get over yourself!"

Betty jumped off the bed, hands in claws. "You want to try that again?" she snapped.

"She saved your life," Maria said. "On the bridge. Now, you've returned the favor."

"I guess that makes us even."

"It makes you more than that. I know it's important for you to be the outsider. You go out of your way to paint that picture, and that's fine. I was the same way not long ago. But I never stopped asking 'what's next?' You better start asking that question, Betty."

Betty wilted just a hair.

Vincent felt a jolt against his back, sending him stumbling forward.

The door eased open as Buddy peered inside. "Is this where the party is?"

The entire room turned to stare at Buddy, who took a careful step inside. He gripped a champagne bottle in one hand and a cigar in the other. His eyes drooped in boozy fumes.

But when those eyes found Betty, they shot open.

Buddy dropped the champagne bottle, sending it bouncing off the floorboards as he reached for his gun. He took aim at Betty, and his finger pulled back on the trigger.

The gun dry-clicked.

Buddy shook his head, lifting his gun to inspect it.

Vincent held up a flat palm, cradling six bullets he'd just plucked from the weapon in a time pinch.

"I'm sure you can still nail a target even when you're drunk," Vincent said. "So, I'm going to hold on to these until you sleep it off."

Buddy stared at the faces in the room. "What is this? Who are you people?"

"Associates," Lefty said as he pulled a chair from the tiny card table. "Why don't you have a seat, kid."

Buddy pointed to Betty. "She's with them. She's one of Maranzano's."

"Not anymore," Lefty replied. "Thanks to you."

He shook his head. "She's still the enemy."

Betty cackled. "Oh, see? He gets it."

Vincent picked the bottle off the ground, holding it up to the light. "Better not open this for a little bit. We'll all be wearing champagne."

Buddy stepped away from Vincent. "How can you…why's everyone making jokes?"

"You need to calm down," Vincent urged as he strode across the room to set the bottle onto the table. "The fight's over. And now the rules have changed."

Buddy held a hand to the side of his face, pressing his revolver against his own cheek. "I'm confused."

"Hey," Lefty said. "You did good tonight. Corbi's gonna be over the moon."

A flicker of a grin lifted onto Buddy's lips.

"But you really need to take a load off. Uncoil that spring inside your chest before you snap."

Buddy shuffled past the girls, wandering to the chair to take a seat.

Hattie said, "Right, well. Where does that leave us?"

Betty turned for the door. "Leave us? That sounds pretty good to me."

"Where are you going?" Maria asked.

Betty stabbed out her cigarette on the wall, dropping it onto the floor before reaching for the door knob. "Elsewhere. I don't feel like sharing a room with a psychopath."

She blew a kiss at Buddy.

"You don't have to leave," Hattie urged.

"Please stop. Stop…this. Stop trying to save me. It's annoying."

Hattie stepped past Vincent. "Then stay in town, at least one more day. Give me a chance."

Betty's eyes darted back and forth between Hattie's. She struggled for a comeback, some crack to give her distance. But nothing came.

Instead, she just nodded and left.

Vincent shook his head. "If she welshed on Catena, she's going to be worse off than before. He'll put her down like a rabid dog."

Buddy snickered. "Good."

Maria reached behind Buddy's head and gave it a solid slap.

"Ow."

"Leave this to the grownups," she chided.

Vincent said, "I hate to admit it, but Lefty might be right. It's time we got you two out of New York."

Hattie sighed. "But we're so close. I can't believe this was all for nothing."

"It's better than losing your life over a lost cause."

She blinked at his statement. "A lost cause? Is that what it is?"

Buddy blurted, "What're you talking about?"

Maria brandished the back of her hand, and Buddy lifted his hands in defense.

Vincent replied, "No, that's not what I meant. Floresta's pulled his support."

"What about Luciano?" Hattie asked. "Isn't he the one calling the shots?"

"I assumed Floresta was speaking for Luciano."

"How well do you think a man like Luciano appreciates having someone else make up his mind? A lot's changed in the past few hours. Give Luciano time to cool off. He'll want to save this. The bastard's too greedy to give up so easily."

Vincent looked to Lefty. "What do you think?"

"She's right," Lefty replied. "If you're utterly devoted to this, then sticking around until Luciano makes a new play isn't the worst idea. But he needs to know you're still on the table."

Vincent nodded. "I'll find him tomorrow. Get a word in without Floresta hanging onto his neck. I bet I can dangle the carrot."

Hattie laid a hand on Vincent's chest. "It's worth trying. This is bigger than any of us."

Vincent smiled, then peered at Buddy, who was admiring the hem of Maria's dress.

"What about him?"

Lefty lifted the champagne bottle. "I think maybe half a bottle, and he won't remember much."

Lefty dropped the bottle into Buddy's lap. "Come on, kid," Lefty declared. "You're going to share that champagne. And I'm going to tell you all about Cezanne's Orchids in White."

Buddy lumbered to his feet. "The what?"

"Cezanne, boy," Lefty explained as he held the door open. "His rumored Orchids in White, a painting that went missing during the War. Nicked from the Musee d'Orsay in the middle of the fighting." Lefty added as he closed the door behind them, "What if I told you I knew exactly where it is?"

Vincent took a seat on the bed. "Sorry I got you two thrown out of your room."

Maria sighed. "I'm exhausted."

Hattie nodded. "Aye."

"Listen," Vincent said. "I'm going to confiscate Buddy's room. Leave you two alone to get some rest."

Hattie reached for Vincent's hand, gripping it tight. "Please tell me there's hope."

He smiled at her and winked. "Always."

CHAPTER 29

*E*ven though Hattie didn't wake up in Vincent's arms like the last time they'd shared a room together, she still found herself blinking away the fog of sleep with gratitude. Vincent had spent the night in a chair by the door. As Hattie sat up in bed, stretching and noting how badly she needed a shower, Vincent stirred and slumped forward to rub his neck.

"Good morning," she whispered.

Vincent nodded, wincing at the stiffness he couldn't seem to work loose.

Hattie pulled herself out of bed, wandering over to the man to massage his shoulders.

Maria stirred on the bed, glancing in their direction with a sigh. "You two want privacy?"

Vincent groaned as Hattie hit a knot.

Hattie replied, "I'd rather clean up. This is a hotel, right? Hall bath?"

Vincent nodded without comment, pawing at her to keep rubbing.

Maria shuffled off the bed, straightening her dress that

she really shouldn't have slept in. Deep wrinkles had set in. That would be work getting pressed. But Vincent wouldn't leave the two alone with the entirety of Masseria's gang on the hunt, and Maria wasn't the sort to strip down with an audience.

With an eye-roll, Maria nudged past the two, reaching for the door. "I'll see if the bath's free." She opened the door and froze. "Uh, Hattie?"

Hattie turned to see that pinned in the center of the wood was a handwritten note.

"I think this is for you," Maria said as she pulled the paper off its pin and handed it over.

Hattie took the paper and Vincent stood, reading over her shoulder

Malloy,

Meet me at Grand Central.

Noon.

Just you.

Hattie squinted at the looping script. "What's the point in leaving ominous notes if one doesn't sign it?"

Maria gripped the pin still lodged in the door, gritting her teeth as she pried it loose. "It was Betty." She handed over the pin, a tiny glass bulb with a sharp, spiraling tail.

Vincent asked, "Why's Betty calling you out alone?"

"Search me," Hattie replied.

"Well, we can clear this up right now—you're not going alone," Maria grumbled.

Vincent nodded in agreement as Hattie shook her head.

"She's asked for just me. You both know this woman. She's smart. And if she sees either of you, she'll go to ground. No, I trusted her with my life before, and she came through. No reason she'd change that now."

"Sure there is," Vincent said as he stood up. "She said it herself. She cut a deal with Catena."

"A deal which she broke at the Julietta."

Maria said, "All the more reason to cut a new deal. This could be her way of serving you up to save her own skin."

"Didn't I just say she was smart?" Hattie retorted. "No way she'd be this ham-fisted if that were her plan."

Vincent nodded. "Good point. Besides, she'd just have shredded the door and throw glass at the problem, like usual."

Maria scowled. "I don't like this."

Hattie reached for her arm. "I'm going with my gut."

Maria nodded. "I'll…I'll check that bath."

As she left, Vincent faced Hattie to wrap his arms around her.

"No lectures?" she muttered.

"Just coming to this city meant taking risks," he said. "What's one more?"

"Do you think she's salvageable?"

"I think you're gonna try, no matter what I say."

She peered up at him with a reproachful scowl. "Well, you could answer my question anyway."

"She's disturbed," he said, pulling away. "Damaged… I don't know how to put it. Something's wrong with her, and if she were a regular person, she'd have gone to a doctor by now."

"She doesn't have doctors. All she has is us."

Vincent nodded. "I hope you can help. I just know I'm not the one to do it."

Hattie stepped up and kissed Vincent sweetly on the cheek. "Why don't you go see how much damage Lefty did to that boy?"

* * *

A HEFTY CROWD piled through Grand Central Station as the

noon hour arrived. Hattie stood on tiptoes, trying to peer over the shoulders of the crowd in search of Betty Sharp. Sunlight poured through the high windows running in lines on either side of the barrel dome overhead, slanting like buttresses of light through the cigarette smoke that swirled through the open space above. A man nearly stepped on Hattie's foot, lifting his hat with an apologetic nod as he swept past her.

This was as easy a place for Hattie to disappear as any. If need be, she could become anyone with a minimum of effort. Assuming, of course, that Catena's trick to seeing through her illusions wouldn't work in a place like this.

As the minute hand clicked past noon, Hattie became panicked. She couldn't find Betty amid the travelers—if she was there at all. Had something spooked her? Did Vincent or Maria end up following Hattie to the train station against her specific demands to the contrary?

Or were they correct, and this was just a trap?

Hattie moved for the stairs leading to the street entrance, climbing to the top to gain a better view. It was a give-and-take. She'd be better equipped to see Betty, but at the price of being more visible for Masseria's people. Surely, a train station would be high on their list of stakeouts.

Hattie squinted as she peered over the crowd. Nearly everyone wore a wide-brimmed hat, concealing their faces as she squinted through the hazy sunlight.

She nearly jumped out of her skin when someone tapped her on the shoulder.

Hattie spun around to find Betty standing in front of her in a lavender floral-print dress and a cloche perched atop a short-bobbed mop of brunette curls.

"You came alone." The woman grinned. "Thanks for that."

Hattie nodded as she regarded Betty's hair. "What happened to the blonde?"

"This is my idea of laying low."

"You look rather glamorous for laying low."

Betty shrugged. "Won't matter much longer."

Hattie shook her head. "What's this about? What's wrong?"

Even as Hattie asked the question, her gaze fell to the ground next to Betty, and the suitcase beside her feet.

Betty said, "I thought about what you said."

"I've said lots of things. Only half of which I regret."

"You'll regret this one." Betty tilted her head. "Seeing as I'm part of something, now."

"That's a good thing."

"Is it?" Betty turned away, looking at the travelers below. "And is it worth it?"

"Is freedom worth it? Through history, people have sacrificed their lives in pursuit of freedom. It's the only thing that matters."

Betty smirked. "That, and some quality gin."

"You have a place with us. If you want it."

Betty turned to Hattie. "I don't want it."

Hattie's face drooped.

"I wanted everything. I wanted to take control. I wanted people to respect me. Now? I just want to disappear. Thing is, I do want to be part of something." She gestured to the crowd below. "I want to be part of that. The faceless. There's freedom there."

Hattie shook her head. "There's only fear, there. Fear of being found. If you run, you never stop."

"I've spent my whole life fighting, Malloy. Look where it's got me."

"That's because you were alone. But you have us, now."

Betty smiled. "You're adorable, you know that? You should run for office one day, if you get your free pincher state."

"Please don't go," Hattie pleaded. "We need you."

Betty clenched the railing, her jaw working side-to-side.

Hattie added, "Just think of how heartbroken Vincent would be."

Betty bent over and laughed. "Oh, I'm sure. Who would he have to scare the wits out of him?"

"So, you'll stay?"

Betty peered through the long, vaulted space, and the lines of ticket tellers. "What do they say? Go West, young man?"

The two stood in silence for a long moment watching as people bustled in and out of the station.

"We send people to Utah," Hattie finally said.

"What's in Utah?"

"We call it Eden."

"A little obvious, isn't it?"

Hattie turned to face Betty. "If you make it to Eden, Utah, ask for a man named Orson. Tell him the Charge sent you. No, tell him I sent you."

"You know, that's fine and all, but I think I'll try Nevada."

"What's in Nevada?"

"Not Eden." Betty grinned.

Hattie nodded. "I suppose this is it, then?"

Betty nodded, then reached for her suitcase. "I'm not hugging you." Then she added with less sarcasm, "Good luck with your great plan. And tell Calendo I'm still coming for him."

The woman turned and marched down the steps, quickly fading into the throng below as if light had pinched her into oblivion.

CHAPTER 30

*V*incent grinned as Buddy stepped out of Floresta's car with a wince. The youth lifted his hand to shield his eyes as they gathered by a corner delicatessen bearing a white sign with "Dominick's" in wide red-and-green letters.

"You going to make it, kid?" Vincent chuckled.

"Shut…up," Buddy mumbled.

"Hero of the day. That comes with certain responsibilities."

"Shut…up."

Lefty shouldered Vincent. "Knock it off. He's doing you a favor, remember."

As they approached the deli storefront, Buddy wheezed, "What was in that champagne?"

"Suffering, son," Lefty replied as he held the door open.

They filed inside to find Luciano peering through the glass case at a slab of mortadella. The butcher handed over a paper-wrapped bundle, waving off Luciano as he tried to pay. When Luciano turned to spot the group, his eyes became razors.

"You," he stated.

Floresta swept around the Baltimore men, pointing to the back for the butcher to make himself scarce. Once they were alone, Floresta returned to the door to lock it.

Luciano leaned against the glass case, setting his meat aside.

"So," Vincent began. "Fifty percent success."

Luciano's face tightened. "You think this is a joke?"

"I do not."

"Maranzano was easy," Luciano snapped. "It was Masseria that was the task."

"Hey," Vincent grumbled. "We had everything set up. Things happen. The unexpected."

"*Si*," Luciano said, turning toward the case to distract himself. "This woman. She was unexpected. And she was not a part of the plan."

"What plan?" Vincent countered. "You left everything up to us. We had to come up with the plan."

"Exactly. And your plan failed."

Lefty lifted his chin. "What now?"

"Now," replied Luciano. "You leave. Go home."

"And Masseria?"

Luciano shook his head. "It is what it is. And there will be no second pincher for Baltimore." He added with a lift of his finger at Buddy. "In fact, I think I keep this one."

Vincent balled fists. "Like hell, you will!"

As Buddy paled, Lefty stepped forward.

"Vincent? Go watch the door."

Vincent spun on Lefty, his blood boiling. But as he glanced at Lefty's face, instead of the usual disdainful sneer he found a half-smile couched in a calm, confident face.

Vincent nodded and stepped away.

Lefty cleared his throat. "You're disappointed, I see that. But you don't get to make that sort of decision. I know you think very highly of yourself, but you're essentially just a handler. Like me."

Luciano scowled at Lefty.

"So," Lefty added, "shall we speak as men?"

Luciano released a long breath from between his teeth. "Let's."

"If Masseria goes back on his offer to Corbi, there will have to be an explanation. No second pincher? I can see you selling that. Things are tight. There were losses. No one would blame you. But if you renege on Buddy?" Lefty shook his head. "That communicates something dangerous."

Luciano pursed his lips, then nodded. "You understand such things. Perhaps you should join us?"

"I have a job, thanks."

Luciano waved his hand at Buddy. "Fine. Keep him. But you leave. Today."

"Are you sure?" Lefty asked. "You've come so close. I refuse to believe that a man like you doesn't have a backup plan."

"Perhaps I do. Perhaps it does not involve you."

Lefty shrugged. "So be it. Throw away an opportunity like this when you have pinchers at the ready. Your call." He turned to the others. "Let's go, boys."

Floresta eyed them all, waiting for some cue that never came. They lined up in front of the door, and finally Floresta unbolted the storefront.

"Unless," Luciano said.

They froze, and Vincent caught a triumphant smirk on Lefty's face.

"Unless, you have a way to deal with Catena."

Lefty turned back to face Luciano. "Giving up on Masseria, then?"

"Catena is a *porco*," Luciano spat. "Without him, I can take my time."

"He's clearly smarter than you," said Lefty. "That's not an insult, just a statement of fact. You need him gone. Then you're second in line and Masseria won't have anyone watching his back."

Luciano grinned. "So it is."

Lefty glanced back at the others, then said, "If we take care of your Catena problem, you'll take care of Masseria on your own time. And you'll leave Baltimore to us."

"Is this a question?" Luciano asked.

"It's terms."

Luciano thought it over. "Then, I accept these terms." He stood. "Masseria has a meeting tomorrow with the families to declare his title. Catena will be left behind to do the, uh… the accounting. There will be little guard. You will have this one chance."

Lefty sighed, then nodded. "In which case, we'll meet again in two days."

The Baltimore boys filed out of the deli, Floresta bolting the door once again behind them as they stepped into the sunlight.

"What just happened?" Buddy muttered.

"Lefty kept us alive." Vincent glanced back to Lefty as they walked up the street to hail a cab. "You don't have to do this."

"Clearly," Lefty answered. "But if you think I'm leaving you in Luciano's tender graces, you're exactly as stupid as you look."

"I hope you have a plan."

"When don't I?"

Vincent chuckled. "Sometimes I wish you were in charge of the Crew. You'd make a fantastic Capo."

Lefty grumbled, "That'd be the day. Watch the kid, will you? I gotta make a call."

Vincent nodded as Lefty withdrew to find a phone.

It almost felt like old times, the two of them. And Buddy makes three. How long would that last, Vincent wondered. When they got back to Baltimore, everything would change forever.

"I know this isn't what we wanted," Vincent said as he and Hattie stood one last time at the Red Hook wharf overlooking the bay. "It'd be easier if it was a sure thing."

"And if we had help," she added.

"So, Betty's gone for good?" he asked.

"I believe so. She found what she wanted. Well, maybe what she needed."

Vincent nodded. "You were right about her, I think. Maybe she'll turn into a human being one of these days."

"I wonder if we'll live long enough to see that?"

He turned her to face him. "Let's not assume the worst. Masseria's going to survive this. It's Catena we're after now."

Hattie frowned. "But what good will it do us? The gangs will still be in power."

"It helps to think of Masseria as another Vito Corbi. It hadn't occurred to me until I saw his gang in action, but he's no better than Vito. He relies on the men behind the throne. If we chisel away at them, he'll be another stuffed shirt whose name means more than he does."

"I hope you're right. And I hope this isn't some elaborate ruse from Luciano."

He squinted. "I thought we weren't assuming the worst."

"What about Lefty?" she asked, guiding Vincent back onto the street to walk back into Brooklyn. "Hasn't this pushed him too far?"

Vincent chuckled. "I think I wore him down. He's too tired to fight us on this. All the same, I'd rather keep him at a distance, if just to make sure we're not putting his neck on the block."

"What about the kid?"

"I think the past few days have served to dismantle some of the Ithaca doctrine. He's getting a healthy dose of the real world. With any luck, he'll choose to stick with the people who stuck with him."

Hattie lifted a brow. "And if he doesn't?"

"Well," Vincent sighed, "I guess we'll see."

They returned to the Monarch Hotel to find Lefty, Buddy and Maria huddled together over a table, the brilliant smell of bread, herbs, tomato and cheese filling the air.

Hattie's stomach grumbled. "What is that?"

"Pizza," Lefty told her. "Not the most elegant food, but it reminds of when I was a kid in Naples. I grabbed a couple in Manhattan, thinking everyone might be hungry."

Maria kicked a chair toward Hattie. "I keep telling you to eat. Now, you have no choice."

Hattie took a seat as Buddy handed her a half-folded slice. Vincent stood behind Lefty, who exchanged glances with Maria. Vincent lifted a brow at the two of them.

"Everyone playing nice?" Vincent asked.

Buddy pointed to Maria. "Did you know she's from Cleveland?"

"I did, actually," Vincent replied. "What, are you from Cleveland too?"

"Akron," he said. "Originally."

"Well, there you go," Vincent declared.

Hattie chewed, closing her eyes as she indulged in food for the first time in almost a day. The strain of the soul trap had eased over the past few hours as she spent time with Vincent. Her body responded by demanding sustenance and sleep.

As they ate, Hattie glanced back and forth at the faces too busy eating to talk, and a gloomy thought crossed her mind.

"Here, now," she muttered. "I do hope this isn't some Last Supper."

"Any of you planning to betray me for thirty pieces of silver?" Vincent quipped.

"Oddly messianic of you," Lefty said.

The others grinned at Vincent, who replied, "I have no intention of getting crucified today, thank you very much."

Buddy dropped a length of crust onto the table, leaning back with a thoughtful glance. "I have a question."

They turned to look at Buddy.

"Why're we doing this? This Catena fella. He's the number two, right?"

Vincent nodded.

"So, where's this comin' from? Corbi? Or Masseria? Because that mook at the deli didn't look like either of them."

Vincent lifted a hand. "Relax, it's all above board."

Lefty shook his head. "Don't lie to the kid."

Hattie straightened a little.

Lefty said, "We're taking out Catena to give Luciano a leg up. That's all."

Buddy's eyes narrowed. "That's not why we're here. Is it?"

"Long run, kid?" Lefty said. "It's exactly why we're here."

"The Capo didn't give us specific—"

"The Capo relies on us to be his eyes and ears. Sometimes

you gotta take the shot before being told to. That's real life, kid. You can't be sure all the time."

Buddy glanced down to his lap, frustration painted on his face.

Vincent sighed. "Look. I don't think you or Lefty should get involved with this."

"Oh," Lefty grumbled, "we're involved already."

"It's a simple hit. I can do this easier on my own."

Lefty rolled his eyes. "Would you shut up with this? If it was gonna be easy, Luciano would've done it himself. Right?"

Vincent thought about it. "I guess so."

"The three of us will go together. You'll want the kid there if things go south."

Hattie said, "Us, too."

Maria nodded. "All hands on deck."

Vincent fought off a lump in his throat as faces beamed at him. This was what *famiglia* was supposed to feel like.

"Okay, then," he said.

* * *

THE BANK LOOKED quiet from the street. Only a few lights were on downstairs, with the second floor dark. The usual cars parked in front were gone. The meeting to install Masseria as *Capo di tutti Capi* had drawn most of the muscle away, if not all. Vincent nodded to himself with satisfaction. The needling thought that Luciano was somehow setting him up was hard to shake.

"Looks good," Hattie whispered.

"I want you to stay outside. Catena's got some work-around for your powers. We can't risk it."

"Aye, but at the first sign of trouble, we're coming in to save you."

"Save me, huh?" he said with a smirk.

Hattie nodded to Maria. "The woman's kin to a general. You'll literally be calling in the cavalry."

Maria muttered, "He was regular army, not cavalry and definitely not a general."

Vincent turned to Lefty and Buddy. "Alright, you mooks. Ready for this?"

Lefty nodded. Buddy stood stiff-armed, face sour.

"I'll take that as a yes."

He gave Hattie a quick peck on the forehead. She reached for his head, pulling him in for a long kiss, gripping him hard.

When they parted, she muttered, "You be careful, boy-o."

"I will."

As Vincent turned to cross the street, Buddy said, "Wait. The two of yous are a couple?"

Lefty sighed. "The kid's finally caught up."

"Hey, it's not like you people tell me anything. I'm still not even sure who that woman is."

"Simple," Lefty replied. "She's the brains of this outfit."

"Alright, settle down," Vincent grumbled as they approached the front door to the Bank. "We go in like nothing's out of sorts, right? When we find Catena, I'll pinch time and…"

Vincent pulled a knife from his pocket, triggering the blade. It slung from the handle with a quick snap.

Lefty spied it. "You sure you want to do this? It's hands-on wet work. You're not used to that."

"I've killed before, Lefty," Vincent said. "I don't think I'll ever get used to it. But it's easiest this way. With luck, we'll be in and out before anyone notices."

"Suit yourself," Lefty replied.

Vincent eyed him for a half-second. There was a weird sort of finality in Lefty's words, as if something had finally come to a significant conclusion.

Vincent folded the knife, slipping it into his pocket as he pulled open the door to the Masseria headquarters. The rows of desks were empty and quiet, dark except for a few lamps left on. The mezzanine and upper offices were similarly dark. There were no voices.

Only footsteps.

The door to Catena's office opened and the man emerged, a stack of papers tucked in his hand. He paused as he spotted the Baltimore boys, giving them a cursory nod.

"Gentlemen," Catena muttered.

Vincent returned the nod. "Evening. Damn quiet in here."

Catena shrugged as he stepped to one of the desks to drop the papers into a drawer. "I could use the peace. You boys about to leave our fair city?"

"Baltimore calls," Vincent replied. "Looks like things are well in hand for you people."

Catena pulled a ledger book from the top of another desk. His eyes ran down the figures distractedly.

"Safe travels," he mumbled as he turned to his office, not even looking up from his book.

Vincent looked to Lefty, then Buddy. He gave them a nod, then pinched time.

The silence in the building barely shifted as the flow of time slowed to an imperceptible crawl. Vincent pinched his bubble wide enough to capture Catena. The man stood in the middle of the doorway to his office, book held in both hands, eyes buried in the figures.

This was it.

Vincent pulled the knife from his pocket, triggering the blade as he pushed his way between the tellers' desks. Step by step, he stalked toward the time-frozen Catena. His back was to Vincent. This was as simple as it could ever be.

Best to get this over with, then find a way to live with himself, just as he'd always done.

Vincent swam through the time bubble, pushing his legs against the turbid air until he reached Catena.

He lifted the knife, aiming it for the left of the spine. Straight through to the heart. One motion. That's all it would take.

A motion caught Vincent's attention. Catena's arm drifted to the doorway. Before Vincent could put together the impossibility of that motion, he felt a weight slam into his midsection.

Vincent dropped the knife as he doubled over, sucking in time-frozen air as Catena turned with the ledger book gripped in one hand, and a baseball bat in the other. He looked up to see Catena glaring dispassionately at him as he lifted the bat, swinging it hard against his shoulder.

Vincent tumbled to the side, his cheek smacking against the stone floor.

Pain shot like lightning through his arm as he coughed, struggling for air. His pinch faded, and the air ran thin once again. Footsteps clacked all around. Vincent gazed up at the mezzanine as gunmen poured out of Masseria's office, their weapons trained on Vincent.

He tried to push against the ground to a seated position, but Catena knocked his arm away with the baseball bat, sending him crashing onto his back.

Vincent glanced back at the front door, where Buddy was lifting his revolver at Catena. Lefty stood beside him, laying a hand on the kid's arm to lower the weapon.

"Easy, kid," Lefty said.

Vincent's brow creased as Lefty stared at him with emotionless eyes.

Catena cleared his throat as he stepped over Vincent to drop the ledger back onto a desk. He thumbed the ring on his left hand as he brandished the bat.

"Well, Mancuso," Catena finally said. "Looks like you owe me five dollars."

Lefty did not respond.

As Vincent glared up at Catena, the man explained, "He bet me a fin that you couldn't go through with it. But I know a killer when I see one."

Buddy glanced back and forth between Lefty and Vincent, face losing its color.

Vincent coughed, forcing air back into his chest from the blow he'd taken to his midsection. "How…how are you… doing this?"

Catena cocked his head in confusion before finally nodding. "Ah. Your powers."

He shook his left hand, fanning his fingers in and out. "These null trinkets from old Absalom do come in handy. They get blazing hot, though. Especially between you and Miss Malloy. Your powers are…considerable. Such a waste."

Vincent glanced back at Lefty one more time. A gunman approached Buddy with an outstretched hand. Lefty urged Buddy to surrender his weapon to the thug and as the thug turned around, Vincent recognized the face.

Pockets Polizzi.

The man slipped Buddy's gun into his endless jacket pocket, his expression blank.

Catena nudged Vincent with the toe of his shoe. "Get up. You're just in time for our meeting."

Vincent struggled to a seated position, cradling his shoulder.

Catena pushed the door to his office open. Someone was seated in front of his desk, back turned to Vincent.

"Shall we finalize the paperwork, Mancuso?" Catena called.

Lefty stepped through the Bank for the office, pausing as

Vincent finally got to his feet. He squinted at Lefty, words failing him.

Lefty nodded to the office and Vincent straightened up, turned to the office, then stepped inside, finally laying eyes on the man seated there.

"Tony?" Vincent gasped.

Tony glanced up at Vincent. "Heya, Vincent."

"What are you doing here?" Vincent blurted.

Lefty said, "I called him."

Vincent refused to look at Lefty, instead searching Tony's face for some meaning in all of this.

Catena took a seat behind the desk, pulling papers from his drawer. "Simple transaction. Masseria will absorb Maranzano's old Ithaca contracts. That'll be three more pinchers by year's end. In the meantime, due to your complicity with this…scheme of yours…Corbi has agreed to return Seiler to our organization."

Buddy shuffled into the office. "What's going on?"

Vincent shook his head. "You're getting sold, kid."

"Huh?"

Lefty turned to hush Buddy.

Vincent looked back at Tony. "This is true?"

"I, uh, I don't know what you've been doing here, Vincent. But it looks bad. Real bad. For the Crew."

Vincent nodded. Checkmate.

"What about me?" he muttered.

Tony replied, "You're being handed to us. For liquidation."

Vincent clamped his eyes shut. This was it. At least Hattie was safe.

Buddy shook his head. "Hold up. This isn't right."

Catena sighed. "I didn't ask your opinion, Mister Seiler. You'll report to Luciano in the morning for orientation. Mister Polizzi will accompany you."

"But…"

No one seemed eager to explain the situation to Buddy, least of all Vincent.

Vincent finally mustered the will to look Lefty in the eye.

"So, this is how it ends? Liquidation?"

"You had to know this was coming," Lefty stated. "I tried to warn you, but you seemed so committed to this lunacy."

"When it happens, will it be you?"

Lefty didn't reply.

Vincent pressed, "That's the least I could ask. That it be you to pull the trigger."

Catena declared, "Alas, that cannot be."

Vincent turned back to Catena as he signed the papers and stood up to hand the pen over to Tony.

"I'm afraid I must be the one to do the deed, if you will."

Tony sat forward. "The deal was we'd take him back to Baltimore."

Catena shook his head. "I understand this seems discourteous, but considering Mister Calendo's abilities, sending him with you will only facilitate his escape."

Lefty scowled. "You're worried he'll pinch time and run."

"I must keep him close," Catena said with a lift of his ring hand, "for this talisman to be effective. If I let him much more than five feet away, he's as good as gone."

Tony looked back at Lefty in frustration.

Catena snapped his fingers as two gunmen slipped past Buddy through the doorway. "Help me gather him. We'll take this outside…for the mess."

Lefty looked back at Polizzi and Buddy, eyes tracing a line from their position at the door along the floor tiles back to Catena.

"About five feet, you say?"

Catena lifted his brow. "What?"

"Five feet," Lefty repeated. "Or that ring on your left hand won't work."

"What are you—"

"Take it out, kid," Lefty said.

Polizzi reached into his jacket to pull Buddy's gun from his endless cache. He tossed the weapon into the air in front of Buddy, who snatched it deftly. He lifted the gun, pointed it level with Catena's hand where he was gripping the corner of his desk, and pulled the trigger.

The gunshot hammered in the room, and thugs drew guns.

Buddy pivoted left, then right. Two more shots.

Two bodies hit the floor.

Catena stood white-faced, head swiveling down to his hand. A pool of blood gathered on the desk top, leaking from the wound where his ring finger, and its talisman, once were. He sucked in a pained breath as he lifted the ruins of his hand.

Tony eased his foot away from the pool of blood dripping down the desk as he lifted the contract and tore it in half twice while Polizzi pulled a Tommy Gun from his jacket, angling it out the office door.

Buddy aimed the gun at Catena's blanched face. "Want me to finish it?"

Lefty stepped up to face Catena. "I think we should leave that honor to Vincent." He turned to Vincent with a grin. "Seems fitting."

Vincent shook his head. "What's going on?"

"Sorry, son," Lefty said. "Had to play this close to the vest."

Vincent released a single, disbelieving laugh. "Huh?"

Lefty explained, "We knew he had some way of nullifying pincher magic. Just didn't know how."

Catena gripped his hand tight to his chest, blood soaking his suit as he staggered back behind his desk.

Vincent put a hand on Lefty's shoulder, letting out a

pained breath as his shoulder throbbed. "You always have a plan, don't you?"

Catena dropped into his chair. "Y-you'll pay...all of you..."

Lefty lifted a finger to his lips in a shushing gesture. "Have some dignity, Catena."

"I'll have more than that." The man sneered.

He reached below his desk, hand gripping something out of sight.

Vincent pinched time as the front of the desk blew out in a shower of buckshot and splinters. Some of the wood made contact with Vincent's hand, sending the force into his arm. He maintained focus, however, grabbing Lefty by the shoulders and pulling him aside, free of the blast from the shotgun tethered to the underside of Catena's desk.

As Vincent released the time pinch, the blast filled Vincent's ears in a deafening roar. He landed on top of Lefty, who grunted as their weight smacked against the floor.

Buddy fired and the back of the office splattered in red as the bullet made contact with Catena's forehead.

The gunmen at the mezzanine opened fire at the office and Polizzi shouted, his Tommy Gun peppering the Bank with lead.

A bullet caught Polizzi in the shoulder, spinning him back into the office. Buddy turned and fired the last two shots in his revolver into the mezzanine before kicking the door closed and diving for cover.

A tremor rumbled through the marble floor just as the office door began to splinter with gunfire. The tremor became a teeth-rattling quake. Marble tiles cracked and the entire building shook. The gunfire in the center of the building petered out, replaced with cries of agony and terror.

Vincent helped Lefty to his knees, and they both steadied

themselves against Catena's desk while the shouts from inside the tellers' area fell silent.

The ground fell still. All Vincent could hear was the labored breaths from Polizzi as he shifted the gun out of his wounded arm. Then he heard the sound of footsteps as they clacked toward the office.

A silhouette appeared outside the ruined door, a shadow falling over bullet holes.

Buddy reached for his fast loader, fishing in his pocket and pulling it out, only to find it empty. Vincent tensed as the ruined door swung open, then let out a relieved laugh as he saw Hattie standing in the doorway.

Her eyes swept the room, and she caught her breath as she saw him. "Are you hurt?" she asked, running forward then crouching down before him.

"Just a little. My ego, mostly." He gave Lefty a quick jab. "And this one about gave me a heart attack."

Maria stepped into the office. "Did it work?"

Vincent shook his head. "Wait, you knew about this?"

"Yeah, she knew," Lefty grumbled. "She's nosey."

Hattie ran her hands along the sides of Vincent's face before standing up, her gaze falling on Catena's corpse slumped in his chair.

"It's done, then?"

Vincent nodded. "Looks that way. Now it's up to Luciano."

Maria crouched beside Polizzi to inspect his wound. He shook his head and stood up, cradling his arm as he turned to the others. They filed through the doorway and into what looked like a war zone. The marble floor had erupted in places, granite spikes slicing through the room and into the ceiling. More of Masseria's gunmen lay dead, facing one another, dead from their own gunfire.

"I figured they could thin themselves out," Hattie explained. "A little trick I learned from Galloway."

Buddy stared at her in awe. "I'm glad you're on our side, lady."

"Me, too," she replied with a grin.

The doors opened and Vincent stiffened, putting a hand in front of Hattie as a lean, tall figure strode into the building. Augustus Henry removed his Stetson and surveyed the damage. His eyes moved from mezzanine to the desks, and then to Catena's office. He released a long, low whistle when he spotted Catena's corpse.

Vincent cleared his throat.

Augustus shook his head. "Well, y'all made a hell of a mess in here."

Buddy searched for bullets in his pockets.

Maria cracked her knuckles. "Augustus?"

He glanced at her. "Maria."

"What, uh…what's your move?" she asked.

Augustus took another look at the bodies hanging from the mezzanine.

"Well," he replied with a heavy sigh, "I suppose I'll move back to Texas."

Hattie asked, "You'll step aside?"

"Step aside, miss?" he chuckled. "I plan to give all y'all a wide berth."

Vincent squinted. "Just like that?"

"Take a look 'round ya. What do you think's the point of sticking around here?"

Vincent stepped toward Augustus. "You know Masseria will hunt you down if you run. There could be a place for you in Baltimore."

Augustus eyed Maria, then smiled. "Naw. I think I've had enough of this gangster life. Y'all have a good day, now." He set his hat back onto his head and tipped it in salute then stepped out the front doors, disappearing into the night.

Hattie released a long breath. "That was…" She didn't finish the thought.

"Yes, it was," Vincent added.

"You know," Lefty said, "when Masseria gets back, he's going to be in no mood to hear explanations."

"You're right about that," said Vincent. "What you say we don't be here when that happens."

CHAPTER 32

"Time to face the music."

Vincent should have been in a panic over this meeting, but surprisingly he felt nothing but a calm resolve. Maybe it was the stoic note in Lefty's voice. Maybe nothing felt particularly life-threatening after what he'd been through in New York City. Maybe it was because stepping off the train in Baltimore filled him with warmth. Everything was familiar. Comfortable. Like coming home.

Vito knew he'd been double-dealing, conspiring not only with free pinchers but working to unseat him. This meeting should have been the end for him, but even though he had no idea what Lefty was planning, his trust in the other man had been renewed. It might be an ending, but he got the feeling that for him, it was a beginning.

They went straight from the train station to the Old Moravia. The lobby with the jazz quartet thumping away while couples danced. The bar with lightly-soused Baltimore socialites untroubled by prohibition. The bellhops with their red suits and click-clack shoes.

Lefty walked alongside Vincent, decked out in a new

black suit that he must have bought when he was up in New York. It looked strange on Lefty, who almost never wore black. It aged him, made him seem more venerable, less surly. Buddy followed, lingering as he smiled at a young woman in a knee-length ruby dress. She, in turn, smiled back.

Tony waved to them from the bar, setting aside his seltzer water as they huddled together.

"Gents," he greeted them, voice low and conspiratorial.

"Is he here yet?" Lefty asked.

"In the war room. He's waiting."

Lefty turned to Buddy. "I want you to stay here. This is going to take a delicate touch."

Buddy shrugged. "Suits me."

Lefty added with a nod. "You did good, kid. Real good."

Buddy's face flowed with pride. He grinned, then turned and stepped back out into the lobby, making a straight line for the girl in the red dress.

"What's his mood?" Lefty asked Tony.

"The usual. He's angry that Vincent betrayed him, and he's confused by the conflicting reports out of New York. Masseria still wants Buddy back, and that's adding fuel to the fire. Basically he wants everyone's head on a pike."

Lefty stepped past both of them. "Then let's get this over with."

Vincent followed, indulging in a last moment of peace before stepping into the path of Vito Corbi's wrath.

Inside the war room, the single bare bulb hummed overhead as Vito Corbi pawed over several sealed documents. When they stepped inside, he slapped his palm against the table.

"Sit down. All of you!"

Lefty reached for a chair across the table from Corbi, face stony and resolute. Corbi never rattled Lefty and Vincent had always admired that. Tony seemed calm, as well. Vincent took heart in their demeanor. If Corbi was prepared to explode, they'd have shielded Vincent, or at least betrayed a notion to hunker down.

Corbi tossed a handwritten letter into the middle of the table with a sour face. "These are not men. These are children."

"Masseria?" Lefty asked.

"Luciano, his new consigliere." Corbi prodded the letter, easing it farther away. "He makes demands as if he were Capo. Who is he but some *soldier*?"

"Indeed," Lefty replied.

Corbi shifted his gaze to Vincent. "And you. What is this? I am told you scheme against us. That you tried to have Masseria killed."

"Masseria has one pincher he inherited from Maranzano and Luciano's pincher," Vincent told him. "You have two. That is, unless you believe the lies and kill me, and then you have one. I think Masseria would be very happy if you had one pincher, Capo."

Corbi scowled. "I thought of that as well. This request for Buddy's return will be denied. I am not giving up my *stregone*. Even you, as exhausting as you are. Magic is power, and now I have two *stregone*. Maybe now the families in New York will pay me my due respect."

"I'm happy to serve," Vincent lied.

Corbi nodded, then turned to Tony. "Antonio, I wish to speak about this woman shipping our product. This Irish woman, O'Toole?"

Tony looked to Lefty.

Lefty gave him a nod, and the other man reached inside his jacket.

Corbi continued, "She must be eliminated. I am not satisfied with—"

Tony pulled his gun from his jacket, and pulled the trigger. Corbi blinked at the gunshot, stiffening as his eyes widened. Vincent launched out of his seat, his heart racing.

A rattling noise rose from Corbi's throat as a bubble of blood emerged from the corners of his mouth. A crimson stain spread across his vest, and a tremor shook his chest, calming as quickly as it came. With a wheeze, Vito Corbi slumped forward, nose smacking against the table.

Tony lifted his pistol, emptying the remaining bullets and handing it out to Lefty.

Vincent glanced back and forth between the two in shock. "What have you done?" he asked.

Lefty stared at the far wall, eyes focused on some distant thought, image, or memory. He reached for Tony's gun, setting it onto the table.

Vincent gripped Tony's shoulder. "What did you do?"

Tony glanced up at Vincent, a bit pale. Eyes wide, slightly breathless. But his expression held no fear, only exhilaration.

The door to the war room burst open. Crew gunmen had their pistols out, searching back and forth, taking in the scene.

Tony lifted his hands. "Vito Corbi is dead." He nodded to Lefty. "Viva il Capo!"

Stunned eyes fell onto Corbi's body, still slumped over the growing puddle of blood on the table.

Lefty's face remained stiff and resolute, unblinking. Vincent stared at him, worried that he'd just signed his own death warrant. The gunmen lifted their weapons at Lefty. Some lowered their guns, while others kept them trained on him. Hammers pulled back. Then, one by one, they eased the guns down. Each looked to one another, searching for their next step.

Finally, Lefty rose from his seat.

"Tony, I release you from all consequence for the death of my predecessor. Furthermore, I hereby name you as my consigliere." Tony bowed and Lefty then turned to the others. "The rest of you, clean up this mess."

The goons exchanged looks one more time before they holstered their weapons and began collecting Corbi's body.

"Vincent?" Lefty said as he turned for the door. "A word, if you would?"

Vincent looked to Tony, who gave him a cheerful nod.

He followed Lefty out of the war room and through the middle of the lobby, avoiding the gaze of everyone gathered. The band had stopped playing. There were no more conversations in the bar. The entire hotel seemed wreathed in silence.

Lefty pushed his way through the revolving door, stepping out into the Baltimore evening air and pausing. Vincent walked up to stand beside him, both looking over the rooftops at a moon rising to the east.

"I don't know what to say," Vincent announced.

Lefty nodded. "Nor do I." He added as he turned to face Vincent and patted him on the shoulder, "But between the two of us, and Miss Malloy of course, I think we'll figure something out."

They stood on the street, side by side, as the promise of opportunity sank in. No more need to run from the Crew. No more pincher hunting. No more having to hide his relationship with Hattie. He was free. He was free to do as he wanted—free to marry. This was the dawn of the first free pincher state in human history.

Vincent laughed at the suddenness of it all, even though it felt like he'd been working toward this end his entire life. "Yeah, I guess we'll figure something out."

CHAPTER 33

Hattie squinted as sunlight spilled through the glass of the Charge warehouse a sliver at a time as Blake and Charley scraped off the black paint. The more the interior was illuminated, the older and more disheveled it all seemed. Had they really lived in such squalor? Could they rebuild all of it now that there was no need to hide?

The front doors opened, and three children rushed into the space, gawking at the converted warehouse as they walked in a circle. Adults followed, faces more reserved and dubious.

Hattie nodded to them. "Welcome!"

This new clutch of pinchers had come from the Outer Banks, courtesy of Raymond. Just as Hattie wondered how her friend had fared, Raymond Bowles stepped into the warehouse.

"Damn, girl," he declared. "This is where you've been hiding?"

"More or less," she replied with a grin, rushing up to give him a hug. "How'd it go?"

Raymond took a seat in a chair by the front door with a

groan. "We pushed hard. The Charleston boys got more boats, now. Makin' it real tough to outrun 'em."

"We'll need to send pinchers with you from now on. Once you're north of Newport, you'll be safe. But outside the Chesapeake, you'll need magical assistance."

He laughed. "Can you hear yourself? You sound like old Lizzie."

Hattie leaned against the stairs. "Heard from her since she left?"

He shook his head. "I'm just hopin' she's doing fine in the oil business."

Hattie reached into her overalls. "Speaking of business, here's your payday from last week."

Raymond took the envelope from her and weighed it in his hands. "Been wantin' to talk to you about somethin'. You got a minute?"

"Sure." Hattie led him upstairs to her office and motioned for Raymond to take a seat. "What's on your mind?"

The man took a deep breath. "I'd like to offer to buy a share in the business. Half, if it suits."

Hattie blinked in surprise.

"I've been thinkin'…" Raymond went on. "This prohibition probably ain't gonna last for much longer. Time for us to make hay, as the farmers say. I got a couple men with fishing boats who would make a run or two a week and be quiet about it. We can increase our runs, now that the Crew is working with us and the West Virginia shiners are on board. Double, or even triple our distribution."

Hattie nodded. "Go on."

"You got a lot going on." Raymond twisted his hands together in his lap. "What with the Charge, and helping with the Crew, and pinchers coming in from south and north. Can't be easy to keep your eye on this side of the business. I know the income helps fuel the Charge, so I'm thinking I become a managing partner. I buy out half the business and earn half the profits, and I take a salary for managing the whole lot of it. You don't have to think twice about it at all, and still get income from your investment to run the Charge."

He dug a wad of cash out of his pocket and handed it to Hattie.

Her eyes widened. "I thought you and Nadine were saving to buy a house?"

"This is a sight better of an investment." He grinned. "And as much as Nadine wants a new house, she knows this won't just buy us a house, it'll get our kids the best schooling and help us set them up for their futures."

Hattie shook her head and took the stack of money. "Brigid O'Toole's busted anyway. Everyone up and down the East Coast knows she was a sham. Won't do Lefty any good to deal with a ghost. We can put the business in your name, and I'll be a silent investor."

Raymond sat back in his chair. "Then we have a deal?"

Hattie stood and reached out to shake his hand. "Absolutely. Partner."

"Partner." Raymond clasped her hand in a crushing grip. "Although you're still a brat."

Hattie laughed. "And you're still a bully."

* * *

Cleanup continued in the warehouse, bolstered by the willing industry of the newcomers. Gossip had spread about the new gang in town, and how the fact that they hadn't officially declared pinchers to be equals didn't make it less true.

Maria and Charley huddled over the kitchen table, his girls practicing their handwriting as they looked on. Hattie caught Maria staring at Charley as he ran his finger along their lines, giving patient correction.

She caught Hattie looking at her and reached out to give Charley's arm a squeeze before getting up.

"He's glad you're back in one piece?" Hattie asked.

"Looks that way. Embarrassing, really."

"Oh, don't try that. I know better. And I see the way you look at him."

"Am I that obvious?" Maria sighed and grinned. "The way he is with his daughters. He never talks down to them. Never tells them they can't be whatever it is they want to be. He's a good, kind, loyal man."

Hattie smiled. "Sounds like my da."

"Now that we don't have to worry about the Crew, I wonder if we can find them a proper school," Maria mused.

Hattie turned to her, motioning for her to follow. "I hate to be the bearer of bad news, but that might not be as easy as you think."

"Why not?"

Hattie led her up the stairs to her office. She closed the door behind them and gestured for Maria to take a seat. "As you know, there's a veritable flood of pinchers looking to stream in from Pennsylvania, now that word's out."

"We already have volunteers with the newcomers. No one's talking about going west anymore. They want to stay here."

"Aye. And that's good. But we're going to run out of room, and quickly." Hattie tapped the papers on her desk. "I've done the numbers, and this sort of growth won't be sustainable unless we look to the future."

Maria nodded. "Plus, Charleston is continuing to be a challenge, from what I hear."

"They are. Now that the power in New York has settled, and Lefty's not giving them quarter to edge into our territory, they're desperate to sponge up as many free pinchers as they can."

Maria squinted. "What does this have to do with Charley and his daughters?"

"In a word, Richmond."

"Richmond?"

Hattie took a seat. "No one's filled the power vacuum in Richmond—not since Betty Sharp was removed. Charleston's looking to absorb Richmond into their territory. I suggest we beat them to the punch."

"How?"

"By setting up another Charge in Richmond."

Maria's mouth drew into an appreciative smirk. "That's ambitious."

"We can do it," Hattie said. "We have the numbers. I spoke with Lefty and we have the financial backing of the Baltimore Crew. All we need is a strong leader with a military mind. One we can trust."

Maria snickered. "Uh…okay. Listen, I like Charley as much as anyone, but I don't think he's exactly leadership material."

"I agree," Hattie said. "Which is why I want you to take over Richmond operations."

Maria blinked. "What?"

"I took you to New York not to test your loyalty, but to test your ability. I'm convinced there's no one else who could hold everything together in Virginia. It'll be difficult. You'll be closer to Charleston, with the heat rising. But you're more of a fighter than I am." Hattie added with a wistful smile, "You remind me a lot of Sadie, to be honest."

Maria sat in stunned silence for a moment.

Hattie lifted her eyebrows. "Well, then?"

"I…guess that makes sense."

"Will you do it?"

Maria blinked again. "Of course, I will. It's just a lot to take in."

"You'll have help," Hattie said. "I'm sure if we ask for volunteers, a red-haired pincher will be the first to step up, and I don't mean me."

Maria chuckled. "What about you and Vincent? What does that future look like for you two?"

Hattie waved her off. "Oh, I'm sure we'll think about that when there's less to do."

"Are you kidding me? Now's the time to make things official between you two."

"The timing's not right." Hattie squirmed. "Yeah, Lefty's in charge here, but there's someone in Philadelphia who might not be too enthused over what's going on with the Crew now. And then there's Luciano. And Boston. And Pittsburgh. There's plenty of work left."

Maria leaned forward. "There will never be a perfect time to share a life with someone. If you wait for that, it'll never come."

Hattie stared at her desk. The truth was that Vincent hadn't asked, and she wasn't sure when or if he would.

"Time will tell, I guess," she finally replied.

CHAPTER 34

*H*attie adjusted the gloves on her forearms and tucked a stray strand of hair behind her ear. A couple passed her on the street. The woman gave her a warm smile.

Hattie returned it, marveling at the feeling of walking the streets of Baltimore without an illusion wrapped around her. No more fear that the mob would grab her and drag her into slavery. Here she was, a pincher, living like a normal person.

Vincent's invitation had given a simple address. As Hattie ventured down Orleans Street, she discovered the street address was leading her to a place that was all too familiar.

The Fontainebleu's windows were lit from inside. A tinkle of jazz piano slipped into the evening air. It had been almost a year since Hattie had been to the Fontainebleu. She'd spent so much time running from the Crew, from Vincent, from Galloway… This was perfect.

Hattie straightened her gloves again and pulled open the door.

The interior of the Fontainebleu was completely empty, save for several tables, the bar as usual, and the old upright piano. No customers. Hattie smiled to herself. Vincent must have rented the entire club just for tonight. She approached the bar and took a seat on a stool, setting her clutch in front of her. The bartender turned to face her with a grin.

Hattie gasped. "Leon?"

Her old friend laughed, reaching over the bar to pat her on the shoulders.

"Hattie." He snickered. "It's been a way too long!"

"My God, what are you doing here?"

He shrugged. "I got a call from an old friend. Dey tell me dere was a special occasion, so I made da trip."

"I don't believe this. How's Chicago, then?"

"Oh," he said with a roll of his eyes. "Too much for one man. Good thing I got so many men, yeah?"

She slapped his arm.

"By da way," Leon said, reaching into his pocket. "I brought ya something."

He set a glass dram onto the bar. The brilliant blue liquid inside glimmered in the candlelight.

"Is that…"

He nodded. "Aqua vitae. For your father."

She reached out to hug him once again. "You're a saint among men, Leon."

"Well, let dis saint pour ya a drink."

"Gin, please," she replied.

As he poured some gin on ice and gave it a shake, Hattie turned to look at the piano. Instead of one pianist, there were two.

"Really pulled out the stops, here," Hattie mumbled.

"Ya like dem?" Leon asked as he set her drink in front of her. "I hear dey don't do requests."

Hattie squinted at them. They seemed familiar, somehow. The young man on the right flowed up and down the keys with an almost bored grace. The older man beside him only played with one hand.

She straightened on her seat, then glanced back at Leon. "What are…"

Leon shrugged again with a smile, leaving Hattie to slide off her stool and approach the piano.

"Mister Mancuso," she said as Lefty eyed her quickly. "What brings you to a low-brow establishment like this?"

Lefty focused on his playing. "A favor for a friend."

"And where might this friend be?" she asked.

The door to the kitchen opened, and a tall dark-skinned man in a chef's hat pushed a service trolley bearing a large silver dome into the room.

Hattie rolled her eyes. "You, too?"

Raymond grinned at her, folding a towel over his arm with a bow. "My lady. If you would?" He gestured to the corner, where a single table was set with two candles.

Hattie gathered her gin and gave Raymond a curtsy, crossing the room as he followed with the service trolley.

She sat and looked around once more. "Alright, then. Where's my boy-o? All this drama had better be worth it."

"I hope it is." Vincent walked out of the kitchen wearing a tuxedo, his hair trimmed and combed back. She watched as he approached, and thought back to the first time they'd been here. She'd been soaked from the rain, still worried that Vincent might turn her in to Corbi, and more than a little jealous when Fern showed up.

One year ago. Her life had changed so much in just one year.

Vincent took a seat across from Hattie, nodding for Lefty and his accompanist to continue.

She leaned forward. "Why, Vincent Calendo, if I didn't know better, I'd think you were trying too hard."

He shook his head, that cocky smile on his face that she loved so. "But you know better, right?"

Hattie laughed. "Oh, aye. This is precisely the fussy nonsense I've come to expect from you."

He lifted his hands. "Guilty."

She glanced back at the bar. "You seriously called Leon in all the way from Chicago?"

"Lefty's making inroads with Capone's organization. I took advantage of an opportunity."

Hattie shifted in her seat. "He said this was a special occasion."

Vincent looked down to his plate as a blush rose on his cheeks.

"What's going on, boy-o?"

Vincent nodded to Raymond who reached for the service trolley, pulling the dome away from the plate. Instead of dinner, the trolley held a single plate—a plate with a ring at its center.

Hattie sat dumbstruck for a second, then fidgeted with her clutch as Vincent slid off his chair to one knee, reaching for the ring.

"Hattie Malloy, I've been carrying this damned ring in my pocket for almost a month, now."

She lifted a hand to her mouth.

"Even in New York," he added. "Which, well... I figured it wasn't the right time. We were, you know, about to die. Or get captured. Anyways, I couldn't figure out how to even talk about the future, and us. It always seemed so impossible. But it occurred to me, if I wait for the right time..."

"It'll never come," Hattie finished.

He smiled. "Hattie Malloy, will you marry me?"

She looked around to find the music had stopped. All eyes were on her. Then she looked back down to Vincent, who still had that adorable cocky grin.

"It's about damned time, boy'o."

Hattie placed her hand in his. Vincent slid the ring onto her finger, then held her hand tight. It was a beautiful ring—silver filigree nestling a diamond in the middle. Gorgeous as it was, the man who'd put it on her finger was what she wanted the most.

Vincent stood up and scooped Hattie into his arms. "I love you. I think I loved you that first night."

She smoothed a hand down his chest. "Even after I insulted you and slapped you."

He grinned. "Yes. Even after you shot at me. And I seem to recall I insulted you, too."

"I love you. And yes, I loved you from the first moment I saw you."

He bent his head to hers, kissing her. Applause filled the air, accompanied by a few hoots and whistles. When they finally pulled apart, Lefty and his assistant began to play once more, pounding out a bouncy tune.

Vincent wrapped a hand around Hattie's waist and she took his other hand, admiring the ring in the candlelight, as they swayed with pep to the jazz.

"I have dinner and drinks for everyone," he murmured in her ear, his breath brushing against her hair. "Afterward, we should go over to your parents' house. I asked your father's permission, you know? Your mother's, too. I was never so scared in my life. I was sure she'd say no, and I'd have to bribe her with a phonograph or something."

She chuckled at the thought of Vincent sweating as he asked her for her mother's blessing. "Very proper of you."

He kissed the side of her head. "And I'm about to be very improper. Hattie Malloy, I'd like it very much if you spent the night at my house."

"Before we've exchanged vows?" she teased.

"Well, I hear Roscoe is an excellent chaperone."

The doors to the Fontainebleu suddenly swung open and a cold breeze flooded into the room, sending the candles into a wild flicker. Hattie turned to see a figure stagger inside, dropping to his knees with a grunt.

The music stopped. The smell of soot filled the room, and something more acrid. Raymond rushed forward and Lefty jumped to his feet, hand inside his jacket.

Vincent lifted a hand for him to hold as Raymond bent over the man.

"He's alive," Raymond turned the man over.

Hattie released a gasp as she stared into half of the face of Assam al Ghasawi. The other half of his face was burned beyond recognition, his chest rising and falling with a sick rattle.

"Leon!" she shouted.

Leon swept around the bar, gripping the dram of Aqua Vitae as he joined Raymond on the floor beside the Janissary. The water pincher pulled the stopper and fed three drops of the elixir into Ghasawi's burned lips.

The man's chest jerked with a spasm of coughs. His eyes fluttered open, and he reached out for Hattie.

"The Hell Pincher. He's here."

ACKNOWLEDGMENTS

A huge thanks to our copyeditor Kimberly Cannon whose eagle eyes catch all the typos and keep Debra's comma problem in line, and to Damonza for cover design.

Special thanks to all our readers who have individually followed us to Hel and back, and enthusiastically cheered us on during our first collaborative project. May there be many more ahead!

Debra and J.P

Debra lives in a little house in the woods of Maryland with her sons and two slobbery bloodhounds. On a good day, she jogs and horseback rides, hopefully managing to keep the horse between herself and the ground. Her only known super power is 'Identify Roadkill'.

A Louisiana native, J.P. relocated to the vineyards and cow pastures of Central Maryland after Hurricane Katrina, where he lives with his wife and son. During the day he commutes to the city of Baltimore, a setting which inspires much of his writing.

For more information:
www.debradunbar.com/white-lightning or
J.P. Sloan's Author page
Debra Dunbar's Author page

Accidental Witches Series
Brimstone and Broomsticks
Warmongers and Wands
Death and Divination
Hell and Hexes
Minions and Magic (July 2019)
Fiends and Familiars (2019)
Devils and the Dead (2019)

White Lightning Series
Wooden Nickels
Bum's Rush
Clip Joint
Jake Walk
Trouble Boys

The Templar Series
Dead Rising
Last Breath
Bare Bones
Famine's Feast
Royal Blood
Dark Crossroads (Fall 2019)

* * *

<u>IMP WORLD NOVELS</u>

<u>The Imp Series</u>
A Demon Bound
Satan's Sword
Elven Blood
Devil's Paw
Imp Forsaken
Angel of Chaos
Kingdom of Lies
Exodus
Queen of the Damned
The Morning Star

* * *

<u>Half-breed Series</u>
Demons of Desire
Sins of the Flesh
Cornucopia
Unholy Pleasures
City of Lust

* * *

<u>Imp World Novels</u>
No Man's Land
Stolen Souls
Three Wishes
Northern Lights

Far From Center

Penance

<u>Northern Wolves</u>

Juneau to Kenai

Rogue

Winter Fae

Bad Seed